AND

SPIDER-MAN

TIME'S ARROW
BOOK 2: THE PRESENT

MARVEL COMICS

SPIDER-MAN: THE VENOM FACTOR by Diane Duane
THE ULTIMATE SPIDER-MAN, Stan Lee, Editor
IRON MAN: THE ARMOR TRAP by Greg Cox
SPIDER-MAN: CARNAGE IN NEW YORK
by David Michelinie & Dean Wesley Smith
THE INCREDIBLE HULK: WHAT SAVAGE BEAST by Peter David
SPIDER-MAN: THE LIZARD SANCTION by Diane Duane
THE ULTIMATE SILVER SURFER, Stan Lee, Editor
FANTASTIC FOUR: TO FREE ATLANTIS by Nancy A. Collins
DAREDEVIL: PREDATOR'S SMILE by Christopher Golden
X-MEN: MUTANT EMPIRE Book 1: SIEGE by Christopher Golden
THE ULTIMATE SUPER-VILLAINS, Stan Lee, Editor
SPIDER-MAN & THE INCREDIBLE HULK: RAMPAGE
by Danny Fingeroth & Eric Fein (Doom's Day Book 1)
SPIDER-MAN: GOBLIN'S REVENGE by Dean Wesley Smith
THE ULTIMATE X-MEN, Stan Lee, Editor
SPIDER-MAN: THE OCTOPUS AGENDA by Diane Duane
X-MEN: MUTANT EMPIRE Book 2: SANCTUARY by Christopher Golden
IRON MAN: OPERATION A.I.M. by Greg Cox
SPIDER-MAN & IRON MAN: SABOTAGE
by Pierce Askegren & Danny Fingeroth (Doom's Day Book 2)
X-MEN: MUTANT EMPIRE Book 3: SALVATION by Christopher Golden
GENERATION X by Scott Lobdell & Elliot S! Maggin
FANTASTIC FOUR: REDEMPTION OF THE SILVER SURFER by Michael Jan Friedman
THE INCREDIBLE HULK: ABOMINATIONS by Jason Henderson
X-MEN: SMOKE AND MIRRORS by eluki bes shahar
X-MEN: EMPIRE'S END by Diane Duane
UNTOLD TALES OF SPIDER-MAN, Stan Lee & Kurt Busiek, Editors
SPIDER-MAN & FANTASTIC FOUR: WRECKAGE
by Eric Fein & Pierce Askegren (Doom's Day Book 3)
X-MEN: THE JEWELS OF CYTTORAK by Dean Wesley Smith
SPIDER-MAN: VALLEY OF THE LIZARD by John Vornholt
X-MEN: THE LAW OF THE JUNGLE by Dave Smeds
SPIDER-MAN: WANTED DEAD OR ALIVE by Craig Shaw Gardner
X-MEN: PRISONER X by Ann Nocenti
FANTASTIC FOUR: COUNTDOWN TO CHAOS by Pierce Askegren
X-MEN & SPIDER-MAN: TIME'S ARROW Book 1: THE PAST
by Tom DeFalco & Jason Henderson
X-MEN & SPIDER-MAN: TIME'S ARROW Book 2: THE PRESENT
by Tom DeFalco & Adam-Troy Castro

COMING SOON:

X-MEN & SPIDER-MAN: TIME'S ARROW Book 3: THE FUTURE
by Tom DeFalco & eluki bes shahar
SPIDER-MAN: VENOM'S WRATH by Keith R. A. DeCandido & José R. Nieto

X-MEN AND SPIDER-MAN

TIME'S ARROW
BOOK 2: THE PRESENT

Tom DeFalco & Adam-Troy Castro

ILLUSTRATIONS BY
TOM GRUMMETT & DOUG HAZLEWOOD

MARVEL COMICS

BYRON PREISS MULTIMEDIA COMPANY, INC.
NEW YORK

BERKLEY BOULEVARD BOOKS, NEW YORK

If you purchased this book without a cover you should be aware that this book is stolen property. It was reported as "unsold and destroyed" to the publisher and neither the author nor the publisher has received any payment for this "stripped book."

Special thanks to Ginjer Buchanan, Steve Roman,
Howard Zimmerman, Michelle LaMarca, Emily Epstein,
Ursula Ward, Mike Thomas, and Steve Behling.

X-MEN & SPIDER-MAN: TIME'S ARROW Book 2: THE PRESENT

A Boulevard Book
A Byron Preiss Multimedia Company, Inc. Book

PRINTING HISTORY
Berkley Boulevard paperback edition / August 1998

All rights reserved.
Copyright © 1998 Marvel Characters, Inc.
Edited by Keith R. A. DeCandido.
Cover design by Claude Goodwin.
Cover art by Jim Burns, based on a sketch by Tom Grummett.
Book design by Michael Mendelsohn.
This book may not be reproduced in whole or in part,
by mimeograph or any other means, without permission.
For information address: Byron Preiss Multimedia Company, Inc.,
24 West 25th Street, New York, New York 10010.

The Penguin Putnam Inc. World Wide Web site address is
http://www.penguinputnam.com

Check out the Byron Preiss Multimedia Co., Inc. site on the
World Wide Web:
http://www.byronpreiss.com

Check out the Ace Science Fiction/Fantasy newsletter,
and much more, at Club PPI!

ISBN: 0-425-16415-2

BERKLEY BOULEVARD
Berkley Boulevard Books are published by The Berkley Publishing
Group, a member of Penguin Putnam Inc.,
200 Madison Avenue, New York, New York 10016.
BERKLEY BOULEVARD and its logo
are trademarks belonging to Berkley Publishing Corporation.

PRINTED IN THE UNITED STATES OF AMERICA

10 9 8 7 6 5 4 3 2 1

This one's for Mark Gruenwald,
who's been called to soar the spaceways
with Quasar and the gang.
The old MU just isn't the same
without you, buddy.
—TD

To Zachary, Kate, and Ari: the super heroes of the future.
—ATC

PROLOGUE

F*ace it, Tiger. You just hit the jackpot.*

They were the first words the love of Peter Parker's life had ever spoken to him, at the moment they first met. They were also the first words she'd spoken on their wedding night, and the first words she'd spoken after their baby was born.

Today, as he strolled through the park with his wife, Mary Jane, and their beautiful daughter, May, he thought (not for the first time) that they'd been a self-fulfilling prophecy. Because his life had become the best of all possible worlds.

He gazed at his wife: tall, beautiful, blonde (she was actually a natural redhead, but dyed it for the lead role in a hit TV series just renewed for its fourth year). It was a beautiful summer day, of the sort that the gods only visit on Manhattan when they're in an especially generous mood; the sun was high and the air was clear and the temperature was in the narrow range of perfect comfort that separates New York's frigid winters from its broiling summers.

The zoo was crowded, but not unpleasantly so. Everybody Peter knew seemed to be here. Not too long ago they'd run into *Daily Bugle* publisher J. Jonah Jameson, for whom Peter had worked briefly during his teens; the kindly old man, one of the warmest and most generous souls Peter had ever met, had surprised Peter by not only recognizing him after all these years but also running up to greet him with a hug.

Jameson had beamed at Mary Jane. "Did you know that this fine young man used to be a professional photographer? Did he ever tell you that?"

Mary Jane's eyes had twinkled. "I think he mentioned that once or twice."

"He showed promise too. Journalism lost a great talent the day he decided to go into science instead. Broke my heart! But I'm sure he's doing great things. Great things!"

Now they were stopped in front of the polar bear cage, where he'd proposed to her on an equally sunny day almost two years before. It was Peter's favorite for that rea-

THE PRESENT

son alone, but today the bears were in fine form; there was one big fella who seemed to be having a grand old time swimming endless laps around the pool, and little May, who'd been fussing, completely forgot that she was overdue for her nap and instead announced, "Gahg. Gahg, Daddy. Gahg."

Mary Jane laughed. "Some zoo, Tiger. We've been to ten cages already and all she's seen is ten different varieties of dog."

"Well," Peter said, "you must admit, it's still more species of dog than we have at home." He knelt by the stroller. "It's a bear, honey. Can you say bear?"

"Bah?" May asked doubtfully.

"That's right, May. Bear."

May shook her head vigorously and repeated her own hypothesis: *"Gahg!"*

Peter gave up: he didn't have to be a scientist every day. She could think it was a dog for a little while longer. She could say it was a rhino, or a scorpion, or a puma. She was his daughter, and he'd defend her position to the death.

She held out her arms for some "doose," and as he handed her the drinking cup from the knapsack in the back of the stroller, he noted out of the corner of his eye that Mary Jane was being asked for her autograph again. As always, he automatically looked over the fans in question to make sure that they were safe: he had always been a little afraid that, someday, they might find themselves faced with somebody too crazy to handle. It hadn't happened yet, which was a good thing for Peter, since he'd never been a fighter. But no: these were sixteen-year-old girls, bubbling at length over how much they loved *The Black Cat* and how they thought Felicia Hardy was just the coolest character on television. Mary Jane thanked them warmly: not blowing them off as another celebrity might have done, but actually chatting, asking their names and what schools they went to and talking to them about the various other actors on the show.

Until May, jealous at how much attention her mommy

TIME'S ARROW

was getting, began to fuss. Then Mary Jane immediately excused herself to pick up her daughter, cooing in her ear and playing the whoopsie game that never failed to make May forget she was upset.

At which point the tallest of the three teenage girls surprised Peter by saying, "What about you, mister? Are you an actor too?"

Peter was embarrassed. "Well, uh . . . actually, no. I'm a scientist."

Mary Jane, who now bore little May on her shoulders, broke in: "A great scientist."

"Wow. What kind of science do you do?"

"Biochemistry," said Peter.

"Sounds complicated," the tall girl said.

"And important," Mary Jane said. "My hubby's one of the most brilliant men in his field."

Peter found himself turning red at that. Mary Jane was overstating the case—as far as he was concerned, he was only beginning to establish his reputation—but the federal government, led by a science-friendly President Sagan, had just shown what seemed an excessive amount of faith in him, by giving him an open-ended grant to study the mutagenic effects of increased solar radiation. Starting Monday morning, he'd be able to devote himself to cutting-edge research. He already had some ideas about using the controlled release of radiation to transfer genetic characteristics from one organism to another, though it would probably be a long time before he worked up the nerve to try it on anything more advanced than simple arachnids. But that was a far cry from considering himself a celebrity, and when his wife started going off about his supposed brilliance, he had to protest. "Honey—"

She smiled mischievously, and kissed him. "He also has one of the cutest blushes in the business. Doesn't he?"

The tall girl, enjoying herself, said, "I think so," which of course made Peter blush all over again.

He ended up giving away a few autographs himself.

"That was very naughty of you," he scolded Mary Jane, as soon as the three girls were out of earshot.

THE PRESENT

She laughed saucily, as she checked on little May (now asleep) and began to push the stroller in the direction of the sea lions. "I keep telling you, Tiger . . . this modesty thing of yours has got to go. Why do you think you got this project, instead of somebody like Bruce Banner or Otto Octavius?"

"Because I work cheap?" Peter guessed.

She slapped his arm. "No! Because the powers that be asked everybody whose opinions they respected and found out what I knew the first time I met you—that you're about fifty times better than you think you are. They knew that there wasn't anybody else in the field, even Octavius, who could take this project as far as they want to take it. And they knew that if there was anybody smart and dependable enough to trust with power of decision on a project they clearly consider top priority, let alone creative enough to make it worth the funding, it was you. So stop being surprised when I act proud of you. Because you deserve it. And as soon as we get home I'm going to remind you of that all over again."

Peter was awed. "When was the last time I told you I love you?"

"About an hour ago. But you can say it again if you want to."

"I love you."

They kissed.

It was the best of all possible worlds, and Peter Parker was living the best of all possible lives. He was married to the greatest woman in the world, he had a daughter who amazed him anew every single day, and he was about to embark upon a project with the potential to yield the most important scientific advances since the astonishing discoveries made by the crew of the space shuttle *Challenger*. Nothing could possibly ruin it.

But then something did.

It was a little like seeing a cloud passing over the sun. It was a little like hearing the squeal of brakes when he stepped off the curb without first checking for traffic. It was a little like feeling an icicle stabbing him at the base

TIME'S ARROW

of his spine. It was a little like all these things, and it was worse, because in that first instant, when all around them the animals in their cages began to wail in total elemental terror, part of him already knew, as they did, that the best of all possible worlds had just ended.

As the crowds around them rumbled with the beginnings of panic, Peter looked up at the sky, and saw that the sun had disappeared. It had been swallowed whole by a vast, formless darkness, which even now billowed across the sky, swallowing up all traces of warmth and light. It descended so fast that it seemed to be falling, with a force capable of crushing everything that lay beneath. As Peter watched, a low-flying 747 passed along the edges of that darkness, and disappeared: neither entering it nor being destroyed by it, but simply ceasing to be, like something that had never been there at all. In the few seconds of life remaining to him, Peter couldn't help knowing that the airplane wasn't the only thing that was gone, for so was everything behind the darkness, including the sun and the moon and all the stars behind them . . .

The zoo around them was chaos in the form of people praying, people screaming, people going mad, people running even though there was no place to run. Somehow, Peter recognized one of those sounds as the wailing of his own beautiful daughter, who knew only that she was afraid and that her mommy and daddy were helpless.

Mary Jane scooped up the baby, in a final, futile attempt to protect her. "Peter! You've got to have some kind of explanation! What is that thing? What's happening?"

There wasn't much time for an answer, before the darkness was upon them, but he managed to get it in: "I don't know . . ."

The wave rolled across the Earth, splitting the planet like a ripe melon hurled against brick. Peter Parker had one last thought: that it shouldn't have happened. That he should have been able to stop it. That he should have been able to protect everything he loved.

Face it, Tiger. You just lost it all.

Oblivion.

THE PRESENT

• • •

There was a place that would have been ennobled by the word *oblivion*: a place of sooty gray clouds that swirled together in complex eddies and currents that failed to hide the nothingness that lay beneath.

It was called Limbo, and it existed only because the multiverse needed something to occupy the gap between time and physical reality.

It should have been completely uninhabited, but it did have a ruler, whose castle was an edifice imposing enough to reflect the dreams of a man who wanted to conquer everything. It was an impossibly huge structure, with hallways that doubled back upon themselves, windows that looked out upon oceans of madness, and chambers that seemed to go on forever . . . but somehow it did not seem too grandiose a place for the armored man who sat on his throne in the central court. It seemed too small. He needed more—but then, it was part of his nature that he would always need more.

Before him stood his albino servant. Lireeb: tall, cadaverous, and devoted to him in every way. Lireeb bowed, as he always did, and then reported the latest victories in a voice that betrayed neither joy nor satisfaction, but instead wry amusement.

"Another alternate timeline has been eradicated, with no resistance from its inhabitants."

Kang the Conqueror rested his head on folded hands. "Excellent."

"Well," Lireeb qualified, "if you like that sort of thing."

Kang paid him no mind. He knew that he still had much to do, but he couldn't resist basking in this, the moment when his master plan seemed to be finally developing a momentum of its very own. After all, he had enslaved entire populations, razed entire continents, used the powers of time travel to make destiny itself the chisel with which he sculpted history itself . . . but all of that paled beside this, his greatest achievement.

Soon, he would be like the great Alexander: he would

see the width and breadth of his realm, and he would weep, from the knowledge that there were no more worlds to conquer.

But then, he would have something even more precious than conquest. The only thing other than conquest that he'd ever truly loved.

Lireeb was saying something. Kang stirred himself from his reverie and asked, "What?"

"I was saying that you should feel free to rant out loud, if you wish. Silent megalomania isn't nearly as edifying as a nice prolonged bout of self-congratulation."

Kang grunted. "Time enough for that."

"Was that supposed to be irony, sir? I'm afraid I don't have the knack."

Kang said, "I mean that we are still unacceptably far from my goal. From the current rate of collapse and the sheer number of alternate timelines still in existence, it will still take a few hundred thousand subjective centuries to prune away all I still consider... unmanageable. And, subjectively speaking, the mechanism that is holding the timelines in stasis will have broken down long before then. So it's time to step up the program... and lend my Time Arrows a little help they didn't have before.

"You'll find that we won't have to wait nearly as long as you think..."

CHAPTER ONE

It was the same day, the same park, the same city, the same world: the same perfect weather, the same blue skies, and many of the same people wandering around beneath the same sun. Aside from that, everything was different.

For one thing, it was the dead of winter: a bitterly cold day, redeemed only by the relative lack of any exacerbating wind. There was no snow on the ground, but the trees were bare, the pedestrians were hidden beneath warm hats and gloves, and every spoken word became visible as vapor dissipating in the air. The park was still crowded, but only because the sun was shining, the weather was otherwise clear, and today's mercury level actually represented a substantial improvement over what New Yorkers had become used to in the past month. There were a lot of people, enjoying the wide open spaces of the park. But there'd be a lot of runny noses and chest colds to deal with later.

For another thing, this Peter Parker's clothes were itchy.

He wore battered snow-boots, patchy corduroy trousers, a stained and oily goose down jacket, a wool scarf, and a black woolen cap over something that most passersby just naturally assumed to be a funky ski mask. It was actually his Spider-Man mask, and he wore it partially pulled up, exposing his nose and mouth. The gestalt was not an outfit designed to make him look prosperous, or even reasonably intelligent. He'd chosen the clothes because they were available, which is to say that he was able to nab them from a charity clothes drop. He did not want to know why they were itchy.

At that, he was much better off than his traveling companion, Bishop, who was larger and bulkier and more difficult to dress in clothes scavenged from storage bins. Bishop wore a tattered green sweater, a green military jacket, a pair of camouflage pants, a red wool cap, and an ankle-length trench coat with a rather disconcerting blood-stained hole where the heart would have been. He carried

THE PRESENT

a hefty cardboard box, wrapped in a mesh of sticky gray webbing.

Together, they didn't exactly blend. But that was okay. Even in an alternate universe, this was still New York. Most people didn't even give them a second look.

But though they were all dressed up, they still had no place to go, for though this looked like Earth, it was not *their* Earth: not the one where Peter Parker prowled the rooftops in the guise of the amazing Spider-Man, not the one where Bishop fought for humanity as a trusted member of the uncanny X-Men. This Earth was a far stranger place ... a far more dangerous place ... and the two of them had been trapped on it since the Time Displacement Core dumped them here two days earlier. Oh, there was no reason to believe their plight was permanent ... not when Bishop's teammates were back on the real Earth, and probably spending every spare minute searching for them. But there wasn't much they could do while they waited to be rescued, except get to know each other.

Yeah. Right.

All in all, Spider-Man missed Venom.

He said, "Hey, Bish. You know what really kills me?"

The massive X-Man rumbled, in a voice like a freight train waking up from a nap. "I most sincerely wish I knew."

Spider-Man managed to press on. "No. I mean it. Really."

"I know. And I'm sure you insist on telling me."

Daredevil, Spider-Man thought. *Captain America. Reed Richards. Even (and I'd never tell him this to his face) the Torch. These are guys I get along with. If I was temporarily trapped on a parallel Earth with one of those guys, it wouldn't be that bad. We'd have stuff to talk about. But this guy makes the Punisher look like Jim Carrey. He could depress a Shirley Temple movie. What do they put in his breakfast cereal and where do I go to have it declared a dangerous substance?*

Spider-Man shook his head, determined to keep up the conversation at all costs, and said: "*Cats.*"

TIME'S ARROW

Bishop stopped in midstride. "Cats?"

"Yes," Spider-Man said, with grim satisfaction. "*Cats*."

It was fun to watch Bishop's face at war with itself. The guy was usually one big scowl—except when he screwed up his attitude enough to attempt a grimace instead—and normally betrayed his thoughts about as much as Spider-Man's full face mask did. But now his emotions were churning visibly: the simple human need to ask battling the dread certainty that he'd be sorry if he did. It was only after a seeming eternity of conflict that Bishop slumped, surrendered to the inevitable, and said, "All right. What about cats?"

"Look at the skyline," Spider-Man said. "I take a serious interest in where all the tallest buildings are—"

"Naturally. You have to know your battlefield."

"—so I know the skyline better than anybody this side of the Tourist Information Board. And since we've been on our feet for the past two days, I've been paying close attention to which buildings are different."

Bishop was intent now. "I don't believe it. You actually sound like you're going to say something useful. Go ahead."

"Well, the first thing I see is that hotel, off to the south. Back where we come from, that's a Helmsley apartment building: very elegant, very fancy, and very old. It wasn't the thirty-story mirror it is here. Over there's the Roxxon Corporate Headquarters. It looks exactly like it does on our Earth, but it's on the west side of the street instead of the east: meaning that though the architect was the same, they erected it on a different lot. I don't recognize that short building over there; my guess is that the skyscraper I'm used to never got built, which to me means that the corporation that owned it didn't prosper quite as much as it did where we came from."

"Or," Bishop mused, "that they built their corporate headquarters in another city, which would no doubt have any number of repercussions. Go ahead. What else did you see?"

THE PRESENT

"That the *Daily Globe* and the *Daily Bugle* have switched addresses. That the Baxter Building never got destroyed and replaced with Four Freedoms Plaza. That the Pan Am Building is still the Pan Am Building, which on our world it's not. That there are fewer *new* buildings, and that the older ones seem to be in slightly better shape. That there are still foreign banks all over Madison Avenue, which confirms that there's still a thriving international economy. That Damage Control, Incorporated, appears to be out of business, when back home they're the most lucrative growth stock since IBM. That Avengers Mansion is in the same place, but it doesn't seem occupied by Avengers..."

"And how do you know that?"

"Because they moved it back from the sidewalk right after they started occupying the place in order to accomodate their quinjets. And the mortar is all the exact same color all across the building, which isn't true on our world 'cause of all the times they've had wall damage. Either they never occupied that mansion and therefore never needed to move the place and replace the walls... maybe they were there once, and something happened to them... and maybe, for once, they broke up and actually stayed broken up, like the Beatles did. Then there's the matter of the weather."

"I noticed it's cold," Bishop said dryly.

"Exactly. But what exactly does it mean to us, that it's cold here, when it's summer back home? Is it possible that this Earth rotates on a reversed axial tilt, making the summer months back home the winter months here? Or can it be that there's no direct correlation between the passage of time in one universe and another? Maybe the days we're experiencing here only correspond to, let's say, a number of hours back home. Maybe the whole reason the X-Men haven't summoned us back yet is that they haven't even had time to realize we're overdue!"

Bishop nodded with reluctant admiration. "You really do have a functional brain in there. I'm impressed."

Spider-Man, in response, gave a slight bow. "Thank Kyew."

"The only thing I don't understand is just what this has to do with cats."

"Everything," Spider-Man said. "Because that's the part I was talking about, the part that really kills me."

"Tell me."

"Well, with all these major differences, and all they mean to us..." Spider-Man hesitated.

"Yes?"

"Even on this world, *Cats* is still playing!"

Bishop stared. And stared. And stared some more. And emitted a not-very-pleasant sound somewhere deep in his throat: a sound that reminded Spider-Man of nothing so much as a gear grinding itself to slivers because somebody forgot to add the oil. "I really don't understand you," he said at last. "We're trapped on a world far from home, where we may have to stay if Blaquesmith can't call us back, where we may have to face dangers we're not even equipped to understand, and you make jokes?"

"Can you think of a better time?" Spider-Man asked.

Bishop shook his head and walked away.

Spider-Man, who followed close behind, knew the big guy had a point. Inside, he was frantic; it was impossible not to think of Mary Jane, and how desperately he wanted to see her again. He joked about it for the same reason he fired off wisecracks while fighting monsters like Carnage, or Dr. Octopus, or the Hobgoblin... because sometimes they were the only thing that kept him from being afraid.

He followed Bishop onto the Great Lawn, which, given the temperature, was only sparsely populated with pedestrians and diehard joggers. There was somebody flying a kite on the other side of the field, at the spot where stages were erected whenever somebody decided to do a concert in the park. The kid was flying it so high that it was little more than a speck in the sky. Spider-Man watched it bob and weave in the wind, and found he envied it; the need to keep a low profile had stuck him at ground level since arriving on this world, and he'd been denied the simple

THE PRESENT

exhilaration of being able to travel across town at skyscraper height. He didn't miss it as much as he missed Mary Jane, but he still missed it. He wondered what Bishop missed. If Bishop missed anything.

And then he wondered about the one thing he'd tried so hard to avoid wondering about. Namely: why weren't they back home?

Spider-Man's adventures hadn't taken him time-traveling as frequently as, let's say, the Fantastic Four's—which was fine with him; he much preferred life as a friendly *neighborhood* Spider-Man—but he had been back and forth a little, enough to take it more casually than it merited. (He'd fought Martians in the future and Puritans at the Salem Witch Trials—after that, one's sense of awe tended to operate wonkily if at all.) When he agreed to go along on this trip, he hadn't devoted nearly enough thought to the kind of things that could go wrong. He hadn't wondered what Mary Jane was going to do if he wasn't able to find his way back.

But then he hadn't had much choice, had he? The whole mess had been dropped in his lap as suddenly as a fat lady falling from a theater balcony.

It had begun at the museum, when Peter Parker ran across that photograph of Bishop and himself, beside that covered wagon in the Old West. There had been a message from himself carved into the back of an antique silver serving tray:

CABLE!
IT'S JUNE 26, 1867, AND WE'RE STUCK HERE! SEND HELP TO THE PLACE WHERE IT ALL BEGAN! HOPE TO SEE YOU SOON!
YOUR PAL,
WEBS

Cinching it was the discovery of one of his spider-tracers on the underside of the tray: rusty and covered with dust, but still functional.

When Peter Parker saw that, he'd known for a fact that he and Bishop were fated to travel to that particular era, at

TIME'S ARROW

some point in their mutual futures. On Mary Jane's urging, he'd changed into Spider-Man and contacted the X-Men to investigate . . . whereupon he discovered that the journey had to take place immediately. Because their pet time machine, a thingie they called a Time Displacement Core, had already picked up evidence that somebody, somewhere, was bent on destroying entire parallel universes. Several had already been wiped out, along with their populations— a body count so immense that it beggared the imagination. Missiles had already been fired from four separate alternate futures, into an equal number of places in Earth's past, carrying bombs that, if permitted to explode, would annihilate not only all life but all history.

Only Spider-Man and the X-Men were in a position to stop them.

With no other choice, they'd broken up into teams and used the Time Displacement Core to send themselves into the past. They'd each brought along recall devices, so they could get back home once their missions were accomplished. Of course, thanks to the clues already provided for them, it was preordained that Spider-Man and Bishop had to be the pair sent to take out the bomb in the Old West . . . and they managed it with little trouble, thanks to the aid of the famous gunslinger known as the Two-Gun Kid.

The only problem was that the recall devices hadn't survived the fight . . . hence the necessity of scratching the message onto that serving tray.

And once a replacement recall device was provided for them, and they were summoned back to the future, or the present, or wherever, Spider-Man and Bishop discovered that their problems were just beginning. They hadn't landed back home, where they could say seeya later and return to their own lives. They'd landed on some strange alternate Earth where the X-Men were fascist enforcers intent on capturing and imprisoning everybody else with super-powers. No sooner had they landed than they found themselves forced to flee an encounter with nastier versions of Iceman, Wolverine, and the Beast.

THE PRESENT

Obviously, something had gone terribly wrong. But was it the Time Displacement Core? Or history itself? Had the other X-Men succeeded in tracking down and disarming the other bombs? Were they even alive, and if they were, had they given Spider-Man and Bishop up for dead?

They had suffered two long days without answers, without any way to fight back aside from getting on each other's nerves.

Bishop was right. It was no time for jokes.

But Spider-Man knew no other way to stay sane . . .

He caught up with Bishop just in time to feel a certain buzzing sensation in the back of his head. "Uh-oh."

Bishop said, "Another joke, web-slinger?"

"No." Spider-Man didn't bother to explain about his spider-sense. "Trouble. Somewhere up ahead."

Bishop's eyes narrowed as he scanned the trees at the other side of the meadow. It was true. Something was going on over there. All the people on the walkways were whirling around, reacting to something behind the trees. Something very startling, and very frightening, and very unexpected. Spider-Man heard their distant cries a second before he heard the source of the disturbance itself: a certain high-pitched humming—

—and then he spotted the lone figure moving through the air over the trees.

He was a tall, athletic young man in a warmup suit. He wasn't flying, at least not in any way that Spider-Man was used to. He was . . . running? No, *skating*. He moved in the rhythmic side-to-side manner of a pro hockey player going for speed, his legs driving hard against open air, treating it like solid surface instead of open space. It was obviously a physical effort for him; as he sped through the sky over the Great Lawn, moving faster than anybody skating across mere ice, his arms and legs pumped with the desperation of a man giving the race everything he had. Almost immediately after he cleared the trees he descended to within a few feet of the ground, and doubled over, now moving so quickly that most of the onlookers must have seen him as a blur; Spider-Man, who was used

TIME'S ARROW

to people capable of moving even faster, caught a good look at his face as he passed by and saw that he couldn't have been older than sixteen.

About as old as Peter Parker had been, when he first became Spider-Man.

Bishop didn't flinch as the Air-Skater sped by, merely turned his head, to follow his progress. "He's terrified."

"He's not the danger," Spider-Man said. He knew it for a fact. His spider-sense was tingling stronger than ever now, but not because of the Air-Skater: because of something else yet to make its appearance from behind the trees.

And then he saw them.

Men and women in black uniforms. They looked like cops, but their uniforms were darker, and more severe, and cut along paramilitary lines. There were dozens of them, coming into view behind the trees; they moved quickly and professionally, but without any particular sense of hurry. Some carried slender weapons with transparent barrels; others carried little boxy machines with something that resembled a parabolic antenna mounted on the front. There were so many of them that the electronic beeping emitted from all those boxes was audible all over the lawn. As they fanned out over the lawn, the civilians in their path hurriedly got out of their way; Spider-Man did not need to be an expert in body language to know that the people seemed more frightened of this army than they were of the young man skating through the air. One look at their faces—and the terrified hunted expression on the face of the young man who seemed like a younger version of himself—and he knew why. He tensed up, ready to lend the Air-Skater a hand—

—only to stop when he felt Bishop's hand close tightly around his wrist.

"No," Bishop said.

Spider-Man stared at the hand encircling his wrist. It couldn't hold him here; not physically. He was stronger and faster than Bishop and could break the grip in the time it took to sneeze. But that would mean ignoring the ur-

THE PRESENT

gency in Bishop's voice... "Bish, can't you see what's going on here?"

"I see," Bishop said. "Probably even better than you. I'm a mutant. I've been in that young man's position."

Spider-Man twitched his wrist, freeing it from Bishop's grip. "Then why—"

"Because this isn't our world," Bishop said. "It may look like our world, but we don't understand anything that's going on here... and anything we do to interfere runs the risk of making matters a thousand times worse. No. Painful as it is, the most we can do right now is watch, and learn, and figure out the rules, in case we need them."

Spider-Man didn't like it. It went against everything he stood for. And standing idly by while something wrong happened had once proved the single greatest mistake of his life. But Bishop was right... and so he remained in place, helplessly watching as the Air-Skater sped around in circles in the air three stories above their heads.

That was a bad sign. The kid moved much faster than the cops. If he wasn't fleeing the scene, it could only mean that he considered himself trapped... and that he'd chosen this place to make his last stand.

Come on, kid, he prayed. *You may think you're alone up there, but you've got a rooting section.*

Most of the civilians had fled the Great Lawn; those that remained seemed either frozen with indecision or rapt with curiosity. Spider-Man saw a few taking pictures, and found himself wondering inanely whether any of them were stringers for the *Daily Bugle*. He saw a few others shouting at the Air-Skater, either taunts or words of encouragement. The cops took no notice, but just fanned out around the lawn, their weapons all trained on the Air-Skater. The officers who carried the little boxy machines looked neither at the crowds nor the Air-Skater; instead they just kept their attention firmly riveted on their machines, obeying readouts that seemed the world to them.

"Cerebros," Bishop said.

Spider-Man glanced at him. "What?"

"It's a device invented by Professor Xavier when he

TIME'S ARROW

founded the X-Men. He designed it to detect and track down mutants. He built his because he wanted to recruit allies before his enemy Magneto did. This wouldn't be the first time I saw somebody use the same basic technology to try to hunt mutants down. They're all focused on the boy right now, but it won't be long before somebody realizes he's not the only mutant here. We should—''

And then it was too late.

There was always one in every gang of thugs: a trigger-happy idiot who wasn't content to be one of the many faceless soldiers pointing a weapon, and had to be the big glorious hero who actually fired the weapon. Spider-Man hated those guys even more than he hated thugs in general. After all, a guy who can't obey the rules even as a hired thug is a guy you can't depend on for anything.

This one fired his shot from somewhere in the middle of the field. A burst of flaming yellow energy rocketed into the air and exploded next to the Air-Skater with a force that might have incinerated him. But his reaction time was almost as fast as Spider-Man's own . . . and by the time the fireball swallowed the place where he'd been, the Air-Skater was already twenty yards away, zigzagging so quickly that he seemed less a man and more a multi-colored streak in the shape of a man.

Some people cheered. A hot-dog vendor some thirty yards away from Spider-Man and Bishop cried out, "You go, bro!" Somebody shouted, "Do it again, fella!" Somebody else yelled, "Shoot him! Shoot him! Shoot the sponkie!"

Spider-Man was in agony. *Don't get cocky, kid. Keep an eye on the ground.*

Another half-dozen fireballs exploded in midair, lighting the sky brighter than any sun. The Air-Skater flew a ragged course between them, staying just one step ahead of the explosions, at times buffeted by them, but remaining unharmed. The last one detonated over his head, and the Air-Skater had to descend to less than ten feet over the earth to avoid the shock wave; he passed close enough to Spider-Man for the web-slinger to see that he was covered

THE PRESENT

with sweat, and shouting in mingled fear and anger. He flew directly over the head of one of the cops, who was stupid enough to actually try to jump up and grab him; the glancing impact disturbed the Air-Skater not at all but sent the cop tumbling to the ground with what looked like a pair of broken wrists.

Smart, Spider-Man thought. *Stay low. Stay between them. They can't fire their weapons if you're that close.*

The Air-Skater seemed to realize that even as Spider-Man thought it. He descended to within a few short feet of the ground and skimmed the earth at dizzying speed, scattering the cops as he went. He didn't actually collide with any; he seemed to have way more self-control than that. Instead, he just picked his target, and let the normal human tendency to avoid rapidly moving objects do most of the work. Some cops fell all over themselves to avoid being run down. The ones that stood their ground were bowled over by the air pressure when the Air-Skater changed course at the last minute.

Bishop cried out, "Cartwright!"

It took Spider-Man a fraction of a second to remember that this was the alias he had used with Bishop during their mission in the Old West. He had already told Bishop that that wasn't his real name, but perhaps the large mutant thought calling him by such an obviously false name as "Spider-Man" would be unwise under the circumstances.

He yanked his gaze away from the battling Air-Skater and saw what Bishop was so upset about. One of the police officers, a skinny fellow with a pencil-thin moustache, was standing only a few feet away, and staring at his portable Cerebro with no small amount of shock. The officer glanced in their direction with wide eyes and immediately went for a communication device strapped to his wrist. "Frants here! Code—"

Bishop crossed the distance between himself and the police officer in three short steps, and took him out with a single blow to the neck. The officer stiffened and fell to the ground without making a noise. In the chaos on the Great Lawn, nobody even noticed. Bishop crushed the

TIME'S ARROW

portable Cerebro with a single stomp of his boot, then turned on his heels, and walked away as quickly as possible, grabbing Spider-Man by the arm as he went.

Spider-Man said, "You didn't—"

"He'll have a sore throat for a while," Bishop told him. "I try not to war against people who are only doing their jobs. But we may have to do a lot worse soon, if we don't get out of here now. The rest of them may be too busy to notice anything strange about their readings, but that won't last. They'll notice us and call for reinforcements. Maybe super-powered reinforcements, and probably lots of super-powered reinforcements."

The Air-Skater was up in the sky again, dodging another fusillade of exploding fireballs. Spider-Man protested, "We can't just leave him, Bishop!"

"And what are you going to do, if you take up his cause? What are you going to do, if we're summoned home while you're still fighting everything that's wrong with this world? Are you actually irresponsible enough to raise the stakes of a battle you know you might not be here long enough to finish?"

Spider-Man wanted to fight. He really did.

But his spider-sense was shrieking like an air-raid siren gone rabid, and the air above the park was filling with police helicopters, some of which were equipped with what looked like high-tech weaponry, and some of which had larger versions of the Cerebro device mounted on their fuselage. They flew above the Great Lawn in tight formation, hemming the Air-Skater in, preventing any attempt at escape. With dozens of police weapons now aimed at him, and the whirling blades of the helicopters threatening to carve him into slices if he moved outside a very restricted airspace, the Air-Skater could only move in circles, like an animal probing for weak spots in its cage.

Loudspeakers broadcast the police ultimatum at a volume that must have been audible all over the park: *"Attention, the individual in the air! You are in violation of federal law! Surrender now and you will not be hurt!"*

THE PRESENT

Bishop pulled on Spider-Man's arm. "Come on. Before they detect us again."

And Spider-Man, hating himself, made a decision as difficult as any he'd ever known. "All right." *But I'm not done with this. I swear it.*

Spider-Man and Bishop were not particularly conspicuous as they fled the open spaces of the Great Lawn. All around them, the civilians who hadn't already run away—who had preferred to enjoy the spectacle of the Air-Skater making fools of the police—were also belatedly realizing that this had become a show too dangerous to keep watching. Spider-Man and Bishop were just two out of the dozens running away from the battlefield.

For Spider-Man, who could have hopped to the front of the crowd in three giant leaps, the act of will it took to keep himself down to merely human speed was not quite as difficult as what it took to restrain himself from lending the Air-Skater a hand.

They ran through a clump of trees and onto a paved walkway, just in time to hear a young woman shout, "Look! It's him!"

He and Bishop stopped just long enough to see that she was pointing at three men running toward the Great Lawn. Two of them were police officers clad in the same militaristic black uniform as the troops in the park; the third, leading them, was a tall athletic man in a strangely altered version of a costume that both Spider-Man and Bishop otherwise knew quite well. The one they were familiar with was a blue bodysuit with yellow trunks, gloves, and boots, topped with a hood and a gleaming gold visor; this version had all of that, but the colors were yellow and black, and the uniform was padded and bulked up, with unidentifiable military insignia along one side of the chest.

"Cyclops," the young woman said breathlessly.

A kid stopping for rest near a tree said, "He'll stop that sponkie. You'll see!"

Spider-Man and Bishop glanced at each other. This wasn't good. Their Cyclops was the co-leader of the X-Men. He was totally professional in battle, and totally ded-

TIME'S ARROW

icated to Charles Xavier's dream of a future where normal human beings and super-powered mutants could live together in peace. If this world's Cyclops was here, now, then their own situation was more precarious than ever.

Bishop said, "See what I mean? You probably didn't have a problem fighting the police, but are you ready to take on Cyclops, and maybe the rest of this world's X-Men as well?"

"You've made your point," Spider-Man rasped. *But I'm still not done with this.*

He hesitated only an instant before joining Bishop and the rest of the fleeing spectators in the mass exodus from the park.

For Scott Summers, aka Cyclops, taking down the Air-Skater was a minor challenge. He was moving fast, of course, and there were a number of helicopters up there that would have been even more vulnerable to an optic blast than the boy himself. It would not do to miscalculate, and send the shattered remains of a chopper crashing down upon the people below; that might be acceptable behavior for movie directors, but not for the nominal leader of the X-Men's Super-Power Registration Enforcement Action Detail. Cyclops needed to be considerably more precise in his work.

Still, it was essentially just skeet-shooting.

All Cyclops had to do was stand unseen by the trees at the edge of the Great Lawn, watch the Air-Skater for maybe ten seconds, then activate the mechanism that controlled the ruby quartz lenses in his visor. As long as the lenses covered his eyes, his force-beams were contained; when the lenses were retracted, however slightly, the terrible destructive power was allowed to burst free. It was a power that made him a potential threat to everybody around him; that was precisely what he liked most about it.

He tracked the speeding figure from a distance, under conditions that might have challenged the world's greatest sharpshooters, then fingered the controls in his palm to

THE PRESENT

open his visor just a tiny notch. The force-beam left his visor at the speed of light, piercing fifty yards of open space to strike the Air-Skater in his solar plexus. The impact immediately knocked the breath from the fugitive sponkie, who emitted an astonished "Whuuuufff!!" He spun out and crashed into the ground, tearing a twenty-foot furrow as he went.

The two cops accompanying him both whistled in appreciation. "One shot," said Sergeant Vossoff. "Excellent work, sir."

"It certainly hadda hurt," agreed Sergeant Nimmitz.

"That was the point," Cyclops said. He spoke into his communicator. "All right, people. I want that sponkie handled, and I want all our procedures followed to the letter. No medical attention until *after* he's secured, understand? And even then I want him stashed at Pegasus until we can get a proper team assigned to his case. Move it!"

All over the lawn, cops began to converge on the fresh scar in the earth. Cyclops watched with deep satisfaction. Yes, from the reports he'd heard on his way here, their performance against the Air-Skater had been pathetic—but what they lacked in paranormal ability they certainly possessed in numbers. They'd been able to engage the boy repeatedly, at several different points throughout the city, preventing him from finding a safe haven, wearing him down until they finally cornered him in the park. Even without Cyclops, they would have captured him in another hour or so. Spending another couple of million of the taxpayers' money, but still.

There was nothing like a well-oiled machine to make the day run smoothly.

One of the cops at the crash site gave a hand signal. Target secured. Cyclops relaxed, but not by much.

"Sir?"

Cyclops turned. "What?"

Sergeant Vossoff was listening to a coded transmission on his ear-speaker. "The observation team's been inspecting their readouts . . . and they say the Cerebros picked up an anomaly during the operation."

TIME'S ARROW

There were times Cyclops wished he didn't wear a mask: a single raised eyebrow would have spoken a thousand words right about now. "What kind of an anomaly?"

"They say there's a better than 75 percent probability of more sponkies among the civilians we scared off. Not latents or inactives, either. Full Class A's, operating in the open. Kirby's hacking the data to make sure it wasn't doubling caused by the kid's flight speed, but says that if he's right, it looks like there may have been two." Vossoff hesitated, and listened to a clarification as it came in. "One standard-issue mutant, one situationally enhanced—who didn't seem to possess a reading. Moving in concert. Kirby—well, he sounds pretty sure."

"Are they still in range?"

"Not at the moment. Apparently they fled the scene with the rest of the civs."

Cyclops grimaced. This couldn't be good. Sponkies had once congregated in teams, but these days they rarely travelled together in public, since staying together only increased the chances of being picked up by Cerebro. Most of the ones still at large were individuals like the Air-Skater, who'd developed their powers only recently and had yet to forge any alliances with others of their kind. Sponkies travelling together, looking out for each other, usually avoided capture a lot longer. And tended to do considerably more damage before being run to ground...

It wasn't totally unexpected. Iceman, Wolverine, and the Beast had encountered a pair of sponkies only two days ago. One was a muscular black man with an M tattooed on his face, the other an acrobat type in a gaudy red-and-blue bodysuit. They'd both proven surprisingly resourceful, and they'd both gotten away. If that was the same pair Kirby was talking about, then they were either reckless, crazy, stupid, suicidal—or so sure of their own abilities that they just didn't care.

And if one didn't possess a reading... maybe he was Registered. Which was bad news for everybody.

Vossoff spoke again. "I think we just got independent confirmation, sir. They just found Officer Frants knocked

THE PRESENT

out, with his Cerebro inoperative on the ground beside him."

"Not dead?" Cyclops asked.

"No, sir. Just unconscious."

"What a relief," Cyclops said. "That means when he wakes up, he'll be able to give us a description." He activated his own communicator, and sent out a broad-based signal to every police officer in range. "Attention! This is Cyclops! We have a Double Class-A situation here! Repeat, Double Class-A. Two sponkies of unknown abilities and unconfirmed description, believed to be fleeing the park. I want wide-angle scans from every chopper, full-intensity readings at every park exit. I don't want anybody leaving unless they've been checked. This is top priority, people. These are unknowns we're dealing with here, which means that they are to be considered dangerous and a threat to human life."

He didn't pause at all before he said the next part.

"If you find yourself in a survival situation, don't hesitate to kill . . ."

CHAPTER TWO

The short, stocky man crept along the upper branches of a one-hundred-year-old oak, feeling them tremble beneath his weight, willing them not to break, not to move, not to make any sound.

There were three hunters, spread out at ground level. They had to know he was somewhere above them. More than once they'd looked up and seemed to stare him right in the eye. But though they were about as good in their jobs as anybody the stocky man had ever known, they didn't register his motionless form, lying in wait. Their eyes just moved on, toward other trees, other hiding places.

A sly smile crossed his face. It was a rough-hewn face—a fighter's face. Some might even say a bestial face. It wasn't his best feature. He didn't mind too much, because it wasn't his worst feature either. Not many people appreciated seeing his worst feature. Not many even survived it.

His name was Logan. That was it. He didn't need any more name than that, unless you counted the one that had made his reputation: Wolverine. Anything else just took too much time to say. Wolverine didn't have the patience.

Unless, of course, he was hunting. Then he could stay rock still for hours. Then he made himself one with his surroundings, until even the savviest opponents—which the three down below were—could look right at him and not realize what they saw. For that he had an unlimited supply of patience.

He caught a flash of movement in the branches just a few inches to his right, and checked to see that it wasn't one of the hunters, pulling something funny. The answer was considerably more mundane: a squirrel.

It was less than three feet away, and it didn't know he was here either.

Wolverine inhaled, sifting the squirrel's scent from all the others that surrounded him on all sides. It was a healthy well-fed male in its early adulthood, that had lived a life relatively free of stress and was right now fairly contented to remain where it sat. It was an animal at peace,

THE PRESENT

and for a moment, living through its perceptions, Wolverine was at peace as well.

Then, with one swift, sure movement, Wolverine reached out with one gloved finger and tapped it twice on the top of its head. It froze, then bolted, a flash of gray leaping for safety on another branch.

Good luck to ya, pal. He smirked. *Pay a little more attention and maybe you'll live longer.*

He heard a chuckle, directly above him. "Enjoying the local wildlife, Logan?"

Aw, nuts.

Wolverine jumped from the branch just as a battering ram of pure ice struck the spot where he'd been. He allowed himself to fall roughly, paying no heed to the dozens of other branches that raked his skin on the way down; they were cutting the hell out of his arms and legs, but they didn't hurt nearly as much as the grating awareness that with a moment's unthinking carelessness, he'd allowed himself to be caught like a rank amateur.

Up above, Iceman's mocking voice called out to the others. "Hey, guys! I think I found Logan's weakness! The guy thinks he's Dr. Doolittle!"

Wolverine scowled. Bobby was gonna be sorry he said that.

He caught hold of a lower branch, spun around, and scrambled around to a higher position, to get a closer look at the odds he faced. What he saw appeared to be a man of opaque crystal, sliding along in a controlled skid along a roller-coaster bridge of solid ice. Iceman, as Bobby Drake was called, moved impressively fast. His temperature-reducing powers allowed him to spin that ice bridge ahead of him as he sped along, and as he circled the tree again and again, in a smooth spiral that resembled the express ramp at the local mall's parking garage, Logan realized that Bobby had no intention of coming in to finish the attack at close range. He wanted to keep circling the tree until it and Logan were completely caged by ice.

Logan had to blame himself for having been taken by surprise. True, when Bobby was in his ice mode, it was

TIME'S ARROW

more difficult to pick up his scent; but the kid couldn't move without making a constant cracking noise. Powered up, the man was almost incapable of stealth. Logan would have been prepared for him, if he hadn't grown bored and stopped to chat with squirrels...

"Hey, Logan!" Bobby called, merrily enough. "Maybe when we're done I'll drive you into town so you can rent *Bambi*!"

"That's enough, Bobby." It was a regal woman's voice, coming from somewhere up above. "This is a serious exercise, you don't have to mock the man."

Wolverine smirked. *That's okay, Ororo, darlin'. Let the kid mock me all he wants. It makes this easier.*

Snikt!

The sound signaled the spring-loaded release of the six razor-sharp claws, built out of the indestructible alloy adamantium, that spent most of their days safely hidden in the recessed shafts on the back of Wolverine's wrists. They were part of him—the nastiest part. They'd cut anything, if Wolverine was so inclined. As he often was.

He leapt from the tree, launching himself, not at Bobby, but at the closest pass of Bobby's mammoth ice-sculpture. He leapt with no concern for the great height, or the seemingly uncrossable distance between himself and the ramp; instead, he just aimed himself straight out, and trusted in his momentum to carry him the rest of the way throughout the arc of his descent. When he smashed into the ice ramp, only a few feet off the ground, it was with an impact capable of breaking another man's ribs. Wolverine didn't even grunt; he just stood up and with a slash of each arm sliced the level immediately above him in half. He scrambled through the opening, onto the next loop of the spiral, and ran along the icy ramp slicing chunk after chunk out of the levels above him. Bobby had built in plenty of supports along the way, but the whole couldn't stand if the structure wasn't sound....

Somewhere, Ororo's regal voice cried out: "Watch out, Iceman! Your ramp's becoming top-heavy...."

The ice ramp shuddered and began to list. Somewhere,

THE PRESENT

high above him, Bobby Drake cried out, "Oh, noooo . . ."

Wolverine jumped away from the structure just as it collapsed all around him. He was almost hit by a fragment the size of a car that would have done him serious damage, but was carried out of the way at the last second by a gust of powerful wind that dropped him the instant he was clear. That would be Ororo, forgetting for the moment that she was supposed to be an opponent. He cleared the wreckage just in time to face the next attack, a series of ground-level explosions that peppered his already stinging arms and legs with gravel.

Gambit called to him from about thirty feet away. "You done good wit' de walkin' snowball, man. Mebbe you do better wit' a body from a warmer climate."

Wolverine brandished his claws. "I'll make it as hot for you as you want, LeBeau."

The opponent who faced Wolverine now was a tall Cajun from New Orleans, whose love of cards had led him to adopt the code name Gambit. He wore an unbuttoned ankle-length duster, and the merest outline of a hood, which had been perversely designed with cutouts that hid absolutely nothing of his face. Like Iceman, he carried a roguish sense of humor around with him wherever he went . . . but unlike Iceman, he didn't ruin it by constantly trying to be funny.

The two men circled each other warily, each looking for the best moment to press the attack. This time Wolverine paid more attention to his heightened senses. He respected Iceman, and regretted having underestimated him . . . but also there was something about Bobby Drake that had never lost its innocence. Much as Wolverine respected that, he still considered Remy LeBeau a much more dangerous opponent.

After about two seconds, Gambit demonstrated why.

In a movement so fluid that even Wolverine was taken by surprise, Gambit darted to one side, pulled six ordinary playing cards from a hidden pocket somewhere inside his long, flowing coat, and flung them Wolverine's way. By the time they left his hand they were no longer ordinary:

TIME'S ARROW

they were glowing with explosive kinetic energy. They would explode with deadly force as soon as they hit another solid object—and at the moment, the only solid object in their trajectory was Wolverine himself.

Wolverine leapt over the glowing missiles, slashing them with his claws as they passed below him. The explosions didn't harm his adamantium claws in the slightest; they did burn his arms and wrists, but that wasn't important; what was important was that the shock wave buffeted him about the chest and added lift to his flight. He hit the ground within a few short feet of Gambit, too close for the Cajun to risk another missile attack. He tucked, rolled, and jumped to his feet, already pressing his advantage with a fresh swipe from the blades on his left wrist.

Gambit easily deflected the swing with a blow to Wolverine's forearm. Even as Wolverine drew back his right arm for another attack, Gambit drove his knee into Wolverine's midsection, then deliberately fell backward and used the momentum of Wolverine's assault to flip the scrappy Canadian over his shoulders.

Both men got to their feet simultaneously, circling each other exactly as before, but with increased respect dawning in Wolverine's eyes. "Nice move, Cajun."

"You t'ink Remy jus' know 'bout dealing cards?"

Wolverine searched for another opening, but already he knew he was too late; he could hear the familiar crackling sound approaching from directly above him and to the right, and knew that Gambit had only been giving Iceman time to recover. Instead of attacking Remy again, which would have given Bobby his opening, Logan fled just as a pylon of solid ice pierced the ground where he'd been standing. He continued his serpentine path across the grass, dodging battering rams of ice and energy weapons made of playing cards, keeping alert for the one moment when he'd have an opportunity to turn the tables on his opponents.

It didn't come.

THE PRESENT

Instead, Wolverine was attacked by the air itself. Between one step and the next, it simply went mad, enveloping him in an insane maelstrom of howling wind. *Tornado*, he thought dizzily. The funnel had struck ground only a few feet away from him, and its powerful suction was even now threatening to pull him off his feet and hurl him into open air. He flung himself to the ground, stabbing it with all six of his claws in a futile effort to anchor himself to the earth. It wasn't enough. When the funnel passed by, it tugged first at his legs, then at his chest, and then at his entire body, yanking him and his claws from the ground with a violence that left clods of dirt following close behind.

As the winds hurled him high in the air, and spun him around in circles, Wolverine retracted his claws, and stewed in frustration. He hated bad weather. It was an enemy that could surround him on all sides, and pummel him from up close . . . but that his abilities were absolutely ineffective in fighting. There was nothing he could do but endure the ride, try not to get dizzy . . . and wait for Ororo to make her move.

When she did, he was four hundred feet straight up.

The tornado simply disappeared, as if it had never been there at all . . . and he found himself dangling high above the earth, held only by the two strong hands wrapped tightly around his wrists.

The hands belonged to one of the most beautiful and regal women Wolverine had ever known. She was a tall black woman, with soft blue eyes, flowing white hair, and confident bearing that might have been a large part of the reason that the natives in one part of Africa had once worshiped her as a goddess. Sometimes, just listening to her deep but musical voice, Wolverine wondered if they'd come to that conclusion before or after witnessing her uncanny control over the wind and rain; certainly, her presence alone had impressed every single person who ever met her, up to and including the notoriously unimpressable Dr. Doom. Her birth name was Ororo, but the name she'd adopted when she joined the X-Men suited her even more: Storm.

Hovering atop a cushion of cooperative air, and holding on to Wolverine with no apparent show of effort—more a measurement of her own strength than the strength of the winds she employed to support a portion of his weight—she simply said, "So: Logan."

"So: 'Roro."

"What did you think of my tornado?"

"Honestly?" He grinned evilly. "I thought it sucked."

She groaned. "I ought to drop you."

"I was about to suggest somethin' like that. Wanna put me down?"

"I don't think so."

"Why not?"

"Because you set the rules of this exercise. Gambit, Iceman, and I had not only to find you, and fight you to a standstill, but also get you to say uncle. Now, I'll admit I don't understand why you would have picked that word, in particular, over any other . . ."

"Tradition," Wolverine said. He looked down at the ground, and saw a growing ice-ramp slowly rising toward their position. Iceman was at the formation point, of course; Gambit was following by holding on to the back of Iceman's belt. They'd both be here in less than a minute: a fairly long time, to spring what he had in mind. He sighed and took quick stock of his wounds—which were all healing quite nicely, thank you; another half hour and nobody would even be able to tell where they'd been.

Storm waited the few remaining seconds it took Iceman's ramp to reach their altitude.

"Hey, Ororo," Iceman said. "How long are you two going to hang around up here anyway? I'm itching to get back to Professor X and the others, to see if they managed to repair our pet time machine yet."

Gambit concurred. "What's de holdup, *cherie*? Ain't de man said uncle yet?"

"Actually," she said, "we were just getting to that." She turned her attention back to Wolverine. "Well, Logan,

THE PRESENT

are you going to say 'uncle' now? Or must I drop you and see how well your healing factor deals with a fall from this height?"

"Neither." Wolverine grinned. " 'Cause I ain't gonna say uncle. You are."

"Really." Ororo was amused. "And why would I do such a silly thing?"

"Because all this time we been here, you ain't once stopped to think how dangerous it is to hold *me* by the wrists."

There was a moment of stunned silence.

"De man's bluffing," Gambit said.

"You know me better than that, Cajun. I'm crazy. I'll do anything. And while I *know* Ororo's bluffing—she wouldn't drop me just to win a game—ya gotta know that sometimes I forget myself. Question is whether I'll forget myself enough to pop my claws right through her hands. And ya gotta know how much that would have to hurt. She'll prob'ly lose a finger or two, an' whatever she's got left gonna be a long time healin' . . . if it heals at all, which is doubtful. Even if you're *almost* sure I won't do it . . . are ya so certain you're willing to risk it? Are ya?"

Gambit shrugged. "Ain't my hands. Dat's up to de lady to decide."

Iceman's gaze was darting from one deadly-serious face to the other. "You guys gotta be kidding me! Logan, I—for Pete's sake, this isn't funny!"

Ororo's voice was grim. "No, it's not." She lowered her voice, and spoke with the deadly seriousness of a woman who had decided she was no longer playing a game. "Logan, you're my friend. And I know you're only saying this because you want to win the exercise. But you should know by now that I'm every bit as capable of ruthlessness as you are. And I'm warning you that if you don't renounce this insane tactic right now, I will indeed drop you . . . and do whatever I can to keep Bobby and Remy from catching you."

"Your option, darlin'. Course, if you do that, you'll never know if I was bluffin' or not." He chuckled. "Guess we got ourselves a nice Mexican standoff."

"I will count to five."

"That's dumb. I might pop my claws when you reach five."

"And I might drop you when I reach four."

"People," Iceman said, "I'm really not enjoying this."

"You ain't involved," Wolverine told him. He looked at Ororo again. "Five don't give either one of us a lot of time to back down, does it?"

"No," Ororo said. "It doesn't. One."

"Two," said Wolverine.

"Three," said Ororo.

Iceman shouted, "Uncle! For God's sake, *uncle!*"

Both Ororo and Wolverine looked at him before looking at each other.

And Wolverine grinned. "Game, set, and match, kids."

Scene: a rubble-strewn subbasement beneath the winery where Wolverine and the others had just completed one of their more sedate training exercises.

One of the wonderful things about technology is that when the machines break down, none of them are any better than any other. They're all, in the eyes of the people who needed them running, equally worthless pieces of junk.

This was even true of the Time Displacement Core, the superscientific device designed to facilitate travel to and from other eras of history. The principles that governed its operation were as advanced as anything the human race had ever seen. The thousand and one finely tuned mechanisms that controlled its power were beyond the comprehension of any but the most brilliant scientific minds on the planet. The forces that kept it running were a miracle of quantum mechanics and theoretical physics. And now that it was broken, the silver-haired mutant known as Cable needed all his considerable willpower just to suppress the urge to kick it.

"No good," he said, as he emerged from an access panel beneath the control center. "Blaquesmith and I have

THE PRESENT

tried rerouting the power, activating its auto-repair capabilities, even boosting the redundant systems . . . but, for now, the time-travel capabilities appear to be shot."

"Unfortunate," said Professor Charles Xavier, once again demonstrating his fine gift for understatement. It could not have been easy for him; as the world's greatest expert in the field of human mutation, the world's most powerful telepath, and the founder of the X-Men, understatement must have taken a conscious act of will. Still, as a man paralyzed from the waist down, he knew his limitations; and though he'd been following the repair attempts very closely, he'd carefully kept his hovering alien "wheelchair" out of the way of those doing the actual work. "What is functioning?"

"The monitors are still up," Cable said. "We can scan timelines, past, future, and alternate. And the teleportation grid's working again—we can still use it for instantaneous travel to anywhere on the planet. But the temporal displacement matrix is shot, and without that, the TDC simply isn't a time machine anymore. Unless we manage to fix that, retrieving Bishop and Spider-Man is totally out of the question."

A new contributor loped over from another control deck on the other side of the lab. He was the Beast: Dr. Hank McCoy, a brilliant biogeneticist whose most unusual features were his enlarged hands and feet, his enhanced strength and agility, and the bright blue fur that covered every inch of his body. He said: "Loath as I am to dwell on the ramifications of this misfortune, I must reiterate that we're also bereft of any offensive capabilities against the architect of said damage."

"That's right," Cable said grimly. "We may have barely stopped Kang's troopers from blowing up the TDC, but we still weren't able to prevent them from crippling us. Now we can't even stage a counterattack. He launched that last group of packages from four separate future timelines . . . and if we can't get to those eras, then he can send as many time bombs as he wants, to any era or timeline

TIME'S ARROW

that he wants, and we won't be able to do a thing to stop them."

"That's unacceptable," said Cyclops, who was one of the founding members of the X-Men and had been the official battle leader for almost as long. He spoke more harshly than he'd intended, but then everybody in the room expected it from him. He had a penchant for excessive seriousness born of constant awareness of the danger his eyes posed to everybody around him. The visor he used to control his optic blasts made him look stern at the best of times; today he was even grimmer than usual, since he wasn't sufficiently versed in the technology to help with the repairs, and he felt thoroughly useless—something that all the other X-Men would have happily testified he'd never been.

"There must be another option," said Phoenix—Scott's wife, Jean Grey, who'd also been with the X-Men almost since the beginning. She was a lovely redhead who just happened to be one of the most powerful telepaths and telekinetics on the planet. "If we can't use the TDC, then we'll just have to use something else."

"An easier suggestion to make than to implement," said Blaquesmith. Many of the others weren't sure just what he was; Iceman had once referred to him as Cable's Yoda, and it was easy to see why, since he was an indeterminately aged nonhuman with slits for eyes and a penchant for wisdom doled out in aphorisms. He leaned most of his weight on his walking stick, as he turned his attention to Xavier. "There aren't many other places in this era where one can find working time machines."

"Actually," the Beast said, "I can reference several, and just to guard against suspicions that we haven't explored every alternative, I've already weighed the difficulties of obtaining access to those. The Fantastic Four have one at Four Freedoms Plaza, but they're apparently off-world right now, doing their cosmic thing, so I have not been able to reach them to ascertain its suitability. And the ranting miscreant known as Dr. Doom also has one in his possession, which I believe to be of the same

THE PRESENT

design . . . but given his notoriously misanthropic disposition, I would strongly counsel against any impulse to show up at his front door to ask for a cup of sugar and a time machine. There may be others, but I doubt they're conveniently listed in our database. For better or worse, we must unravel this conundrum with the the tools we already have."

"That may take more time than we have," Cable said. "The whole universe might be destroyed while we're still discussing what to do." The pain in his voice was so palpable that he had to catch his breath, and wonder if anybody else in the room realized that this was more than just another world-threatening crisis to him. This was personal: very personal. After a moment, he said, "If the Fantastic Four aren't home, then maybe we should break into their headquarters. The Beast was an Avenger once, so he should have access. Maybe—"

"That's no good," Blaquesmith said, with so much frustration that he appeared likely to stamp his foot with rage. "We're running out of time as it is. I examined the records made by the TDC when you were in the past, going after Kang's previous missiles . . . and as far as I can ascertain, it took you far too long to destroy them. They had already been active long enough to damage the timestream: the chronotons they emitted were more than enough to set off a cascade effect that is claiming uncounted other timelines even as we speak. The situation is so unstable that we don't dare bring in other time-travel technology. It might destabilize the multiverse even further."

Xavier grimaced. "What's the margin for error in that analysis, Blaquesmith?"

"Twenty-five percent. Which is unacceptably high, I know—but that still means I'm seventy-five percent sure the timestream's already been damaged beyond repair. We can't risk making things even worse!"

Phoenix said, "Under the circumstances, we might have no other choice. Shouldn't we dispatch somebody to see if the other time machines are available? At least then we'll know. At least then we'll have the option of—"

TIME'S ARROW

She was interrupted by an alarm from one of the monitors. Blaquesmith shuffled over to investigate, and the look on his face was enough to tell the others that whatever he saw may have signaled the end of all hope. Cable and the Beast rushed to his side, with Professor Xavier piloting his hoverchair right behind them.

"It's academic," Blaquesmith said. "Three more massive payloads, evidently bombs like the last ones, each fired from a different alternate future. The same futures he fired the last missiles from. And these missiles are all being sent to the same timeline. This time he wants to destroy *us*."

"Oh, my stars and garters," the Beast murmured. "Daddy Kang's becoming obsessive-compulsive."

"Indeed," said Professor Xavier. "He evidently sees us as a threat, which is the most encouraging news we've gotten all day. Where are these bombs being sent?"

Blaquesmith hesitated, performed a few calculations, and said, "The physical locations . . . are varied. The locations in time . . . are all the same. They're all being targeted to a point . . . one week ago."

"He's taunting us," Cyclops said. "He knows the TDC isn't functioning, and he's sending his missiles someplace just beyond our reach."

"Indubitably," said the Beast. "However, is that all he's doing?"

"No," Professor Xavier decided. "It's not. Not this time. If that's what he wanted, he'd send his missiles to some bygone era, a hundred or a thousand or a million years ago, and detonate them knowing that without the TDC we'd be absolutely powerless to stop him. No. This time he's sending us an invitation. He's giving his forces a week to get ready for us . . . and *daring* us to stop him before the bombs go off. It's a trap, of course . . ."

"Or his notion of entertainment," Phoenix suggested.

"Maybe," said Professor Xavier, though he looked doubtful. "But that doesn't make sense. After all the trouble he's already gone to, just to take out the TDC . . . and the sheer scale of his insane plan . . . why would he now

THE PRESENT

suddenly want to give us back our chance to win? Can it be that he actually has something to gain by this?''

Cable couldn't believe they were still mired in discussion. He had already crossed the room to a workbench where he and Blaquesmith had been performing some of the more intricate repairs. He picked up the ion cannon that was his most powerful weapon, pulled back the safety, then returned to Xavier and the others. His expression, which was almost always grim, now crossed the threshold into murderous. "Who cares?" he said, simply. "It's not like we have a wealth of other options. If we do nothing, he's already won. This world becomes the next to fall, and he goes on to destroy another and another and another. If we accept his invitation, then we have a chance to stop the bombs, and maybe figure out a way to go after him. It's a shot. And we can use it to teach that butcher the meaning of underestimating the X-Men.''

Professor Xavier studied the image on the computer screen. It was now a two-dimensional representation of the planet, marked by three blinking lights to mark the places where the missiles had landed. Staring at those lights, he reminded himself that each represented a battlefield that had been chosen a week ago . . . where even now, preparations were being made for the arrival of this timeline's defenders. He wondered, *Are we too late? Is Kang waiting for us to arrive, just so he can detonate the bombs in our faces?*

But Cable was right. It didn't matter. The X-Men did not have the luxury of allowing it to matter. For now, they had to play this by the enemy's rules, and hope that the rightness of their cause would still give them the edge they needed to win.

"You'll have to hurry, whatever you do," Blaquesmith said. "Those missiles are probably functional already. There's no way of counting all the alternate timelines they're destroying."

Cyclops decided it. "Let's go."

Xavier spared one second hoping that Bishop and Spider-Man, wherever they might be, weren't being faced with any situations this dire. Then he turned to Cyclops. "Agreed. Call Storm and the others. Tell them we're back in the game."

There was a special chamber, somewhere in Kang's castle, filled with objects that the master considered treasures and Lireeb dutifully cared for as treasures, but which seemed to have no useful function whatsoever. Items as varied as a black statue of a bird; a dinner menu from a seagoing vessel called the *Lusitania*; the complete contents of the Library of Alexandria on microfiche; a stack of film canisters that his master proudly said contained "the complete *Greed*" (whatever that meant); a flat pad enscribed DON'T PANIC; and a strangely beautiful transparent globe which contained both the tiny model of a house and a quantity of white crystals that fell like snow whenever the globe was vigorously shaken. The globe was the most mysterious of all the master's treasures; Lireeb could not discern its function, but found the snowfall effect one of the most perversely addictive delights to be found anywhere in the universe.

The master was occupied in that chamber, engrossed by a terrarium inhabited by the half-mad, miniaturized crewmen of the *Marie Celeste*, when Lireeb entered and cleared his throat. "It has been done," he said. "The missiles have reached their destinations, and the X-Men are already making plans to interfere."

"Excellent!" Kang crowed. "Excellent!"

"So much so, apparently, that you had to say it twice. But I should ask why. You do have all of time at your whim. Why give the mutants even the slightest chance to stop you?"

Kang reached into the terrarium, picked up one struggling sailor, and placed him in another terrarium inhabited solely by an American aviatrix missing since the 1930s. True love, of a sort: the kind that motivated Kang, that made him misty-eyed with longing. "You have no poetry in your heart, Lireeb."

THE PRESENT

"I would hope not, sire. Iambic pentameter would give me chest pains."

The tiny sailor was now chasing the tiny aviatrix around the little island. Watching intently, Kang said, "It is not enough for me to win. I must also have enemies who lose. If they do not have a chance to oppose me, then they do not have a chance to be humiliated and crushed."

"Ah," Lireeb said. "So you're doing this out of a sense of fairness. I understand now."

The tiny sailor had cornered the tiny aviatrix, who seemed to be helpless—until she decked the little randy fellow with a punch to the jaw. Kang *tsk*ed, reached into the terrarium with a pair of tweezers, and returned the poor fellow to his shipmates. "Actually, I am giving them the chance to give me something I very badly need. They'll be making my dreams possible—even though they won't have any idea what they're doing until it's too late."

"As opposed to us, of course," said Lireeb. "We're totally in control of the situation. Will you be needing any more androids for them to fight?"

Kang drew a black velvet curtain over both terrariums and said, "I suppose that would be the easiest way, but no . . . the battles they had with the previous androids seemed so cold and unsatisfying. There is, after all, no glory in fighting a machine, is there?"

"I wouldn't know, sire. I surmise it would depend on what battle hymns were playing in the background as I fought one."

Kang moved among his exhibits, examining them one by one: the child's sleigh enscribed ROSEBUD, the devil doll, the triluminary pendant, the gold watch stopped at one hour to midnight, the bejeweled ring that glowed ominously when—and only when—he drew near. Lireeb followed close behind, ready to accept his orders at any moment.

Finally, at long last, the conqueror said, "There were, in that time period, certain super-powered individuals who styled themselves super-villains, even though many of them were generally nothing more than common thugs willing to work for the highest bidder. Go send an agent to contact some of the more avaricious types, and arrange for them to meet our opponents at the various missile sites. You may, if you wish, supplement their power with androids when necessary—but I want individuals capable of giving our mutant friends a substantial degree of trouble, with or without android help. Is that clear?"

"Let me check," Lireeb said dryly. He closed his eyes and furrowed his brow, then opened his eyes again. "It appears to be, sire."

"Good. Then this shall be clear too. Make sure that there's one android capable of telling them what's really going on. I want to mock them with my superior intelligence."

Lireeb shook his head. "A good game of chess would accomplish that."

"Do it!" Kang thundered.

Lireeb bowed, mimed the zipping of lips, and left the room, not so much by walking through the only door as by . . . sliding sideways through one of the more dimensionally compromised alcoves.

Kang stared for a long time at the spot where the albino had been, muttering to himself with aggravation and more than a little confusion. He was still studying the spot when he picked up another miniaturized trophy from the past—a mutant hybrid of *stegosaurus* and *tyrannosaurus*, granted fire-breath from exposure to atomic wastes. From his records, it had once laid waste to much of Japan and the western coast of North America, before being stopped by a concerted counterattack by the champions of the time. Shrunk down to this manageable size, it was just large enough to provide an interesting opponent for the similarly shrunk-down sailors of the *Marie Celeste*.

Grinning beneath his mask, Kang moved toward the terrarium, to see what kind of fun he could have.

CHAPTER THREE

As they wandered through the streets of Greenwich Village, Spider-Man and Bishop looked, if anything, even more bedraggled than they had earlier that day in Central Park. They'd been on their feet for hours, following a more or less random course through the city, staying in motion at all times to prevent Cyclops and his forces from getting a fix on their location. But though they were tireless men, with stamina capable of dizzying a marathon runner, the constant running was beginning to take its toll.

"We need to take a break," Spider-Man said.

Bishop bristled. "I'm not sure we can afford a break. We're exposed."

"Come on. We're two raggedy men who look like any other pair of derelicts in the neighborhood. The only thing that's exposed is our embarrassment."

"Cyclops—"

"—lost our trail long ago. It must have taken him a couple of hours just to confirm we'd escaped the park."

"He'll find us again," Bishop said.

"Probably. Which is why it makes sense to take a break. The last thing we should do is run ourselves ragged."

Bishop looked like he was about to protest further, but the events of the day must been wearing heavily on him as well; without visibly relaxing one iota, without showing any of the stress or weariness that must have been weighing on him as heavily as it weighed on Spider-Man, he still conveyed the impression of a man who was willing to let himself be persuaded. "What do you suggest?"

Spider-Man flashed a ten-dollar bill that had been burning a hole in his pocket for hours now. It was the one piece of solid luck they'd had since landing in this insane timeline; that and Bishop realizing, as they made their way out of Central Park, that the changing deployment of cops and helicopters could only mean that the Cerebros had picked up their presence, and that the hunters were now after them.

Bishop had wanted to fight his way out. But Spider-

THE PRESENT

Man had turned around, and led Bishop back into the park, to a sewer entrance he knew about. From there it had been two hours underground, making their way to the subways, which they used to travel fifty blocks downtown, and at least temporarily out of Cyclops's clutches. At the end of that journey, when they were tired and hungry and beginning to snipe at each other again, the filthy ten-dollar bill fluttering near the third rail looked like a gift from heaven. Even if the president on its face was Gerald Ford.

Spider-Man snapped the bill at Bishop, and said, "Come on. I'll buy you a cup of coffee—if we can find a place sleazy enough to serve people who look and smell like we do."

The place they found was on the corner of Thompson and Houston, and it was not one of the trendy gourmet coffee places that had become ubiquitous in most major American cities, even in this timeline. It was called Krakatoa Cup of Java, and though it pretended to be a coffee shop, it was really the most downscale tavern in the neighborhood. It sat a full flight of cement steps below street level behind a filthy picture window decorated with a painting of a bearded man regarding a steaming mug with an expression of near-religious awe. Inside, they found a dimly lit place redolent of cigarette smoke. There were about two dozen other customers, some of whom made the sewer-crawling Spider-Man and Bishop look like a walking public service announcement for good hygiene. Some were playing chess; a couple were nursing coffee or tea while taking furtive sips of booze from the paper bags secreted in their ratty clothing. Back home, Spider-Man would have taken one look at the basic ambience and walked back out the door. Here, it seemed like a little slice of heaven. The perfect place to hide when you didn't want to be spotted by anybody capable of caring.

Behind the counter stood a pear-shaped man with a beard, a moustache, and a filthy apron. "Yeah?" he said.

"Two coffees," Spider-Man said. He pointed at Bishop. "Better bring him decaf."

"Any partic'lar flavor?"

"Hot," Spider-Man said.

"Siddown. I'll bring it out."

Spider-Man shrugged at Bishop—who did not quite curl his lip, but looked like he wanted to—then joined him at a booth chosen for its distance from anybody else in the place. There were pie crumbs on the table. Spider-Man wondered if he should order some, but decided not: he might have been willing to take a risk on the coffee, but had already gotten the impression that the food here ranked with Doc Ock, the Green Goblin, and J. Jonah Jameson's editorial meetings as one of the greatest dangers he'd ever have to face.

Still, what Krakatoa lacked in ambience it clearly possessed in service: the counterman brought their coffees almost as soon as Spider-Man and Bishop sat down.

Bishop took his black. He tried a sip, swallowed it, and pronounced his judgment: "Bitter. How's yours?"

Spider-Man reached toward his cup, hesitated, and said, "I dunno."

"What's wrong?"

"I guess it just hit me all of a sudden. You know, one of those moments when the bravado just fails you, and you feel the size of the mess you're in? I have family back home, Bish. Somebody I care about more than anything. I'm worried about whether I'll ever get to see her again."

Bishop said, "Does she, ah, know about—"

"Yes."

"Has it ever kept you away this long?"

"Sometimes longer." Spider-Man's fingers danced around the coffee cup without quite working up enough courage to attack it. "One time a villain I'd fought about a dozen times before kidnapped me and buried me underground for two weeks. All that time, she didn't know whether I was alive or dead. She's not like us, Bish. She doesn't have any special powers, and she's not used to fighting for her life. She's been through a lot in her life with me. Sometimes I think I don't give her enough credit for that."

THE PRESENT

Bishop said, "You're going to have to do that, when you get home."

"Yeah." Spider-Man reached for his cup, and hesitated. "You miss home, Bish?"

Bishop considered that, and came out with an answer that clearly surprised him. "No."

"You're kidding."

"No," Bishop said. "I want to be there, but I don't miss it."

"Why not?"

Bishop responded with what was clearly a lie. "I don't know."

There was very little Bishop could say after that. Peter thought about Mary Jane, considered all the times his activities as Spider-Man had brought such terror and uncertainty into her life, and for a moment there was very little he could say either; he could only sit there, stare at his untouched coffee, and wonder for about the ten millionth time whether his super-powers had come with too high a price.

The silence stretched until Bishop rumbled like a long-dormant engine coming back to life, took another sip of his coffee, and said, "Since I suppose this qualifies as a heart-to-heart, may I ask you a personal question?"

Spider-Man regarded him warily. "You can ask. I can't promise I'll answer."

"I'd like to know what makes somebody like you fight the good fight anyway."

It was uncomfortably close to what Spider-Man had just been asking himself, but he bristled nonetheless. "What's that supposed to mean—somebody like me?"

Bishop shrugged. "I'm a soldier, Spider-Man. I've been trained to be blunt. And the more time I spend with you, the more I learn about who you are. And my thumbnail perception is that you're pathetically self-absorbed. You're impulsive, hotheaded, and amused by just about everything you say. You don't strike me as the kind of person who'd react to super-powers by putting on a costume and dashing out to save the world. I know what made

51

TIME'S ARROW

me do it. I came from a time and a place where the world was beset by troubles worse than anything you can imagine. I had to learn to fight, just to survive . . . and I had to become a soldier so I could persuade myself that the fight made sense. But what made you do it? Why do you constantly throw yourself into dangerous situations, when you could use the same powers just to make life easier for yourself?"

Spider-Man almost said, *None of your business.* His secrets had always been precious to him; he had no desire to share them with somebody he didn't even like. But then he slumped, and said, "Why not? We're both so far from home. If I can't talk to you, who else is there?"

He reached for his coffee, and again pulled back before touching the cup.

"It's like a fairy tale," he said, quietly. "Once upon a time, there was a skinny little kid whose parents died when he was three, and who ended up being raised by his aunt and his uncle, who were two of the best people he would ever know. They were kind, and gentle, and they had this . . . well, I guess it's not too corny a word . . . goodness about them so strong that even when he came home upset because the other kids had been cruel to him, he only needed to be with them a little while to feel right about the world again."

Bishop was listening intently. "And why were the other kids so cruel to him?"

"He was . . . well, today, they'd call him a geek. He was a real prodigy when it came to science, and he got good grades in all his classes, and all the teachers thought he was just about perfect, but he had almost no interest in anything the other kids were interested in. Not their music, not their sports, not—" He spread his hands dismissively. "When he wanted to talk to the other kids, he talked to them about school. When he wanted to suggest something fun to do, he suggested going to science museums. He was a good kid, and he meant well. But it's no wonder they hated him."

"Or," Bishop noted, "that he hated himself."

THE PRESENT

Spider-Man drummed his hands by his coffee cup. "Yeah. No wonder." He remained silent for several seconds, lost in the memories of a life where his greatest enemy was a loudmouthed jock named Flash Thompson and his greatest battle was an occasional exchange of insults after school. Once upon a time, it had seemed unbearable; now, it was almost nostalgia.

"So one day, this kid went to a special demonstration at the science hall: specifically a controlled release of radiation under laboratory conditions. He went alone because he couldn't get any of his high-school classmates to go with him. They even laughed at him when he said he wanted to go. But when he was watching the demonstration, he didn't care; he was where he wanted to be, in the place where he thought he belonged. And then a spider dropped between the emitters, got itself irradiated . . . and bit him."

Bishop was incredulous. "That's what it was? You got bitten by a radioactive *spider*?"

"Not the kind of thing that happens every day, is it? Anyway, our hero felt woozy and disoriented. The bite burned. He left the demonstration in a hurry, with some vague idea of getting home before he collapsed; he didn't even have a clue what had really happened until he walked into the path of a truck and jumped three stories straight up just to get out of its way. And when he landed on a wall, he stuck to it.

"It was a big shock for our hero, let me tell you. Between one second and the next, he went from the worst kid in gym class to this walking miracle with the proportionate strength and agility of a spider. All of a sudden, he could climb walls, do flips and somersaults better than any gymnast, lift fifteen tons, and take punishment that could kill a normal person . . . you know. All the skills that teenage science nerds are well known for being mature enough to handle."

Bishop sipped his coffee. "And, of course, he made no mistakes whatsoever."

"None at all. This kid had common sense. He was *right*

on top of things. He didn't have any selfish instincts at all.''

"What did he do?"

"He decided to make a killing as a novelty act."

Bishop winced. "Ahhh."

"He broke out the old home chemistry set, and mixed up some artificial webbing to fire from some doohickeys he designed to be worn around his wrists. This was just so he could play up the spider angle onstage. It never occurred to him—until later, when it was too late—that if he could patent a glue that powerful, he could easily make more money than he ever could in show business; all that was important to him by then was teaching a lesson to all the people who'd laughed at him."

Spider-Man stirred in sudden epiphany. "You know, until now I never realized it . . . but I guess he had a lot in common with the kind of bad guy I never understood before . . . the ones who spend six million dollars building robot suits so they can rob banks. Because, at that point, it wasn't the money—it was revenge. He didn't have any friends, he didn't like himself all that much, and the only two people he cared about were his aunt and his uncle. The rest of the world could go hang; he'd make himself rich and famous, share the money with his family, then unmask, making everybody sorry they'd laughed at him."

"But it didn't work out that way," Bishop said.

Spider-Man looked at him. "Are you sure I haven't told you this story before?"

"I'm sure. But I begin to see where it's heading."

"Well, dressed as Spider-Man, our friend actually did manage to do what he set out to do: he got an agent, got some bookings, appeared on television, headlined a few club appearances . . . all without ever revealing his real name. And he was a genuine hit. People loved him. They applauded him. They told him he was great. They came to him with movie scripts, endorsements, merchandising deals. They told him that if he kept going the way he was, he'd be the number-one entertainer in the world. He even began to think that maybe he should take off the costume

THE PRESENT

and go for glory under his own name . . . maybe as a professional athlete or actor or something. And maybe he would have done that, and gone on to be exactly the kind of selfish, me-first person he was in danger of becoming."

Spider-Man took a deep breath. "But then one day, he was leaving the studio after a taping and this seedy little guy came running down the hall, with a security guard right behind him. The guard yelled, 'Hey, you! Stop that thief before he reaches the elevators!' And our hero did absolutely nothing. Not because he was scared, but because he just didn't care. That one little thief just wasn't important enough for him to deal with.

"He let the bad guy get away. The security man yelled at him for doing nothing. 'You didn't have to hold him! You could have tripped him, or blocked the elevators. . . .' And our hero walked away from him, saying, 'Hey! That was your business, buddy! From now on, I don't go out of my way for anybody! I don't—' "

Spider-Man stopped in midsentence, and covered his eyes. "Does this sound more like the kind of person you think I am?"

"Finish the story," Bishop said.

Spider-Man stared at his coffee, which was untouched and no doubt getting cold by now. He was thirsty, and he wanted to drink it . . . but somehow he could not bring himself to pick it up.

After a while, he said, "And then not long after that our hero went home, to the place where he lived with his aunt and uncle, and there was something wrong. The place was surrounded by cop cars. He ran up and was stopped by a policeman, who told him that his uncle was dead and that his aunt was at their next-door neighbor's. They'd walked in on a burglar, you see. The uncle had been shot, and the aunt had gone into shock. The burglar himself had been chased into some rotting old warehouse not far away—but though the place was surrounded by cops, the killer was armed and dangerous and barricaded in a huge warehouse, and they hoped to talk him into surrendering.

"Our hero was in no mood to wait for him to surrender.

No, he was out for blood. He wanted to punish the bad man for hurting the only people he ever cared about. So he changed into Spider-Man and swung into an upper window of the darkened warehouse, where he used his powers to absolutely terrorize this pathetic third-rate thug... knocking him out and dragging him into the light.

"It was the thief from the TV station. The one who hadn't seemed important enough to bother with. The one who would have been in jail... if only our hero had done the right thing."

Spider-Man reached for his coffee—and once again, stopped. "He learned something that day. Something that led him to spend much of his life swinging around in a silly costume, getting shot at by thugs and villains... something that became so much a part of him he can hear it in his sleep. And that something was, with great power comes great responsibility. You want to know why he puts on a costume and rushes out to save the world? Because he knows that every day he doesn't, somebody dies who he could have saved. Does that answer your question, Bish?"

Bishop said, "Yes, it does. And I apologize."

"Why?"

"For misjudging you. You're a much better man than I gave you credit for. You made a tragic mistake, and honored your vow to put it right. And for all the good you must have done over the years... you should be proud." Bishop drained his coffee to the bottom. "Even if I still find you about as annoying as anybody I've ever met."

"Thanks," Spider-Man said. "I think." This time he actually picked up his cup, intending to drink... but without even being aware of it, put it down like a man burned. "What about you? What makes you do what you do?"

"That's... a little bit harder to explain."

"Tough," Spider-Man said. "It's your turn."

"Well," Bishop said, "to begin with, the world you call home... it isn't where I came from, any more than this is. I was born in a future where there were horrors I can't even describe to you. It was a place where you

THE PRESENT

couldn't trust anybody, where death could come at any time, and where all our fears were embodied by a contagious strain of genetic vampirism, which turned mutants into murderous energy-absorbing monsters we called emplates. The world swarmed with them. I saw them corrupt my friends, my family, and the people I believed in... and I fought back as a member of a group called the XSE—Xavier's Security Enforcers—which tried to keep Charles Xavier's dreams of peace alive in a world that desperately needed something that noble to believe in. When I came to your time, I found a world where it was still possible to make a difference. I have friends on that world... but it's not home, and I suppose that explains a lot about why I don't miss it. If I never get back, I suppose I'd be just as content fighting here as anywhere else... but, all things being equal, I'd rather..." He blinked several times. "I'd rather..." His eyes closed. "Hell."

"What?"

"S-something's wrong. I can't—"

And then Bishop suddenly stiffened, and collapsed face-first onto the table.

Sparing a quick glance at the other patrons (who were all watching him with a vague interest that did not go so far as actual alarm), Spider-Man reached across the table and grabbed the big man by the wrist. Bishop's pulse was strong and steady but much slower than it should have been. But what—

With a surge of dread, he grabbed his own untouched coffee and immediately felt a stab of warning at the base of his skull.

Drugged.

He remembered the way he'd repeatedly reached for the coffee, and just as repeatedly pulled his hand back. No wonder he'd felt so uneasy! His spider-sense had been trying to warn him about the sedative all along... but because he'd never actually tried to drink, the tingle had never grown powerful enough to register as anything more than a vague, instinctive avoidance. It wouldn't be the first time ambiguous or inadequate warnings from his spider-

TIME'S ARROW

sense had allowed him to walk into a trap . . . but this time he'd brought Bishop into the trap with him.

The counterman wasn't even bothering to hide his portable Cerebro anymore. No, he held it in plain view, pointing it at Spider-Man and Bishop, with the bored, overconfident expression of a bully who believed he'd already won.

"What do you think this is?" the counterman asked. "Some kind of dump? You thought I wouldn't have one of these babies behind the counter, readin' the stats on everybody who comes through that door?"

Spider-Man stood. "Well, that depends, bunkie."

"On what?" the counterman asked.

"Just who I have to go to to complain about the lousy coffee around here."

He took a step toward the bar, and the counterman cried: *"Stop him! He's a sponkie!"*

Most of the other patrons jumped up at once, converging on Spider-Man with the graceless animosity common to all mobs. Spider-Man regarded them in the couple of seconds it took the first wave to reach him, and saw that there didn't seem to be any genuinely capable of giving him trouble. Only half looked like veterans of previous fights, and only half of those looked like the kind of people who might have won. No, by and large these were just the kind of idiots silly enough actually to obey a bartender's order to beat up a patron with unknown super-powers.

Under normal circumstances, Spider-Man might have been inclined to go easy on them.

But he had spent the last few days being shot at in the Old West, trapped in an alternate timeline where he had to refrain from helping people in trouble, wondering if he'd ever get to see his wife again, and crawling through the sewers in the company of a man who might have been the least likable guy to ever call himself an X-Man.

These were not normal circumstances.

The first three guys to reach him were unshaven, unwashed gents of the sort who wear woolen caps all year round. They arrived first only because they happened to

THE PRESENT

be sitting closest, and they wore aghast expressions that seemed to indicate they hadn't realized they'd be first until they were actually upon him. Spider-Man gave them what they wanted most by immediately relocating them to the back of the line—admittedly, at a higher altitude than they might have wanted to travel.

The second wave consisted of a pair of massive thugs with matching leather jackets and matching shaved heads. Spider-Man immediately pegged them both as proud graduates of the prison exercise yard body-building academy. He waited until they were almost upon him, then hopped six feet straight up and landed with one foot on each of their glistening foreheads. As they went down, Spider-Man freed his retracted web-shooters with a flick of his wrists, and gave a nice spritz to the faces of the next two in line. Three fell to the ground in panic, their cries muffled behind gags of sticky webbing; the one that was still able to speak tumbled over a chair, shouting, "My face! My face!"

"I was about to say," Spider-Man snapped back. "Your parents should be sued."

There were only a handful of volunteers left after that; Spider-Man jumped from one to the other like a pinball using human beings for bumpers, knocking most of them aside before they could even raise their fists for an attempted attack. One of the smarter ones saw which way the wind was blowing and fled back to his booth, pretending that he'd never been part of the mob in the first place; one managed to land a punch that hurt Spider-Man about as much as a playful pat on the cheek; a third emitted a high-pitched shriek that might have been a poor man's attempt to imitate Bruce Lee, and attempted a karate kick that might have done some serious damage had Spider-Man not grabbed that leg by the ankle and stood there holding it in midair.

"What do you know!" Spider-Man cracked. "Skanky, the master of Dumb Fu!"

The man hopped in place on his free leg. "Hey! Let go of that!"

TIME'S ARROW

"If you insist," Spider-Man said.

His opponent was unconscious and airborne when Spider-Man turned his attention back to the bartender. White with amazement at Spider-Man's speed in taking down his customers, the man was already clutching for something under the bar. Spider-Man, who had seen the same panicked move from other stunned bartenders in other underworld taverns, knew that there had to be a gun or a baseball bat under there. He jumped the twenty feet between himself and the bar in a single leap, landing on the bartender's chest even as the man managed to aim his gun at Spider-Man's heart.

Fortunately, Spider-Man managed to bat it aside before the man could fire. Unfortunately, the man's fingers spasmed before the pistol was completely out of the way. The gun went off, and Spider-Man felt a jab of impact in his upper right arm. It was followed a heartbeat later by the pain . . . which was itself followed by a cool tingling sensation as frightening as any agony could possibly be.

In the instant before the pistol went flying, Spider-Man saw a tiny feathered shaft protruding from his arm.

The two men fell in a heap onto the grating that was the floor behind the bar. As the pistol skittered away, the bartender tried to reach for a drawer beneath the cash register, which no doubt contained another weapon; Spider-Man grabbed him by the wrist and physically pulled him back to a standing position. The man stopped fighting as soon as Spider-Man crushed the fallen mini-Cerebro with a single kick of his right foot.

"I want to know," Spider-Man gasped. "Did you call anybody? Did you trigger a silent alarm? Is anybody coming?"

The bartender, who had been cringing in anticipation of the killing blow, now broke out in a wide relieved smile. "I got you."

Spider-Man grabbed him by the lapels and lifted him off the floor. "Answer me! Is anybody coming?"

"It don't matter. That was a sponkie dose. You'll be snoring louder than your friend in a second or two. You

THE PRESENT

might as well close your eyes and enjoy it...."

Spider-Man felt the perspiration beading on his forehead, and the numbness spreading down his arm, and he knew that the bartender was telling the truth. It didn't matter what alarms might have been sounded. If the authorities hadn't been summoned already, they certainly would be as soon as the dart knocked him out. Whatever it was, it felt strong enough to have been brewed by his old enemy Kraven; despite his considerable powers of resistance, he could already sense his thoughts turning sluggish, his survival instincts sinking in the narcotic fog that would soon swallow him whole.

He had to gather up Bishop and bring him somewhere where it would be safe for them to sleep off the effects of the drug—that is, if there was someplace safe, and if it was a drug and not some poison....

He lifted the bartender by his collar and marched him to the wall, holding him tightly three feet off the floor.

"Wh-what are you doing?" the bartender managed.

It was a great straight line, and had Spider-Man been his usual self he would have come up with any number of snappy rejoinders. "The *macarena*," for instance. Or "Decorating the walls! You should see what I have in mind for the game room!" Or "Gee, I'm sorry—I thought you said you were a fixture of this place!" But Spider-Man remained dead silent as he used most of a web cartridge to cement the man in place. He couldn't think of anything funny to say. It was all he could do just to remember what he was doing.

By the time he realized the bartender was securely in place, the numbness had affected his entire right side. He wasn't surefooted enough to hop over the bar, so he had to climb over, taking so much care not to fall that he could feel his hopes of escape vanishing with every second. His knees buckled when he lowered himself to the floor on the other side. Once he recovered, it took him a couple of seconds to remember what he had to do next; he knew it was important, and knew that he had to get it done before he was able to claim the sleep he craved, but couldn't

TIME'S ARROW

dispel the fog long enough to remember what it was....

Then he spotted Bishop, slumped in a booth about a million miles away.

It seemed a totally unreasonable distance to walk. He wouldn't be able to manage it until he got some rest. But something—a distant sense of urgency—kept him on his feet as he shuffled toward the faraway booth. His destination seemed to recede a little bit farther with every step he took. There was something wrong with the floor too; it seemed to be veering off in random directions, turning every step he took into a new adventure in disorientation. Once the entire building turned on end and the booth containing Bishop seemed to be hanging over him, like an outcropping twenty feet straight up; and Spider-Man felt a moment's relief, because he was Spider-Man and he was used to climbing walls.

He was almost upon Bishop when he sank to his knees.

Somewhere, worlds away, a sweet old lady named Aunt May rose from her sickbed and scolded him for being such a quitter. A high-school bully named Flash Thompson stood behind her, laughing at the good-for-nothing pantywaist Parker. A hate-filled face he vaguely recognized as J. Jonah Jameson's loomed greater than both of them, assuring them that he'd been right all along, that Spider-Man was just another glory-seeking vigilante, who caved in whenever the going got tough.

He was on all fours now, facing the floor, seeing it as a landscape a thousand miles below him, refusing to let himself fall the rest of the distance, holding himself up with nothing but the little strength that still remained in his arms. But he was so very heavy, and the rewards of sleep so impossible to resist....

Another dart hit him in the shoulder.

Impossible. It couldn't be the bartender. He was immobilized. And all the patrons were beaten. It had to be somebody else. Somebody who'd just come in.

Cyclops? The police?

He collapsed, and was claimed by the darkness.

CHAPTER FOUR

There was no such thing as silence in the canyon of ice.

A past geological cataclysm had cracked the glacier in two, forming a wedge-shaped depression four miles long and a thousand feet deep. Bordered by vertical walls of ice, gradually narrowing to a crevasse at its farthest end, the canyon was one of the most inhospitable places on Earth, with winds that frequently approached hurricane velocity and temperatures that rarely topped seventy below zero. The ice that loomed on all sides was a restless beast, constantly on the move; it cracked and groaned and sometimes screamed. If there were any laws that governed the landscape here, one was that solid ground was just an avalanche waiting to happen. The other was that the hairline crack which might be practically invisible now might yawn wide enough to swallow mountains tomorrow.

It was a place that had never known the heedless footsteps of humankind. Which also made it a place that, up until now, had never been a battlefield.

The two figures materializing at the valley's base knew that that was about to change. They were Cable and the Beast, and they had teleported there using the Time Displacement Core.

They did not look like their usual selves. Despite their respective tolerance for extreme conditions, they'd both come prepared for their journey into this little corner of hell, wearing bulkily insulated overalls over a thin inner layer of heated thermal insulation. They also wore fur-lined hoods pulled up over faces covered with fur-lined leather masks, and they hid their eyes behind wraparound smoked goggles. Despite all this, the Beast—and his own personal layer of insulating blue fur—wasted no time exclaiming, "Oh, my stars and garters! It must be close to a hundred below!"

Cable said nothing.

The Beast glanced at him, and said, "We can only hope that our esteemed opponent believes in showing his guests the warmest of receptions! If we don't locate his bomb within a reasonable period, we may need to use these re-

THE PRESENT

call devices, to return to the TDC for periodic warm-ups!"

Cable emitted a grim snort. "I don't think we'll have to wait that long."

"Neither do I, actually. Super-villains are such a notoriously impatient breed. In any event, the sooner we engage his forces the sooner we'll be able to return for hot cocoa with marshmallows. I say we boogie."

Cable didn't respond; he merely started walking.

The two men trudged across the landscape with the slow and careful gait of old men, leaning into the wind, the nailed soles of their boots gripping the jagged ground with every step, for now using almost none of the advantage they might have gained from their respective mutant abilities. They were both sapped by the cold, despite their protective clothing; there was just too much cold for any amount of precaution to keep it out entirely, and simply continuing to put one step in front of the other used up as much energy as a brisk run at room temperature. The canyon was like that: a great leveler.

The Beast knew he could take it. This wasn't his first trip to Antarctica—not counting his various journeys to the Savage Land, a hidden subtropical valley that was the frozen continent's great meteorological anomaly. He'd once endured hours lost in an Antarctic blizzard, suffering temperatures at least as cold as this, with nothing but his own fur to keep him warm. He'd survived that . . . but only barely, and he hadn't enjoyed it much at all. It would have been nice if, when the teams were assigned, Storm had been tapped for this particular trip; her weather-controlling powers might have made enduring this cold a good deal easier.

Or Iceman, for that matter. But Bobby's abilities worked by drawing heat from his surroundings; in temperatures *this* cold, he simply didn't have all that much ambient heat to work with, and the effectiveness of his powers was severely curtailed. He also made his ice sculptures by acting on the moisture in the air, and since most of the humidity around here had already crystallized as ice, he wouldn't have much ammunition in that area either.

The Beast considered this yet another argument in favor of the proposition that the DNA molecule comes equipped with a sense of humor.

There was a low jagged shape hugging the ground ahead of them. As the Beast approached, he saw that it was a natural barrier, formed by tectonic buckling in the ice flow. The ice had disintegrated into shards, risen upward, then frozen again—forming a wall of jutting slabs and protruding shelves that was probably as treacherous as it was beautiful. Climbing it the hard way would probably be a mistake; the thing was liable to collapse underneath them. The Beast looked around for his teammate, and saw him ten yards away, staring at the barrier with his trademark look of grim determination. "Hey, Cable, want a lift?"

Cable shook his head and said nothing.

The Beast hesitated. It was so hard to tell with Cable; like Bishop, he had never been one of the world's sunniest guys. (He made Cyclops look like the life of the party.) But this was even more taciturn than usual. . . .

He was about to lope over and ask Cable what was wrong . . . when Cable began to run up the barrier, taking the entire climb in four great leaps. The Beast's heart leapt to his throat at the sight—*He's crazy, the going's too treacherous, even somebody with my superhuman agility would need to take it slow*—before he understood that Cable was using his telekinesis to keep most of his weight off the ice. For all the impact his steps had, he might as well have weighed as much as a mouse.

It was a slick move. The Beast grinned appreciatively, and tackled the barrier in his own inimitable manner: with a single great leap that carried him all the way to the top. He could have cleared the barrier entirely, but that would have been a most unfortunate choice if terrain on the other side included anything as inconvenient as a bottomless chasm. He hit the summit prepared to leap again if he felt it begin to shift beneath his weight . . . but it held, and when he saw that it was safe to proceed he jumped over the sawtooth-shaped shelves of ice for a safe landing on the unbroken ice field that lay beyond. He even beat Cable there, which gave him a certain guilty pleasure, since nobody likes a show-off.

Even so, when Cable landed by his side without a word, the Beast had to say, "Are you all right?"

Cable glanced at him only briefly. "Yes."

"I'm afraid I don't believe you, Nathan. You've never been an unusually loquacious individual, but your demeanor since your return from your mission in the past has been sullen to the point of rigidity. And if you keep on gritting your teeth that way, you're in serious danger of reducing the enamel to subatomic particles. Because I believe you're in pain, I, as your teammate and comrade, must strenuously insist you divest yourself of any secret you might be carrying."

Cable nodded. "You're right. I should." He took a deep breath and, as they resumed walking, said, "We're not the only ones involved in this, Hank. I met . . . somebody else when I was in the past. Somebody who was also traveling through time. Somebody I used to know, where I come from . . . somebody who meant everything in the world to me, who still means everything in the world to me. My Aliya."

The Beast, who had heard Cable speak of his murdered lady love before, stopped in midstride. "Oh, my stars and garters. B-but . . ."

"Oh, it's not *my* Aliya. My Aliya is dead. But this Aliya is identical to her in every way. She comes from some alternate world where I died and she lived . . . and she still feels the same way about me. If we get the Time Displacement Core fixed, we might actually have a chance to be reunited, and live the life that was taken from us."

The Beast could only stammer out his answer. "Cable, I can't even imagine how you feel . . . but we're dealing with truly universal forces here. Time, and history, and probability, and factors we can't even name. There's no way of knowing what'll happen if you start using the TDC to—"

"I don't care!" Cable snapped. "Everything I ever

TIME'S ARROW

loved was taken from me. My parents, my sister, Aliya, they were all taken from me. I never had a normal childhood, I never had a normal life, I've been hunted and hounded and infected with this technovirus that I'll have to actively resist until the day I die. All I've ever had is my warrior training. All I've ever known is a series of wars that I've been fighting for more years than I can count. And all I've ever had for a home is a battlefield. And that's no life for a man. I tell you, Beast, if Aliya and I can find each other again, and claim one scrap of happiness after everything we've been through, then I'm not going to worry about how. The universe owes us that much."

The Beast was stunned. He'd never heard Cable string together so many consecutive sentences before. "Back at the TDC...when you argued in favor of accepting Kang's challenge...you weren't really concerned about saving the world, were you? You just wanted to get your hands on his time machine. All you really cared about was finding Aliya."

"And if saving the world is the way to accomplish that, then I don't see anything wrong with the world repaying the favor for once." Cable's eyes—one blank, one glowing—took on a faraway look, as he said, "I want to settle down with her. I want children. I want a life. I just hope I'm still fit, after everything I've seen. I hope...I'm even one half the man she deserves."

And with that Cable turned his back on the Beast and marched ahead into the cold Antarctic night.

The Beast honestly didn't know what to say. He had never given much thought to the forces that drove Cable; the man had always been closemouthed and hard to know, his closeness with X-Force, the younger students at the Xavier Institute, impossible to see as anything but an anomaly. Somehow, he had never once considered the possibility that Cable got along with the kids precisely because he saw them as the family that had always been denied him. It just wasn't the kind of epiphany that came easily, when thinking about Cable.

THE PRESENT

He could only sympathize. He'd been pretty lucky himself; despite the genetic accident that had left him furry and blue, the frequent crises that went along with being a member of the X-Men, the social stigma that went along with being a mutant, and a few dark patches here and there, life as a whole had been pretty good to him. He had a career, a reputation, family, friends . . . and a sense of perspective that kept him sane even in the face of total chaos. Everything he'd ever wanted was available to him on this planet, including the opportunity to change it for the better. But even in his own case, he'd never had anything like a normal life. He'd missed one. He couldn't even imagine what it was like to be a man like Cable, who had never known happiness of any kind, and who now needed to place all his faith in a distant possibility, just to have what other men could take for granted.

He hoped Cable found what he was looking for. He really did.

But that couldn't stop his misgivings. . . .

They entered the narrowest part of the valley, where the mountains on either side of them formed a funnel that amplified the force of the howling wind. The visibility was close to zero here. There was almost as much ice in the air as there was on the ground, and anything more than a few yards away was rendered an indistinct shape, moving through a universe of pure white. Cable was just close enough to be visible as a gray portrait of battle readiness; he stood stock still, aiming his gun into the emptiness. He was shouting something, too, but any meaning it might have possessed was swallowed up by the wind.

The Beast didn't need to know what it was. Not really. He'd been in enough battles to already know. Here, where they were effectively both blind and deaf, they were in perfect position for the ambush they expected. That's why Cable had stopped. He knew it was about to happen.

He spotted a patch of darkness, amid the white. A trick of the wind?

No, it was a humanoid form. A big one. Barrel chested, wider than most doors, with arms as massive as tree

TIME'S ARROW

trunks. Running too—each step a pounding assault upon the ice, reverberating like cannon fire, making tremors that the Beast could feel right through his insulated boots. The Beast came up with two likely possibilities without even thinking hard: the Hulk or the Juggernaut. Either one meant a battle capable of exhausting the entire X-Men team, much less the two of them.

The figure stopped in midstep, just outside the boundaries of visibility. He stood there, facing the Beast, his steam-train breath audible even over the wind. The Beast couldn't see his face, but it was impossible to escape the subliminal impression that he was smiling.

Juggernaut. It had to be. But if so, what was he waiting for?

A second later, the Beast saw: a second figure, emerging out of the wind. This one was a woman—Rubenesque, perhaps a tad overweight, and giving off the heat of a blast furnace. She was the outline of light, to her companion's outline of darkness. If her stance was any guide, she'd chosen Cable as her opponent.

The Beast glanced at Cable, to see if he was ready. Dumb question. If the Beast were a villain, facing a guy who looked that ready, he'd rush right out and get the want ads, to see if he could find a less dangerous line of work.

He only wished he could see and hear whoever he was dealing with—

—and then, on cue, his wish was granted.

The wind died. The ice and snow in the air continued swirling about, out of sheer momentum, but with its impetus gone, it had already begun to precipitate toward the ground. He heard a nasal midwestern voice—the woman's—remark, "Well, I guess that means the force field kicked in. That's good. I don't mind the cold, but the wind was a royal pain in the rear."

The giant grumbled. "On, off . . . who cares? I never needed no fancy gizmos."

The voice was unfamiliar. It wasn't the Juggernaut or the Hulk. Who—?

Cable cocked his rifle and aimed it at the woman. "You

THE PRESENT

can both save yourselves a lot of trouble by leading us to the device now."

"No trouble," the woman said cheerily. "Say, before we start, do you mind telling me if Iceman's anywhere around? I figured he'd be here, and I was so looking forward to mixing it up with him. You know, fire, ice, that sort of thing..."

"Sorry," the Beast said. "His dance card's full today."

"Shoot. Aw, well. It's not like anybody made any promises."

The massive form grumbled louder. "Oh, for cryin' out loud, Volcana! The boss ain't payin' us to gab with these jerks! Can we just get *on* with it?"

"Might as well," Volcana said.

She flared, giving off a wave of heat and light that for an instant seemed to turn the already stark landscape as bright as the sun itself. The Beast was dazzled even through his protective goggles. Even as Cable fired blindly into the heart of the inferno, the Beast averted his eyes just in time to see the larger figure bearing down on him, aiming his massive head like a battering ram, driving himself forward with the speed and the power of an express train.

If he had half the mass he appeared to, and was anywhere near as powerful as the animal he resembled, the impact alone would break every bone in the Beast's body.

Of course, the Beast had no intention of allowing that impact to happen.

He waited until the last possible second, and jumped straight up, allowing the behemoth to pass by underneath. The move assumed a fairly poor reaction time, and it turned out to be somewhat riskier than surmised; even as the Beast vaulted over his assailant's back, he barely avoided the pair of impossibly huge arms that had immediately reached up to grab him. The hands at the end of those arms were even larger than the Beast's own; they looked more than powerful enough to rend the Beast into mutant linguini. The Beast was happy to avoid their ac-

TIME'S ARROW

quaintance, especially since he'd now had a close look at the miscreant in question.

"Oh, my stars and garters!" he exclaimed, as he landed on his feet. "It's a grown man dressed like a hippo!"

On the ice, his opponent needed a good twenty yards to slow down and turn around. He covered most of that distance growling: "Not a hippo, you overgrown smurf! Didn't you see the horn? I'm the Rhino!"

The Beast knew that, of course—he'd recognized the Rhino from his file in the Avengers archives. If reputation served, the Rhino was a murderous, surgically enhanced thug whose brute strength and implacable rage placed him well within the Hulk's class; he was capable of derailing freight trains, and winning head-on collisions with Mack trucks. He was also rumored to be, putting it tactfully, not the brightest tactician in this line of work, and he tended to lose what little self-control he had when folks got him riled.

To that end, the Beast called out, "Really? A rhino? What's so scary about a rhino?"

Battling Volcana was a lot like running across an enemy minefield, trying to remember where the the bombs were, when the ground around you was being shelled by both the opposition and the friendlies. She was very good at what she did: she kept after Cable with dozens of bolts of white-hot flame, one after the other, sticking to his heels, keeping him too busy for a clear return shot. She'd shot down the few ion bursts he'd been able to fire, and though he'd managed to avoid being hit, just staying one step ahead of her attacks had kept him from getting close enough to take her down the hard way.

He'd fought more dangerous enemies, even more powerful enemies. But Volcana differed from them in one very obvious respect: She neither stayed silent, nor taunted him.

It seemed she wanted to chat.

"So, where you from, originally?"

Cable saw a massive fireball explode just ahead of him, reducing the ice to a steaming crater. He'd avoided the last

72

ten craters, either by jumping over them or changing direction at the last minute, but this one he leapt into, judging it a perfect foxhole. He hugged the edge, brought his ion cannon to bear, and shot a wide spread of covering fire low across the ice. Volcana fired a wall of flame, to protect herself; the resulting explosions echoed across the valley and filled the air between them with superheated steam.

"I'm usually very good at guessing where people are from," Volcana said, behind that misty curtain. "It's a gift of mine. I have you pegged for Maine. Are you from Maine?"

Cable leapt out of the crater and ran zigzag patterns over the ice, firing random bursts into the steam just to keep her off-guard. By the time he'd covered even half the distance between them his boots were sinking into semiliquid slush. He heard a whistle of wind somewhere high above him and darted for safety just in time to avoid the ball of corruscating flame that she'd blindly fired over the steam.

"I visited Maine once. My ex-boyfriend Owen took me to visit Stephen King's house. It turns out they're old friends. I got his autograph and everything."

Cable could see her now: a sun in the shape of a woman, glowing behind the mists.

"Do you read Stephen King?"

Cable couldn't take anymore. "Are you out of your mind? Do you have any idea what's going on here? Do you have any idea what we're doing?"

"Sure I do," Volcana said—and though Cable couldn't see her well enough to tell, there was clearly a pout behind that endlessly chatty voice. "And what am I supposed to go on about? Am I supposed to shout things like, 'Tremble, mortal, before the invincible wrath of Volcana'? That's stupid! Even Owen doesn't say things like that anymore."

Cable saw her form pulse, the way it did whenever she seemed about to release another massive wave of killing heat. Instead of darting out of the way again, he charged her head-on, firing his ion cannon as he went. The closer he got to her, the hotter the air became. Something very hot passed very close—so close that he knew he'd just passed within inches of being incinerated. He saw another flaming missile heading directly toward him and deflected it with a telekinetic shield—avoiding the flames, but still gasping as a wave of broiling hot air left his protective mask smoking.

He ripped off the mask—fighting her, he didn't need it anyway—and saw, without quite believing it, that she was now running away. Incredible. All her power, and she didn't even want to press the advantage caused by his momentary blindness.

"It doesn't matter what words you use," he said. "You're still a criminal, in the employ of a monster."

"Oh, please," she said "I'm an unemployed woman, and I needed to pay off my credit cards. And when this strange guy came out of nowhere, paying me *exactly* the amount of money I needed in cash, in advance, to spend an afternoon in Antarctica, fighting some super hero who probably wouldn't mind because he did this kind of thing on a daily basis anyway, what was I supposed to say? No? Believe me, when I'm done with this, it's back to macramé and television!"

Cable almost didn't go after her. He had seen a lot in a life of unending violence and strife, but he'd never once fought anybody like this woman who could be friendly and innocent and even perversely likable even as she bombarded an enemy with deadly force. He wondered if she was really as mundane as she liked to pretend. Then he decided, renewing his pursuit, that he really didn't want to know.

She was still a barrier between him and Aliya.

The Beast wasn't experiencing anywhere near the same level of cognitive dissonance—he was causing it.

"I'm serious! You really ought to change your name to the Hippo. Did you know that, despite their gentle reputation, hippopotami are actually considerably more dan-

THE PRESENT

gerous than rhinoceri? Indeed, some rhinos are so docile you can walk right up to them and pet them. You can't say that about hippos."

He said all this while riding the Rhino's back. The Rhino kept trying to grab him and rip him off, but every time those massive arms came up the Beast merely leapt straight up, did a triple somersault, and landed on the Rhino's back again. He had gotten the idea from the little birds that frequently perch on the backs of real rhinos, feeding on insect pests; rhinos were no good at dislodging those, why should this Rhino be any good at dislodging a mutant who acted the same way?

"I mean it," the Beast merrily repeated. "Ask anybody who knows anything about African wildlife. Rhinos are overrated—it's hippos you have to worry about."

"I . . . am . . . *not* . . . calling myself the Hippo!"

"Why not? You want to be accurate, don't you?"

"Hippo's a name you call fat people!"

"Oh, sure. Like you're svelte."

The Rhino bellowed in rage, and charged off in a brand-new direction: toward the barrier of ice Cable and the Beast had needed to cross earlier. It was sufficiently far away that the Beast relaxed long enough to look over his shoulder at the considerably more pyrotechnic battle taking place between Cable and Volcana. From here all he could see was flames and explosions and great big bursts of light, which wasn't all that much to be worried about, since it was precisely the kind of battle Cable was best at. Indeed, it already seemed that Cable had the upper hand—for as the Beast watched, the steam clouds parted just enough to let him see that Volcana was fleeing toward the valley wall, and that Cable was pursuing her.

The Beast felt reassured for all of two seconds before all his mental warning buzzers went off.

Valley walls. Covered with thousands upon thousands of tons of precariously stacked ice. A woman capable of shooting flame.

She wasn't fleeing. She was getting more ammunition.

Aware also that the Rhino hadn't tried to grab him for

some time now, the Beast shifted position and looked ahead to see just what the pusillanimous pachyderm had in mind instead. The Rhino evidently intended to meet the ice barrier head-on—a collision that wouldn't mean much to a gent capable of derailing freight trains, but which might leave the unwanted passenger on his back feeling more than a little flat.

It was a tactic he'd seen used by the Juggernaut, who was in many ways a spiritual brother to the Rhino: if you can't dislodge the hero clinging to your back, walk through a building. Let it collapse on you. You won't be hurt. He, on the other hand, might be a tad inconvenienced.

The Beast smiled, and shook his head.

Some things were just too easy.

The Rhino smashed into the ice barrier. Crystal shrapnel flew everywhere. Ten thousand pieces of hail flew straight up, and billowed outward. The ice barrier heaved twice, like a sleeping giant fighting for its last breath, then imploded, revealing the skid marks of a burly gray behemoth whose momentum had carried him not only through the barrier but another fifty yards beyond it. He'd covered at least half that distance skidding on his belly. Soon he'd come to a stop, feel his back, and confirm that he no longer had a wisenheimer X-Man hitching a ride.

The wisenheimer X-Man had, of course, back-flipped to safety an instant before the Rhino smashed into the ice barrier. He had hit the ground running and chased after Volcana and Cable with all the speed he could muster. He was sure he'd have no problem outrunning the Rhino. But there was no way he'd reach Cable before the flaming woman sprang her trap. . . .

"The worst part of it was my transmission," Volcana said. "I'd always taken such good care of that car, and then all of a sudden, boom, everything hits the fan, I have to spend hundreds I don't have fixing something that wasn't even my fault. It makes me wish I lived somewhere I didn't need a car, y'know?"

THE PRESENT

It was the strangest super-villain repartée Cable had ever heard. And even as he warded off one of her flaming missiles by using his telekinesis to levitate a sheet of ice into its path, even as he continued to chase her into a place where the mountain walls loomed closer and the valley gradually became a narrow crevasse, even as he realized that he was leaving the Beast behind and that Volcana must have been luring him into some kind of trap—he found himself, against his will, responding in kind. "Have you ever considered living in New York?"

"Oh, yuck! You know what the rents are like there?"

She whirled, and fired a wall of flame, not at Cable, but at the air over his head. He had expected such a move—he'd entered the area knowing that the cliff walls were avalanches waiting to happen. But one of the convenient things about warfare is that once you know your enemy's strategy there are no copyright laws that keep you from adopting it as your own. Even as she fired, Cable fired too. His ion burst shattered a pitifully narrow shelf some fifty feet over her head. The valley roared as two thousand feet of stacked snow and ice began tumbling toward her.

By the time Volcana looked up and saw the frozen tidal wave about to engulf her, Cable had already spun on his heels and begun to flee his own personal avalanche. Unlike the one she'd unleashed on him, his was initially lukewarm rain, which made the first few seconds of his flight almost easy. Then—as he pushed himself to run as fast as he'd ever run before—the colder stuff began falling. First he was pelted by slush and then by snow and then by hail and then by a great angry wall of ice, one step behind him as he fled the roaring frozen deathtrap the valley had become. A white haze obscured the view ahead of him, swallowing the whole world, promising to swallow him.

And then something struck him from behind and lifted him off his feet and wrapped itself around his back and swept him a hundred yards in ten seconds, turning the cloudy sky above into chaotic streaks of gray.

But that stopped when the avalanche did.

TIME'S ARROW

After a moment of assuring himself that he was still alive, he sat up, and looked over his shoulder at what he'd just escaped. The narrowest part of the valley was now completely buried in ice; he hadn't managed to outrun the avalanche entirely, but he'd managed to avoid being buried beneath it when it fell. He had covered just enough ground that, when it hit bottom, the edge of its expansion wave had scooped him up and carried him out of harm's way.

It wasn't the closest call he'd ever had. But it was definitely one of the top five.

He searched the horizon and saw that the Beast was on his way, alone, covering the distance in a series of great gravity-defying leaps. The Rhino was nowhere in sight. Cable doubted they could count on that for long; he didn't even think they could count on having heard the last of Volcana. Their type had a nasty habit of getting up.

But there was good news. With the force field Volcana had mentioned blocking out the wind, and the last of the steam clouds stirred up by the battle already precipitated to the ground as ice, the air was much clearer than they'd found it. They had decent visibility for the first time—and with it, their first opportunity to see what they were looking for.

The Beast arrived, in a burst of splattering snow. "Where's your date?"

Cable said, "Snowbound. And the Rhino?"

"On his way. If you can suggest any productive ways to spend our time until he gets here, I'll be most gratified to listen."

Cable smiled, and pointed at the other side of the canyon, toward an opening twenty yards up the western wall. It was just big enough for a man, and just small enough that it could only be seen if you were specifically looking for it.

"Does that look natural to you?" he asked.

The closer they got, the less it did.

The opening was so perfectly circular it might have

THE PRESENT

been drilled with a high-potency laser. The walls were so smooth they looked polished. Even the canyon wall around it seemed deliberately shaped. Though deceptively natural looking, it came equipped with regularly spaced handholds that made the climb up the wall to the entrance positively easy. Cable scrambled up almost as quickly as the Beast did. They both hesitated as they stood at the cave entrance, marshaling their strength for what would almost certainly turn out to be another battle.

"Our opponent's a gamesman," the Beast said. "He gives us the opportunity to stop these bombs. He turns on a force field to cut out the wind so we have enough visibility to fight. He creates a cave so perfectly round that even a blind man could tell it's artificial. I don't like it, Cable. He's clearly arranged this entire scenario to lead us wherever he wants us to go."

"Absolutely," Cable said. "But there's no point in turning around. There's nothing out there but Rhino and Volcana. We'll just have to continue acting like rats in a maze, and hope we see the point of this before it's too late."

The Beast hesitated, not liking it. "Maybe we should question the Rhino first?"

It was an idea; the super-villain was lumbering about at the foot of Cable's icefall, pacing first one way, and then the other, as if thoroughly stymied by it. Which was not saying much. The Beast hadn't known the Rhino for long, but he'd already gotten the impression that the gent was stymied by most things.

Actually, come to think of it, he was probably looking for footprints. If so, good luck; the Beast had carried Cable all the way here, leaping from one crater to another, leaving almost no trail to speak of. Even Wolverine might have had trouble tracking them here. *And you, my dear Rhino, are no Wolverine.*

Cable said, "Do you really believe he knows anything? Volcana was in it for a paycheck. He must have been too. I don't think either one of them would have gotten in-

TIME'S ARROW

volved if they knew there might be no world left in which to cash it."

"You're probably right." The Beast sighed. Although, if personal experience was any guide, the Rhino might conceivably be that stupid.

They turned from the cave opening and proceeded into the tunnel of ice. They found that it remained almost perfectly circular even as it descended into the cliff. As the light filtering in from the outside gradually dimmed, the tunnel itself took such a sharp dip downward that they had to brace their arms against the walls to avoid enjoying a sudden slide down an almost vertical chute. They glanced at each other—silently sharing the observation that their host seemed to be enjoying this a bit too much—then carefully descended, finally entering a dim space large enough to turn their every movement into an echo bouncing off distant unseen walls. Their nailed boots clanked as they took their first steps onto a metallic grating of some kind.

It felt wrong. Very wrong. Neither of them had to speak to know that the other felt the trap, whatever it was, would be sprung now. They stepped away from each other, and faced the darkness.

When the enemy made his next move known, it seemed at first almost disappointingly mundane: a machine gun. When he first saw the flash of muzzle fire at the other end of the chamber, the Beast was almost relieved. As the first wave of bullets impacted against the wall to his immediate left, chipping the ice like shrapnel, he leapt over the strafing fire, somersaulted, rebounded against the wall, and landed unharmed twenty feet away. Meanwhile, Cable threw himself to the ground, whipped out his ion cannon, and returned fire. There was a brilliant flash of light as the resulting explosion lit up the entire chamber, revealing the deep chasm between them and the gun. It was a hundred feet deep and filled with icy stalagmites perfectly positioned to tear great nasty holes in anybody clumsy enough to fall in. The grating was a catwalk that completely circled the chamber, providing the only safe path over the abyss. As the light from the explosion faded, Cable scram-

THE PRESENT

bled to his feet and raised the ion cannon for another shot—

—only to halt when the Beast cried out, in a voice alive with horror: "No! Cable, *don't*!"

Cable froze as the Beast leapt to his side. "What's wrong?"

The Beast was so sickened he could barely manage the words. "That moment of light," he choked. "It was so brief, I don't blame you for not seeing..."

"What?"

"It's a girl," the Beast said. "Fifteen or sixteen years old at most. She was wearing a parka and chained to an automatic gunner. You disabled the gun, but you also got her. I... I saw her go down, Cable. I saw your rounds get her in the belly. It... it doesn't make any sense... but maybe... somehow... all of this is just about tricking us into killing her...."

Cable felt the blood pounding in his ears. "Are you sure?"

"I'm telling you, I saw her go down! We have to get over there and find out if she's still..."

Something wet splattered on the hood of the Beast's parka. He looked up, and was rewarded by another drop landing in his eye. All throughout the chamber, the silence that marked the possible aftermath of a murder was replaced by the even more chilling sound of warming rain splattering against the metal catwalk. They heard a loud gurgling, and whirled, just in time to see the first streams of steaming water pour through the tunnel leading out.

Cable's right eye glowed in the darkness. "Volcana," he said. "She's found us, and she's turning on the heat. We have to—"

But before he finished the sentence, they both heard the choking voice of a frightened young woman, crying out in pain....

CHAPTER FIVE

For Spider-Man, awareness returned slowly: first with the sensation of a cold hard surface beneath his back, then with the dull ache the darts had left behind, then with the realization that he knew the cruel voices he could hear in the darkness.

"—on the tube last night? That guy has an attitude the size of the Big M's."

"Whaddide say?"

A snort. "Whaddaya think he said?"

"The usual stuff?"

"Naturally. Eternal vigilance. Report all sponkies. Same as always."

"I hate that guy."

"Huh. So what else is new? Last time I checked, he felt the same way about us."

Spider-Man stirred. Met resistance. Realized that his arms and legs were shackled to a wall, and frowned in annoyance. He hated when that happened. Pretty soon he'd have to open his eyes and listen to some bozo on a power trip, ranting about his grand design. He had a theory about people like that: shackling other people to walls was the only way they could get anybody to listen to them. He preferred unconsciousness. It was quieter.

"Sleepin' Beauty there's startin' to wake up."

"Sshhh! Not so loud! You'll ruin his dream!"

Dream. It would be nice to have a dream, right about now. Maybe, if he concentrated, he could summon up Mary Jane, the way she looked that night they went to the Alison Blaire concert at the Garden. . . .

Then he remembered where he'd heard those voices before, and full consciousness returned with the suddenness of an explosion. When he opened his eyes, the two men were grinning at him unpleasantly. He knew them both, of course. The one on the left was Electro, the human battery, who stored in his body enough electricity to light up a city. The one on the right was Hydro-Man, who, though he looked normal now, was not flesh or bone anymore, but a humanoid being composed entirely of water. Spider-Man had fought both these men time and time

THE PRESENT

again—they were nothing but common thugs who had both reacted to the acquisition of super-powers by remaining common thugs, on a larger scale. Unless this world's Electro and Hydro-Man were substantially different people, their appearance here—together—was not a happy development. (Especially considering what happened when electricity met water; Spider-Man couldn't imagine how they could feel comfortable even standing next to each other.)

They looked significantly different from the versions he knew. His Electro wore a green costume with a jagged yellow starburst mask; this Electro wore no mask at all, and for his costume wore a jet-black bodysuit patterned with phosphorescent lightning bolts. As for Hydro-Man, he may have been dressed in black t-shirt and jeans, like the version back home—but this version wore his hair long, and tied back in a ponytail. They were minor changes, overall, but they served to remind Spider-Man that he was a long, long way from home.

It was too dark to discern much about their surroundings, but it seemed to be a large, damp chamber, on a platform somewhere between an unseen floor and an unseen ceiling. The platform was lit, but that small circle of illumination failed to penetrate the darkness that lay beyond; the distant echoes that followed just about every word his captors said made the chamber sound about as large as an aircraft hangar.

Hydro-Man said, "Top of the mornin' to you, buddy. 'Bout time you woke up. Your closemouthed friend's been bright eyed and bushy tailed for twenny minutes awready."

Bishop, who was chained to the wall beside Spider-Man, said, "Don't take it personally, Cartwright. From what I can make out, each of the darts they hit you with had two times the sedative they needed to dose me. Your resistance to such things must be phenomenal."

"Yeah," Hydro-Man said. "It's a good thing Electro and I showed up when we did. We hadda give you a second dart just to put you down."

TIME'S ARROW

No, you didn't, Spider-Man thought. *I only had another couple of seconds of consciousness left. But I'm not about to tell you that.*

Now that his head was clearing, he registered (from the welcome absence of itching) that the civvies he and Bishop had scrounged were now gone; the bad guys had chained them up only after first stripping them down to their super hero union suits. Grateful that this was as far as they'd gone—defiance being so much more impressive in a union suit than a birthday suit—Spider-Man said, "Let me guess. I assume you're not working for the authorities?"

"Hell, no, buddy. You're in the hands of the Power Liberation Front."

It had the sound of a big melodramatic announcement, but Spider-Man shrugged. "Never heard of you."

"Oh, you're a cool one, all right. Whoever trained you oughta give himself a medal. But it ain't gonna do you no good. We ain't fooled. You ain't sponkies. You're just pretending to be. You're spies, makin' a whole big show of pretendin' to be on the run, hopin' that we, the last major alliance of free sponkies, show up and recruit you so you can drop a dime for your bosses. Well, here's a flash bulletin for you guys: we've been onto you since the start. And we've had our supporters lookin' for a chance to take you down since yesterday."

"We being the PLF," Spider-Man said.

"Uh-huh." Hydro-Man raised his right arm and transformed it into a churning mass of white water. "The second you walked into that coffee shop, your friend behind the counter dropped a dime on *you*."

"But not to the police," Spider-Man said.

"Yup." Hydro-Man grinned. "Now either tell us who *really* sent you, or grow yourself a pair of gills."

Spider-Man hesitated. He didn't want to gauge his chances of getting two veteran hardnoses like Hydro-Man and Electro to believe a story about alternate worlds and conquerors from the future. If these two were anything like the villains he knew, it didn't matter whether he persuaded

86

THE PRESENT

them or not; they were positively anxious for the chance to, like the guy in the movie said, get medieval on him. But he didn't like his chances of making up anything more believable, so he said, "Can I just ask you a question first?"

"It better be a good one," Hydro-Man said.

"Oh, it is," Spider-Man said. "What's a sponkie?"

It was probably the last thing either super-villain had ever expected to hear. They gaped at him, unwilling to believe he'd actually said what they'd just heard him say—and then, with a quick glance at each other's face, started laughing. Electro's was loud and crackling, like a live wire dropped in a bathtub; Hydro-Man's was liquid and bubbling, like a stopped sink overflowing onto a kitchen floor. Electro recovered first: "Hey, what are you, a moron or what?"

"We're not spies," Bishop told them, "we haven't been sent here by anyone, and we never even heard of the PLF before today. And, yes, I second the question. I've been hearing that word for two days and I'm getting tired of it."

"*You're* tired of it," Hydro-Man murmured.

Electro gestured him to silence, then turned his attention back to Bishop, and raised a fist filled with angry lightning. "If you're not spies, then why were you prowling around our tunnels today? You practically walked right through our front door!"

It took Spider-Man a second to understand what Electro meant. "You mean, when we escaped through the sewers? We weren't looking for your hideout. We were just trying to get away from Cyclops."

"You're lyin'!" Electro shouted. "Nobody as dumb as you're pretending to be could possibly get away from Cyclops!"

"We were in the park when he took down the Air-Skater. We saw it happen. We just went underground when it looked like they were coming after us next."

Again, the two villains laughed—but this time they were not alone, for there were other people laughing in

TIME'S ARROW

the darkness. Spider-Man recognized some of the people by the sound of their laughter. It was a sound he'd heard many times before, when they thought they'd beaten him, a sound that had always stopped when he got back up and beat them down. It had always been that sound which spurred him on to fight the hardest. And here, in this place, when he was literally worlds away from home, he finally connected that laughter to a vow that had been made by a lonely kid less than one hour away from the accident that had turned him into Spider-Man: *I'll show them. Someday they'll be sorry. Sorry they laughed at me....*

Angry now, he said, "All right, bunkies. So I'm a laugh riot. Why don't you just turn on the lights, so I can at least see who I'm talking to?"

Electro loomed close. "You're in no position to make suggestions, buddy-boy."

"Except," Bishop said, "that he happens to be right. There's no reason we should all suffer eyestrain, while you're all deciding whether or not to kill us."

Somebody must have considered that a valid point, because at that moment the chamber was flooded with light. It turned out to be a vast empty space three stories high, encompassing an area about the size of a gymnasium. The walls were broad expanses of crumbling concrete, lined with corroded steam pipes; the floor was a filthy pitted swamp dotted with oily black puddles. It was obviously underground, obviously abandoned, obviously a relic of the subways or the sewers. Spider-Man and Bishop were chained to the wall on the second level, at one end of a catwalk containing a number of people Spider-Man recognized at once.

Most were bad news. Spider-Man had fought their counterparts many times. They were so dangerous individually that he shuddered at the thought of something powerful enough to drive them into hiding as a group.

The closest was a walking mass of silicon brawn called the Sandman. Spider-Man didn't know whether that was bad news or not. He dressed in the same striped shirt and brown trousers as the Sandman he knew—making him, if anything, a welcome dose of familiarity in the face of all this strangeness—but that didn't necessarily mean he was a potential ally. The Sandman Spider-Man knew had started his life as a ruthless criminal named Flint Marko, who, thanks to a nuclear accident, was transformed into a being composed of tens of thousands of separate grains of sand. He'd fought Spider-Man, the Fantastic Four, Nova, and others, for years, and was universally feared for his ruthlessness and his brutality—until he astonished everybody by suddenly deciding to change his life and join the side of the good guys. The Flint Marko Spider-Man knew had turned out, against all odds, to have a fundamentally decent man buried deep within the soul of the murderous criminal he'd been. The only question was: which Flint Marko was this? And would Spider-Man have a chance to find out?

Behind him stood two women who'd both been granted super-powers by the omnipotent alien being known as the Beyonder. Best friends before and after, they'd reacted to their empowerment in completely different ways. Titania, who'd been granted extraordinary strength and toughness, used both to satisfy her grudge against the world. The last Spider-Man had heard, Volcana had just decided the super-villain life was not for her and gone back to an existence largely defined by cable TV. They could both be dangerous when they wanted to be, but Titania was clearly the one to look out for.

They both looked a little different from the versions Spider-Man knew from back home. Spider-Man's Titania dressed in a purple costume, but was essentially just a big girl with an attitude. This Titania had punked out big-time. She wore spiked hair, leather pants, and a torn leather vest over a halter; the only part of her still recognizable was her sneer. The familiar Volcana was a slightly overweight, deceptively sweet-looking woman who preferred shapeless warm-up suits when not out radiating heat and flame; this one was significantly thinner and significantly better dressed in simple white blouse and long skirt. Of everybody in the room, she resembled a murderous super-villain least.

Then there was the glowering man-monster called the Rhino. He was bad news no matter what planet this was, and he looked about the same, except possibly—hard as it might be to believe—a little uglier. Spider-Man might have fought him many times himself, but anybody more at home going head-to-toe with the Hulk was somebody best avoided. The man wasn't just strong, he was *mean*. His favorite hobby was turning buildings, automobiles, and overconfident super heroes into smoking wreckage.

Spider-Man had to forcibly remind himself that they were not the same people he had fought so many times, but their alternate-timeline counterparts, who might have had about as much in common with the bad guys he knew and loathed as this world's tyrannical Cyclops had with the humane, responsible X-Man he remembered from back home. But he still took each new face as another blow against the chances of his and Bishop's ever managing to reach home alive.

Fortunately—though there was no way of telling yet whether it actually was fortunate—three of the watchers on the catwalk were people he recognized as the counterparts of allies, instead of enemies.

One was the gangly, awkward teenager named Speedball, who had developed an aura that enabled him to rebound from any impact. He was a nice kid who'd become a super hero because, for a while at least, he couldn't turn the bouncing off: the slightest shove had sent him rebounding over the roofs of houses. The Speedball Spider-Man knew had developed a little more self-control, eventually—at least enough to qualify him as a valued member of the super team known as the New Warriors. Spider-Man liked him, personally; there had always been something about Speedball that had reminded him of his younger self, almost as if their lives had been drawn along the same lines. This Speedball seemed a little more grim, a little more shell-shocked—as was only reasonable for a kid forced into going undercover with so many more ruth-

THE PRESENT

less characters—and wore goggles about twice as large.

Speedball was accompanied by a young acrobatic crimefighter known as the Night Thrasher, who on Spider-Man's world had been the leader of the New Warriors. Spider-Man didn't know much about him, except that he was competent and dedicated and possessed of a grim outlook that made Bishop look like Jerry Lewis. Night Thrasher was good news *if* he was on the right side—in which case, he could be counted on to stay there. Like the Night Thrasher from back home, this one dressed in a stylized ninja outfit, with the addition of bulging pockets across his chest and down both arms, an indication that he'd armed himself with many more odds and ends.

Finally, bringing up the rear, wearing the ridiculous oversized helmet shaped like the head of a wild boar, Spider-Man saw the towering, almost seven-foot figure whose appearance in this particular lineup provided the final indication that this alternate world was really getting out of hand. It was Buford T. Hollis, the well-meaning, but not incredibly talented, truck-drivin' champion of Arkansas, better known as Razorback. According to the She-Hulk, who'd also encountered him once, Hollis was supposed to be a mutant with the ability to drive anything like an expert. Spider-Man supposed that made sense about as much as anything Razorback touched could make sense. He just knew that Buford was a tough guy with a lot of heart whose greatest victory before teaming up with Spider-Man had been against a gang of outlaw truckers smuggling stolen CB parts across state lines. In this lineup, he would have seemed well out of his league; but then, this Razorback seemed to have toughened himself up considerably. His previously no-frills suit was now augmented by a metalwork that made his entire chest look like the grille of a truck. There was a headlight in the center of his chest, just above what appeared to be a functional winch with a long length of chain. They made him look tougher, all right—even if it was hard to tell exactly why. But the single most overpowering element of his costume was still that huge tusked boar head he wore for a helmet, which

TIME'S ARROW

made his rough-hewn face look like the apple in the mouth of a roasted pig.

After a moment, Sandman stunned everybody present by saying, "Cripes. I know that one."

"Which one?" Hydro-Man asked.

"The little fella." Indicating Spider-Man. "Dunno where, but I seen that costume before. Somewhere. A long time ago."

Titania stepped closer, and gazed at Spider-Man contemplatively. "I think you're right," she said, with growing excitement. "Something about him—like I've seen him on TV or something...."

"I got me a tune runnin' through my head," Razorback said. "Can't name it, though. Drivin' me crazy."

"Who cares?" the Rhino growled. "Just smash 'im."

"Aren't you being a bit hasty?" Speedball protested. "I seem to remember you wanted to smash me once."

"Still do, kid. And still will. Soon as we get this Pegasus thing sorted out."

"Big man," Titania said. "Gets his jollies threatening kids. Why don't you pick on somebody your own size? You can start with me, if you want to!"

Rhino leered. "Anytime, anyplace, babe. I'll bring the mood music."

"Why, you—"

"*People!*" Night Thrasher cried. "This isn't solving anything! Before Speedball makes with the obvious Rhino pun—and don't try to deny it, kid, I can see the urge in your eyes—let's get back to the subject at hand. We don't have to argue about it, there's a faster way of settling this. Give me a few minutes to take their fingerprints and hack into the local Cerebro mainframe. If they're certified, I'll find out. If they're really sponkies, I'll find *that* out. Either way, we take the data to Eric and decide what to do then. All right?"

"Not all right," the Rhino muttered, confirming—as if he really had to—that he was just as charming an individual on this planet as he was back home. "I say smash 'em now."

THE PRESENT

Electro seemed about to echo the Rhino's sentiments, but then he apparently thought better of it. He nodded at Night Thrasher. "Do it."

Night Thrasher emerged from the crowd, produced a miniature fingerprint kit from his belt, and went to work. As he dabbed Spider-Man's fingers with ink, he said, "I'll tell you this much: if you two are spies, your cover's good. The cops have gone to Double Class-A alert, the nets are running Iceman's descriptions of a big black man and his unusually acrobatic partner. Cyclops has made your capture top priority. If it's all an act, designed to make us trust you, they're really pulling out all the stops. But they tried the same infiltration trick just six months ago. It didn't work then and it won't work now."

"Lady assassin named Elektra," Electro said. "No relation. We fixed her hash but good."

"We did, huh?" Hydro-Man snorted. "Excuse me, but weren't you the guy on your knees, begging her, oh, please, please, please, don't kill me . . . ?"

"Hardy-har har. Criticize me again the next time you have any internal organs to bleed with."

Spider-Man rolled his eyes. This was the major problem with eliciting vital information from large groups of super-villains: in his experience, they all had the attention span of two-year-olds. Before they could descend into further bickering, he said, "Excuse me! Tell me this much: if this was a trick, why would we pretend we didn't know what a sponkie was? Which you still haven't told us, by the way."

Night Thrasher finished with Spider-Man's fingerprints. "SPNC. Pronounced Sponkie. Meaning, Super-Powered, Noncertified. As in any paranormal not yet drafted by the government goon squads."

Bishop stared, as Night Thrasher began to take his prints. "You mean, all super heroes have to work for the government here?"

Hydro-Man rolled his eyes. "Where are you people from? Jersey?"

"It's not just super heroes," Night Thrasher said. "It's

TIME'S ARROW

everybody. All mutants. All paranormals. Whether they're mutants, enhanced humans, sorcerers, cyborgs, even people with powers too minor to be of any real use in a fight. If they do something baseline humanity can't, they get put to work tracking down the rest of us. Unless they refuse, in which case they get taken into 'protective custody,' a fancy way of saying that they're never seen again. Just like people who try to spy on us, in case you're wondering.'' He closed his fingerprint kit, and addressed the others. "This shouldn't take more than a few minutes."

"Hurry," said Electro. "I'm looking forward to frying some spies."

As Night Thrasher hurried off, Bishop spoke up, in an uncharacteristically hesitant voice. "I need to know. The X-Men . . . they sanction this policy?"

There was much general hilarity at this.

"What's the matter with you?" Electro demanded. "You don't know the word *sponkie*, you don't know the PLF, you don't know the deal with the X-Men. Is this some kinda new version of name, rank, and serial number? As in don't bother questioning me, 'cause I don't even know what planet I'm on?"

"That's it," Spider-Man said. "Exactly."

Electro's eyes flashed high-current rage. "Why, you smart-aleck son of a—"

"He's telling the truth," Bishop said, in a calm, confident voice that immediately commanded the attention of everybody in the room. "My friend and I are . . . castaways, of sorts. Time travelers. We were on our way back to a world where history followed a different path, where all of you were different people playing different roles. Then something went wrong, and we landed here. I don't expect you to believe this—"

Hydro-Man snorted.

"—but you don't have to. Right now, you can explain our ignorance any way you want. Amnesia. Insanity. Even the naïveté of somebody who, like that young man said, just doesn't get out much. You can call it anything you want. All my friend and I need you to believe, while we're

THE PRESENT

waiting for the results of that fingerprint test, is that we honestly have no idea what you're talking about, and that it won't hurt one bit just to bring us up to speed on the parts that are already public knowledge."

The silence that followed lasted only a second, before Rhino said, "This is boring. I say smash 'em now."

"We can't do that," Speedball protested. "What if they're telling the truth?"

"That dog-and-pony show the truth? Kid, I got dirty socks that smell better than that!"

"No you don't," Titania sniffed.

"Huh? What's that supposed to—"

"Listen to me!" Spider-Man shouted, eager to regain control of the conversation before the bickering began again. "Buford!"

That silenced them. As every eye in the place turned on Razorback, the literally pigheaded Arkansan stepped out of the crowd, suspicion burning in his narrow little eyes. "How d'yew know my real name, son?"

Spider-Man measured his next words very carefully. "I know you won't remember this, Buford, because it probably didn't happen the same way here, but on the world my friend and I come from, you and I once fought side by side against a very nasty bad guy called the Hate-Monger. We were chained up together, just like my friend and I are chained up now, with no way to free ourselves, and save thousands of lives. Then you called Big Pig, and she came to rescue us." Something flickered on Razorback's face. Astonishment? Rage? Disbelief? Spider-Man pressed on. "If that means anything at all to you, Buford—even a little bit—tell us what's going on here. Please."

As Razorback covered his face with his right hand, Spider-Man watched the others to gauge their own reactions. Rhino and Sandman shrugged, Speedball looked concerned, Electro and Hydro-Man rolled their eyes in exasperation, and the two women, Volcana and Titania, exchanged significant worried looks. As for Bishop, he just silently mouthed two words: *Big Pig?* Spider-Man nodded,

TIME'S ARROW

feeling sheepish despite the life-and-death stakes of the moment, then returned his attention to Razorback, who was even now regaining his composure, and facing the others through grimly set eyes.

"Tell the kid what he needs to know," Razorback rumbled. "Now."

Titania gave Razorback's shoulder a friendly squeeze. He shuddered once, then gave her a nod to confirm that he was all right. Perhaps a little too quickly, Volcana moved to his other side, glaring at Spider-Man and Bishop with hostile eyes. "If you two turn out to be spies after all, I promise you I'll make you pay for putting him through this."

"Deal," Spider-Man said.

Titania contemplated his face for a long time, then said, "Okay. It started a few years ago, when the paranormals of the world were still essentially divided into two groups: super heroes and super-villains, some fighting for the law, some against it. The X-Men were on the side of the so-called good guys. They fought to keep the peace between those with powers and those without—"

"As on our world," Bishop said. "Continue."

"Then something happened. I don't know what. It was like, between one day and the next, the X-Men renounced everything they'd ever stood for. They'd always been against government intervention in paranormal affairs. But all of a sudden, they went public, and came out in favor of Senator Robert Kelly's Super-Powers Registration Bill. The bill had died a couple of years earlier, thanks to a presidential veto, but now the X-Men said it was time to dust it off and try to pass it again. They said that the world could no longer afford to have paranormals fighting their battles in the street. That it was time to reign in the madness. That it was time for the government to take control."

"Except," Speedball said, "that when the bill passed, the government ended up taking too much control. It ended up using the X-Men as a private police force intent on locking up anybody who could possibly offer them any resistance."

THE PRESENT

"That meant most super-villains, to start with," Titania said. "Nobody had any problem with that. Guys like the Green Goblin, Dr. Octopus, the U-Foes—they were always driving everybody's insurance rates right through the roof, so the average citizen felt much safer with them carted off in stasis tubes. Oh, Captain America asked some tough questions, until they got him. And the ACLU filed a suit protesting the legality of holding all these people incognito without benefit of trial, but somehow, they couldn't find a judge willing to support the rights of people like Graviton and"—she hesitated, closed her eyes—"the Absorbing Man." Spider-Man remembered that, on his world, Titania and Absorbing Man were an item—he'd even heard a rumor that they'd gotten married. She continued, "Before long, the X-Fascists could bury as many bad guys as they wanted, without anybody asking any questions at all."

"Until they started running out of villains," Volcana said, "and turned on the rest of the heroes."

"They went after anybody who wouldn't join them," Speedball broke in. "They started with the Hulk, just to prove they could. That battle lasted a couple of days, and destroyed much of Monument Valley, but it ended with the big green guy dead."

"Nobody had any problem with that," Titania said. "Not after all the property damage he caused over the years. Then they shut down the Fantastic Four, and the Pantheon, and the Champions, and the Defenders, and all four branches of the Avengers. . . ."

"The Punisher held out for a while," Speedball said, "until they put Wolverine on the case. Rumor has it that there wasn't even enough of the man left to bury."

"Daredevil was the last of the big guns," Sandman said, almost fondly. "Gotta give ol' Hornhead credit—ya woulda thunk, a guy like that, no real powers to speak of, who turned out to be blind, for Pete's sake, he woulda been the first to go. But no, for a few months there it seemed they couldn't catch him no matter what they did. He even put Gambit in the hospital with a broken leg once.

TIME'S ARROW

Folks actually started takin' bets on how long it would be before he shut the X-Men down—and he mighta done it, too, but then his old junkie girlfriend, Karen Page, sold his name to the Kingpin of Crime in exchange for a fix. The Kingpin blew up his house, beat him to a pulp, and turned him in to the feds. I won't say the Fat Man got something in return, but there was a Federal Racketeering Task Force that suddenly lost its funding about a week later.''

Spider-Man couldn't believe what he was hearing. Just as he thought he'd heard the worst of it, they would come up with another detail. "And Spider-Man? What happened to Spider-Man?"

The silence that greeted this question was palpable.

The Sandman said, "Who?"

Titania said, "Never heard of him."

The Rhino sneered, "That's the dumbest idea for a super hero I ever heard."

Emerging from his funk, Razorback grinned. "Well, that makes me feel a whole lot better."

Speedball said, "Are you sure you have the name right?"

"Sure I am!" Feeling more alienated with every moment, Spider-Man searched the faces before him for some sign of recognition, finding only puzzlement and incomprehension instead. "Friendly neighborhood super hero, dressed the way I am? Do you really mean to tell me that none of you have ever heard of Spider-Man?"

Just about everybody shrugged, shook their heads, or murmured no—with one exception. Volcana hesitantly raised her hand and, looking almost embarrassed to admit it, said, "Uh . . . well . . . actually, I have."

Spider-Man could have kissed her. "Really?"

"Uh, sure. I guess I just watch more TV than most of these guys. He wasn't a super hero, though. He was just this old novelty act, who used to pop up on all the talk shows. Don't any of you guys remember him? Spider-Man? Used to spin webs, and climb walls? Did *The Tonight*

THE PRESENT

Show a couple of times, before Elvis Presley handed it over to Howard Stern?"

Sandman snapped his fingers, chipping off a fine spray of grit as he did. "Yeah, that's right!" he said excitedly. "I forgot all about that joker! He was all over the place for a while. You couldn't change channels without seein' him, on some show or another. I even remember that dumb theme song of his, the one they used to play when he came out to do tricks—you know, 'Spins a web, any size . . .' "

Razorback clasped his forehead. "That's the tune! That's the tune!"

Sandman grinned. "Boy. I hated that song. Made me want to smash the guy just on general principles. But he dropped out of sight a *long* time before any of this went down. He's just a trivia question now, I guess." He narrowed his eyes. "You sayin you're him, buddy? That's rich. It's awful convenient of you showin' up now, after all these years. . . ."

There was nothing Spider-Man could say to that. This world had demonstrated itself to be a place where all his basic assumptions were turned upside down and inside out. It was a place where everything had gone wrong, where heroes had abandoned everything they stood for and villains had been forced by necessity to become the heroes. And it was a place where all the risks he'd ever taken, and all the battles he'd ever fought, were now reduced to a rumor, with no more relevance than a trivia question about an old TV performer almost no one remembered. Supervillain threats didn't bother him; he'd heard them hundreds of times before. But this sudden . . . irrelevance was more than he could bear. He was almost grateful to be shackled down; if not, he might have fled the room in panic.

Then, just in time, Bishop said, "Cartwright . . . ? I remember Spider-Man too." It brought Spider-Man back. He shuddered, reminded himself that this wasn't his world, and that though it was unimaginably far away he still had a world and a life and people whose lives had been af-

TIME'S ARROW

fected by his. He had to hold on to that . . . even if it seemed impossible.

Somewhere, a million miles away, the Rhino made a rude noise. "This is stupid. We don't have the time to talk about old TV shows. We got X-Men to stomp. I say we smash these bozos flat and get on with the important stuff!"

"Not until Night Thrasher gets back," Speedball said.

The Rhino whirled. "You're awful anxious to protect those guys, ain't you, kid? You know, I never trusted you! Maybe you're an X-Cop too! I oughta . . ."

"You'll do nothing," Night Thrasher snapped.

He stood in the back of the room, holding the fingerprint kit and—oddly—a rolled-up magazine. Every face turned toward him, even the Rhino's. Spider-Man couldn't believe it, since he was significantly more powerful than Night Thrasher, and had never succeeded in intimidating the Rhino himself—even after defeating him several times. But the Night Thrasher was one of those one-with-the-dark guys with The Look. As he elbowed his way past the Rhino, he gave the larger man a stare that actually made the Rhino step back. *Good for you*, Spider-Man thought.

"What have you got?" Electro asked impatiently.

"Trouble," Night Thrasher said. "I ran a priority search, with the fastest, most powerful program at my disposal. I found no data on the big one. He's in no government records, whether federal or state. And he's definitely not in the Super-Powers Certification files—neither the public records, nor any of the classified databases I've managed to crack so far. If he is an X-Men spy, he's an exceptionally well-hidden one."

"And his smart-aleck friend?" Electro demanded.

"Him, I found." Night Thrasher unscrolled the magazine, which turned out to be an issue of *NOW* magazine.

"Hey!" the Rhino bellowed. "You went through my stuff!"

"Sorry. I figured we could all use a visual aid. After all, our friend there is the cover story."

The chamber was filled with cries of astonishment and

THE PRESENT

disbelief, with Spider-Man's as loud as any of them. Sandman elongated his right arm, snatched the magazine right out of Night Thrasher's hands, and glanced at the cover. "Holy . . . ! I don't believe it!"

"Who?" Titania demanded.

Sandman tossed her the magazine. She caught it, looked at the cover, and blanched. "You gotta be kidding me. They sent *him*?"

"The Park?" Rhino bellowed. He rushed over and grabbed the magazine from Titania, ripping the cover in the process. "It don't make sense. The *Park*?"

Spider-Man, on the other hand, was dying. He looked for Speedball, who had been the only sympathizer among his captors, and saw him slipping out the back. He looked at Bishop, who, like him, was shocked speechless. He looked at the Rhino, who was pawing through the pages of the magazine with the speed of a man accustomed to only looking at the pictures, and cried, "Will somebody please tell me, already—who's The Park?"

Night Thrasher seized the magazine from the Rhino's fists—ripping it yet again—and, opening it toward the centerspread, marched upon the helpless Spider-Man. His eyes were grim and his jaw set, but Spider-Man hardly noticed. He was too busy staring at the full-color shot of a lithe young basketball player in what appeared to be unassisted flight over the heads of three dumbfounded members of the other team. The photo had captured the player just after he threw the ball, which had left his hands so quickly that even the high-speed camera which had captured his superhuman leap had only succeeded in registering an oval blur at the extreme right side of the frame. It was the kind of photograph that defines sports heroes.

It was a photograph of Peter Parker.

"The Park," Night Thrasher said. "So dubbed because of his spectacular ability to park the ball in the hoop, no matter where in the court he happens to be. Most valuable player in the NBA, five years running. Star of TV commercials, talk shows, a top-selling Nintendo cartridge, and the occasional movie; sponsor of his own line of athletic gear; hero to millions and, not incidentally, people, tremendously vocal supporter of both the X-Men and the Super Powers Registration Act. I will also note that he happens to be certified in the classified files of the Federal Super-Powers Registry—a revelation that would no doubt mar all the records he's achieved in a quite remarkable career. Which brings up the very interesting point: since this is *not* public knowledge, just what services does he supply in exchange for the government's silence?"

Razorback was downright appalled. "Say it ain't so, Park!"

"It's so," the Rhino said regretfully. "Maybe we can get his autograph on a basketball before we smash him."

"This is crazy!" Spider-Man cried, as they drew closer. "If I was somebody as famous as this—Park—do you really think the government would be crazy enough to send me undercover? Wouldn't they have to know you'd recognize me this quickly?" They weren't listening; aside from Volcana and Razorback, who were holding back, unsure how to react, and Speedball, who was still nowhere to be seen, they were all moving toward him and Bishop, their raised fists rendered deadly weapons by their various paranormal abilities.

"Come on!" he shouted desperately. "Don't you see that there has to be something else going on here?"

"Yeah," the Rhino sneered. "We do. And we're gonna tear it from your lying face, one piece at a time. . . ."

CHAPTER SIX

The island had enjoyed many names, in the century since its discovery. The captain of the first ship to drop anchor there called it New Pitcairn. A British mapmaker updating government records in the years after the first World War called it Victory. A freighter that rediscovered it during the 1950s called it St. Joseph's. An atlas published in 1967 called it Vespuccus. None of the names stuck, because nobody ever got around to living there. It was just another uninhabited island, poking its head out of the ocean: a lush and verdant place that would have been settled long ago had it been large enough or strategic enough or wealthy enough to attract the uncertain benefits of modern civilization.

The island was shaped like a snake that had just swallowed a pig—one long, narrow strip of land, just barely one mile wide for most of its length, with an almost perfectly circular place at its midpoint where it broadened to about three. That was also the island's highest point: a bare volcanic mountain rose one thousand feet above the surface of the Pacific. Choked with rain forest (except for a dead zone immediately surrounding the volcano), surrounded by hundreds of miles of ocean, the island might as well have been a nation unto itself, on a world that had never known the coming of humanity. If so, it was a nation on the verge of revolution, for the ground was covered with a thin layer of ash, and the volcano was belching clouds of thick white steam.

The two X-Men who had just materialized on the beach at the widest part of the island gazed up at that smoking crater with a significant amount of respect.

"Figures, dat," Gambit said. "Tell me, *mon ami*... what is dis t'ing between super-villains an' volcanoes, hey? You t'ink maybe dey all got togedder and got some kind of special deal on de real estate?"

"Wouldn't put it past the suckers," Wolverine said. He sniffed. "'Cept it looks like our buddy with the time bombs actually got himself a bargain, this time."

Gambit looked at him. "Why's dat?"

"All this ash, coverin' everything. An' the thick per-

THE PRESENT

fume of all the wildflowers in the jungle. It's so overpowerin' that I can smell it over the sulfur. It's like breathin' through a handkerchief doused with cologne. Long as we're on this stinkin' rock, my sense of smell's gonna be next to useless."

That was bad news. Normally, Wolverine's sense of smell was as accurate as any bloodhound's. It was exceptionally useful in battle, where it kept most opponents from sneaking up on him. If he had to operate without it now ... Gambit regarded him with concern. "You gon' be okay wit' dis, Logan?"

Wolverine flashed his singularly unpleasant version of a confident grin. "You oughta know me better than that, LeBeau."

And with that he popped his claws and marched into the jungle, using his claws to slash a path through the overgrown vegetation. Gambit followed close behind, eyeing the jungle carefully, in constant search for the sneak attack Wolverine was now less likely to anticipate.

Wolverine wasn't particularly worried. He had had his nose broken twelve times. All on different occasions, fortunately—and each time the damage had mended quickly, thanks to his mutant healing factor—but each time, it had shut down the old sense of smell a lot worse than this. It wasn't even the first time somebody had deliberately overloaded his powers of scent to gain an advantage; he still winced at the nauseating memory of the one occasion, many years ago, long before he'd joined the X-Men, that a self-important trophy hunter named Sergei Kravinoff— or, as he pretentiously had started calling himself, Kraven the Hunter—had sprayed him with a particularly nasty concentrated extract of skunk. That had thrown him off, until he rallied, got the drop on Kravinoff, and made the fur-wearing jerk drink the rest of the pint bottle all the way to the dregs.

Cherished as the memory was, the afternoon wiled away watching Kravinoff retch wasn't the point. The point was that it wasn't Wolverine's powerful sense of smell that made him the warrior he was. It was his skill, his adapt-

TIME'S ARROW

ability, his ability to compensate for any barriers fate might choose to place in his way.

The lack of scent was a problem. But he'd overcome much worse.

"Dis bomb," Gambit said. "Mebbe we should split up and look for it, no?"

Wolverine scowled. He respected Remy too much to say so, but he preferred to conduct his hunts in silence. It was one of his major complaints about people in general: they all spent far too much time filling up perfectly good silences with empty little snatches of conversation. And Remy's question had already been asked and answered back at the winery, when Cyclops and Professor X assigned the teams. "No," Wolverine said. "It ain't gonna be that hard to find. It's either in plain sight, or set up someplace obvious where we're bound to look sooner or later."

"Dat's what de Professor said. But Remy don't buy it."

Wolverine slashed at the underbrush. "I know why ya wouldn't. It doesn't make any sense."

"But—"

"But the sucker let us see where his bomb was going. He practically sent us a flamin' telegram. He wants us to find it. An' he won't be able to spring his trap if we have to trip all over creation just lookin' for it." He slashed again, and grumbled. "You comin'?"

Not long after that, they reached the base of the volcano. The closer they got to the mountain, the sparser the jungle became. Many of the trees were choked beneath a thin layer of gray dust; many others were damaged, even splintered, by what looked like the force of an explosion even more terrible than anything Remy could possibly muster with his explosive mutant powers. Many were fallen, so violently wrenched from the ground that it looked like a petulant giant had swept them all aside with a single swing of his powerful fist.

Even worse was the ash. A noticeable presence down

THE PRESENT

by the beaches, it was here so thick that Gambit could feel his eyes and lungs burning. If this was just the aftermath of a recent blast, he couldn't imagine what it would be like to be in the neighborhood when the mountain was in full swing.

He turned to Logan, to ask how he was holding up, and was surprised to see the little Canadian lighting up one of his trademark thin cigars.

Logan puffed a cloud of smoke. "Helps me think," he said. "I been feelin' the earth, Remy. Feelin' it right through the soles of my boots. And what I feel ain't good. Neither you nor me nor this hunka rock got much time before it all goes bang."

Gambit thought of the household pets that start going crazy in the hours immediately preceding major disasters. If their senses warned them, then Wolverine's senses could warn him. "What kinda time are you talkin' about, *mon frere*?"

"I ain't a flamin' seismograph, how am I supposed to know? But that volcano's angry, Remy . . . with the kind of anger that builds for millions of years. Pretty soon, this island's gonna be a smokin' hole fillin' up with seawater."

"Great," Gambit said. And something occurred to him, something so very obvious that it would be fatally dangerous to overlook. Kang would know to the second just when the volcano was set to blow. He could very well use the volcano's explosion as an almost simultaneous cover for his own.

He was about to share his fears with Logan when he turned and saw that Logan wasn't there anymore.

It took him a second to see where his fellow X-Man had gone; Wolverine had scrambled up a thirty-foot rise and was now prone on the ground, peering at something on the other side. Whatever he saw there was giving off steam. Given all the splintery wood underfoot, he must have needed all of his uncanny powers of stealth in order to rush that hill without making a sound; Gambit was pretty good at that kind of thing himself, but he was still impressed. He scrambled up the rise as quickly as he could

TIME'S ARROW

without snapping every twig he stepped on along the way.

Typically enough, Wolverine didn't give him credit for trying. "Blast it, Cajun!" he whispered. "Why don't ya just bring along your own marching band and be done with it?"

"Left 'em at home," Gambit whispered back. He sank to the ground, and belly-crawled the last few feet, ready for any sight that might be awaiting him on the other side—

—except for what he actually saw.

On the other side of the rise, the land formed a natural bowl which sheltered a volcanic hot spring. The water was steaming lightly, but not bubbling: it was probably no warmer than a nice hot bath. Certainly the four beautiful native women frolicking in that water didn't seem to be finding it unpleasant at all; they were doing long, languorous laps around the center of the spring, splashing each other mischievously whenever they got close enough to get in a good shot. They were all young, tan, and athletic, with long shiny hair as black as any Gambit had ever seen.

"Heard the giggling," Wolverine explained.

Gambit barely listened to him. Sights like this did not come along often, and when they did, they were almost enough to make a red-blooded Cajun forget little things like the end of the world. "Ooh la la," he murmured. "Logan, we have time to take a dip, too, *non*?"

"Get your mind out of the gutter, LeBeau."

"But it's so perfect, *mon frere*. An uninhabited South Sea island...four lovely mademoiselles...a pair of lonely castaways...it is so classic!"

Wolverine grimaced. "Life ain't a cartoon, bub."

"Our life sometime seems like it," Gambit said merrily. Then, with more urgency: "Leastways, we oughta t'ink about findin' some way of evacuatin' dose beauties from dis island. Dey might not have deir own way off, and Remy would hate for dem to get trapped when mean old papa volcano decide he want to blow his top."

"Those ladies ain't ladies," Wolverine said.

108

THE PRESENT

"Huh?"

"Think with your brain. Look at that water. It's sparklin' clean. If it was natural, it'd be covered with a thin layer of ash like the rest of this place . . . an' those ladies would be muddy with it. 'Steada that, they're all scrubbed an' fresh-lookin'. It's like we ain't lookin' at potential volcano fatalities, but a swimsuit layout from *Sports Illustrated*. It stinks on ice, Remy . . . an' I don't need my sense of smell to know that stink means a trap."

Feeling singularly stupid, Gambit said, "You t'ink dis de place with de bomb? Underwater, maybe?"

"Seems a bit too obvious," Wolverine replied. He thought furiously, then grinned. "You're the ladies' man . . . why don't you amble on down and do what you do best? I'll keep an eye from up here, an' cover you in case of an attack from above."

Gambit grinned back. "I'll remember dat strategy next time we hit de French Quarter." He hopped up, brushed the volcanic ash from his long coat, brushed an errant lock of hair back into place, and began his jaunty, unthreatening walk down to the hot spring. His boots kicked up clouds of gray soot with every step; the air itself so thick with it that he needed all his self-control just to avoid sneezing. He was halfway down when one of the native women saw him coming and jabbered excitedly at the others. They all turned to look, and regarded him with smiles of frank approval. He fell helplessly, unreservedly in love with all four of them at once.

Not for the first time, he reflected that super-villains were much crueler than they had to be.

He stopped at the water's edge, and saw that Wolverine was right: it was impossibly clean. It almost looked distilled. He could see the stony bottom of the spring bed, glittering with polished stones. When he failed to take off his clothes and dive in, the native woman who'd noticed him first *tsk*ed impatiently and splashed him experimentally. He still stood his ground. She gave up and walked to shore, with the hot water rising in little tufts of steam from her perfect, glistening skin.

TIME'S ARROW

Her high kick almost took him by surprise. It was aimed at his neck, and driven with a force that could have snapped a vertebra. He backpedaled just enough to avoid being struck, then brought up his right arm to block another roundhouse kick aimed at the side of his head. The woman fell back, then pressed her attack once again, driving Gambit back with a series of jabs and punches delivered with consummate martial arts skill.

He wondered why Wolverine hadn't entered the fray, and decided that Logan was probably having too good a time watching this happen to him.

The thought irked him so much that he actually let one kick get through. It struck him in the belly, just hard enough to knock the breath out of him. He fell flat on his back, and looked up just in time to see his opponent leap into the air and hurl herself toward him, with both feet aimed for a potentially fatal impact at the place where his rib cage sheltered his heart.

Gambit rolled out of the way. The native woman landed in soft dirt. He scrambled around in a circle, sweeping her legs out from under her with a kick. She stumbled, came very close to falling, compensated, and regained her balance just as he came up behind her and pulled her right arm behind her back.

"You're lovely, *cherie*," he said, "but Remy don't care much for your idea of *l'amour*."

She struggled powerfully, trying to hook her foot around one of his ankles. He sidestepped, tightened his grip, and danced her around in a circle, just so he could check on her friends. As he might have predicted, they were also striding from the water, at equidistant points around the steaming lake, approaching him with the same wide, seductive, inviting smile fixed on their exotically beautiful faces.

Yes, super-villains truly were far crueler than they had to be.

Silently begging the gods that governed the karma between men and women to forgive him what necessity required him to do now, he shoved the struggling woman to

THE PRESENT

the ground. She had to run to remain on her feet, but stumbled after the first two steps, and fell facedown into the soft mud by the shore. Even as she pressed her palms into the dirt and began to rise, Gambit whipped out three playing cards, charged them with kinetic energy, and hurled them at her three friends. He was careful not to target the women themselves, but instead aimed at the soil by their feet. The three explosions that rocked the area around the hot spring knocked all three of them to the ground. If luck was with him, they'd remain stunned for a few minutes at least.

But when the dust cleared, they were all rising to their feet, dusting themselves off, and smiling at him with the kind of affection that suggested they'd like to know him better.

The average super-villain, Gambit decided, deserved a good smack.

"Wolverine!" he shouted, as he parried a high kick from the one he'd shoved into the mud. "Dere's plenty of action down here, in case you're wondering!"

Wolverine's response came from some indiscriminate point behind him. "More than ya think, Cajun!"

Before Gambit could wonder just what Logan meant, he caught a glimpse of something moving very quickly. He whirled to see what it was, and saw a man tumbling uncontrollably down the slope. The man wore a strange starburst mask and a skintight green suit. Errant lightning played around his hands and feet as he somersaulted head-over-heels toward the shore. He was cursing quite impressively, too. But only when he came to a stop at the edge of the hot spring, and dizzily struggled to rise to his feet, did Gambit recognize him as a figure whose criminal behavior had rendered him a regular on the front page of the *Daily Bugle*: namely, Electro, the human power battery.

Wolverine came running down the slope after him. "He was circlin' around the top of the ridge, tryin' to get a bead on ya. Just like a great white hunter, 'cept he ain't any good at it."

TIME'S ARROW

The crazed super-villain seemed to take mortal offense at this. "Not any good at it? You're looking at a guy who fought Spider-Man over a dozen times!"

Wolverine grinned condescendingly. "Slow learner, huh? Ya wanna impress me, say you beat him once."

Electro howled with rage, and charged—

Gambit would have liked to lend his scrappy Canadian friend a hand, but at the moment, he was too preoccupied with his other dancing partners.

It seemed they'd toyed with him enough, and were now intent on attacking him all from all sides at once. The one he'd fought off before was the first to go for him. The kick she aimed at his right knee would have shattered the bone and crippled him for life. Fortunately, he wasn't still in the same place when it arrived. Instead, he was dodging off to the right, aiming a kick of his own at her midsection. The impact drove her back, but did not make her fall. Which was okay; he didn't want her to fall, he just wanted her off balance. As she stumbled, he darted toward her, clapped a hand on each of her shoulders, and somersaulted upward, driving his legs into the air above his head.

The effect was a lot like doing a handstand on a set of parallel bars, except that the bars were her shoulders, and she wasn't about to stand still for the experience. That was okay with Gambit; although he remained in position for a full two seconds just to show he could do it, he quickly allowed gravity to take over so he could complete his somersault just in time to land on the two women who had been moving into position directly behind her. The maneuver was so perfectly controlled that he even spared their lovely faces—but he was still able to drive the heels of his boots against their respective shoulders with a force that certainly had to hurt.

All three of his dancing partners hit the ground. By the time Gambit landed, he realized that he'd lost track of the fourth one.

He didn't wonder about her for long.

Because a second later he heard something move be-

THE PRESENT

hind him, and her long lovely fingers closed around his neck....

Electro's lightning bolt fused the sand into glass, but it didn't fry Wolverine.

That's because Wolverine was already in the air, leaping. The Canadian felt the current as it passed through him—and even he felt a jolt of surprise when he saw the jagged sparks dance up and down in the spaces between his outstretched claws—but he wasn't grounded. The killing bolt didn't do all that much more than make his hair stand on end—which it did already, anyhow.

When all was said and done, Electro was not really much to worry about. He had power, all right—so much power that if he had half a mind he might have become as world shaking a threat as somebody like Magneto—but he was so dependent on that power that he'd never bothered to learn any of the other fundamentals of combat, like strategy, or self-defense, or just getting out of the way. Instead he stood his ground, fired lightning bolts at moving targets, and had the colossal nerve to act surprised when he was laid low by a right to the jaw.

Before being mellowed by the X-Men, Wolverine might have cut the poor loser wide open with a single swipe of his claws.

But sometimes it was good enough to let poor losers know he could.

Moving faster than the speed of thought, in a single economical movement, he passed his blades through the air over the startled Electro's head, instantly slicing off three out of five points on the man's star-shaped mask.

The pugnacious mademoiselle was much stronger than she looked. Her grip around Gambit's neck was as solid as iron and as unbreakable as one of Magneto's vows.

Gambit reached into his duster's pocket and pulled out a small metal rod. With the touch of a stud, it telescoped into a bo staff, which he then drove into his opponent's belly, hoping she'd loosen her grip if he knocked the breath out of her. The impact drove her off her feet, but didn't seem to deter her in any other way; she even giggled like a schoolgirl as the gray spots gathered at the edges of Gambit's vision.

Time slowed to a standstill. He saw the other native women, walking like models on a runway, smiling like game show spokesmodels, but bearing his death in their murderously skilled hands. He saw something white and bubbling rising from the waters of the hot spring. He saw Electro firing one volley of wildly uncontrolled electrical blast after another as Wolverine's claws tagged him again and again. He saw a bolt strike one of the women approaching him in the head, briefly lighting her up like a miniature sun, before fading away to reveal a face that had cracked and bubbled and revealed some of the metallic sheen underneath.

In what would have been his last few seconds of consciousness, Gambit actually smiled. *Oh. I see. They're androids. Why didn't you say so?*

He dropped the staff, grabbed the one strangling him by its wrists, and focused all his will on charging it with kinetic energy. The glow that started on her wrists traveled up her arms and spread to her shoulders before she realized that something was wrong. She wasn't stunned enough to release him, but her grip relaxed just enough for Gambit to twist free, drop to his knees, and leap away.

He knew she was just a machine, but she looked so good that he was glad to be facing elsewhere when she exploded.

Shrapnel peppered the beach behind him, tearing holes in his coat. He ducked, rolled, and stood just in time to see her three friends still advancing upon him. They had all been struck with debris from the explosion, their tremendous beauty now severely compromised by all the places where their metal skeletons now shone through the rips in their skin. The smiles on their faces were no longer alluring, but ghastly fixed rictuses that displayed far too many teeth. They were all still dangerous. But they moved

THE PRESENT

with more caution, now that Gambit had proven himself capable of taking out their sister.

He wasn't worried about them anymore. Not really. Given the chance, he was sure he could deal with them in a manner of minutes.

The problem was that the architect of this battle wasn't giving him that chance.

Because the white bubbling thing rising from the waters of the hot spring had just resolved itself into the shape of a man made of water, with great enlarged fists that looked like they possessed all the destructive power of tidal waves.

In the instant before it engulfed him, it spoke in a cruel, distorted voice. "Whatsamatter, mutie? Ain't you never heard of Hydro-Man?"

Electro's costume was in tatters, and his skin wasn't much better. Dodging lightning bolt after lightning bolt, hopping around a landscape that was now more fused glass than oasis sand, Wolverine had slashed at the super-villain again and again, peeling off one scrap of clothing after another, in an assault meant more to humiliate than to hurt. Though there was plenty of the hurting too; Electro's chest and arms were now crisscrossed with shallow wounds, all of which cauterized themselves as they bled sizzling supercharged blood. His counterassault against Wolverine hadn't been nearly as successful, limited to a few small electrical burns and a smoldering shock that had driven the Canadian to the ground for a fleeting instant or two.

At the moment, Electro was on his knees, shooting off sparks as the feral Wolverine circled him like a hungry dog. "It's true what they say about you!" he spat. "You're nothin' but an animal!"

Wolverine shook his head. "Sorry, bub. That may be a sore spot with me, but I ain't about to take offense hearin' it from a lowlife mercenary who sells his powers to the highest bidder. Do you even know what you're fightin' for? Or care?"

TIME'S ARROW

"Why should I? With what they're paying me, I could retire from now till the end of the world!"

Wolverine decided not to dignify that with the obvious response. It wouldn't do any good on somebody like Electro. Besides, he didn't have any more time to waste on this sucker anyway. Every animal instinct in his body was rebelling at the feel of the ground beneath his feet—ground that seemed to be tensing up, preparing itself, gathering all its strength for an explosion that now seemed minutes away. And he wasn't alone in sensing it, either, because all of a sudden the sky was filled with tropical birds of every color and shape, all of them flying away from the island with a haste Wolverine understood all too well.

As if that wasn't enough, some kind of walking tsunami had just sauntered out of the hot spring and swallowed Gambit whole.

So he turned his attention back to Electro and said, "Awright, bub, listen up! We're runnin' out of time here, an' I can't afford to say this more than once! You may be a big-shot bad guy, who fights Spider-Man all the time—but that's 'cause Spidey's a nice guy who lets you live when he's done. I ain't. An' if you don't get out of my way *right now*, all six of my claws are gonna be in your stomach, gettin' intimately aquainted with whatever it was you had for lunch. It's your choice. Which way is it gonna be?"

Electro surprised him, then, in a way that few sane people would.

He sneered, "Go for it."

Wolverine leapt.

Gambit was having the devil of a time catching his breath today. First some robot lady had to go and strangle him, and before he could completely recover from that, Hydro-Man surrounded him in an impenetrable sphere of free-standing water. Gambit had tried to swim free, but the sphere simply moved when he did, leaving him at its center, drowning on dry land.

THE PRESENT

The water churned all around him, turning what would have been the random movements of water into a coherent human voice. "Like my powers, mutie? The girl who hired me sure did. That's why she told me to wait until you thought you had a chance of winning."

Gambit saw a flash of daylight behind a shimmering curtain of water. He launched himself toward it, and saw it recede from him. Air seemed a distant friend, one he most sincerely missed.

The bubbling voice chuckled. "An' just to make sure you don't die lonely, I'm gonna make sure some lovely ladies get to spend your last few minutes with you."

The three remaining robots all dived into the sphere of water, surrounding Gambit on all sides with a gauntlet of kicks and punches and unwavering smiles. . . .

"Gotcha!" Electro cried.

He had just accomplished the impossible and seized Wolverine by the wrists, just behind the openings where the razor-sharp claws emerged from their sheaths. Wolverine immediately stiffened with agony as the killing electricity coursed through his flesh, as if a million tiny claws as sharp as his own had all struck home in every single nerve of his body, all at once.

"You're as dumb as the web-head!" Electro ranted. "He ain't the easiest guy in the world to grab either. My reaction time ain't exactly the best, but when I'm supercharged, I'm as fast as any of you creeps!"

Wolverine tried to answer, but the only sound that emerged from his mouth was a low growl. He smelled burning flesh, and realized it was his own.

But as Electro turned on the juice, he realized it didn't even matter—for the ground was shaking, and the volcano was starting to blow.

The picture window overlooked a certain spot in the North Atlantic, at 2:17 A.M., on April 15, 1912. The ship in question had hit an iceberg a little bit more than two hours earlier; now, it was foundering, its head slipping beneath

TIME'S ARROW

the waves while its bow rose for one last defiant stab at the night. Most of the fifteen hundred people who hadn't made it into the underoccupied lifeboats were still on board, clutching for the last useless handholds as the decks turned into steep ramps capable of delivering them down to the black and freezing sea.

The window, a new addition to the palace decorations, occupied one entire wall of the room containing Kang the Conqueror's swimming pool. Kang—or at least, the flesh-and-blood man usually hidden within the armor usually recognized as Kang—kept the chamber dimly lit, to avoid distractions from the view; he was nothing but a shadowy figure doing endless luxurious laps. He broke surface just in time to see Lireeb enter carrying a tray; the tall albino did not come to him directly, but instead paused before the spectacle, studying it for all of ten seconds before finally shaking his head with his usual dry mockery. "Well. I must say *that's* cheery."

"It's one of the most ironically fateful moments any timeline has ever known," Kang proclaimed. "It has a terrible beauty to it that I find . . . inspiring."

"That is a relief indeed. I would hate to think it was just inherent sadism. Your wine, sir?"

"What year?"

"None in particular, sir. It's a Limbo vintage."

"Ah," said Kang. "Leave it there, I'll take it directly." He dunked his head under the water, imagined just for an instant that it was a few degrees above freezing and that he was a lowly steerage passenger surrounded by screams, and broke surface, luxuriating in the awareness that he, at least, was master of his own fate. "Before you go, is there any further progress on this little game we're playing with the X-Men?"

Lireeb was a silhouette backlit by the lights of a ship about to sink beneath the waves. "All is going precisely as planned, sir. The various members of the X-Men are already in place, battling their respective foes; the pair that got sent to Antarctica are within minutes of finding their Time Arrow; and the pair at the volcano are not far behind.

THE PRESENT

I will obtain an update on the third team as soon as I'm done with this ever-so-fascinating conversation."

Kang smiled. It was fortunate for Lireeb that his master kept this chamber so dark, for Kang's smile was a sight almost as terrible as the one that dominated the wall. "Excellent. And the power siphoners?"

"Fully operational. They're fully primed on each bomb. If the X-Men perform as predicted, you should have no trouble collecting all the extra energy you need."

Kang smacked his lips in satisfaction. It didn't get much better than this. After all, energy was the whole point of this exercise; destroying universes one at a time was a pretty good trick if you could manage it. Unfortunately, the timelines had to be kept in a sort of stasis while that operation took place. The apparatus that kept the timelines stable would only last so long—a shorter time-frame than the amount necessary to wipe out all the timelines Kang wanted destroyed. This didn't leave nearly enough time to accomplish Kang's goal.

But if he had enough energy to fuel an explosion capable of shattering all the unwanted alternate timelines at once—that would be a memory worth treasuring. That would be an accomplishment worthy of Kang.

And these posturing mutant fools were about to hand it to him.

Lireeb cleared his throat. "Will that be all, sir? Is there anything else you'd like before I leave? A towel? A snack? A baby in a stroller, with some candy ripe for the stealing?"

Kang was in far too good a mood to feel his usual smoldering annoyance. "Just let me know when the X-Men are all in place. Oh, and also when our agents at the winery make their move. I want to watch."

"As you wish, sir." Lireeb bowed, clicked his heels, and glided from the room, his movements as smooth as the mirrored waters of the Atlantic on the night the great ship went down.

CHAPTER SEVEN

"**G**et away from them!"

The voice was imperious, commanding, and carried by a will strong enough to change the course of nations.

It cut through the lynch-mob fervor of the powerful figures converging on Spider-Man and Bishop. In an instant, they were transformed from grim-faced executioners to children who'd just been caught doing something dangerous without their parents' permission. They traded looks of fear, then averted their eyes and moved aside, like waters parting at the command of a prophet.

Spider-Man didn't blame them, because he'd recognized that voice. He'd only encountered it a couple of times, but he knew that it was not a voice one defied lightly.

It was the voice of Magneto, so-called master of magnetism.

The Magneto Spider-Man knew was one of the most feared men on the planet: founder and leader of the sarcastically named Brotherhood of Evil Mutants, a one-man army fighting a never-ending war on behalf of the mutants he saw as the natural successors to the human race. Depending on who you spoke to, Magneto was either a terrorist, a freedom fighter, a conqueror, a mass murderer, a teacher, a barbarian, a tragic hero, or a symbol of evil incarnate. The only point of agreement in all those conflicting portraits was that Magneto was a being whose dedication toward his cause had rendered him more force of nature than man.

The one time Spider-Man had fought the man, he'd triumphed only because his own substantial abilities as Spider-Man had been temporarily boosted to nearly cosmic levels. He'd emerged aware how lucky he'd been—and grateful that his adventures as a friendly neighborhood super hero usually kept him out of Magneto's way. He glanced at Bishop, aware that as an X-Man, Bishop must have been obliged to face Magneto far more frequently—and was unsurprised to note, from the tension in the man's eyes, Bishop was in no way relieved by this rescue.

THE PRESENT

Magneto entered in full armor, his long purple cape billowing behind him. This Magneto had a helmet that was similar to that of his "real-world" counterpart, but the facial aperture was wider to reveal more of the face, now displayed behind a clear shield of Plexiglas. He came striding in midair, each step reflecting the infinite self-confidence of a man who had lived his life as absolute master of one of the basic binding forces of the universe. He was so awesome a sight that the breathless Speedball, who entered behind him, seemed almost invisible in his wake.

As for the other assembled members of the PLF, they all moved aside to avoid obstructing Magneto's path—with the predictable exception of the Rhino, who remained where he stood, glaring up at Magneto with what could only be interpreted as open defiance.

"They're spies," the Rhino said. "We was takin' care of them for you."

"And I appreciate your kind consideration," Magneto said contemptuously. "But you don't have either the intelligence or the authority to make decisions. Hydro-Man, Electro—release them now!"

The interval between the command and the opening of the clamps was so short that even Spider-Man, with his preternatural reflexes, found himself surprised to be free. He leapt from the wall, and landed in a fighting stance, ready for anything. Bishop joined him a second later, and it was clear from the look in his eyes that it was as if all the other potential threats that surrounded them didn't even exist. He only had eyes for Magneto.

Magneto didn't seem bothered. "I have been informed that you two claim to be—to coin a phrase—new in town. Is this accurate?"

"We're from an alternate timeline," Bishop said. "We came here by accident, and we have no personal stake in any power struggles you might be waging here."

The Rhino snorted. "You're not gonna believe that horse hockey, are you?"

Magneto lifted his head slightly. "In fact—yes. I even

TIME'S ARROW

believe we might find some mutual profit in discussing this matter in my private chambers." To Spider-Man's surprise, he lowered himself to the catwalk, and removed his helmet. What lay beneath was a distinguished-looking man of indeterminate age, whose white hair and aristocratic features instantly made him seem more diplomat than terrorist. "Follow me, gentlemen. Speedball, Razorback, Night Thrasher, Volcana—I'd appreciate it if you came along as well. As for the rest of you—no harm done, this time. Get yourselves some rest. Further information will be forthcoming only when you need it."

Spider-Man expected the others to grumble, but they all remained respectfully silent—hiding any resentment they might have felt behind a flurry of hurried departures. Only the Rhino lingered, just long enough to flash Spider-Man a glare filled with thoughts of smashed flesh and broken bones. Spider-Man met the glare evenly, with a look equally clear: *Whenever you want, bunkie.*

The route to Magneto's sanctum was a five-minute walk through dim subterranean corridors, all of which (judging by the wildly different materials used in the stonework, and the significant variations in the decay of the metal) must have been built at different times, by different hands. Most of the way, the path was wide enough for Magneto's group to walk in twos. Magneto and Volcana led the way, with Volcana using one upraised hand as a makeshift torch. Magneto ambled along unhurriedly, not bothering to turn around to confirm that the recently released prisoners were still following. Spider-Man and Bishop walked side by side behind them, trading frequent glances that communicated nothing but shared confusion and the willingness to support the other in a fight. Razorback and Night Thrasher brought up the rear, observing a mutual silence.

It was that silence which led to Spider-Man's one attempt at making conversation. He turned toward Razorback and said, "Hey, Buford, I want to thank you for giving us the benefit of the doubt back there."

Razorback smiled. " 'Twasn't nothin'. Back where I

THE PRESENT

come from, we judge folks by what they do."

"How *is* Big Pig, anyway?"

A dark cloud passed over Razorback's face, and he faced the ground for exactly five seconds before he looked up again, with a distant anger in his dark brown eyes. Facing that gaze, Spider-Man felt a hollow, aghast lurch at the base of his spine. *I don't believe it. This Razorback is grim 'n' gritty.*

"They took her away," Razorback said. "They took her away and ... destroyed everything that was special about her. And there was nothing I could do to stop them. Nothing." He shuddered, tormented by the memories, then faced Spider-Man again, with the look of a man who had once been almost destroyed by his sorrow. "This universe you come from," he said. "When you saw Big Pig, was she still fast? Still beautiful? Still the best there ever was?"

Overcome with a particularly goofy form of empathy, Spider-Man came up with the only possible answer. "Yes. There wasn't anything that old girl couldn't do."

And, surprisingly, Razorback found his smile again. "I'm obliged, son. Knowin' that makes losin' her a little easier to bear."

The Arkansan had fallen about ten paces behind by the time Bishop, seeing his opportunity, sidled closer to Spider-Man, lowered his head, and spoke beneath his breath. "All right. You win. I suspect that I'm going to sincerely regret asking this, but who was this 'Big Pig'? His wife? His girlfriend? His sidekick?"

Spider-Man almost didn't want to respond. Loss, after all, is loss, and as deeply as he respected this Razorback's pain, he wasn't sure he was capable of answering Bishop's question while still maintaining a straight face. But Bishop was so serious and so concerned and so ... so ... well, so *Bishop* ... that Spider-Man honestly couldn't resist. So he made sure he had a good view of the X-Man's face and said, "His truck."

Bishop was just barely self-possessed enough to mouth his aghast response silently: "His *truck*?"

TIME'S ARROW

• • •

Magneto's private chambers turned out to be located behind a heavy steel slab with no visible doorknob or handle. Magneto moved the slab to one side with one peremptory flick of his fingers, and gestured for Volcana and Razorback to guard the entrance. That last touch struck Spider-Man as pure egotism—after all, if the slab was so heavy that only a master of magnetism could move it, then exercising his authority was the only possible reason Magneto would need to assign anybody to guard duty. Obviously, this Magneto was on as big a power trip as his counterpart back home. Spider-Man filed that little epiphany away for future reference, just in case he happened to need it.

The chamber itself was big, well lit, and comfortably furnished, with fine art on the walls and a luxurious shag rug that actually complemented the twin sofas. There was a TV, a VCR, a gray-market cable box (prompting in Spider-Man the disconcerting realization that one of the most feared super-villains on Earth actually thought to steal the premium channels), and what looked like a fully stocked kitchen and wet bar. It was better than most apartments Spider-Man had lived in, even if it didn't have a view. But he couldn't help noticing that both Speedball and Night Thrasher seemed ill at ease here; they both had the look of school kids on their first trip to the principal's office. Clearly, Magneto was not the kind of boss who encouraged his underlings to consider him just another one of the guys.

Spider-Man was back to wondering just whose side any of these people were on when a strikingly beautiful woman with spiky black hair and chevron markings on her cheeks emerged from a back room and waited to be introduced.

"Gentlemen," Magneto said, "I give you the lovely Aliya. One of the best-kept secrets of this little revolution of ours."

Aliya nodded slightly. "A pleasure, Spider-Man. And Bishop. I wish I could have briefed Magneto about you a day or so earlier, and therefore saved you both a great deal

THE PRESENT

of wandering around this city, but I only just arrived myself. I've just been telling Magneto here where you come from, why you were traveling in time, how you came to be trapped here . . ."

Before Spider-Man could retort that that was an awful lot for one woman to know, Bishop spoke, in the stunned voice of a man who had just reached his saturation point. "Aliya," he whispered. "Not Cable's—"

"The same." Aliya nodded. "I see my reputation precedes me."

"Not anywhere I've been wall-crawling," Spider-Man said. "No offense, Bish, but can you please bring me up to speed on what reputation she's talking about?"

"Cable speaks of her sometimes," Bishop said, his gaze firmly fixed on the woman before them. "He describes her as the one great love of his life—and from the look in his eyes I know it's true. But the Aliya he knew was murdered, and he was never able to put that one terrible loss behind him. Which means that this Aliya—"

"—is the Aliya from this timeline," Aliya finished. "The one who saw Cable die, instead of the other way around."

"What a perfect setup," Spider-Man murmured. "We should introduce you crazy kids."

"Already taken care of," Aliya said calmly.

"We have much to discuss," Magneto said. "Make yourselves comfortable, gentlemen—and lady, of course. Speedball, I know you've already been of tremendous service today, but would you please gather some food and drink for our new arrivals? They must be in dire need of a hot meal, after all their time on the run."

"Absolutely," Speedball said. "Long as they know I can't make anything but grilled cheese."

"It will do," Magneto said.

Speedball gave a little bow and literally bounced off to the kitchen.

Spider-Man had seen many super-villains who insisted on being gracious hosts while explaining their nefarious plans. The kind offer of refreshments was usually better

127

TIME'S ARROW

left refused, because they were always too quickly followed by the arrival of paramilitary types instructed to dump him into a shark tank or something. But today, after everything else he and Bishop had been through, he was in just the right mood to be genuinely grateful for the invitation. He and Bishop took one couch, Night Thrasher the other, while Aliya claimed the recliner. Magneto, being Magneto, remained standing, imperious as ever despite the barest hint of a smile flickering at the corners of his lips.

Even as he sat, Spider-Man said, "Don't bother waiting for the leading questions. We want to hear this."

Aliya bowed slightly. "I'm sure you do. The long and short of it is that I was just briefing Magneto about the trouble involving alternate timelines when Speedball alerted us about the trouble you two were facing out there."

"Which begs the question," Bishop said, "just how you know about alternate timelines at all?"

"How else? I'm a time traveler. I still have access to the Time Displacement Core, and I've spent the last couple of years using it to gather intelligence for the PLF. I never expected to discover evidence of a war raging across time, or run into a Cable from a world where he never died—"

"Wait a minute!" Spider-Man yelped. "You have a Time Displacement Core?"

"Yes."

"In working order?"

"Like it just left the factory," Aliya told him.

Spider-Man and Bishop exchanged glances. Bishop said, "I presume you'd have no objections to letting us use it to get back home?"

"None at all, Mr. Bishop. If you do something for us first."

Spider-Man grimaced beneath his mask. "I shoulda known. There's always a price."

Aliya averted her eyes. "I'm truly sorry about that, Spider-Man. I know you have loved ones waiting for you. And I want to see Cable again just as badly. But I can't

THE PRESENT

leave this timeline until I take care of my responsibility here—and it's as important to me as yours is to you.''

Responsibility. There were days when Spider-Man hated that word. He set his jaw, nodded, and said, "So tell me."

"I was investigating why our X-Men came out in favor of the Kelly Act. It was so out of character for them—so much an abridgement of the freedom that the X-Men of almost every other timeline have devoted their lives to defending. And I found out that it wasn't entirely their idea. They were lied to—by a being from the future called the Scarlet Centurion."

Spider-Man remembered hearing about him from Captain America, during his own brief association with the Avengers. "Omigosh. The Scarlet Centurion. Bishop, the whole mess with the time bombs is beginning to make sense."

"How's that?" Bishop asked.

"It's another name for Kang—this time-travelling conqueror-from-the-future type the Avengers must have fought about a dozen times by now. If I remember right, he's also known as Immortus and Rama-Tut. The man changes outfits more often than Vanna White."

Night Thrasher frowned. "What does the senator from Rhode Island have to do with this?"

"The senator from—you mean, *Vanna*, she's—"

"Cartwright," Bishop warned. "Let's not get sidetracked here."

It was only with the most extreme difficulty that Spider-Man resisted the temptation. "Sorry. I keep colliding with this alternate-world thing. Go on."

Aliya regarded him oddly for a moment, then went on. "The Centurion told the X-Men a story that seemed to make sense, in light of all the battles they'd fought over the years. He told them that the proliferation of superbeings like them, the Fantastic Four, the Avengers, and the various super-villains of the world, would only continue escalating into endless open warfare, with humanity living under a constant state of siege. He said that by the turn of the twenty-first century, all major governments would fall, all major cultural centers would be reduced to rubble, and all human existence would be reduced to the day-to-day reality of cowering in shelters and hoping to survive while self-styled super-powered gods fought endless cataclysmic battles over turf. He said the wars would finally grow destructive enough to turn the world into an almost lifeless cinder."

"I've had days where I half believed it was getting that bad," Spider-Man admitted. "Usually when Carnage or the Sinister Six blow into town. What about you, Bish?"

"The future I came from," Bishop said, "was awful in a completely different way. I take it, however, that there was no truth in this story? That it was just the Scarlet Centurion's way of manipulating the X-Men?"

"I can't speak to its truth," Aliya said, "but from what I could tell, observing over the TDC, the scant evidence he provided didn't seem nearly convincing enough to win them over. But they bought his story almost immediately, without asking any of the obvious questions. He may have boosted his persuasiveness with some help from mind-control technology—it would certainly explain why they now perform their self-appointed duties with some uncharacteristic ruthlessness. But however you justify it, they immediately threw their support behind Senator Robert Kelly, got the Registration Act passed, and went to work rounding up any paranormals who wouldn't join them."

"The only thing that doesn't make sense to me about that," Bishop said, "is how come Senator Kelly even accepted their support. After all, people hate mutants. They think of us as monsters. My X-Men are hunted outlaws, who have to fight off any number of government plots to destroy us."

Aliya shook her head. "You must be mistaking our timeline for yours. There is anti-mutant prejudice here, but it isn't nearly as bad as all that. Our X-Men always worked openly, just like the Fantastic Four and the Avengers. They had a government liaison—a General Fredericks—and mutants who needed help dealing with their powers could

THE PRESENT

even look them up in the phone book. They were heroes, in public opinion as well as fact."

Bishop was stunned. "What about Bolivar Trask? Reverend Stryker? Graydon Creed?"

"Never heard of them," Aliya said.

"On . . . on my world . . . they were all people advocating the extermination of all mutants. They routinely murdered children . . . innocents. There were lynch mobs, and riots in the streets, and talk of concentration camps. Trask started it, with his hateful propaganda. He built giant robots called Sentinels, which were programmed to kill mutants on sight. The X-Men I come from had to spend most of their time just battling to stay alive." He glanced from one horrified face to another. "I . . . do you truly mean to tell me that none of this means anything to you?"

In the ensuing silence, only Night Thrasher managed to find his voice. "It means something, all right. It means that this isn't the worst of all possible worlds after all."

"It means," Bishop said, "that even with pointless bigotry removed from the equation, humanity will still find a way to inflict suffering and misery on others."

"But even on this world," Night Thrasher said, "we never—"

"That's enough of that," Magneto rumbled. He faced Bishop. "No. As Aliya says, there are always hatemongers, here and there, and they always need watching. But they never arrived at the level of influence that you indicate here. On this world, the X-Men had actually achieved what their founder, Dr. Charles Xavier, had in mind for them: they were role models, and educators, and advocates, whose efforts succeeded in easing the vast majority of mutants into the mainstream of American society. They even had an attaché office in Manhattan, and an eight hundred number for anybody who wanted information on mutant affairs." Magneto grimaced, and for just one instant looked terribly, heartbreakingly old. "They did good work. I have to admit that. Personally, I never believed it would last—which is why my own efforts were always a trifle, shall I say, more radical than theirs. But I never

TIME'S ARROW

imagined that the danger, when it arrived, would originate with them. Never."

Spider-Man boggled at the sight of a disillusioned Magneto. *Now I really know I'm on an alternate world.*

Aliya said, "Except that it now turns out not to have originated with them after all. They were being manipulated by the Scarlet Centurion."

"It doesn't make them any less dangerous," Magneto told her.

"I agree," she said. "If anything, it renders your next official act as the Power Liberation Front even more critical. You have to win this country back from the X-Men, so we have the freedom to stop this Kang from wreaking havoc with our history again."

Magneto nodded, and turned his attention back to Spider-Man and Bishop. "You see our position now. We know this isn't your fight. We don't expect either one of you to join us for the long haul. But tonight, some six hours from now, the PLF will embark upon the single most important battle of our existence. We're going to put everything we have into a single all-out assault on the facility where all the most important paranormals—heroes, not villains—are being held in stasis. If we can free the Avengers, the Defenders, the Fantastic Four, the Inflictors, Daredevil, and anybody else they might have secreted away up there—then we can take the first steps toward stopping the X-Men and their reign of terror once and for all."

Spider-Man boggled again. "And this is what you need our help to do?"

"Consider this," Aliya said. "The X-Men know about us. They've been whittling away at our ranks for months now. We still have many sympathizers, like your friend the bartender, but in the past year we've gone from a core group of about thirty to the few remaining members you've met today. If we can engage the enemy with a couple of recruits they haven't met before—whose capabilities are unknown to them—then it might just make the difference between defeat and victory." She lowered her

THE PRESENT

eyes. "I'm sorry I have to hold this over your heads. But if you help us, I promise I'll personally see to it that you get sent back home."

"And how do we know you'll keep that promise?" Bishop asked. "What's to stop you from continuing to hold this over our heads indefinitely, just to keep us as obedient members of your private army?"

"It's a fair question," Aliya said. "And the answer is, in the first place, if we succeed in freeing the Fantastic Four and the Avengers and the rest of America's imprisoned heroes, you'll just be a couple of foot soldiers in the middle of a great army. Your own efforts will no longer be critical, and the PLF won't need either of you anymore. In the second place, they won't need me, either, and I'll be able to go with you and reunite with Cable, which is next to this the most important thing in my life. And in the third place—"

"In the third place," Magneto said, with eyes that stabbed like daggers, "you have *my* word."

Spider-Man was still trying to come up with a polite way to ask just how he and Bishop were supposed to know Magneto's word meant anything, when Bishop stood and said, "I think we've heard about enough, for now. If you don't mind, my friend and I would like a moment's privacy, to discuss what we've heard."

Magneto indicated a door. "By all means."

The door led to an immaculately kept bedroom, with a king-sized bed and a wall-to-wall bookcase featuring hundreds of shiny leather editions, showing just enough wear to confirm that they were actually there to be read instead of just looked at. Spider-Man spotted the Oxford Mark Twain, Spengler's *Decline of the West*, and forty bound volumes of a scientific journal called *Theories and Mechanisms of Paranormal Mutation*. There was also a special glass case containing an open first edition of Charles Darwin's *The Origin of Species*, signed by the author. Any other time, Spider-Man would have given a week's earnings just for an afternoon in this room. Today he just wondered how Magneto kept his collection from being damaged by the bad underground air.

Bishop sat on the bed. "Remember what I told you back at the coffee shop? About how I didn't miss home?"

"Yes," Spider-Man said.

"Now it's worse. Now I feel like I *am* home. The open warfare, the paranoia, the feeling that I can't trust anyone and might be stabbed in the back at any time—I keep getting the strangest feeling that I've just returned to my natural habitat, after too many years in a cage. I'm not sure how I feel about that."

Terrific, Spider-Man thought. "How do you feel about Magneto? Can we trust him?"

Bishop rubbed his forehead. "The Magneto I know stands by his promises. He may be a murderous, power-mad fanatic, but he always keeps his word. If we were dealing with that Magneto, I'd trust him in a second. But we're not dealing with that Magneto. This one might be completely different. Just look at the X-Men."

"Yeah," Spider-Man said. He took a deep breath. "Unfortunately, Bish, I don't think we have any choice. Not if Aliya can send us home."

"There's still Cable and Blaquesmith."

"I know. And if nothing's happened to them, I'm sure they're doing everything possible to pull us back. That will either happen, or not happen, no matter what we do. In the meantime, we should do everything we can to improve our chances. Which means that we have to deal with Aliya, and keep our eyes open for a trap."

"Of course," Bishop said. "And I concur. But this does raise one very interesting question, Spider-Man."

"Which is?"

Bishop's eyes bored into his. "Even under these desperate circumstances, would you have been so willing to join her cause if you didn't believe it was just?"

Spider-Man considered about a dozen wisecrack answers to that, but ended up discarding them all. In the end, he just shrugged ruefully and said, "I guess we've been spending too much time together, Bish. You're beginning to understand me."

They rejoined the others, only to be assaulted by something neither one of them had expected: sudden ravenous hunger, brought on by the smell of melted cheese. Spider-Man wanted to leap for a sandwich, but he just stood his ground beside Bishop, and said, "I guess you have a deal."

"Great!" Speedball exclaimed. "I knew you guys would come around!"

"I wasn't quite so sure," Night Thrasher said.

"I was," Magneto said, with considerable amusement. "After all, it's not like they have any other choice. But it serves our purposes to be grateful. Is there anything we can do to make your stay easier?"

"I just want my cannon back," Bishop said. "I'll want to look it over to make sure it isn't damaged."

"I'll see where the others have hidden it. And you, Spider-Man?"

"I'll need two things," Spider-Man said. "First, access to chemical supplies. I use an artificial web-fluid, and if we're going into battle, I want to be fully stocked."

Magneto nodded. "I'll have Night Thrasher introduce you to our quartermaster. What else?"

"Your help finding an address. And four hours of freedom to get there and back."

Nobody liked that. Spider-Man hadn't expected them to. The members of the PLF were wanted fugitives; the last thing they needed was to let such a reluctant ally out of their sight. Aliya spoke for all of them. "This isn't even your world. What kind of personal errand can you possibly have here?"

"Hey, you're the lady who sets new records in long-distance relationships. You figure it out."

Night Thrasher looked like he was about to raise serious objections, but he didn't have a chance—because by the time he opened his mouth, Magneto had stunned them all by breaking into deep and hearty laughter. It wasn't

TIME'S ARROW

the insanely megalomaniacal kind of laughter Spider-Man was so used to hearing from super-villains—but a genuine belly-laugh, neither threatening or forced. Spider-Man would never have expected to hear such a sound coming from Magneto, and from the looks on the faces of Aliya, Bishop, and the others, they all felt the same way. Even so, what Magneto said next shocked Spider-Man as much as anything he'd seen since a hundred-thirty-year-old photograph sent him on this adventure: "I enjoy this fellow. Of course, Spider-Man. I'm sure we can trust you to take care of yourself. Just take Razorback along as lookout, and make sure you're back in four hours." The master of magnetism nodded at Aliya. "Come, my dear. We have to brief the others about our new inductees."

Spider-Man watched them go. He had a bad moment immediately after Aliya and Magneto left, when the metal slab slid back into place. "Oh, no. Are we locked in?"

"There have been prisoners here who thought so," Speedball said. "But there's a back door hidden behind one of the bookcases."

"Oh." Maybe this version of Magneto could be trusted after all. "Who has that copy of *NOW* magazine?"

Night Thrasher handed it over.

The front cover photograph of himself made Spider-Man feel lightheaded. He moved to the couch, shakily sat down, and flipped to the feature article on page twenty-two. It was headlined "PARK IT!" Written by Eddie Brock, it was ten pages of gushing, uncritical hero worship, waxing rhapsodic about Peter Parker's nearly blinding speed on the basketball court. There were photographs of him outleaping Magic Johnson and Shaquille O'Neal. There was a photo of him shaking hands with President Gingrich. There was another photo of him clowning around on a talk show hosted by Millie the Model. There was a two-page spread of Peter wearing nothing but a pair of Jockey shorts, which seemed to be there only because, as the middle of the magazine, it permitted the too-cute-to-live caption CENTRAL PARK. There was an interview,

THE PRESENT

which seemed to be nothing but the usual celebrity clichés. Most telling was a picture of himself in a jogging suit, signing autographs for scruffily dressed youngsters in a low-income neighborhood. *Seen here greeting fans on Yancy Street, Parker attributes his spectacular skills to "practice." "I've been lucky," he says. "It's not easy, being the shortest superstar in basketball."*

Spider-Man handed the magazine to Night Thrasher. "I need his street address. It'll be unlisted."

Night Thrasher pulled out a laptop computer. "Got it."

Bishop, who'd been quietly reading over Spider-Man's shoulder, said, "Is this wise?"

"No," Spider-Man said. "It's not. But a lot of things in my life aren't wise. Putting on a silly costume and swinging from rooftops isn't wise. Fighting sociopaths on a nightly basis isn't wise. Gallivanting around time when you've got one of the world's great ladies at home waiting for you isn't wise. But this isn't about wisdom. This is about needing to know how come this version of me does what he does, while I do what I do." He looked at Bishop. "I need this, Bishop. I need to make some sense out of all this."

Bishop studied him contemplatively. "Then you're wrong on one thing, at least."

"Huh?"

"It is wise . . . Peter."

Hearing Bishop use his real name for the first time was like a little electric shock. It didn't come as a surprise, after everything that had happened, but it was a lot like feeling the shaky barriers that kept his two lives safely separated once again weaken and threaten to fall. He averted his eyes and said, "You know . . . of course, that I've never been too happy . . . about other people knowing . . ."

Bishop cut him off. "I know all about the necessity of keeping secrets, Spider-Man. Secrets are what keep the X-Men alive. And as long as I live, yours is safe with me."

"Thanks," said Spider-Man. He lifted his mask free of his mouth, and fumbled for his sandwich, mostly because

TIME'S ARROW

he needed something to do with his hands. "I guess I . . ."

Night Thrasher's computer beeped. "I've got it. He has a penthouse on Sutton Place, overlooking the East River. Razorback will be able to show you a quick route through the tunnels that won't force you to spend too much time exposed on the surface."

"Good," Spider-Man said. He took a bite of his sandwich, swallowed it, and suddenly realized that he wasn't hungry at all. "What about your quartermaster? I should give him a list of chemicals before I leave."

"He's not far," Speedball said. "Magneto's got him set up in some abandoned steam tunnels about a quarter of a mile from here. You won't believe the dude's operation—he has untraceable phone lines hooked up to half the supply houses in the city. He can have anything you want safely delivered by the time you return from wherever you're going."

"Good," Spider-Man said.

"I should warn you, though: you'll both be in for one tremendous shock when you meet him. He's a duck."

Both Spider-Man and Bishop said it out loud: "*Howard?*"

"Oh," Speedball said. "You've met him?"

It was maybe forty minutes later. Peter Parker stood on a street corner, facing a fashionable apartment building. He was unmasked, and dressed in civvies: the ratty goose-down jacket now replaced by a comfortable old leather jacket that Speedball had offered to lend him. It was warm enough to protect him from the cold, but he'd already found himself shivering more than once.

He didn't mind admitting to himself that he was scared in ways that he'd never been scared before. It was one thing to face Spider-Slayers or mad scientists or even irascible newspaper publishers; it was another to know that he was about to face the life that might have been. He blew on his hands to keep them warm, aware that the chill at the base of his spine wouldn't go away nearly as easily.

So he took a deep breath and crossed the street.

THE PRESENT

The doorman, a pudgy bald man with a pronounced lower lip, quickly moved to intercept him. When he saw Peter's face, he started. "Mr. Parker? Good Lord, sir, I didn't recognize you in those clothes!"

Peter grinned weakly. "I . . . uh, needed to go for a walk. . . ."

"And incognito, too, from the looks of it! Are you all right, sir?"

"Never better, uh"—he glanced at the man's name badge "—Adam."

"Forgive me, sir, but you don't look all right."

Peter retreated to the all-purpose excuse of twentieth-century America. "Something I ate."

"Oh, I see. Shall I call a doctor?"

"No need. I'm sure if I just lie down awhile I'll be perfectly—"

The doorman glanced at something over Peter's shoulder. "Ah, Mrs. Parker! You're just in time."

Peter whirled, expecting—hoping—to see Mary Jane.

But it wasn't her.

He was shocked to see who it was: so shocked that for a second he just stood there dumbly, thinking, *But that's not my wife!*

Once upon a time, before the accident that had turned Peter into Spider-Man, he'd nursed an almost painful crush on the blonde and beautiful Liz Allan, who had always ignored him in favor of the bullying jock Flash Thompson. She'd been thoroughly beyond his reach. Then Peter became Spider-Man, and something interesting happened. His brash, wisecracking Spider-Man persona had begun to affect his day-to-day civilian personality—making him more confident, more outgoing, less concerned about the opinions of the kids. Liz had noticed the changes in him and responded—but Peter was by then interested in someone else. They'd drifted apart, and dated other people, Liz marrying Harry Osborn and Peter marrying Mary Jane Watson. Oddly enough, Harry and Mary Jane had been a fairly serious item themselves at one point; since Harry eventually went mad and became the murderous super-villain known as the Green Goblin, Peter honestly preferred not to think about it.

But that was in the world Peter knew. The idea of actually being married to Liz Allan seemed as alien to him as anything he'd encountered so far—especially since this Liz Allan, with her fur coat, flashy earrings, and armful of gold bracelets, seemed so different from the one he knew.

She pecked him on the cheek. "You're home early. Is something wrong?"

"Uh—" Could he possibly start a sentence without saying *Uh*? "No. Just a little tired."

"The way you're underdressed, I wouldn't be surprised if you've gone and caught yourself a cold. Where on Earth did you get those things?" She handed him a pair of big boxes from Neiman's. "Here. Help me upstairs with these and I'll make you chicken soup."

Bishop had been right. This wasn't wise. This Liz thought he was her husband, and here he was as distant as any stranger. But the conversation had taken on a terrible momentum of its very own, and as she took him by the arm and led him toward a special private elevator on the other end of the fashionably appointed lobby, he found himself nodding and smiling and pretending that the names she dropped actually meant something to him.

There was one especially uncomfortable moment when he spotted a slot beside the elevator; he had to pretend to fumble with the boxes so she'd use her own card key instead of waiting for him to produce his. "Oh," she said, as she remembered something. "Mr. Burstein called—from the school? He says he needs to see you about Richard's aptitude test."

Richard had been the name of Peter's father. He actually swallowed at that, as they both got into the elevator. This Peter had a son named Richard. "Is there anything wrong?"

"Are you kidding? The kid's brilliant, just like his old man. Burstein just wants to put the boy in advanced placement classes. He says Richard shows a real talent for bi-

THE PRESENT

ology. I told him about the microscope you gave him for his birthday, and he said he's pleased to see how much we encourage the kids."

"Kids," Peter said, with a neutrality he didn't feel.

"Yeah. I think the poor guy's smitten with us. He has Mary's photographs all over his office."

Mary. His mother's name. On this world he had a son named Richard and a daughter named Mary. He thought of how much he'd always mourned never getting to know his parents, how frequently he'd thought about them, even with Uncle Ben and Aunt May in their place. He nodded, a fixed smile on his face, forcing back a tidal wave of emotions through sheer force of will.

This was crazy. This was crazy. This was crazy. What was he going to do if his other self was upstairs? Would he be able to talk to him without a big fight? And if not, how would he ever get away from here without compromising Magneto and the others?

Against all that, the single unanswerable question: How could he just walk away without knowing?

The elevator doors opened into the entrance hall of a vast penthouse apartment. The walls were covered with photographs: some of the Park, sailing over the heads of his opponents on the basketball court, others of Peter, Liz, and family. A pair of sliding glass doors, visible from the elevator, led out to a spacious patio overlooking the East River. The TV set was roughly the size of a small Cineplex movie screen. Peter forced himself to move casually, in the manner of a man who had seen this apartment a thousand times before, instead of indulging the impulse to race around staring at everything.

He placed the Neiman's boxes on a table by the entrance and said, "Listen, I'll be right back, there's something I have to do in the other room," figuring that even if he didn't know what other room he was talking about, then his alleged wife would pick up the slack and assume.

She obliged. "Hurry back, okay? I'll put on that soup!"

He fled down a hallway, past two open doors that he quickly identified as the children's rooms, past another

TIME'S ARROW

door that was clearly the master bedroom (shag rug, huge four-poster bed, gleaming nautilus equipment, another huge television), and into a room that turned out to be—
—the Park's study.

It was a shrine to an unparalleled athletic career. There were photos of the Park at the Olympics, photos of the Park slam-dunking one basket after another, photos of the Park making mincemeat of the other players, all lovingly framed and gathered together in tribute to the athlete who could do no wrong. The idea of the Park sitting in here, surrounded by so many tributes to himself, made Peter more than a little ill. It showed a narcissistic self-absorption that might have left room for nothing else.

He was almost relieved when he found photos of the kids. Richard was about ten, Mary nine. Richard looked a lot like Peter had at that age: skinny, bespectacled, and intense. Mary looked like a younger version of Liz.

My children, he thought. It was so unreal it made him dizzy. Peter was most startled by their ages. On his world, he and Mary Jane hadn't gotten around to attempting children until fairly recently; based on the ages of these kids, this world's Peter Parker and Liz Allan must have gotten married right out of high school. Something about that bothered him, too, but he wasn't sure why. . . .

Surveying the photos, he found a shot of his high-school nemesis, Flash Thompson, who had in his own world gradually become a friend. There were pictures of him beaming as he and Peter hoisted trophies together. One of the pictures came from a magazine, complete with caption: PETER PARKER WITH PERSONAL TRAINER FLASH THOMPSON. Another data-point, and one that only added to his unease. Why was that? After all, Flash was his friend, wasn't he? There was nothing wrong with this world's Peter Parker sharing his success with friends . . . or was there?

But Peter was bothered by more than the spectacle of his life, reshuffled like a deck of cards. There was a picture forming in the back of his mind—something dark and twisted, behind all these images of a perfect life. He didn't

THE PRESENT

know what it was; he only knew that for the first time he wasn't sure he'd like this world's Peter Parker.

The photo that finally persuaded him he'd had enough was a group shot of two couples sharing dinner at a fine restaurant. One of the couples was Peter and Liz, the other was Harry Osborn and Mary Jane Watson. Harry was relaxed, comfortable, and smiling: so different from the man Peter had known, whose life had descended in a great spiral from drug addiction to homicidal insanity. From the ages of everybody in the picture, it seemed clear that none of that had ever happened here. Both couples had lived happily, with the only price paid a small matter of unwittingly reversed marriages.

Peter had seen more than enough. He had to get back to Magneto and Bishop and the others, and try to put all of this out of his mind. He turned, already planning how he'd get past Liz without being seen.

There's an old vaudeville gag, best done in the Marx Brothers movie *Duck Soup*, where two people who look more or less alike encounter each other in a doorway, and try to deny it, pretending instead that they're facing a perfect reflection in a mirror.

Facing the door to the hallway, Peter knew exactly how Groucho and Harpo felt.

At least until the Park backed him into the room and said, "I don't know who you think you are, you half-baked imposter, but you just made the very worst mistake of your life!"

CHAPTER EIGHT

In an Asia that sometimes seemed to have long ago run out of wild places, the Devil's Crescent was one of the last great remnants: a vast overgrown swamp, shrouded by a thick forest canopy. Once, it had been two hundred miles across, and home to an uncounted number of plant and animal species that existed nowhere else. Now, thanks to the rapid encroachment of humanity and the mixed blessing of land reclamation, it was less than half its previous size. The area was bracketed by a pair of sooty factory towns most notable for the way they'd gone from virgin wilderness to slum in less than fifty years. Both towns were expanding, thanks to the vast numbers of poor and the equally vast numbers of industrialists anxious to relocate somewhere with relaxed pollution standards and workers willing to labor cheaply. It wouldn't be long before they grew together and became one big, stinking, overcrowded city, with the Devil's Crescent naught but a memory. Until then, it was still wild, still a place where life and death and the daily struggle for survival proceeded as they always had: according to their own inexorable, but still somehow preferable, equation.

Until then, it was still a paradise, at least for the mosquitoes and the snakes.

The two figures materializing on one of its few outcroppings of undeniably dry land had wildly differing assessments of its natural beauty.

Storm took a deep breath, and said, "Goddess! Just look at those trees! The way they link together, like a great sculpture . . . the way the sun filters down through the forest canopy—it's positively primeval."

"It's a swamp," Iceman said flatly. "It's filled with bugs and mud, it's as humid as an underarm at rush hour, and it smells like something that curled up and died."

The look she gave him was not far removed from pity. "Come now, Bobby. Doesn't all this natural beauty hold some appeal for you?"

"Nope," Iceman said. "It just reminds me of the appeal of the nice, comfy, climate-controlled mansion. I'm not exceedingly fond of hot places."

THE PRESENT

She frowned. "Heat and humidity allow your powers to work at peak efficiency."

"I know, I know," Iceman said. "And I know that's why you guys thought I should come here. But I'm still never gonna pick a place like this as my ideal summer home." He sighed. "C'mon, let's just hurry up and find that bomb, so we can get back to someplace where I'm not the only air conditioning."

"Agreed," she said. She spread her arms, summoning the winds to grant her flight. They obeyed at once, as they always did. She rose into the air, her long white hair billowing around her face as brilliantly as the starbursts radiating from an alien sun. She was, as always, the most beautiful sight in a landscape filled with natural wonders. Iceman had seen her in flight more times than he could count, and he was always impressed by the sight. He'd known many men and women who could fly, starting with his old buddy Warren Worthington III, aka the Angel. He had known some who made it look majestic, and many who had made it look fun, and quite a few who had made it look like a thrill the rest of humanity was missing. But Ororo flew with so much confidence and grace that she actually made it look easy. He almost followed her on one of his trademark ice-ramps, but then she signaled him to stay at water level—an instruction that made sense, since she was better equipped for a high-speed aerial search.

So he projected his ice ramp a mere two feet above the fetid swamp, keeping one eye on the water as he zigzagged back and forth between the trees. He didn't see much worth mentioning. Oh, at one point, some kind of crocodile or alligator, attracted by the swiftly moving object just over its head, lunged out of the water in an attempt to take a bite out of him. And a few minutes later he encountered some bizarre species of tree with multiple trunks and branches so ornate that they were more like embroidery than plant life. When he passed close to that, figuring it just creepy enough to hide something as nasty as a time bomb, a colony of bats swarmed out of a hollowed-out section of trunk, circled him warily, and flew off into the darkening tropical sky. But he didn't find anything actually worth commenting on—certainly nothing that even resembled a dangerous weapon from the future.

In fact, he couldn't help wondering just how he and Storm were supposed to find the time bomb at all. It would be different if this *were* the Antarctic ice canyon where Cable and the Beast had been sent, or the tropical island where Gambit and Wolverine had gone. Both those locales were so inherently straightforward that Iceman couldn't imagine either of the other two teams having any special problems finding their respective devices. But the swamp was almost all water—and none of that clear. Iceman could have passed over the bomb a dozen times by now, and not seen it; he could have a map to its precise location and a guide willing to show him exactly where he needed to look, and still not be able to see it. He could only hope that this Kang character played fair, and that the device was not so cunningly hidden that they'd have to rip up the entire swamp to find it.

It was only after fifteen minutes of high-intensity searching that Storm descended to talk to him. She landed on his ice bridge, her face a portrait in worry.

"We have a problem," she said.

It was an interesting way to put it. "You mean, aside from needing to find a time bomb capable of destroying the universe in a swamp where you could sink a dozen eighteen-wheelers without anybody ever noticing?"

"As a matter of fact," Storm said, "yes. I have been examining the patterns of the wind, and I know why our foe chose this spot for his little game. Look at the sky, Bobby. Do you see how dark it's becoming?"

He looked up at a sky the color of slate. "Yeah. I noticed it was looking pretty grim up there, but I didn't think much of it. What's wrong?"

"In about five minutes this whole region is going to be hit by one of the worst monsoons in recorded history. I can feel the forces behind it gathering. They're not nearly as powerful as they're going to be once they cut loose,

THE PRESENT

and they already harbor enough destructive potential to scour the earth. We're going to be in the middle of it, Bobby, and for us it will be like being at the heart of a force-five hurricane, with everything that implies.''

"Yowch." Iceman winced. "Smells an awful lot like a setup, doesn't it?"

She nodded. "We were expecting one, after all. And I'd be very surprised if the monsoon were all of it."

"Why don't you just use your weather powers to drive it away?"

"I could, but it would take some time—and it would require all the concentration I could muster. You'd be left alone to find the missile, not to mention deal with anything else our foe might have in store."

He understood her worry now. Storm was not the kind of person who liked to abandon her friends in a crisis; far from it. Her sense of responsibility was one of the most highly developed of anybody he knew, and Iceman's circle of friends was composed pretty much exclusively of people with an overdeveloped sense of responsibility. He smiled. "Don't worry about it, Ororo. If it comes to that, I can take care of myself. After all, I was an X-Man before I was old enough to drive."

She smiled. "That doesn't make me feel all that much better, Bobby. I've seen your driving."

"Hardy har har. I'll have you know—"

Iceman never got to finish the rejoinder, as suddenly something big and black and heavy and round burst from the underbrush with the force of a mortar blast. Even as Storm instinctively ducked back down to get out of its way, she swung her arms around and fired a pair of lightning blasts at the oncoming missile. The bolts deflected it not at all, merely making it glow white hot, like a hurtling ball of flame. Iceman didn't even attempt to project a shield; he simply lowered his head, tackled Storm, and knocked her out of the way just as the glowing, crackling missile smashed into his ice bridge, reducing it to slivers.

As the two X-Men plummeted toward the water, Iceman looked down and caught a glimpse of a leering croc-

TIME'S ARROW

odile, surfacing just in time to claim the morsels from above. Half a second was more than enough time to deal with that. He pointed at the critter and gave it a nice tasty mouthful of slush, right in the gullet. As reptiles are not the target market for slurpies, it did not appreciate that at all; so little, in fact, that it convulsed, twisted, and got out of the way before the dispenser of frozen treats became its guest for dinner.

Storm arrested her fall and skimmed low over the swamp water, just as Iceman projected an ice bridge that did the same for him. They both came to a stop almost simultaneously, as four bulky, colorfully clad men emerged from the trees, with cruel grins on their grizzled, rough hewn faces. The one in front, who carried an oversized crowbar, was dressed in a loose-fitting green jumpsuit, with purple gloves, boots, and mask. From the way he preceded the others, he obviously considered himself their leader; certainly the three men behind him all held back, waiting to see what he was going to do. The only one who moved was the black man immediately behind him, who nonchalantly raised one arm to pluck his returning missile—which Iceman now recognized as a decidedly unaerodynamic ball-and-chain—right out of the air.

The leader sneered, an expression perfectly at home on a face that might not have been much good doing anything else. "Surprised, muties? Well, you oughta be! You ain't gettin' out of this godforsaken jungle alive. Not with the Wrecking Crew on your tail!"

Iceman and Storm looked at each other. He thought he saw the shadow of a smile twitch at the corners of her lips, but, fortunately, she held it back—a good thing, since this would not be an advantageous time to lose it. He said, "Forgive me for saying so, fellas, but you all look a little too . . . urban . . . for this to be your usual neighborhood. Are we safe in assuming that you've been paid to meet us here?"

"Paid to stomp ya into the mud!" the guy with the crowbar said succinctly.

The bulkiest of his companions, a bare-chested gent

THE PRESENT

with a bulky steel helmet and shoulder plate that appeared to have been bolted on, cried out, "You tell 'im, Wrecker!"

Iceman looked at Storm. "You're right. Definite setup."

"And not a very good one," she agreed. "Our foe must have been running short of cash, to scrape the bottom of the barrel like this."

"Must have been a labor shortage at the flunkie supervillain union hall," Iceman said.

"Must have been." Storm nodded.

Of course, Storm and Iceman weren't really anywhere near as overconfident as all that. They'd both heard of the Wrecking Crew, a quartet of brutal thugs who'd been mystically granted enough strength to take on the likes of the Hulk. Any one of them would have been tough to beat. Fighting together, they were formidable enough to level entire city blocks.

But the exchange between Storm and Iceman did serve one very useful purpose: it immediately isolated the stupidest and most easily baited individual among their foes.

The blond one dressed in the red-and-white costume rushed forward, yelling, "I'll show youse bottom of da barrel, ya geneckital freaks!"

He certainly did. He lunged at Storm and Iceman with the single-minded determination of a lummox so blinded by his anger that he'd forgotten that there were a limited number of solid places to step on in a swamp. Even as the Wrecker shouted, "Piledriver, no!" his super-powerful minion sank to his shoulders in muddy swamp water, with a force that radiated waves five feet high. Iceman wasted no time freezing that entire section of swamp solid, waves and all. Piledriver, trapped like a fly in amber with only his head protruding above the surface, immediately cried out, "Hey, boss! Help! Dey *homogenized* me!"

Iceman smirked. "I've got to tell you, Wrecker. I'm really impressed so far."

The Wrecker was fuming. "You really think you're hot stuff, don't ya, Frosty?" He snapped out his orders:

151

TIME'S ARROW

"Thunderball! Bulldozer! You take out the woman! I'll get the Silver Surfer wannabe!"

The Wrecking Crew barreled toward them, utterly ignoring the plaintive, malaprop-infested cries of their trapped companion. The Wrecker came brandishing his thick iron crowbar. Thunderball came swinging his iron ball by its chain. Bulldozer simply lowered his steel-encased head and came using the top of his own skull as a battering ram. Storm and Iceman reacted immediately: Storm by rising another thirty feet into the sky while unleashing a hurricane-force wind against Thunderball and Bulldozer, Iceman by projecting a gigantic battering ram, which he intended to ride all the way into the Wrecker's face.

As a visible illustration of an irresistible force meeting an immovable object, it couldn't have been better. As another phase of a battle, it left the two heroes worse for wear. The Wrecker simply shattered Iceman's battering ram with a single swipe of his oversized crowbar, sending the X-Man somersaulting over his head into the bushes. And while Bulldozer was indeed blown away by Storm's pocket gale, sliding aross the frozen section of swamp with all the grace of a driverless Zamboni, Thunderball stood his ground long enough to hurl his ball and chain at Storm. It stayed on course despite the force of the wind marshaled against it, as if all the elements in all the world were simply irrelevant. And when Storm took evasive action, swooping low to the ground and then back up into the air again, the ball-and-chain simply altered course to intercept her, splintering a tree in its way like kindling.

As the Wrecker sauntered over to where the stunned Iceman lay in a heap, he chuckled. "Seems like magic, don't it? Well, here's a news flash for you, Frosty—it *is* magic!"

Before he could continue his rant, another icy battering ram burst from the underbrush and hit him dead-center, knocking the breath out of him and driving him fifty feet into the air. His flight described a wide parabola over the small frozen section of swamp, carrying him over deep,

THE PRESENT

still water. As he fell, he swung his crowbar in all directions, as if daring the universe to hand him something he could smash. He still hit the water so hard that the splash resembled an underwater explosion.

Iceman emerged from the bushes with a broad smile on his face. Maybe he shouldn't have complained about the swamp after all. Because a swamp did have one tremendous advantage in a fight like this: it was mostly mud and water. Fighting the Wrecking Crew on concrete city streets, where they had room to build up a good head of steam and couldn't get bogged down by the landscape, would have been a much tougher proposition. Here, the Wrecking Crew's weight and momentum worked against them. The advantage went to people who could fly, or soar along on ice bridges. He didn't know how long it would be before the Wrecker managed to slog clear of the mud where he'd landed, but he was willing to bet it'd be a while.

A worried expression crossed his face as he searched the sky for Storm.

Storm had given up trying to lose the hurtling wrecking ball with evasive action through the trees, and was now flying straight up, in an attempt to outdistance it.

It wasn't working. Even as she summoned the winds to propel her at the greatest acceleration her body could take, even as she assaulted the ball and chain with wind, rain, hail, lightning, and waves of alternating heat and cold, it continued to gain on her. It pursued her as relentlessly as a thing with a mind of its own, its smooth metallic surface taking on the look of a hungry ravenous blind idiot face, that wanted only to smash her bones to kindling.

Its pursuit seemed to last an hour.

In truth, it took less than thirty seconds.

As it soared out of range of its master, the wrecking ball slowed, stopped, and surrendered to gravity. As it plunged, Storm hovered, watched to make sure that it truly was falling, and paused just long enough to focus all her senses on the approaching monsoon. She saw all the weather patterns within a two-hundred-mile radius clearly, with a depth of understanding that made a joke of satellite photography. She saw not only the movements of the air but also the gathering energy behind them, and she knew that the monsoon was going to be even greater than she'd thought. The horizon was already black with it, representing a wave of onrushing destruction that to Storm represented nothing less than Nature's murderous rage at everything in Her path.

She saw a patch of ugliness at the distant edge of the swamp. A town. The loss of life was going to be catastrophic.

But it was going to be immeasurably worse if the Wrecking Crew prevented her and Iceman from finding Kang's bomb.

Her eyes narrowed with determination as she began her controlled descent back to the swamp.

Bulldozer, unable to get his meaty paws on Storm, had turned his limited attention span on Iceman. As he ran across the ice, each step sent cracks radiating across the surface, like a preview of what he intended to do to Iceman himself. Iceman took the hint, fleeing the rampaging super-villain on a flat ice-shelf he projected ahead of him as he ran. Bulldozer didn't hesitate to follow, pursuing Iceman across the shelf at top speed.

"There's something I want to know about you guys!" Iceman yelled, as he drove his ice-bridge upward, on a serpentine path through the trees. "I mean, are you all fans of old-time spy movies or what?"

Bulldozer, who was gaining, yelled back, "Whaddaya mean?"

"Well, *Thunderball* was James Bond, and *The Wrecking Crew* was Matt Helm. Did you plan your names deliberately, or was it just a coincidence?"

Bulldozer grunted as he poured on the speed. He seemed to have no trouble keeping his footing on the slippery surface; he was a human missile, proceeding on a

THE PRESENT

predetermined course, and he wouldn't ruin that course for anything as undignified as a pratfall on the ice. "You ain't gonna be worried about no movie trivia once you got your skull smashed like an egg!"

"Probably not," Iceman agreed. They were now a good fifty feet over the water, and Bulldozer was almost upon him. "But y'know, there's one funny thing about being able to make ice sculptures in any shape..."

"Yeah? What's that?"

"I'm able to make *thin* ice."

Bulldozer almost stopped. Almost. But like a car locking brakes on an icy road, he was doomed by his own momentum. Though his legs stopped moving, he continued to slide forward, at a speed that would have made a very respectable all-out run. When he finally came to a halt, it was over a patch as transparent as glass, which promptly cracked in two and left him falling into one of the deepest parts of the swamp.

He bellowed in rage all the way down.

Iceman shouted one last piece of advice. "Hey, Bulldozer—*Get Smart*!"

Storm arrived just in time to see Thunderball insouciantly catch his wrecking ball as it obediently returned to his hands. He was awfully casual about it—almost bored, as if the fight itself wasn't interesting enough to occupy his attention. Indeed, he seemed to have barely exerted himself—unlike Piledriver, who had worked up a good sweat freeing himself from the ice, and the Wrecker, who was still laboriously sloshing his way back to relatively dry land. When Thunderball turned to face her, she saw that he displayed no bloodlust whatsoever, merely a determination to do what needed to be done.

He raised his wrecking ball for another throw, but stopped when she said, "Wait."

He actually obliged, lowering his weapon. "All right. Why?"

She landed fifty feet away, prepared to attack the second she had to. "I want you to know that in a few minutes this entire fight will be irrelevant. We're about to be hit with a monsoon capable of killing everything in its path. Even with your powers, you and your friends need to seek cover now, or you might not survive."

He nodded. "I appreciate the warning. Unfortunately, there is the matter of all the money we've been paid for killing you."

"You may not know this," Storm said, "but if you kill us, or even keep us from doing what we've come here to do, then your employer destroys the world, and none of that money will mean anything."

Thunderball smiled. "There's only one problem with that, lady."

"What's that?"

"You see, unlike my friends, who I freely admit embarrass me from time to time, I really *am* a rocket scientist. I used to work for the government, designing doomsday bombs. And if arguments about the end of the world didn't stop me then, then why would they stop me now?"

He raised the wrecking ball high above his head, and lunged. He did not charge blindly into the water, but instead leapt from one patch of solid ground to another, in a seemingly chaotic but perfectly planned advance that brought him closer to Storm with every step. Watching him almost analytically, Storm saw that he wasn't nearly as dispassionate as he let on. He might not have been the same kind of thug his friends were, and he might not have been as deeply ruled by rage, but he was still looking forward to smashing her with his ball-and-chain.

She did not feel at all bad about what she did next. She only felt bad that it was too easy, the local weather patterns being at that moment already too predisposed toward tornadoes. The funnel formed around him in an instant, rising from the muddy earth as quickly as a flower whose growth had been captured via stop-motion photography. For a split second, there was nothing but wind, leaving the tornado itself transparent. In that split second his face remained visible, with his eyes wide and his mouth agape in a rictus of instinctive terror. Then the dirt and mud

THE PRESENT

sucked up by the funnel turned the tornado as opaque as the ground itself, and Thunderball was only visible as a mass of flailing arms and legs, rising up into the sky like a child's toy yanked hard by an invisible string.

He did try to throw his wrecking ball, of course. But his throw was wild. It sailed off into the distance, in search of a target that didn't exist. Storm wondered just how far it would go before it decided it had missed and came back to him. She supposed it didn't matter. The good thing about starting tornadoes was that once started, they didn't need her constant concentration to keep them going. They had a momentum of their very own.

This one would keep Thunderball occupied for a while.

"Hey, lady!"

It was Piledriver, who'd succeeded in digging his way out of the ice, and was already back on more-or-less dry land, pounding the earth with his impossibly powerful arms. The shock wave made the ground itself seem to whip up and down like a jump rope shaken by a child; it threw her off her feet with a suddenness that did not give her the time to recover in flight. She sailed into the water, swallowed a mouthful of something muddy and foul, and regained her footing just in time to see Piledriver towering above her, swinging a massive tree trunk like a club.

In the instant before the giant tree filled her field of vision, she had just enough time to realize sheets of hard driving rain were assaulting the landscape as far as her eyes could see.

The monsoon had arrived.

It hit too hard and too suddenly to feel strictly natural. To Iceman, racing to Storm's rescue on one of his ice ramps, it felt like the kind of thing she might have been responsible for. He couldn't be sure whether it was the cataclysmic blowout she'd warned him about, or one of her tactics against the Wrecking Crew. It confused him just long enough that he paused, temporarily unable to find her behind the curtains of driving rain.

He wasn't worried about her. She was Storm, and she

TIME'S ARROW

knew how to take care of herself, especially in bad weather. But the monsoon was particularly bad news for him. This rain was as warm as bathwater, and coming down in buckets. Under that kind of assault, anything he built with his ice powers wouldn't last for more than a few seconds. His ice ramps would be next to useless as transportation; he wouldn't be able to gain any decent altitude, and he'd have to do all his fighting on or near the ground, well within reach of the Wrecker and his band of sociopathic goons. He hoped the storm handicapped them as much as it did him.

No sooner had the thought crossed his mind, than it was proved wishful thinking.

Approaching from underwater, the Wrecker broke surface, and swung his mystic crowbar at the ice bridge just above him. It shattered like plate glass, plunging Iceman into the water. Iceman rocketed through the brine and hit bottom—a slimy ooze that made him feel unclean even in his ice form. There was no visibility whatsoever; he knew the Wrecker was nearby but could not see precisely where. Momentarily disoriented, he planted his legs in the mud and stood, finding himself in water waist-deep.

By the time he realized that the Wrecker was behind him, it was too late to do anything about it.

A powerful arm wrapped around his neck, bending it back, with a strength capable of snapping his spine. He struggled, but his strength was merely human; it was not nearly enough to outwrestle a man capable of trading blows with the Hulk. Bobby tried sending waves of subzero cold down the Wrecker's arms, ready to freeze them brittle if necessary, but the Wrecker didn't even seem to notice; he merely laughed that cruel bullying laugh of his, and cried, "You miss the point, Frosty! I only have to take the cold another second or two! Your neck ain't gonna last nearly that long!"

The futilely struggling Iceman realized he was right.

At just about the same moment, on the other side of the world, Professor Charles Xavier was lying on his back

158

THE PRESENT

beneath the control circuitry of the Time Displacement Core. The board he was lying on came equipped with casters, and he'd been using it to move about in the huge but compartmented and claustrophic confines beneath the great machine, replacing the time displacement rods fried by the assault of Kang's troopers. It was tremendously exacting work, which strained the limits of his enormous intellect. He couldn't be entirely sure he was doing it right, since the Time Displacement Core was technology well beyond his understanding, and even picking up telepathic instructions from Blaquesmith wasn't enough to help him understand much of what he was being told to do.

He kept asking Blaquesmith whether the repairs were proceeding well or not, but Blaquesmith wasn't much help there either. Answers like "Well, so far, not bad, considering," didn't bestow a great deal of confidence in their ability to get the machine back online in time to stop Kang. Not to mention rescue Bishop and Spider-Man, whose predicament had been eating at him since they went missing.

Charles Xavier feared for them even more than he feared for the three teams he'd sent out. He feared that he might have sent them to their deaths.

Too many people had already died, fighting wars under his banner.

He pried loose a section of incomprehensibly futuristic circuitry that appeared to have been fried black by some kind of internal fire, shifted position on his platform, and wheeled himself over to one of the power conduits. The thing was, he'd never intended to subject his students to this kind of mission. He'd wanted them to be ambassadors of understanding, who'd spend more time teaching than fighting; who'd be able to devote their days to addressing the shared problems of *Homo sapiens* and *Homo sapiens superior* instead of battling megalomaniacs and bigots and exotic menaces to all life on Earth. But it hadn't worked out that way. Their lives had instead become an unending succession of crises, arriving closer together with every year—and his determination to contribute toward the solv-

TIME'S ARROW

ing of humanity's problems had been reduced to an endless battle just to keep humanity alive while the problems got progressively worse.

He wondered whether the Time Displacement Core could show him a world where he had succeeded in doing what he'd once set out to do. And he decided, almost immediately, that it was better not to ask. He had to live in this world, not another where things were different.

He was about to telepathically ask Blaquesmith whether anything needed to be done to the power conduits when he picked up the man's sudden outpouring of dismay.

"Blaquesmith," he said out loud, "what's wrong?"

The voice was muffled by various layers of arcane machinery, but clear enough to understand: "I just picked up a reading on one of the monitors. All three of Kang's devices have just been triggered. They're channeling an immense amount of chronal energy into the timestream—more than I've ever seen!"

Xavier felt a cold, dark hand grip him by the heart. He knew what was happening, of course. The X-Men had failed, and this reality was about to perish like so many others. Everything the human race had ever done, every dream that they had ever dared, was about to be reduced to a forgotten joke, erased from the pages of history. Somehow, he managed to find his voice, which echoed pathetically in the small coffinlike space where he found himself. "Tell me. Is there still a chance?"

Blaquesmith's voice was equally strained. "I don't know."

CHAPTER NINE

Peter Parker felt a lot like a character in a French bedroom farce: circumstances had conspired to place him in the most suspicious situation imaginable, and the person whose trust he needed most wasn't even giving him a chance to explain himself.

Instead, the Park continued to advance, backing him into the room. He was a far more prosperous-looking version of himself, whose bright red warm-up suit was a sharp contrast to Peter's cast-off grunge. But the visible differences between them were more than just the clothing, more than just Peter's status as a fugitive on this world—it showed on their faces too. Peter had struggled with money problems all his life. He'd had to save, to scrounge, to worry about stretching his paychecks from one week to the next. It had, he realized now, become part of his face, part of who he was. But this Peter—the one the sports pages called the Park—had never needed to struggle. He'd never had to worry about paying his tuition or finagling extensions on his rent. He'd never had to turn a bottle of ketchup into ersatz tomato soup. And as a result, though everything else about his face was identical, there was something missing in his eyes—something that Peter had never noticed in the face he'd always seen in the mirror.

Hunger.

Far from it: the Park's eyes were comfortable. Self-assured. The eyes of a man used to getting what he wanted.

Stunned, backed up against the desk, Peter found it was several seconds before he could manage speech. "Park," he said. "Listen to me—"

The Park grabbed him by the collar. "Why should I? Am I supposed to be impressed, just because you look like me? I'm a celebrity, you idiot! I deal with doubles and imposters all the time! What's your secret? Plastic surgery?"

Peter didn't struggle, though he couldn't credit that to presence of mind. He was just too dumbfounded by the situation. "No, not at all! Listen—"

THE PRESENT

The Park's eyes flashed dangerously. "And just what were you planning to do with my wife?"

Oh, boy. Peter hadn't even considered *that* little nasty implication. "Nothing! I never said I was you! She just assumed—"

"I see." The Park seemed determined to interrupt his every sentence. "And you just happened to go along with it after you just happened to show up at my house just happening to look exactly like me while I just happened to be in the Nautilus room downstairs. I guess I'm wrong in assuming that's first-class, A-one stalking. You won't get your hands on her, mister. I've already sent her down to a friend's apartment. She won't come back until I tell her it's okay. Now give me one good reason why I shouldn't give you various scrapes and contusions before turning your sorry ass in to the cops."

Sick and tired of this, Peter reached up with both hands and broke his double's grip on his collar. Surprised, the Park grabbed for him again; Peter placed a palm against the Park's chest and gave him what for them qualified as a hard shove. Unprepared for the unexpected demonstration of super-strength, the Park staggered two steps back, and recovered his balance, a fresh caution burning on his familiar face.

"I know about the radioactive spider," Peter said. "I know about how distracted you were when you were walking home . . . about the truck that almost hit you . . . and how you jumped twenty feet straight up just to get out of its way."

The Park's eyes narrowed. "Who sold you this information?"

"Nobody sold it!"

"You used your looks to sneak a peek at my file, didn't you? Why not? You've already proved you can fool my wife . . . and that you're in good enough shape to pass for me . . . why not use this against the government? Why not walk right into the Super-Powers Registry and wrangle a look at my file? After all, they wouldn't stop you. They

163

know me. And they know everything in that file's an open book to me."

"Remember the drainpipe?" Peter asked. "How you grabbed it for support, and crushed it flat in your hands? Remember that first moment when you looked at what your hands had done and you didn't know whether to be thrilled or terrified? How for just a moment you wondered if everything in the world would always be tissue paper to you? Does your file say that?"

The Park lunged. *"Who are you?"*

It was a fast attack, one that would have overwhelmed any street hood and many super-villains. But for Peter, who'd been expecting it—whose spider-sense had pinpointed the exact moment of the Park's attack—it was so late that the Park might as well have phoned it in. By the time the Park passed through the place where he had been, Peter's somersaulting leap had already brought him to the ceiling. He clung there, in an upside-down crouch, blinking impassively as the Park whirled, looked for him, and finally, painfully, registered where he'd gone.

"I don't expect you to believe me," Peter said, "but I promise you, that if you took my fingerprints, you'd find them identical to yours. I'm you, Park. And you're me."

The Park flashed at least five separate facial expressions, one after the other. Anger. Shock. Denial. Bargaining. And, finally, acceptance.

He needed to support himself against his desk in order to make it to the plush leather chair. "My God." He sat down. "What are you? Some kind of . . . clone?"

Peter winced. "Oh, please. If we get started on that we'll be here all year."

"Then what?"

"I'm the Peter Parker who might have been."

The Park's eyes were very wide and very round. "What is this? *A Christmas Carol* or *It's a Wonderful Life*?"

Peter dropped from the ceiling, landing lightly on his feet. His counterpart visibly tensed, as if the move had once again placed Peter in the category of threats he could handle. Peter hesitated, momentarily unsure how to pro-

THE PRESENT

ceed, then said perhaps the least threatening thing he could come up with. "Listen. I've been trying to get a cup of coffee all day. The way this week's been going, I really need some. But things have been so crazy I haven't had a drop. Can we just sit down and talk about this reasonably, one Peter Parker to another? I promise you, we can always have the obligatory fight scene later on, if that's what you want."

The Park stared. "You've got to be kidding."

"What's the matter," Peter asked, "haven't you ever made yourself a cup of coffee before?"

The Park continued to stare. And then, unwillingly, begrudgingly, fighting it every step of the way, he smiled.

It wasn't the kind of smile that bestowed friendship, or even respect. It was still backed with wariness, still fueled by potential threat. It did nothing to thaw the ice behind the Park's cold eyes. It was only a smile of recognition— formed by the awareness that he would have handled the situation the same way.

"Come on," the Park said. "I might as well show you the kitchen."

The coffee was rich and aromatic, and Peter supposed that it was probably delicious. But even as he sipped, he was in no mood to appreciate the taste. He was too busy trying not to avoid being creeped out by the spectacle of the Park, speaking in Peter's own voice as he used the cellular phone to offer his excuses to Liz.

"Yeah, it's okay," the Park said, speaking into the phone. "Guy gave me a scare too. . . . I almost bopped him one before he told me who sent him . . . Harry Osborn. . . . Yeah, Harry. . . . Spotted the guy shooting hoops on some street court downtown, told him he could make big bucks playing one-on-one with me in some commercial for the shoe line, sent him up here to give me a surprise. . . . Yeah, I was surprised all right. . . . I thought it was another crazy, like the guy from two years ago. . . . Yeah . . . yeah . . . yeah, I certainly will have a word with Harry. . . . I'd retaliate with a look-alike for *him* if I knew where to find another guy with that rusted-Brillo hairline. . . . Uh-huh . . . uh-huh . . . right. Yeah. Um, listen, honey, would you terribly mind staying at Keith and Marina's for a while? Me and handsome here have some negotiating to do. . . . I don't know, an hour, maybe less. . . . I'll call you. . . . Fine. What's that? How will you know it's me?" For a fleeting moment the Park looked worried. "I'll tell you what Flash used for a visor, that Halloween he and Sha-Shan did Halloween as Cyclops and Phoenix. . . . Yeah, no imposter could possibly come up with something *that* stupid. . . . Right. See you in a couple of hours. . . . I love you too. . . . Bye-bye."

He clicked off his cellular phone, placed it on the counter, and for several seconds just stood there staring at it, as if expecting it to hop like a frog.

"She doesn't believe a word of it," Peter guessed.

"No." The Park didn't take his eyes off the phone. "But she knows I'm handling it."

Peter hesitated. "Does she . . . know?"

The Park looked exasperated. "Get real, why don't you? How long could she be married to somebody who can walk on walls without knowing?"

"Um." Peter took a sip of his coffee. "Good point." *And I should have known. After all, Mary Jane knew long before I got around to telling her.*

The Park poured another cup from the same pot, lifted it, and put it down hurriedly. "You even drink the way I do. I never knew I'd recognize the way I held a cup . . . but that's *me*, that's the way I do it. If you are a fake, you're certainly a good one."

"I'm no fake," Peter said. He put down his coffee and looked his counterpart in the eyes. "I lived the things you lived. I remember that little house in Forest Hills. The microscope Aunt May and Uncle Ben gave me, the chicken soup Aunt May insisted on cooking up every time the temperature outside went below sixty-five. I remember how, once upon a time, I thought they were the only people I'd ever care about—and how, when I got my powers, I decided to get rich so they'd never have to worry about

THE PRESENT

money again. Isn't that what happened for you, Park?"

The Park leaned against the counter and folded his arms. "Go on."

"I remember testing myself at that wrestling match. Remember? One hundred dollars to the first person who could last five minutes with Crusher Hogan. I remember twirling him like a baton, carrying him up that pole, making an absolute fool of him. I remember silk-screening my Spider-Man outfit, getting an agent, and performing on TV. And I remember the burglar."

The Park seized that with the desperation of a drowning man. "What burglar?"

Peter felt something cold fluttering at the base of his spine. "You don't remember?"

"I have some beach property in Santa Monica that got robbed a couple of years back, but the insurance took care of that. What was so special about that?"

My God, Peter thought. *He really doesn't know.* "Don't you remember, that day at the TV studio? You had just finished your act, and a funny-looking freckled guy in a mac ran right past you."

"Him?" The Park rolled his eyes incredulously. "Oh, man, it's been years since I thought about him. Yeah, he was a burglar, all right; he'd just robbed the gate receipts. But he never ran past me. That old security guard tackled him before he even got close. As I recall, we paid off the guard and the skell and planted an item in the papers saying it was me who tackled him. But that was all. I repeat, what was so special about that?"

Peter had taken gut punches from some of the strongest beings alive. None had affected him quite as profoundly as this. The blood pounding in his ears like an angry beast, he somehow managed to find the voice to ask what he was afraid he already knew. "And he never murdered Uncle Ben?"

The Park stepped away from the counter, his face a mask of sudden anger. "My uncle Ben and aunt May are both alive and well and living in a luxury condo in Boca Raton. He's a literacy volunteer and the treasurer of the local Everglades Preservation Society, and she runs night classes on physical fitness for senior citizens. They'll both live another twenty years; we should all be as healthy as they are. Now, will you please tell me what this is all about?"

Peter's voice was a dry croak. "I told you. I'm you. And you're me."

"I see. And since we've already established that you're not a clone..." The Park's eyes narrowed. "Please. Don't even try to tell me that I'm the clone. I'll throw you right out of here."

"And I wouldn't blame you." Peter shook his head. "You're no clone. At least... if you are, I don't know about it, and that's your own business anyway. We're just ... different versions of each other. I come from a place where that security guard ran a little slower. Where the burglar ran past me, and I was so full of myself I couldn't be bothered to stop him. Where he got away—and later murdered Uncle Ben in front of Aunt May's eyes."

"You're talking about an alternate universe," the Park said.

"Well, basically, yeah."

"And I'm supposed to believe this crock?"

Peter averted his eyes. "I know it's hard. But you're looking at the proof. Think about it. How many people look exactly like you and can do all the things you do?"

The Park tried to take another sip of his coffee, but his hands were shaking too badly. "So you became a basketball player too?"

"No. The death of Uncle Ben taught me that with great power comes great responsibility. I stayed Spider-Man, but I used my powers to protect people."

"This is getting better and better," the Park said. "You became a costumed super hero. Like the X-Men."

"Like my X-Men," Peter said. "Not like yours."

"Ah. We finally get to the point. You don't approve of my world's X-Men."

"They've imprisoned a lot of good people," Peter said.

"And a lot of bad," the Park countered.

THE PRESENT

"But at what price?" Peter asked. "Maybe it's just because you're rich and you're comfortable and you have everything you could possibly want. Maybe you're too insulated here, and too attached to your fame and your money and the way people treat you like some kind of hero. But I've seen the way your world works! There are people out there living in fear. People who are hunted and terrorized just because of what they are. People who have to decide whether they want to sell their souls to the government or never be seen again! It's not right, Park! Don't you feel any sense of responsibility whatsoever?"

The Park stood there for several seconds, his eyes closed and his fists tightly clenched at his side. Eventually, he looked up, and flashed something that was more grimace than smile. "I see what alternate world you come from. The one where I turned out to be a real jerk."

"Now, wait just one minute—"

"No," the Park said, "you wait. You've talked long enough, and now it's my turn."

Peter fell speechless.

"In the first place," the Park said, "I do feel a sense of responsibility. A responsibility toward my wife, and toward my children, and toward the people who come to see me play, and toward the kids who look at me as a role model, and toward the government that pays me to be its spokesman, and toward the country that gave me opportunities I wouldn't have found anywhere else. I live up to those responsibilities every minute of every day, mister, and you do *not* have the right to tell where they start and where they end. All right?"

Peter just stared at him.

"In the second place—assuming this whole alternate-world story of yours is on the level—what makes you think that putting on a silly costume and fighting crime is handling your responsibilities in life any better than I've handled mine?"

"The people I've protected," Peter said. "The lives I've saved—"

"Oh, really. Well, let's talk about that. We've already

established that you set free the man who killed your uncle Ben. What happened to your aunt May?"

Peter averted his eyes. "She died a couple months back. She'd been . . . ailing for years."

"Okay," the Park said. "And as I've already pointed out, my aunt May's in terrific shape. I guess having her loving husband at her side, and not having to worry about money all the time, makes a difference with a woman that age. Let's go on. Are you married?"

Peter seized on that happy fact like a drowning man. "Yes. To a woman I love very much."

"But not to Liz."

"No."

"All right. Fair enough. I won't ask who. I'm sure you feel just as strongly about her as I do about Liz. But you knew Liz before the spider bite, right? What happened to her with you out of the picture? Did she get married?"

"Yes." He did not add that it was to a man who turned her life into a nightmare of violence and madness.

The Park nodded. "I don't need any details. I can see from your face that it wasn't a pretty picture. Which is too bad, because you saw how happy my Liz is. Let's move on. We won't even count my children, because if you never married Liz, they were never born. What about your love life? If you didn't marry Liz right out of high school, like I did, I suppose you played the field awhile."

"A little," Peter said. "But what does that have to—"

"Answer this truthfully, hero: were they all better off for knowing you?"

Peter thought of Betty Brant, whose heart he had broken, and whose husband he had been unable to save. He thought of Gwen Stacy, who had seen her father murdered, and who had then herself been killed. He thought of Deb Whitman, who had almost been driven mad by the suspicion of his life as Spider-Man. He thought of Jean DeWolff, who he'd only seen as a friend, but who had carried the secret of her love for him to her grave. And finally, he thought of Mary Jane, whose life with him was

THE PRESENT

best described as fleeting moments of perfect happiness interspersed with long days and longer nights of uncertainty and fear. And he said nothing.

The Park was on a roll. "Well, I can see the answer to that question. Let's ask about your other friends. Flash Thompson, for instance. You knew him in high school, didn't you? You didn't like him—and back then, I didn't either—but he turned out to be an okay guy. Well, my Flash is a successful personal trainer, with celebrity clients all over the country. He's married to a woman who's nuts about him, he has two kids he adores, and a reputation for being the one responsible for my success. What happened to your Flash?"

Peter thought of his Flash, who had drifted since his stint in the army, unable to give his life direction or maintain any long-term relationships. His Flash had struggled with a drinking problem and a tendency toward explosive anger. His Flash had never been happy, and may have been constitutionally incapable of being happy. He thought of his Flash and again he said nothing.

"Can't say anything good about Flash, either, huh?" the Park said. A demonic light had entered his eyes; it was as if part of him enjoyed this, and part of him viewed it with the horrified fascination he'd accord a train wreck. "What about Harry? Did you ever meet Harry?"

Yes, he'd met Harry. Harry had been his roommate and his best friend. His Harry had been the son of the insane super-villain known as the Green Goblin. Abuse at the hands of his increasingly unstable father had led to a drug problem, a nervous breakdown, and ultimately his own adoption of the Green Goblin's insanity. It was Harry who'd married Liz and turned her life into hell on Earth. Like his father, Norman, Harry had eventually been consumed by his hatred for Spider-Man, and eventually died, but not before he'd killed, looted, and left random terror in his wake.

When Peter failed to answer, the Park pressed on. "My Harry's one of the most sought-after business managers in the country. He and Mary Jane are as happy as two human beings can be. But you wouldn't know that, would you? Because I guess you weren't any good for him either. How many ruined lives does that make, Peter? Should I start making a checklist?''

"G-go to hell."

"Why should I? I have heaven right here. Hell's more your neck of the woods, isn't it? At least, that's certainly the picture I'm getting . . ."

Peter couldn't take any more. He leapt out of his chair and went for the Park's throat.

But this time the Park was ready for him, sidestepping the blind lunge, grabbing Peter by the arm, and adding his own strength to the charge. Peter hit the countertop with enough force to knock the breath out of him. He tried to toss the Park aside, but it was impossible. His counterpart had him in a thoroughly professional headlock, and was pressing his advantage for all it was worth.

"Don't stop now," the Park said. "I'm sure we're only skimming the surface. Let's take a closer look at all the people you've helped, and all the lives you've saved. Think of them, Peter. Add them up together, and tell me right now that there are enough of them to balance out the mess you must have made of everything else."

And something happened. For a heartbeat, Peter was no longer fighting his alternate-world double in a kitchen larger than some of the apartments he'd rented. He was in a realm of his own, watching a parade of familiar faces condemn him with accusing looks. He saw Captain Stacy, crushed to death by the wreckage of a battle between Dr. Octopus and Spider-Man. He saw Professor Miles Warren, a good man driven mad by deaths he believed Spider-Man had caused. He saw J. Jonah Jameson, so consumed by his inexplicable hatred for the wall-crawler that at times it overshadowed almost everything else in his life. He saw Ned Leeds, who had been murdered only in order to be framed as the man behind the mask of a particularly murderous villain known as the Hobgoblin. He saw Venom, the merger of two creatures, one human and one alien, united into a psychotic killing machine by a hatred for

THE PRESENT

Spider-Man. He saw the people Spider-Man hadn't been able to save; the people who might have lived full and sane lives if they hadn't wanted to fight Spider-Man, or befriend Spider-Man, or be like Spider-Man, or prove themselves in front of Spider-Man, but who were instead swept up in the circle of madness that seemed to follow Spider-Man wherever he went.

He saw all that, and more, before he realized that the Park was no longer restraining him. Instead, the NBA star was at the opposite end of the kitchen, cellular phone in hand, watching him tremble beneath the twin demons of shame and guilt. The Park was watching him carefully, obviously waiting for another attack—but he was also grinning mirthlessly, in the cruel way common to all bullies who understand that they've scored a direct hit.

And Peter Parker realized what had bothered him so much about the photographs in the Park's study.

They were more than mementos of a life lived.

They were souvenirs of a revenge lusted after and achieved.

Once, less than an hour before the spider bite changed his life forever, he had faced the backs of some laughing high-school bullies and said, *Someday they'll be sorry. Sorry they laughed at me.* He remembered that moment as clearly as he remembered the spider bite itself: the hopeless, but sincerely meant, vow of the teenage boy who considered himself unappreciated and alone. He remembered meaning that vow as, up until that point, he'd never meant anything else.

It had taken a single senseless murder to teach Peter Parker that some vows were more important than others. But the Park had never lived through that awful night—and so he'd devoted his entire life to making them sorry.

He'd started with Flash Thompson. Flash had been the big man on campus, the object of everybody's admiration, and the boyfriend of Liz Allan, the prettiest girl in school. He'd also been Peter Parker's worst enemy since they were both small children: bullying him, calling him names, leading the other kids in their ostracism. What better re-

TIME'S ARROW

venge for a high-school wimp than suddenly becoming a better athlete? Than stealing the bully's girlfriend and marrying her? Than going on to fame and fortune, and seeing to it that the erstwhile bully owed him everything? Than dooming the high-school football star to spend his own life trapped in the shadow of the skinny kid whose life he'd once made miserable?

It was a marvelous revenge, as such things go; total wish-fulfillment always is.

But it was still nothing more than revenge.

And even if it did leave the people in the Park's life better off than they would have been in a world where Peter Parker became Spider-Man instead—it would always carry that taint.

Peter said, "I'm not sure you'll buy this, but I feel sorry for you."

The Park's grin faltered. "Why?"

"You used to be heavily into science. You used to know more than your teachers could tell you. You used to be a total egghead on the subject. It was the one thing you were proud of, the one dream you shared with Uncle Ben and Aunt May. It was part of what the other kids hated about you. But when was the last time you even thought about it?"

Did it take the Park a few seconds to answer? "I gave up that dream. I found another."

"But whose dream, Park? Did you give up everything that was special about you, just to live up to what some stupid high-school bullies thought was important?"

This time the Park didn't answer at all.

"Don't you remember?" Peter asked. "Almost as soon as we could read, science was everything to us. Our heroes were Galileo, Newton, Darwin, Einstein. We dreamed of standing in their shoes, of changing the world for the better, of learning something that nobody ever knew before. Now, I won't pretend I managed it any more than you did—though I have gone back to grad school, so I still might. But we were sidetracked by different things. You were sidetracked by money and the need to impress people

THE PRESENT

whose opinions never mattered. I was sidetracked by the awareness that I couldn't ever stand still when there was something I could do to help. And if some people have paid the price for that . . . well, their faces haunt me every day, but at least I also know I've rescued uncounted numbers of people in danger. I've even saved the world a few times. And right now you have the opportunity to do the same."

The Park's eyes grew dangerous. "I hope you're not talking about what I think you're talking about."

"Face it, Park. You've bought this little patch of heaven with lies. You tell your fans that the X-Men are right and that the government has the right to imprison super-powered people without trial, and I bet you don't even believe it yourself, but you just go on saying it, because they pay you to say it, and because it keeps them off your back, and because they need voices like yours to make it all possible. You're as much a part of this as the X-Men are, because you allowed them to buy you, body and soul."

"Nobody owns me!" the Park snapped.

"Then prove it! This is your moment of truth, Park. Do you just go on letting it all happen, because you're too afraid to get involved—or do you join Magneto and the PLF and stand up for what's right?"

It may have been the most impassioned argument Peter Parker had ever made.

But it was for nothing.

The Park merely sniffed, and opened up his cellular phone. "I don't want anything to do with Magneto. Anybody who'd even think of supporting him and his band of goons should be locked up. And that even includes you. I'm calling nine one one."

Despite everything the Park had said, this was perhaps the last thing Peter would have expected. He'd looked at the Park and seen only another version of himself—somebody who had avoided some of Peter's own mistakes and made others of his own, but who could still be made to see things Peter's way.

TIME'S ARROW

"Hello?" the Park said.

Peter ran past him, and into the opulently appointed living room, aiming for the spotless white sofa beside the sliding doors to the patio. He leapt over the sofa and, shielding his face with his arms, dived right through the doors, surrounding himself with an explosion of hundreds of shards of shattered glass. The leap was so blindingly fast that he'd passed over the terra cotta balcony before the first pieces of glass began to impact on it. Even as he fell, he could hear screams from the street below. No doubt pedestrians who'd looked up, spotted his plunging form, and imagined this a suicidal leap to his death.

Peter flipped in midair, landed against the building across the street, and leapt again, in the next leg of a rapid zigzag descent toward the street.

It took him maybe ten seconds to reach the ground. Not much more than it would have taken if he'd just allowed himself to go splat. But he landed on his feet, among an astonished gaggle of pedestrians who were as disturbed by his safe landing as they would have been by his reduction to pavement pizza.

A woman in a green dress pointed at him. "It's a *sponkie*!"

Peter didn't stick around to protest the political incorrectness of the slur. Instead, he just ran, faster than anybody human could possibly follow. There was a subway station only a couple of blocks away. Once he got underground, it wouldn't be long before he was once again among the allegedly more sympathetic faces of Magneto and the PLF.

But why was his vision so blurred with tears? Why did his heart hurt so much more than the hairline cuts from his passage through the glass door?

Could it be that he'd learned just how bad he'd been for everybody in his life?

Or was it something worse?

THE PRESENT

Like the realization that he'd looked in the face of the man he might have been, and seen only the cold, pitiless stare of a stranger?

CHAPTER TEN

The world had become a clock, inexorably counting down to zero.

With the revelation that Kang's devices had been activated, Blaquesmith and Professor Xavier had plunged back into their repairs with a haste that left care, safety, and human endurance in its wake. Xavier burned his right hand realigning an energy conduit. Blaquesmith tried to reroute the quantum overrides on the timeline isolators and caused a power surge that almost sent the top half of his body into the future while shipping the bottom half into the past. One of them—and if they lived through this day, they'd always argue who—made a software error and ended up wiping out an entire encyclopedia's worth of historical data. But the repairs went on. And while all the timepieces within earshot were atomic and therefore made no noise at all, they could both still imagine they heard the ticking that represented a universe approaching death one second at a time.

For Charles Xavier, who understood only a small part of the technology he was being required to repair, despair loomed especially close. The tasks he'd been set to perform may have been within his capabilities, and he may have been performing them as efficiently as just about anybody on Earth could, but the complexity of the Time Displacement Core was beyond anything he'd ever known. Every time he dared to believe he'd begun to comprehend its basic functions, he came across another component that placed the basic technology farther and farther into the realm of the arcane. He couldn't even tell how well the repairs were going, or how much more remained to be done. He could only hope that Blaquesmith, who was working on the primary systems, understood the science involved even half as well as he let on—and that the automated repair systems were still functioning well enough to complete what he and Blaquesmith could not.

He was still trying to figure out the fastest way to wheel his platform out of the current dead end and closer to the positronic sequencers, when Blaquesmith said to him,

THE PRESENT

from somewhere else in the vast machine, "Professor, we have a problem."

Actually, Charles Xavier thought, *we have several. You're just referring to the newest one.* "What?"

"There's a psionic focusing system that's been totally wiped out by the attack. The backup is still being reconfigured from the bottom up, and it's going to take at least six hours to reboot."

Xavier wasn't sure whether the burning sensation in his eyes came from sweat or blood. "We don't have six hours, Blaquesmith. We're lucky if we have one."

"I know that—which is why we might have to risk hooking you and your Cerebro up to the terminal. If we're lucky, we may be able to use your mind to run the subsidiary computing—and if we're luckier still, you might not be permanently brain damaged by the experience."

Hidden in his claustrophobic little niche, Xavier actually smiled at that. He opened his mouth, to ask Blaquesmith how much time that would shave off their deadline—

—and for a moment remained silent, because he was too lost in thoughts not his own.

The first he sensed were like boiling quicksilver.

(Watching the rain. Individual needles of water. Each one inching downward as slowly as a maggot on a pane of glass. Each one malformed by the wind: visibly flattened on one side, like a little mirror. It's so boring—why don't they hurry up? Don't they already know where they're going? Don't they know that the ground is there waiting for them? Ha. I could slow my reflexes and turn them back into ordinary rain, but I hate not moving—it's too much like standing still, too much like death. Think of the money. Yeah. A hundred grand just for offing some bald guy in a wheelchair. . . .)

And then another mind: crueler, coarser, more arrogant.

(Hope it's Wolverine. Yeah. I love the way he moves: his lurking, his snarl of warning, his full-throttle leap. Wolverine's as good as they come. Knowin' his tricks is almost as good as knowin' Captain America's. An' expensive too. He ain't a public figure, and there just ain't that

much visual sourcing available. Yeah, I hope it's him, 'specially after the way I prepared. But I wouldn't mind it being any of 'em—anythin' that boosts the ol' rep boosts the ol' school. An' I'm nothin' if not a booster of the school. In fact, it's about time I jacked tuition again. . . .)

Blaquesmith practically had to scream it: *"Xavier!"*

Xavier realized that the other man had been calling his name for the better part of a minute now. He shouted back, "I'm all right," even though in truth he was more than a little nauseated. If there was one thing about telepathy that he'd never gotten used to, it was the unrelenting ugliness he found in some minds—especially when contrasted with the unbelievable heights of nobility he found in some others. "I just picked up some thoughts from outside. Kang's sent a pair of professional assassins after us."

Blaquesmith muttered a curse. "It's the worst possible time, Charles. The repairs may be going well, but we still have a lot to do. We can't abandon our work now."

"And we don't have to," Xavier said grimly. "I've already taken precautions."

Night had come upon the winery, bringing with it a cold torrential rain. The saturated ground had swallowed all that it could, and the ankle-deep puddles forming beneath the vines were already beginning to merge into a great black mirror that shimmered and boiled madly from the impact of all the raindrops hammering down from above. It was not the kind of night that most people would have chosen for a walk in the country—even if they were being paid to commit murder.

Nights like these were one of the reasons the two figures in the dark preferred to leave the hands-on fieldwork to those with the proper temperament.

One of the two hunkered down beneath a tree, wincing beneath his hood and skull-face mask as the cold rain soaked through his cape and into his costume. The weather shouldn't have been bothering him as much as it did; his outfit was made of a highly expensive insulating weave

THE PRESENT

with bulletproof Kevlar inserts for added protection. But armor it wasn't, and once saturated, it tended to hold in the water, making it about as comfortable as a wet bathing suit in motel air-conditioning. He wouldn't let it slow him down, of course—true professionals suffered discomfort as just part of the price of doing business. He'd get the muties with the same kind of efficiency that he'd always been able to get anybody else he ever went after. But once this job was over, it would be back to the classroom for him.

He had always much preferred teaching to doing.

He raised his arm and spoke into a transmitter on his wrist. "Hey," he whispered. "Jackrabbit! You in position yet?"

The voice that came through his ear mike seemed to speak all in a rush, without any discernible pauses between the words. He sounded like that guy in the old Federal Express commercials—except that guy probably slowed down once in a while, at least off camera. Taskmaster's partner on this mission spoke like a hyperactive chipmunk *all the time*. "Don't call me Jackrabbit, you skull-headed sap. That's not my name and you know it!"

"Ain't a bad name, speedy. Certainly sounds better than that first one you had." He chuckled nastily. "The Whizzer. Ain't ya got any command of slang at all? I swear, you're the only bad guy I ever heard of that picked hisself a name worse than that fella Paste-Pot Pete."

"Get off my back, Taskmaster, or I'm warnin' ya—"

"Warn me all ya want," the Taskmaster said, his voice suddenly cold and dangerous. "But never forget, Speed Demon—or whatever you're callin' yourself today—your fancy footwork don't impress me. Remember why the boss put me in charge? 'Cause I'm the guy who took you out five times in a row in practice."

Speed Demon emitted a high-speed string of curses too quickly for any of them to be discernible as individual words.

The Taskmaster wasn't impressed. But then, he was never impressed. "Just get your overrated rear in gear and

TIME'S ARROW

do two more circles around the perimeter. We'll go in soon as the place is swept."

"You got it...." Speed Demon said. For one fleeting instant, wind noises wailed through the little speaker. Then his partner's voice returned, and this time he spoke at a more normal speed. "Did three circles, not two. Nobody in sight. If there are any defenders, they're hiding."

Showing off again, Taskmaster thought. "Ain't no Defenders here," he said. "They broke up years ago. We're expecting X-Men."

"You know what I mean," Speed Demon cried angrily.

"Only 'cause I'm a smart guy," the Taskmaster said. "But if you was one of my students, I'd still give ya two demerits for the error in identification." He took a deep breath, basked in the priceless entertainment afforded by the frustrated imprecations coming through his communicator, and decided that he'd baited the Speed Demon enough for one night. "I'm gonna go in and draw 'em out. You hold yourself in reserve and wait for the fireworks. *Capisce*?"

"*Capisce*," his partner said. Though he clearly didn't like it.

The Taskmaster took a deep breath and ran for the house.

A veteran observer of super heroic lore watching his shadowy form race across the winery grounds might have mistaken him for Captain America. After all, there weren't many men with that much grace, that much perfect economy of motion. Even the greatest athlete in the world could have devoted years of training just to learn how to run through the dark with such uncanny skill.

It had taken the Taskmaster half an hour and a ten-dollar videotape of *Great Super Hero Footage*, fished out of the cutout bin at Al's Corner Video.

It was that simple. Some people had photographic memories. The Taskmaster had photographic reflexes. He could learn how to do anything, as long as he got to watch somebody else doing it first. Thanks to that and the miracle of cable television, he was now a true Renaissance man:

THE PRESENT

he could pole-vault, play classical piano, flamenco-dance, perform open-heart surgery, perform amazing feats of prestidigitation, fight like Bruce Lee *and* Jackie Chan, and demonstrate the Joy of Painting, complete with happy little trees. There literally wasn't any field of endeavor that hadn't been wide open to him.

But once he reached a certain age and it came time for him to decide just what he was going to do with his life, anybody who knew him as a kid would have been utterly unsurprised by what he found as his calling.

Specifically, he wanted to teach.

Even more specifically, he wanted to teach criminals. He wanted to take his instant understanding of the fighting techniques used by super heroes, and earn big bucks sharing his expert knowledge of the best ways to fight back.

To this end, he'd devoted the better part of a weekend to watching every super hero available on videotape. He'd emerged from his parents' basement teeming with the kind of martial-arts mastery that less fortunate types had needed years of training to acquire.

He had even become adept at using their various weapons—an eclectic set of skills that had resulted in a costume best described as unusually busy. Forget the hood, the cape and the skull mask. He also wore a shield, cut along the lines of Captain America's, on his right arm; a broadsword, designed to match the Swordsman's, sheathed at his waist; a billy club, identical to Daredevil's, strapped to his lower leg; a quiver with collapsible bow, like Hawkeye's, slung on his back; spring-loaded claws, inspired by Wolverine's, set into housings on each wrist. He also had boomerangs, climbing rope, *shuriken*, daggers, *sai*, steel-edged throwable playing cards (all aces of spades), a bolo, and retractable Rollerblades mounted on each boot.

Of course, one of the major reasons he preferred to limit his activies to the classroom is that some days it took him the better part of two hours just to suit up.

He managed to get within forty yards of the house before he heard the woman's voice inside his head:

TIME'S ARROW

The Professor's right, Cyclops. This is a truly disgusting individual.

It wasn't the first time the Taskmaster had encountered telepathy. One of his most popular seminars at his super-villain school was a weekend course on using addictive country-music lyrics to block out psionic attacks. But the temps he'd hired to help him run the demonstrations were all second-raters, recruited from the personal ads in the back of The *Village Voice*. They may have been able to induce migraines at fifty paces, but their shared mental wattage wouldn't have been enough to impress Dionne Warwick. He'd needed to borrow amplification equipment from Hydra just to make them dangerous at all.

This voice was something else entirely. It was pure and strong and reverberated in his head like a cannon blast going off between his ears. A lesser man would have passed out. The Taskmaster weathered the shock; but reacted too quickly: leaping up, performing a perfect triple somersault from a standing position, and throwing his circular shield in the direction where the psychic blast seemed strongest.

He threw blindly, so he didn't see it being deflected. But then, he was the Taskmaster: he didn't need to see. He could tell just from the sudden tonal change in the whirring noise it made as it sliced through the air.

He hadn't heard any impact. Not even energy impact. That, combined with the persuasive demonstration in the fine art of telepathy, strongly suggested telekinesis.

He didn't need a house to fall on him. (Though, like witchcraft, this line of work always left that as a definite possibility.) After all, he'd been briefed. There was only one telekinetic among the X-Men.

"Phoenix," he cried, with great enthusiasm. "I was hopin' to meet you!"

"I know," she said out loud, somewhere above him. "I saw the nauseating mental images. Got to hand it to you, Taskmaster—you're a pretty nasty piece of work even by super-villain standards."

He sensed the air charging directly behind him. It was

THE PRESENT

maybe a fraction of a second's warning, but he took advantage of it, dodging the telekinetic blast and tossing a handful of *shuriken* into the darkness above. It was another blind toss, handicapped as he was by the need to stay out of the way of her mental assaults, but this time he had her voice to guide him. He heard three of the *shuriken* suddenly slow down and fall, heard three others batted aside by some kind of energy blast.

Cursing, he ducked, rolled, and came up in time to see the two of them, floating above his head. One was the woman, Phoenix. A beautiful redhead in big shoulder-pads who just happened to be one of the most powerful telepath-telekinetic combinations of the planet. She radiated confidence. Even facing an enemy, like now, there was something about the way she carried herself (thirty feet off the ground) that to Taskmaster instantly branded her as a babe to be reckoned with. He was sorry he'd have to kill her; the sheer depth of the grim disgust in her eyes turned him on like not many women could.

The other was a tall, muscular man in a blue jumpsuit, whose thick visor marked him as the team leader, Cyclops. He would have been harder to read, since the upper half of his face was obscured by his hood and visor, but there was no mistaking the feelings behind the thin grimace down below. He took personal offense at anybody who dared attack the pretty lady. Real personal offense.

Cyclops said, "All right, mister. Because we're worried about more important things than you right now, we're going to be charitable and assume that you're just in this for the money and that you honestly have no idea what kind of cause you're fighting for. Under the circumstances, if you turn around and leave, we'll refrain from giving you the kind of reception you deserve. You have five seconds."

The Taskmaster ignored him and turned his attention to Phoenix. "Hey, babe, do you actually date this guy?"

It might have been interesting to hear her response to that.

But that's when Speed Demon struck.

TIME'S ARROW

Even for Taskmaster, whose reaction time was second to none, there was almost no discernible transition between his absence and his arrival. He just appeared in their midst, as suddenly as a bright spot projected from a flashlight a hundred yards away. By the time anybody realized that he'd come plowing the earth with cupped hands, the shock wave of soaking mud had already lashed into the air and splattered against both of the floating hero-types with a force great enough to knock them out of the sky.

The X-Men may have been taken by surprise, but they were on the ball; they each took separate action even as they fell toward the ground. Cyclops fired a wide beam of scarlet energy at the spot where Speed-Demon stood. It splattered mud in all directions and dug out a crater the size of a small car, but the mercurial one was already way out of range by the time the beam hit.

As for Phoenix, she quickly arrested her fall, righting herself and hovering for the split second it would have taken her to catch Cyclops as well. She was so good at this that there was hardly any noticeable delay at all. Most of her opponents wouldn't have been able to take advantage of it, but most of her opponents were not Taskmaster. In less than the heartbeat it took her to regain her balance, he was already whipping a favorite weapon from his belt and tossing it at her head with an accuracy that would have been deadly had Taskmaster not been more interested in enjoying himself.

The small white object sailed past her head, seemingly missing it . . . then, pulled up short by the cable it trailed behind, looped around her neck three times in an instant, tightening enough to cut off her air at once.

Taskmaster pulled. Hard. She broadcast pain in all directions, lost concentration, and hit the mud barely a second after her visored boyfriend did.

Stunned by the fall, but still concerned for his lady, Cyclops managed to fire a quick optic beam in Taskmaster's direction. But Taskmaster had calculated the probable trajectory of the beam even before it was fired, and leapt over it with ease. A video librarian might have recognized

THE PRESENT

the maneuver as something Spider-Man had been filmed doing seven months before. The energy beam in that case had been a high-intensity laser, not an optic blast, but the basic principle was the same, and Taskmaster's move was in no way inferior to Spider-Man's original.

Taskmaster was about to appropriate a fondly remembered Daredevil clip in order to dodge the follow-up blast Cyclops was about to fire—but then he felt another rush of wind, and saw that Speed Demon had it covered. The onetime Whizzer was running around the sprawled X-Man in ever decreasing circles, no doubt trying to asphyxiate Cyclops with the vacuum.

It was a nice trick, if it worked. Taskmaster had his doubts.

But that didn't really matter. At the very least, it gave him a few seconds to take care of the pretty lady.

He covered the distance between himself and her struggling form in five easy strides, taking up the slack on his cable as he went. With each step, his boots kept sinking a foot or more into the increasingly soft mud. The woman was herself covered with it; her uniform and gorgeous red hair now black with rain-slick filth. The only sign of brightness that remained was her spotlessly white teeth, grimacing for air as she struggled to remove the tightening cable from her throat.

He heard optic blasts cut the night, somewhere behind him, but he also heard the whirring sound of the Speed Demon racing in circles at full speed. He figured as long as he kept hearing that particular sound combination, he was free to deal with the lady at leisure.

And so he knelt down beside her—drawing the cable taut with a force that yanked her head off the ground—and said, "I don't blame ya for being taken by surprise, babe. Most folks woulda been. They see one of these things and they think it's just another toy. Somethin' for the kid to fool around with. Maybe, if they're trivia buffs, they remember it's the gizmo President Nixon did tricks with on the stage of the Grand Ole Opry in Nashville.

"But there's somethin' not many people know about

TIME'S ARROW

yo-yos, babe. Namely—they're weapons. They was developed in the Philippines for street fightin'. Used properly, the spinnin' part hits hard enough to make a real unsightly dent in your opponent's skull—an' it even retracts, so you can bop him again right away. Over there, a tough guy with a yo-yo is more dangerous than a tough guy with a switchblade, 'cause he has somethin' the guy with the knife don't have: range.'' The Taskmaster grinned beneath his skull mask. '' 'Course, this partic'lar yo-yo uses a constricting adamantium monofilament for string. Which means that, soon as I give it the word, it's gonna tighten up even more an' take that pretty mutie head of yours clean off!''

On the word *off* he thumbed the controller in his palm, commanding the cable to do just that.

But though he felt the telltale vibration that indicated the controller was indeed sending the signal, her pretty mutie head remained precisely where it was.

It didn't make sense. The adamantium monofilament was state-of-the-art personal weapons technology, obtained from a certain costumed terrorist group in exchange for two semesters of free tuition for their trainees in the Far East Division. It constricted with the kind of force capable of slicing a diamond like soft butter. There shouldn't have been a paranormal on the face of the planet with skin strong enough to resist it, including the Hulk. And next to them, this slip of a girl was tissue paper. How could she—?

Then he realized.

The monofilament may have been wrapped around her neck, but it wasn't touching her skin.

She was repelling it with her telekinesis, keeping it a millimeter away from her flesh on all sides, so that it constricted nothing but empty space.

"Nice try," he said, meaning it. "But I been studyin' up on you psionic types, an' from everything I hear, all that heavy concentrating's a major strain on your mind. I wonder how long you'll be able to keep this up if I in-

THE PRESENT

crease the pressure to, lessay, a couple of tons per square inch?''

He upped the power slowly, because he wanted to enjoy this. The controllers strained. But so did she. She arched her back, allowing the rain to wash the mud from her lovely face; revealing a contorted grimace that could only be the look of a lady mutie being pushed past her limits.

If she didn't fold in another couple of seconds, he had options. For a moment he considered drawing his sword and burying it in her head, but the Wolverine claws were a much better idea. Killing her with her teammate's own weapon was the kind of once-in-a-lifetime hoot that made this business the thrilling growth industry that it was.

He hesitated just long enough to see what Cyclops and Speed Demon were doing.

It was hard to tell, between the darkness and the rain and the sheer velocity of the battle, but it looked like Speed Demon had Cyclops sussed. He'd trapped Cyclops at the bottom of a pit dug at super speed. Speed Demon's arms blurred in the act of shoveling tons of mud back into the hole. Each new tumbling load of mud hit another optic blast on the way down—an impact that sent it exploding upward, like geysering earth. But Speed Demon was still filling up the pit faster than Cyclops could bat the mud away. Cyclops would no doubt be buried alive in less than a minute.

Taskmaster liked that strategy. It showed originality and style and genuine satisfaction with the work. Maybe he'd misjudged Speed Demon. Maybe, when this job was done, he'd even talk to the guy about signing up as a lecturer at the school.

But first he'd have to finish the job, which he wouldn't even be able to start until he first finished the girl.

He looked down at Phoenix, and saw that she was still resisting the pressure even at the highest setting, but it was taking everything she had. She'd never be able to resist an assault from another angle. Grinning widely beneath his mask, he popped the claws on his right arm, and drew it all the way behind his back, in preparation for the blow that would carve out her heart.

In Limbo, Lireeb descended the spiral staircase that was his least favorite furnishing of the castle. It was a free-floating Möbius strip, that hovered in the middle of nothingness like the bad idea that it was. Many strangers to the castle had wandered onto its literally infinite length and spent all of eternity descending one loop as their past and future selves ascended another loop just out of reach. Lireeb was one of the few beings who could enter and leave the spiral staircase at will—and he had to do so often, since the Möbius staircase was the best way to reach some of the more inaccessible parts of the castle. But he still hated it. Infinitely long stairways took forever to dust.

Not that Kang appreciated it, once Lireeb appeared in the library, a vast room filled with books from timelines that now no longer existed. Kang was lounging in an easy chair, reading a famous science fiction anthology from the early 1970s. The conqueror merely asked, "And is all going according to plan?"

"Yes. I have checked on the other two teams. The Wrecking Crew is keeping Storm too busy to deal with the approaching monsoon, and Taskmaster and Speed Demon are doing a thoroughly professional job with the defenders at the winery."

Kang smiled and flung the book into a corner—where it was intercepted and reshelved by a beeping maintenance droid. He stood, and marched to Lireeb's side. "What about the Time Arrows?"

"They haven't built up even a fraction of the energy they need to achieve the results you want. Are you disappointed?"

"Not at all," Kang said, his leer clearly visible through his purple mask. "They were never designed to do the job alone."

CHAPTER ELEVEN

Spider-Man rejoined the PLF just before their briefing, his churning emotions well hidden beneath his familiar red mask. By then, the little alcove they used for a meeting room was packed with costumed types muttering among themselves. Somebody had set up a slide projector on a rolling table, and a couple of rows of metallic folding chairs facing a plaster wall that, though not strictly white, was still close enough to serve as a makeshift screen. The cliques that formed within even the most tightly knit organizations were clearly visible in the groups that stood apart in the various corners of the room. Sandman, Hydro-Man, and Electro stood whispering in one corner. Night Thrasher and Speedball discussed something serious in another. Titania and Volcana were both competing for Razorback's attention in a third. Rhino sat by himself near the back, muttering. Bishop was the only one who'd already claimed a seat. He sat front row center, stonily watching the blank screen, as if it already bore secrets known only to him.

The room was illuminated by battery-driven floodlights that had been strapped to the ceiling at all four corners. It had the look of a hasty job. Spider-Man had the idea that the meeting room had never been used before, and had only been set up for the specific occasion.

Razorback waved as Spider-Man entered. "Hiya, webhead! Did the duck get ya them chemicals you was lookin' for?"

Both women gave Spider-Man a look that didn't exactly encourage him to join that particular social gathering. So he just shot Razorback a thumbs-up. Actually, he hadn't had time to brew state-of-the-art web fluid for tonight's battle. Instead, he'd been forced to brew up a somewhat older mixture that was not nearly as strong or as stable as the recipe he'd been using for several years now. Given his emotional state, he was surprised he'd managed to complete even that. He still had several full cartridges of the good stuff before he'd need to start using the good-but-not-quite-as-good. He could only hope the difference wouldn't prove critical in tonight's battle.

THE PRESENT

He waved at Speedball and Night Thrasher, nodded warily at Sandman, Hydro-Man, Rhino, and Electro, then made his way to the lone figure seated in the front row. "Bish," he said, with a false joviality that did little to hide his mood. "How goes it?"

Bishop glanced up, showing neither relief nor cordiality. "Spider-Man. You're almost late."

"Where I come from, almost late is the same thing as being on time."

"Not where I'm from," Bishop said curtly. Then his features softened. "Did you find what you were looking for?"

Spider-Man shuddered. "No. I don't like alternate worlds, Bish."

"They take getting used to," Bishop said, with a surprising degree of empathy.

Spider-Man sat down beside him. "Have you learned anything else about our friends here?"

"Absolutely," Bishop said. He lowered his voice to near inaudibility. "And I wanted to talk to you about that. In the past few hours, I have managed to spend some time with everybody in this room, and I've learned that this is an alliance of necessity alone, with the tensile stability of tissue paper. Electro, Sandman, Hydro-Man, Volcana, and Titania don't trust Night Thrasher and Speedball, and vice versa. Nobody seems to like or respect the Rhino, but everybody's wary of him. The only one who seems to get along with everybody is Razorback, though as you can see he reserves his full charm for the women. I can't say I feel wholly confident about the chances of a group this volatile remaining together long enough to do the job that needs to be done. I wouldn't be surprised to find one or more of them working for the government."

"Swell," Spider-Man muttered. "And who would you suspect? The Rhino?"

"He is the most obvious choice. With his every word and deed, he establishes that he's stranger to all and friend to none. He certainly bears no loyalty for anybody other than himself. But everybody's already suspicious of him;

they wouldn't give him any more secrets than they had to. No"—Bishop shook his head—"if I had to pick one person as my hypothetical spy, it would have to be your pigheaded trucker friend."

"Razorback? Oh, come *on* . . ."

"He's uncomplicated, idealistic, friends with everybody, and a lot smarter than he acts—which frankly isn't hard, since he plays up the country-bumpkin act more than anybody I've known this side of Cannonball. People like that never have difficulty learning the innermost secrets of an organization—which makes him a potential security risk. Especially on this world, where he's no doubt been subjected to pressures that the Razorback you know never encountered. There's no evidence one way or the other—yet—but I'm going to keep my eyes on him, and I strongly advise you do the same."

Spider-Man stared at his companion with horrified awe. "You thrive on this, don't you? Suspicion, betrayal, never trusting anybody."

Bishop returned the look with eerie calm. "Yes."

Spider-Man was about to say what he thought of that, when Magneto arrived, entering through the back of the room. He did not greet his troops as he marched up the center aisle, did not even bother to make eye contact—just marched straight ahead, with no regard for anything but his destination. It would have been easy to attribute this to sheer coldness, but Spider-Man, who knew a lot about masks, understood at once that the rigidity was Magneto's way of holding tension in check. There was a lot at stake tonight. And as leader, he did not have the luxury of showing doubt.

Aliya entered behind Magneto, but she did not accompany him all the way to the front of the room. Instead she remained just inside the door, acknowledging the stares of the others with encouraging nods. She spared only the slightest glance for Spider-Man and Bishop before she looked away, and stared long and hard at Electro and his fellow villains.

Beneath his mask, Spider-Man winced. Bishop was

THE PRESENT

right. This wasn't anybody's idea of a tightly knit army. If they were held together by anything, it was a common enemy—and the sheer will of their leader.

Magneto assumed his place at the front of the room, waited for the others to take their seats, and said, "It has been a long and bitterly fought battle for all of us. We've seen colleagues fall, friends taken and imprisoned. Tonight, we finally face the culmination of everything we've fought for. Tonight, we're finally going to face our enemy head-on."

The overhead lights dimmed. Speedball, who was running the projector (just like any other high school nerd, as Spider-Man knew from personal experience), plugged it in by handing the power cord to Electro, who closed his fist around the plug.

The wall beside Magneto lit up with a capital letter P superimposed over the streamlined graphic of a winged horse.

Sandman whistled. "You're not kiddin'. This *is* big."

"The biggest," Magneto said. "Project: Pegasus. Originally a cutting-edge think tank where some of the world's greatest minds were charged with the development of renewable energy resources, it gained a new charter after the passage of the Kelly Act. At that point it became nothing more than a state-of-the-art prison, charged with the incarceration of paranormals who refused to follow the official X-Men line. Slide."

The image blinked and became an aerial photograph of a drab-looking government facility within a vast fenced-in compound. Magneto pointed out a helipad, a water tower, a series of small housing facilities and administration structures, and the old aircraft hangar that housed the motor pool, identifying them quickly and without much interest before moving on.

"As far as the locals are concerned, Pegasus is only a small army facility, operating with a skeleton crew under minimal security. This is a lie, maintained by the federal government in a thin and transparent attempt to hide the true reason for all the activity in the area. In truth, the bulk of the complex is underground, housed in three heavily reinforced—and interconnected—silos that each penetrates a hundred meters underground. The entrances to these silos are hidden beneath these barrack structures, here, here, and here." Magneto indicated the places with his pointing stick. "There has been a continual flow of construction materials and army engineers into the site for years now, but since all the modifications have been underground, well out of sight of my satellite surveillance, it has long been next to impossible to obtain an accurate layout before newer modifications made such intelligence worthless."

Electro was so stunned that the slide dimmed momentarily. "I didn't even know we *had* satellite surveillance."

"Extensive satellite surveillance," Magneto said. "I didn't see the point of sharing that information, since it wasn't providing us the intelligence we needed. It certainly wasn't responsible for obtaining what you're about to see. Slide."

The image blinked and became a detailed diagram of the three silos set in the earth. "Ladies and gentlemen, I give you the blueprints to Project: Pegasus."

That caused a buzz, loudest among the villains. Night Thrasher said, "How current is this information?"

"It was downloaded from their computers less than forty-eight hours ago."

"Wow!" said Speedball. "Who did that?"

"A very reliable source," Magneto said crisply. He glanced at the screen, furrowed his brow, and moved on. "I do not expect you to read these diagrams off the screen, of course. We have prepared hard copies, which we expect you to study on the way to the assault. The important thing to know is this: It took us years of planning just to get to this point. And if we fail tonight, we may never have a chance this perfect again. Which is why it's vitally important that this operation go off smoothly, with each and every operative—including our two newcomers, Bishop and Spider-Man—performing to their utmost capability. Everything—and by *everything*, I very specifically include

THE PRESENT

the future course of history on this planet—will depend on all three teams quickly and efficiently accomplishing what they've been sent to do. Slide."

The new image was a black-and-white ground-level photograph of an undistinguished-looking building with no visible windows and only one visible door. There was a satellite dish on the roof. "First Team will cut off the phone lines and the external power supply, both of which converge through this building near the fenced perimeter. The team that tackles this objective will be the one most isolated from the others, which means, with any luck, they'll also serve the function of diverting some of the security forces away from the main silo. Indeed, if they perform their first task quickly enough, they are to ensure further security involvement by proceeding to loudly and showily destroy as many of the other nearby buildings as possible. Night Thrasher will be team leader, commanding Hydro-Man, Electro, and the Rhino." Magneto permitted himself a smile. "I'm certain that you'll be able to do some impressive damage."

The Rhino laughed unpleasantly. "Hey. Damage is my business."

"I'm sure. Slide." The new image showed a metallic structure with a massive steel door. There were small windows along the sides and a larger structure rising in the background. The foreground was a blurred image of two soldiers in a jeep, caught in the act of driving past the facility. "This is the armory, which conceals the entrance to Silo North, which contains housing, medical, and recreational facilities for the bulk of the Project's considerable security force. Most of their light weaponry is also stored at this location. Any all-out assault on this structure will be met with an equally fervid response, further diluting any forces that may be deployed elsewhere. I will personally lead this team, backed by Sandman, Titania, and Volcana."

"Whoo-eeee!" Sandman exclaimed. "I get to work with the babes!"

There was general laughter all around, except from Titania. "Give it a rest, Marko. You know you'll never get your hands on me."

"I already did, babe. Think back to your last trip to the beach."

This time the laughter was even louder—even from Spider-Man, who couldn't help wondering if it was true.

Magneto permitted the laughter for exactly ten seconds, and then cut it off in an instant, with a single icily-spoken word. "Finally"—and here he glared at the others, commanding their attention by his presence alone—"we have the main assault force, which is assigned to take out the internal stasis generator. Slide." The new image was a photograph taken from some point near the top of the silo, revealing a spiral walkway that descended toward what looked like a featureless white floor. The walls were lined with doors all the way down. The walkways were inhabited with dozens of armed soldiers and white-coated technicians, captured in what looked like a typically boring moment from their daily routine. "The prisoners are all housed in the central silo, but as they're all kept unconscious in a stasis field, we cannot break in to free them directly. Our only hope is to penetrate this doorway at the bottom of Silo South, which houses the research and technical support facilities." Magneto indicated a barely visible opening on the ground level far below. "This chamber houses the internal power source for the stasis grid. The instant we disable that, the prisoners wake up and with any luck start breaking out en masse. Once that happens, we have allies, and this war is won. Lights."

The lights came on. Magneto faced the others. "This location is obviously the most critical objective, and so we have chosen the team least known by the opposition. Aliya will be team leader, commanding Speedball, Razorback, Bishop, and Spider-Man."

"Are you sure that's a good idea?" Night Thrasher asked. "I mean, with their abilities so untested?"

"Yeah," Rhino groused. "We don't even know these guys."

The general murmur of agreement stopped immediately

THE PRESENT

upon a single sardonic chuckle from Magneto. "Do you truly wish to make me repeat myself?"

There was silence of the sort that could precede either further argument, or resentful surrender. Spider-Man honestly didn't know which way it would go.

Then Razorback said, "Why, heck, that's good enough for me. Lookin' forward to kickin' some tail, Spider-Man. An' you, too, Bish."

"Yeah," Electro said. "Way I figure it, we're all in this together."

And the members of the PLF cheered. For Spider-Man, who had so recently been declared enemy by the most familiar face imaginable, who had seen a life he could have lived and been told that the one he had was a lie, being cheered by versions of his past enemies was a heady, disorienting experience. It was encouraging and horrifying, gratifying and appalling all at the same time. He searched for cues in Bishop's face, and found himself confronted by a grimace of pure, helpless exasperation.

When he realized why, Spider-Man was grateful for the mask that hid his own reluctant smile from view.

No matter what world he was on, Bishop just couldn't get away from people who called him "Bish."

His amusement did not last long, because Magneto soon cleared his throat again, and once again everybody hushed. "I will repeat myself long enough to state the obvious: this is a do-or-die mission. We are throwing everything we have into this assault—all our hopes, all our resources, all our secrets as an underground organization. We must not fail. And while we should all do what we can to safeguard the lives of our comrades, we must never lose track of our goal. We are *all* expendable. And if we must give our lives to stop the X-Men from continuing to perpetrate this injustice, then we should all consider death a small price to pay for victory." His words echoed hollowly in the little room. "Good luck to you all."

• • •

TIME'S ARROW

Their transportation consisted of three modified Avengers quinjets, equipped with state-of-the-art cloaking technology. The plan was for the three teams to approach from different directions, with Teams One and Two opting for high visibility, and Team Three (the group Spider-Man and Bishop were in) holding off their assault until the others were already in the middle of theirs.

As Razorback piloted their quinjet through the night sky, Aliya got up from the copilot's position and joined the others in the passenger compartment. She was not dressed in baggy overalls anymore, but in Kevlar body armor that was eerily similar to the outfit Cable wore back on Spider-Man's world. She sat in an empty seat opposite Bishop and Spider-Man, and handed a small jewel box to each.

Speedball grinned. "My, my. We're really making it official, aren't we?"

"What is this," Spider-Man asked, "an official decoder ring?" He opened his box and found a featureless black disk about the size of a quarter.

"No," Aliya said. "It's a vocoder. We use it to coordinate efforts between us and the other squads. Inserted in your right ear, it can pick up signals on the speaker, and transmit messages by subvocalization. They're based on Cerebro technology, with limited psionic reception from even normal minds, so you don't have to worry about transmitting or receiving unless you give the mental command to go ahead."

Bishop examined his dourly. "What happens if I put it in my left ear instead?"

"We consider that one of the basic unanswerable questions," Aliya said, without smiling.

"It's safe, Bish," Spider-Man said before Bishop could object further. His spider-sense would have been screaming if the little discs were anything other than advertised. He lifted the right flap of his mask and put the disk in place, feeling nothing but a vague silliness in return. "But, y'know something, lady? Something about this whole setup doesn't make sense. This PLF of yours has access

THE PRESENT

to satellite surveillance technology, Avengers quinjets, and now these psionic communication thingies. You're obviously more than just a bunch of guys hiding out in a sewer. Hell, Magneto alone is strong enough to take on the X-Men all by himself. Why haven't you gone after Pegasus before?''

She brushed a lock of raven hair away from her face. "In the first place, organizing the PLF wasn't nearly as easy as you seem to think. For one thing, some of our members aren't exactly born joiners, and needed substantial persuasion before they saw the common benefit in banding together. In the second place, one of the first things the X-Men did upon passage of the Kelly Act was seize or destroy as many of Magneto's holdings as they possibly could. They blew up Asteroid M, destroyed his base in Antarctica, and emptied the vault containing what was left of the Nazi gold he liberated from Baron Strucker decades ago. He was left with almost no resources, and with the X-Men searching for him all over the world, he had to be especially careful how he chose to rebuild. It took years of putting everything back together before he was even ready to begin mounting a counterattack that stood a chance of succeeding.''

"He always did have patience," Bishop growled.

"In the third place," Aliya said, "this isn't the first time we've planned this assault. We intended to go four months ago, and again one month ago. Both times, we had to cancel when the Project put itself on full alert at the last minute. They do that occasionally, at random times, just to keep themselves at full battle readiness. But it turned out to be good for us, since the intel we had then was not nearly as complete as what we have now. This time, we're ready, and we have two people on our side we didn't have before.''

"I don't like it," Bishop said. "Perfect battle conditions have a way of turning on the overconfident. Won't Pegasus be equipped with Cerebros? Won't they pick us up before we even get near the place?''

"They would," Aliya said, "if we hadn't prepared for

that eventuality too. You see, all Cerebro units feed off the same main database, which places all registered paranormals on an approved list to keep them from setting off alarms every time they walk five feet in public. Cerebros filter out all registered paranormals unless they've been specifically programmed otherwise . . . tracking down only those who appear on no official lists."

"That makes sense." Bishop nodded. "The X-Men wouldn't want to spend half their lives tracking each other down on a daily basis."

"Exactly," Aliya said. "Which is why we had Night Thrasher hack the database earlier today. As of four P.M., we're all officially certified and legal. Including you, Bishop; I didn't have to make any changes for Spider-Man, whose counterpart is already in the database, and possesses the same readings. Of course, the federal government double-checks the records every morning, which means our readings will no doubt be removed by midday tomorrow. Until then, we're all exempt from Cerebro detection. With any luck that will be all the time we need."

"With any luck," Bishop echoed.

As for Spider-Man, he said nothing. It had occurred to him that if he was immune to detection, then all the pursuit they'd faced had been directed against Bishop alone. He didn't know how he felt about that. He decided that, like most things he'd encountered on this world, it was something better off unexplored.

Up by the controls, Razorback called out, "Five minutes to Pegasus, ma'am. Autopilot programmed and engaged."

"Thank you, Buford." Aliya stood. "One last question, gentlemen: I do trust you have no objection to parachuting from low altitudes?"

The quinjet came in low over the hills, cruising over the fenced perimeter at less than five hundred feet. It was a dark and cloudy night, with no stars, and the quinjet flew so silently that its passage was only audible as a distant rush of wind. To the five figures plunging from its open

THE PRESENT

hatch, over a darkened compound visible only from a few ambient lights, it was—in the literal sense of the phrase—a blind leap of faith. Even Spider-Man, whose webbing had enabled him to survive many such falls with jury-rigged hang-gliders and parachutes, and who routinely spent his days swinging between rooftops fifty stories above the street, couldn't help feeling a moment of uncharacteristic vertigo. He looked down into the darkness and wondered just what sat waiting there.

Then, with a *whooff* of compressed air, exploding from canisters attached to the cables, their parachutes inflated, and the speed of their plunge slowed from fatal to merely terrifying. The wind buffeted their bodies as the ground rushed up to greet them. When they hit the pavement, less than twenty yards from the corrugated steel structure that hid the entrance to the northern silo, the impact was enough to knock the breath out of a normal man. Bishop rolled and was back on his feet in an instant. Speedball absorbed the force of the impact and rebounded a full ten feet before Aliya, who'd landed first, reached up and grabbed him by the foot. Spider-Man simply landed in a crouch and stood immediately, thinking it not much worse than any other leap from three or four stories up.

"Whoo-ee!" Razorback cried, in a stage whisper. "I don't know about you guys and gals, but I wanna do that again!"

"Let's not have to," Aliya hissed. "Everybody stow your chutes and get up against the building!"

Spider-Man detached his chute with a click and began the laborious process of manually stuffing the yards of cloth back into the pack. He stopped as soon as he saw Aliya flip a hidden catch on her strap assembly. A whirring sound came from inside, and the chute slid across the pavement and into the pack, retracting so completely that the flap even resealed for future use. Time elapsed: one second. Spider-Man's first reaction was unabashed admiration for this clever feat of design. His second was the uneasy image of some unlucky parachutist accidentally pressing that catch a hundred feet in the air.

TIME'S ARROW

He banished the image, retracted his chute the same way, and joined the others as they sought cover in the shadows. "Nice gadgets, lady. You ever think of opening a Sharper Image?"

She shushed him with an annoyed gesture. "Quiet! I'm trying to pick up the other teams." Her lips moved silently for about fifteen seconds before she nodded, and permitted herself a smile. "They're down, and moving into position."

"I didn't hear anything," Spider-Man said.

"To hear you have to be willing to shut up long enough to listen. Will the voder to receive. You'll hear everything, just like the rest of us."

Spider-Man glanced at Bishop to see if he was buying this. The massive X-Man merely looked back impassively, his trademark scowl perhaps just a little more grim than usual. Speedball merely blinked through his huge goggles.

All right, Spider-Man thought. *If she can do it, so can I.* He concentrated. *Come in, everybody. Come in, come in, come in. I'm getting nothing. Can you hear me? This is Big Web comin' at ya, scannin' the dial for the latest update in tonight's mutant mayhem. Send me a coupla hot bulletins, already. I'm lost and confused and looking for action.*

Magneto's voice came in through the voder. "In the name of God, Aliya, either confiscate that thing or teach the man how to use it properly!"

Spider-Man was suddenly very grateful for his all-concealing mask. Without it, his blush would have set off heat sensors all over the compound. It certainly didn't help to notice that, for the first time in their forced association, Bishop was actually grinning. The X-Man wasn't alone either; Speedball was covering his face with one hand, and Razorback looked ready to bust a gut.

"Try again," Aliya whispered.

Spider-Man concentrated again, this time on listening. And he began to pick up something. Not yet a signal, but a steady white-noise static that was clearly the silence between signals. He heard a word fragment in Electro's

THE PRESENT

voice, another in the Rhino's; both must have been accidental transmissions, because they faded away as quickly as they began. Then Aliya moved her lips again, and he heard her voice loud and clear, even though the woman standing right next to him hadn't made an audible noise at all. "Third Team, requesting status. Third Team, requesting status. Over."

Night Thrasher's voice emerged, loud and clear. "First Team Here. We have secured a position just outside the main perimeter, and will be penetrating the fence in sixty seconds. Electro will divert the current and Rhino will do what he does best. Expect destruction of prime target within two minutes of mark. Over."

The static returned, only to be replaced, ten seconds later, by Magneto's voice. "Second Team in position as well. Have encountered no resistance whatsoever. Repeat, no resistance whatsoever. Remembering the words of John Wayne. Prepared to initiate on First Team's signal."

Spider-Man frowned beneath his mask. "John Wayne?"

"Cavalry picture," Razorback said. "Forget the name. He's ridin' through Apache territory an' he says, 'It's quiet. Too quiet.' "

Spider-Man knew how he felt. His spider-sense was sending him its single most unhelpful signal: the vague, unspecific, undifferentiated feeling of unease that was just barely strong enough to be noticed. At this intensity, it was almost impossible to distinguish from ordinary everyday nervousness, and it only warned him of potential danger, not yet imminent enough to generate a more powerful vibe. He usually felt this way just before a fight. The only thing the feeling ever managed to accomplish was remind him, if only briefly, that life as a super hero was exactly as crazy as it looked.

"And now," Night Thrasher reported. There was a moment of static. "We're in, and proceeding to the Power and Communications Building. Have encountered no alarms, no sentries—not even any witnesses. This is too

TIME'S ARROW

easy. Expect destruction of Primary Target on schedule. Over."

Magneto came in. "Team Two is initiating attack. We're going for volume; you may hear the side wall of the armory building as it's peeled loose and hurled over the fence. Beginning—now."

Somewhere, off in the distance, metal screamed like a living thing. Spider-Man heard an explosion, followed by shouting. It was all too far away to hear clearly, but it was definitely the sound of Team Two doing their thing. He supposed he should feel encouraged by that, but his vague sense of unease was becoming less vague with every instant. If anything, it was coming into sharper focus, like an instant photograph gradually revealing the details that only seconds before had been too undifferentiated to see.

Then his spider-sense spiked, with a jab so intense it was almost painful. And Night Thrasher's voice came screaming through the vocoder: "It's a trap! Repeat *it's a trap*! The Power and Communication Building's filled with Mandroids! Repeat *Mandroids*!"

Spider-Man's blood chilled. Back where he came from, Mandroids were suits of heavily reinforced armor, so bulky that they resembled the human form only slightly. They were packed with a variety of offensive weaponry that gave their wearers the capability of taking on the likes of the Hulk. While nowhere near as powerful—or as compact—as the Iron Man armor designed by Tony Stark, they were not usually intended to be used singly; most bad guys who employed Mandroids had entire platoons of them, accomplishing in sheer numbers what little they lacked in individual power. If Project: Pegasus had Mandroids lying in wait . . .

"There must be a dozen of them!" Night Thrasher's voice crackled through the voder. "And there are X-Men with them—Storm and Gambit! We're outnumbered three to one! Repeat, *it's a trap! They knew we were coming!*"

Magneto's voice broke in. "We have Mandroids here too. They seem to be . . ." The signal faded out, then returned. "They're plastic—no metal in them at all. They

THE PRESENT

must have been specifically designed to counter me. I can't..." Another pause. "Ending transmission. Cyclops and Phoenix are here, I can't—"

For five seconds, both transmissions ran simultaneously, rendering both nearly incomprehensible, except as vivid illustrations of all their best-laid plans turned to ashes in their hands.

In the brief silence that followed, the members of Aliya's team all stared at one another, suffering a fleeting heartbeat of horrified paralysis.

Speedball spoke the words that none of the others wanted to say. "We have to abort. Run away from here ...regroup somehow...."

Razorback chuckled. "No reason to rush home, son. I got the VCR programmed."

"Agreed," Aliya said. "Nothing's changed. We still have to get to that power grid." She lifted her ion cannon and blasted the building beside her at point-blank range. The explosion shattered the metal wall into fragments, leaving a hole the size of a barn door. For a moment, nothing but smoke and darkness was visible inside. Then the lights came on, and the haze was filled with imposing shapes that Spider-Man instantly recognized as approaching Mandroids.

"Go!" Aliya cried, as she leapt through the opening. "Go! Go!"

She was a brave lady, all right. She charged with the magnificent kind of bravery that was all too easy to mistake for insanity. And Spider-Man was about to leap in after her—as were Bishop, Speedball, and Razorback—when a painful jab from his spider-sense made him jerk back, and in doing so just barely avoid the three razor-sharp claws that suddenly slashed at him from inside. As soon as he was clear of the swing he tackled at the man behind his claws, driving the alternate-world Wolverine back into the building and into the great circular silo that dominated the inside of the bunker.

He leapt away just in time to avoid being flattened by a Mandroid's fist, and while he was in the air saw Bishop,

TIME'S ARROW

Speedball, Razorback, and Aliya, all fighting Mandroids at close quarters. There were two for each of them, and two for Spider-Man himself... a substantial defensive force, even if he didn't count Iceman, Wolverine, and the Beast, who were even now rising from the depths of the silo, riding one of Iceman's patented ice-ramps. Spider-Man was not surprised to see Wolverine snarling with rage—even back home, it was practically his permanent facial expression—but for somebody who'd known his version of the X-Men as long as he had, it was positively unnerving to see pretty much the same look on Iceman and the Beast. On this world, in this place, they were both as prepared to kill as Wolverine was.

The Beast's grin was particularly nasty. The hero Spider-Man knew had always possessed the potential for fearsomeness, but wore a smile and a joking manner more often than not. This version of him was not only blue and furry, but also possessed of dark cruel eyes. He actually looked forward to doing as much physical harm as possible. As he leapt off the ice-ramp, rebounded off a Mandroid's head, and barreled toward Spider-Man, he even laughed. "Nice going, Spider-Man! You've joined the PLF just in time to be arrested with them!"

Off to Spider-Man's left, Razorback punched a Mandroid in the chest. Surprisingly, it staggered—leading Spider-Man to the conclusion that this Razorback was stronger than his counterpart back home. Even so, the Mandroid didn't fall, and Razorback narrowly avoided a blast of plasma fired from one of the Mandroids' gauntlets.

Spider-Man tackled the Beast in midair. "How do you know I call myself Spider-Man? You've never seen me before."

The Beast laughed. "How do you think we know? We were *told*."

And as they tumbled head-over-heels into the silo, surrounded by the sounds of battle on all sides, Spider-Man realized he was telling the truth.

I did it. I revealed myself to the Park. I thought that

THE PRESENT

because he was Peter Parker he wouldn't betray me—but this Peter Parker is one of them.

I led him back to us. I gave him a chance to inform the X-Men. I gave them a chance to get ready for us. I've doomed the PLF to failure.

And I'm about to get all these people killed.

CHAPTER TWELVE

On a volcanic island somewhere in the South Seas, a man who sometimes went by the name Gambit found himself trapped inside a sphere of sentient water that sometimes walked in the shape of a man. Gambit had spent the better part of a minute trying to kick his way free of the creature attempting to drown him, but it moved whenever he did, keeping him imprisoned in its center, far away from the life-giving embrace of warm tropical air.

Had he not been sharing that sphere of water with three killer robots in the shape of beautiful native women, he might have actually been in serious danger of drowning as intended. But the robots were too single-minded to realize that in his hands they were essentially nothing more than prettily disguised ammunition.

He needed only the slightest touch to charge two of them with unstable kinetic energy. And while he survived the concussion that followed, the sphere of sentient water did not. It splattered in all directions, peppering the ground like liquid bullets.

Gambit fell to the ground, gasping. His ears were ringing so badly that it took him several seconds to realize that the ominous rumbling all around was not the after-effect of anything he'd done. It was the island itself, being shaken to pieces by the seismic shockwaves radiating from the volcano at its center. He almost didn't want to know how much time he and Wolverine had left, but he gazed upward anyway—and saw that the crater was once again billowing thick stratospheric clouds of filthy black smoke. One of the quakes had blasted loose an entire section of crater rim, revealing something smooth and metallic that even in the gloom caused by the thick volcanic clouds had still managed to find enough sunlight to gleam for his benefit.

The bomb . . .

He searched for Wolverine, and found him still tussling with Electro about ten yards away. Actually, *tussling* was too strong a word: Wolverine was losing. He was on his knees at Electro's feet, spasming uncontrollably as Electro,

THE PRESENT

who had him by the wrists, fired thousands of volts of deadly electricity into his body. Wolverine's wrists were already turning black from the heat; his mouth was agape in a silent scream, and smoke was beginning to rise from his throat.

Anybody else would have been dead already. Wolverine would be dead in seconds.

Gambit rushed to help him—

—or would have, had the remains of the one remaining robot not chosen that moment to leap on him from behind. Now no longer even recognizably human, its legs paralyzed twisted things, its false skin hanging from its frame in ragged flaps, its smile now a cold metallic gash, it still possessed terrible destructive strength in the ruins of its arms. As it clutched at Gambit's neck, it cried out a single distorted word that may have been *"Die!"*

"I don't have *time* for dis!" Gambit shouted, as he twisted and rolled and flipped the robot back into the hot spring. He jumped to his feet, and rushed to Wolverine's side—

—or would have, if the scattered fragments of Hydro-Man had not chosen that moment to collect themselves and become twelve feet of churning white water standing in his path.

There was a recognizably human head at the top of that wall of water, and it smiled unpleasantly. "Get the picture, freak? I'm Hydro-Man! You can't get ridda me by blowing me up! Soon as I get myself together, I'm back in business!"

"De whole island's about to blow up, man! You t'ink you can survive dat?"

"Why not?" Hydro-Man leered. "Even if it turns me to steam, and blows me a hundred miles from here, all I gotta do is wait for things to cool down a bit. I'll be back together before sunset. *You* won't!"

His body was just transparent enough for Gambit to see what was going on behind him, distorted by the optical effect of all that water. Somehow, even with all that electricity coursing through his body, Wolverine had found

TIME'S ARROW

within himself the will to stand, and lift the shouting Electro over his head. Lightning played around Wolverine's form, arcing into the earth in great blinding streaks. As Gambit watched, in both awe and horror, Wolverine lifted Electro as high as he could, and, expelling all his agony and determination in a scream of primal rage, began lurching forward—toward Hydro-Man.

Gambit was so hypnotized by the spectacle that he was taken totally by surprise when the remains of the last remaining robot grabbed him by the ankles. It had scuttled out of the hot spring and crawled across the sands, yanking Gambit off his feet just as Hydro-Man arced over him like a tsunami about to crash.

The last thing Gambit saw was the water-distorted image of his teammate hurling Electro away from him as hard as he could.

It was a variation of a maneuver Wolverine and another X-Man named Colossus had used often, in the early days of their association with the team. They even had a name for it: the Fastball Special. Essentially, it consisted of Colossus, who was one of the strongest people on the planet, literally hurling Wolverine at the enemy. The only difference with this Fastball Special was that Wolverine himself was doing the toss—and that the person being thrown didn't exactly approve of the idea.

Electro yelled, and thrust out his arms, in an instinctive attempt to protect himself from the impact.

Both his hands hit the wall of water simultaneously.

Hydro-Man's mouth stretched wide as his body bubbled, steamed, churned with glowing energy, and began to shrink. Electro, who was trapped inside him, writhed uncontrollably, the water around him strobing with all the energy of a thousand turbines released in a single instant. He screamed, too, but his voice was only a stream of bubbles rising toward the surface. Gambit didn't have time to watch the rest of it, not with the remaining robot scrambling over him, single-minded purpose burning in its now clearly soulless eyes.

Gambit rolled to get out from under, lightly touching

THE PRESENT

the robot's head as he went. The glow in his right hand was immediately passed to its shiny, sand-speckled skull. The thing grabbed for him one last time, no doubt intent on keeping him close by for the explosion. But Gambit, who'd already experienced ground zero once today, had other ideas. He was already diving for the crater left by a previous explosion when the concussion blast lifted him up and carried him a significant distance beyond his previously planned destination.

He hit the ground hard enough to knock the breath out of him, but he was still on his feet in an instant, ready to return to Wolverine's side.

Wolverine looked like he could have used the help. His costume was in burned tatters, his skin was smoking and covered with blisters, and his wrists were nearly black. Gambit didn't even want to guess about the extent of his internal injuries, how much pain he was in, and just how long it would take his mutant healing factor to repair him to something resembling normal. He could only note that Wolverine was standing, while Electro lay unconscious. The being known as Hydro-Man was nowhere in sight.

Wolverine coughed out a cloud of sickly-looking smoke, and growled in a voice even more gravelly than normal. "Chemistry lesson, bub. Electrolysis. Sink two charged leads into a body of water, an' ya reduce it to its component elements, oxygen and hydrogen. Dunno if big, tall, and wet's gonna be able to pull himself together after that, and I don't care. Right now you 'n' me got too much more important stuff to worry about."

Gambit glanced at the summit high above. "You've spotted de bomb, den?"

"Way today's goin', I woulda been surprised if it was anywhere else. C'mon. We got a mountain to climb."

Gambit ran to Wolverine's side and was almost knocked to the ground by a tremor that turned the earth itself into a bucking animal driven insane by pain. He managed to stay on his feet; Wolverine, who had come closer to death than he would have cared to admit, did not. Gambit paused at Wolverine's side just long enough to be horrified by the extent of his teammate's injuries. Wolverine's face, never pretty at the best of times, was now a mass of blisters and scarlet burns, recognizable only because of the familiar angry eyes that glowered beneath. Gambit only needed one look at him to know he'd never make it up the side of the mountain—not with the entire slope bucking and shaking like an explosion waiting to happen. He needed time to recover—much less time than Electro, who was already stirring in semiconscious stupor.

As for Hydro-Man, there was already a distinctively unnatural haze, coming together in the rancid sulphurous air.

Wolverine read Gambit's mind at a glance. "Don't worry about me, Cajun. I can keep these clowns busy no matter what shape I'm in. You gotta get yer butt up that mountain, take care'a that bomb, and activate your TDC recall so we can get out of here before this whole island goes bang!"

Gambit hesitated.

"Ya gotta do it, Remy! My life ain't important! The universe is countin' on you!"

Knowing Wolverine was right, but hating himself for knowing it, Gambit didn't waste any time with words. He just nodded and ran, not knowing if he'd ever see his friend alive again....

At just about that moment, the alternate-universe Night Thrasher was fighting for his life.

The ambush had completely neutralized his team. The Rhino had managed to take out four of the Mandroids almost immediately, without even breathing hard, but another squad of four had driven him back, and now had him on the ground about fifty feet away, where they were pummeling him unconscious with repeated blows of their armored fists. It was impossible to tell how much of his bellowing was rage and how much of it was sheer desperation to survive. He'd be dead or imprisoned in seconds.

Another four Mandroids had chosen Electro as their target. His electrical powers were next to useless against

THE PRESENT

their insulated suits, so he'd chosen a strategic retreat, shooting lightning bolts over his shoulder as they flew in pursuit, firing blasts that turned the ground all around him into a field of smoking craters. Unless he came up with some brilliant new strategy—doubtful, given who he was—Electro might have had only seconds to live.

Hydro-Man had turned himself into a tidal wave and launched himself at the generator, but Storm had used all her powers to drive him back, repeatedly splattering his liquid form with high winds. Night Thrasher didn't have to see inside her mind to know that this was just her, having a good time. The second she got tired enough to freeze Hydro-Man solid with a blast of freezing arctic air, he'd be permanently out of the game as well.

That just left Night Thrasher himself, grappling with Gambit at the shattered wall of the Power and Communications Building. This at least resembled a fair fight. He might not have Gambit's explosive powers, but he did have the edge in martial-arts skill, and he was keeping the fight up too close and nasty for Gambit to charge anything. As it was, both men had drawn blood; Gambit's left arm was broken, and Night Thrasher fought like a demon despite the sandpapery grinding of his ribs.

But the longer this hopeless fight went on, the more certain the arrival of reinforcements.

He changed tactics, letting Gambit see an opening that didn't exist. Gambit rushed forward, his hands glowing, set to charge something on Night Thrasher's costume with enough kinetic energy to blow a hole in him. Night Thrasher, ducking down beneath the charge, came up with a wrist strike against Gambit's lower jaw. Something—either teeth or vertebrae—cracked sickeningly. Night Thrasher ducked to one side, avoiding Gambit as he stumbled and fell. Gambit hit the ground hands-first, charged the dirt with kinetic energy, and was blown into the air by the explosion he himself had caused. Night Thrasher didn't stick around long enough to see whether Gambit was paralyzed or even dead. Either way, he knew he was as good as dead himself as soon as Storm got around to checking

TIME'S ARROW

up on her teammate. Either way, he had a mission to finish first.

He didn't need to slow down as he slipped the shaped explosives from the pockets on his arms. He didn't even need to place them in position before he activated the timer on his belt, which gave him less than thirty seconds before they went off.

He was probably too late already. If the Project had managed to set a trap this elaborate, part of their plan must have included reinforcements already en route.

But he would not allow concern for his own life to deter him from his objective.

Behind him, Storm's aristocratic voice screamed, "Night Thrasher! You *murderer!*"

She must have disposed of Hydro-Man and found Gambit. At the speed she flew, she'd be on him in seconds, and he was not mad enough to think he could outfight her. Without slowing down, he headed for the main control board, intent on making himself the explosive missile that would destroy it and the Project's external communications. He would not have time to get away—but if he was lucky, there would not be time for Storm either.

When the bright light came, he was not sure whether it was the explosives or Storm come to get her revenge. Either way, the result was the same.

His last thought was a silent plea for Aliya's team. *Please. Let them get through. Everything depends on them getting through.*

On another world, engaged in another battle in the middle of a monsoon-tossed swamp, Iceman felt his spine about to give beneath the weight of the Wrecker's choke hold. He thickened the ice around his neck, prolonging the struggle for another couple of seconds at most—but the Wrecker just put more pressure on his mystic crowbar, continuing to force his head back.

As pressed as he was—literally—Iceman devoted one second to rolling his eyes, in desperate search for Storm. It was almost impossible to find her behind the driving

THE PRESENT

rain. But even that couldn't mask the bright flash of lightning that for an instant lit up the entire landscape, revealing Piledriver's look of idiot astonishment as Storm blasted the tree in his hands to toothpick-sized kindling. Then the rain rolled in again, and all Iceman was left with was a momentary impression of her rising back into the air, her thin silver-black cape surrounding her like a corona.

It was enough. She was Storm. As long as she was still capable of fighting, there was no need to worry about her.

And Iceman had more urgent things to worry about.

He had maybe one second of life left to him. One second of knowing that his powers were useless and that there was no way he could use them to save himself.

So he did the only thing he could.

He defrosted.

The inch-thick coating of ice that covered his entire body vanished in an instant, leaving a smaller, skinnier, and considerably more vulnerable Bobby Drake. In this form, there was no way he'd be able to stand up to the Wrecker's brawn, but in this form, he honestly wouldn't have to. Lubricated by mud and rain, granted a heartbeat of opportunity by the sudden looseness of the grip around his neck, Bobby turned his head and squirmed free of the Wrecker's death grip. He sank beneath the surface of the swamp like a marionette whose strings had just been cut, gagged at the unbelievable foulness of the scummy water, just barely kicked himself out of the way when the Wrecker grabbed for him again, and swam blindly through muddy darkness, pummeled on all sides by currents rendered violent by monsoon winds. He was unable to avoid wondering if the alligator he'd escaped earlier was still anywhere in the immediate neighborhood.

By the time he emerged, five seconds later, once again a frozen man riding his ramp of ice into the storm-swept tropical sky, he had more important things to worry about. Like where Storm was, for one. The monsoon had struck in earnest now, lashing the trees and the swamp waters with hurricane-force winds that made maintaining an ice

TIME'S ARROW

bridge almost impossible. He couldn't get his bearings—he had no idea where he was in relation to where he'd seen Storm last. He couldn't see more than five feet in front of his face, he couldn't hear anything but howling wind, he still had the Wrecking Crew to worry about, and he couldn't stop thinking about the device still ticking away somewhere in the midst of all this unstoppable chaos. He circled around in vain for all of five minutes, barely able to keep his footing against the high-velocity winds threatening to sweep him away, shouting Ororo's name against a storm that insisted on whipping the very words from his mouth. He kept trying to get altitude, hoping he'd be able to spot her from the air, but his ice-ramp was threatening to shatter beneath him, and he had to repeatedly return to ground level to sink new supports into the turbulent waters of the swamp.

He was almost completely convinced he'd lost her when the wind gusted more than he ever could have believed, and his ice bridge crumbled beneath his feet, unable to withstand the force of the hot driving rain. The only thing that kept him from projecting another ice-ramp to break his fall was a nauseating moment of uncertainty over just which way was down.

He hit hard, surviving only because the ground was soft and muddy, and his icy form was more tolerant of punishment than human flesh. That didn't stop the impact from knocking the breath out of him. He gasped, felt himself sinking, succumbed to a moment of terror about drowning, and sucked all the heat from the surrounding earth, temporarily freezing the ground to something approaching solidity. He crawled from the hole with what he imagined to be the last of his strength, yelped as another hurricane gust slid him twenty feet across his homemade outdoor rink, and managed to rise to his knees—just in time to spot a smooth, regular, and metallic shape protruding from a mudbank not too far away.

Kang's missile. No wonder they hadn't been able to find it before; it had been completely buried in mud. Only the power of the monsoon, stripping away much of its

THE PRESENT

concealing earth, had been able to reveal where it was hiding. Letting out a yelp, Iceman used a very low, very securely anchored ice ramp to carry him the twenty yards to its side. Once there he was almost afraid to touch it. The part that showed was almost spookily clean, despite being so recently buried. Though it possessed no visible openings or instrumentation, he could still imagine he sensed the terrible destructive power building inside—power that rendered everything he'd ever known so terribly insignificant by comparison. But now that he was here, he suddenly realized that neither Professor Xavier nor Blaquesmith nor any of the strategicians among the X-Men had ever covered the all-important details on how to stop it.

"*Storm!*" he yelled, his voice cracking. "*I found it! Kang's bomb! It's here! I found it!*"

The winds lessened noticeably, and a familiar aristocratic voice spoke up from just behind him. "No need to shout, Bobby. I'm right here."

He whirled, and saw her. Storm. She was filthy and covered with slime, her luxurious white hair now a tangled, mud-spattered mop, but she looked more or less intact, and the tiny smile tugging at the corners of her lips made him almost grateful he hadn't gotten to see what was left of the other guy. The effort it must have cost her to lessen the storm around her and Iceman long enough for them to share a moment of unshouted conversation did not even begin to show on her face. She said, "I found it a couple of minutes ago. I was canvassing the area for you when you showed up and saved me the trouble."

"Uh—" she was too classy a lady to do it on purpose, but sometimes the things she said made Iceman feel like a real dork—"thanks. My pleasure. Have any idea what we're going to do about this?"

"We have to destroy it completely. That's beyond my power, but with this monsoon, nature herself has provided us with the very weapon we need. I'm going to have to reach into the heart of the storm, gather up all its unima-

TIME'S ARROW

ginable destructive energies, and focus them all in one concentrated assault on this very spot."

Iceman goggled. "Oh. Uh, is *that* all?"

"Unfortunately—" and here her eyes lingered meaningfully on Iceman's—"that's going to take everything I have. Maybe even more than I do have. For however long it takes, I won't be able to do or think of anything else. And just a few minutes ago, a couple of hundred yards south of here, I saw the Wrecking Crew, back together and heading this way. They'll be here any second. I'm going to need you to keep them away on your own."

Had they been different people, Storm would have finished that speech by asking Iceman whether he was sure he could handle it. He would have answered by saying that his powers were next to useless in this weather, but that since he had no other choice he was willing to try.

But they were not different people. They were X-Men. And they were often required to face the impossible, just because it needed to be done. Questioning that would have denied everything they'd ever been.

So they simply shared a moment of eye contact, came to a silent understanding, and went to work. The wind returned in full force. Storm closed her eyes and raised her palms toward the sky. Iceman merely staggered blindly toward the south.

At just about that moment, in a crumbling ice cave somewhere inside a glacier on the frozen continent of Antarctica, a similar silent understanding passed between the two mutants known as Cable and the Beast.

One of them had to rush back outside to take out Volcana before she succeeded in melting this entire mountain of ice down around their ears. The other had to stay here, and do what he could to rescue the wounded teenager shackled to the machine-gun placement. The debate over who got what assignment lasted maybe one second, and amounted to nothing more than a heartbeat of eye contact. Then the Beast somersaulted over the edge of the catwalk and began bouncing his way to her side, while Cable

THE PRESENT

hefted his plasma rifle and launched himself back up the tunnel.

He almost didn't make it, and long before he found daylight again he despaired of being able to go back for the Beast and the girl. The tunnel walls and ceiling were all running enough water to make headway difficult, and the tunnel floor was so soft he sank up to his knees with almost every step. Running was almost impossible. When he stumbled for the third time he realized that impossibility had been achieved some time ago. He focused his telekinetic energies at his feet, rising from the slush and continuing with the added agility of a man who, for the moment, weighed next to nothing.

He made it through the cave mouth an instant before it collapsed all around him, not bothering to worry about the fall. He would find some way to catch himself. More important, right now, was locating his targets. And they weren't hard to find. Volcana was standing a safe distance from the cliff wall, using her arms to radiate wave after wave of blast-furnace heat. The Rhino was standing about ten feet behind her, seeming, if anything, totally bored by the spectacle of an entire glacier melting to nothingness at the whim of one woman. They were both knee deep in water, the melting glacier already filling up the canyon like a basin meant to catch what Volcana sent its way.

She was the more important objective. But something in the Rhino's expression made him too perfect a target. Which is why, against all his soldier's training on the importance of prioritizing the enemy, Cable brought his plasma cannon to bear on the Rhino first. Even as he somersaulted toward the ground, he fired off a round of concentrated destructive energy at the slush by the Rhino's feet, reducing it to steam, and leaving in its place a crater that all the thousands of gallons of flowing water immediately whirlpooled to fill. The Rhino, taken by surprise, was immediately swept in, disappearing from sight so completely that he resembled Oliver Hardy sinking up to his derby in a puddle by the curb.

Cable hit the water in a shallow dive. Its frigidity immediately took his breath away. He knew at once that even with these protective clothes he wouldn't be able to fight off hypothermia for more than a few minutes. It was, for him, a good argument for fighting Volcana in the closest quarters possible. With her radiant heat, she could arguably keep him alive even as she tried to kill him.

He rose expecting an attack, but found her standing in place, smiling at him.

"Wow," she said, shaking her head. "That was really slick! You really know your moves."

He couldn't *believe* her. "Do you have any idea what's going on here?"

"Sure. It's just a fight. You knock me around, I knock you around, I get paid, you get glory, nobody gets hurt, my car gets fixed. What's the big deal?"

"The big deal," he said, advancing, "is that the . . . creature . . . who employed you plans to destroy all life in the universe! And you're helping to make that possible!"

For just the slightest moment, she looked pathetically disconcerted. "How does fighting you make *that* possible?"

He would have given her a condensed explanation, but it was just about then that their time ran out.

All glaciers are, at heart, very, very slow rivers. They're just water, flowing downhill—albeit as great masses of ice that may not manage more than a few inches a year. Even so, their progress is as inexorable as the most raging white water torrent. And because they possess the added strength of their own solidity, they carry within them a sheer power that even the greatest waterfalls on the planet cannot even hope to match.

This glacier consisted of millions of tons of frozen water, sliding down to the sea. Though its progress had been negligible on any historical scale, its weight, power, and momentum was as great as anything the planet had ever known. It was nearly infinite power, which was only held in check by the raging cold.

But the battle in the canyon had disturbed that cold. Great masses of ice that had been frozen since before the

THE PRESENT

dawn of humanity had been melted away or blasted to steam. The mass of ice that stood behind them was suddenly held back by . . . nothing. The pressure was unimaginable. The stresses on the mountains of ice were irresistible. And now, with so much of the cliffside melted away, flowing downhill with the speed of the river it had truly been all along . . . the seismic pressures finally made themselves known.

The rumbling began all around them, coming from every direction at once, a cry of geological pain that Cable could feel at the base of his spine. The ground began to shake. Tons of snow and ice avalanched down the mountain walls in great billowing clouds of white. The shock waves blasted the knee-deep water especially hard, creating waves as high as Cable's waist. He fell, submerged, and got up gasping from the cold, just in time to see the Rhino surface, coughing and spitting, maybe thirty yards away. For a moment, he wondered if he'd have to fight the Rhino as well as Volcana now—but then a gaping fissure opened up all at once, a lightning-shaped scar that traveled from one end of the canyon to the other with the speed of a bullet train. All the water and all the pressure began to flow toward that one immense wound with a finality that could not be resisted.

The Rhino's weight worked against him now. The ice beneath his feet gave way, and the current carried him away bellowing and cursing like a man with a grudge against nature itself. Volcana managed to keep her footing by directing all her radiant heat at the waters immediately surrounding her, reducing them to steam, which crystallized even as it rose toward the gray and pitiless sky.

Cable was taken by surprise and swept away.

He managed to use his telekinesis to keep his head above water and slow his headlong rush to a rate significantly slower than the current. So much so that by the time he reached the edge of the fissure the water beneath him was only inches deep, and much easier to resist. Still, he didn't manage to grab hold until his legs had already gone over the side. What was left of the ice was slick with water and almost impossible to hold on to—especially for a man who also needed to keep hold of his ion cannon—but Cable managed it with a little boost from his telekinesis. He scrambled up and over and, breathing heavily, searched what was left of the canyon for signs of Volcana and the Rhino.

The Rhino was nowhere to be seen. Volcana, on the other hand, was clearly visible. She had turned off her powers, and was now a distant figure huddled on the ice, looking wasted and exhausted, if not particularly cold. Cable didn't suppose she'd be especially interested in starting up the fight again, even if given the opportunity, but he didn't particularly feel like going over there to see how she was. He'd had more than enough small talk for one day.

Right now he was more interested in something uncovered when the fissure yawned wide: Kang's time missile. Smooth and metallic and clearly what the two X-Men had come all this distance to find, it sat protruding from the fissure wall maybe one eighth of a mile away.

Cable wished he could afford to go after the Beast. But he didn't have the time. In any life-or-death situation, he had to prioritize.

First priority was the bomb.

After that, everything else—including the Beast, including that teenage girl, and including all his dreams of being reunited with Aliya—had to content itself with a distant second.

He hefted his ion cannon, took a deep breath, and hit the ground running.

At just about the same moment, in the alternate universe, a battle royal raged at the southernmost silo of Project: Pegasus.

To Bishop, who was in the thick of it, absorbing energy blasts and redirecting them back at the Mandroids who had fired them at him, it was clear that Aliya and the others were not doing anywhere near as much damage as they needed to. Except for Spider-Man, who hadn't been seen

THE PRESENT

since he and the alternate-universe Beast tumbled together into the silo, the entire team had been effectively contained at ground level. Aliya was engaged in a furious martial-arts battle with Wolverine, Razorback had managed to zap Iceman unconscious with a high-voltage shock from his electrified mane, and Bishop himself had managed to take out four of the squad of twelve Mandroids with his plasma rifle and mutant powers. They were faring much better than they might have expected. But it was still taking too much time. When four out of the eight remaining Mandroids broke formation and rocketed down the silo in pursuit of Spider-Man and the Beast, Bishop knew that it was because the team members up here at ground level were already considered contained.

It occurred to him, as he fired a wave of energy at another approaching Mandroid, driving it back but not disabling it, that life with the X-Men had corrupted his battle skills. He was fighting like a super hero trying to protect the other members of his team, not like a soldier intent on reaching his objective at all costs.

Maybe it was time he went back to the old ways.

He darted away from a barbed rocket and shouted, "Aliya, keep them busy! I'm going after the primary target!"

"Do it!" she shouted, as she blocked a thrust from Wolverine's claws. "We'll be okay!"

He made a run for the silo, noting even as he seemed about to make it that Speedball was ricocheting his way. That was good. He hadn't seen much of Speedball in this fight, but had assumed that the young man had been keeping busy. His help would be invaluable in keeping the Mandroids occupied. He turned his back, confident that Speedball would follow him—

—only to reel in helpless agony as something hard and heavy smashed against the top of his head. It wasn't the first time he'd been cold-cocked; assuming he survived this day, it probably wouldn't be the last. But he couldn't remember the last time he'd been less prepared. It occurred to him, distantly, that he would have to try to be even

TIME'S ARROW

more suspicious of strangers in the future. Then his eyes rolled back in his head, his plasma rifle clattered to the floor, and he fell into unconsciousness, mere inches from the top of the silo.

"Surprise!" Wolverine leered. "Didn't expect to see that, huh, lady?"

He had a point, but the number-one rule of combat where Aliya came from was simple: If you want to fight, don't taunt—fight. By speaking he distracted himself. Not a lot, not enough to make a difference against ninety-nine percent of the opponents he'd ever have to fight—but enough for Aliya, who was better than that ninety-nine percent, to make her move with her dagger. When it was done Wolverine was gripping his suddenly perforated throat with drenched scarlet hands.

Aliya smiled. "Didn't expect to see that, huh, Wolverine?"

He croaked something about the lady going to the top of his list when he fell to the floor.

He was Wolverine. He'd heal, probably within minutes. But Aliya didn't have the time or the inclination to dispose of him properly. She had a more important target.

Even as Wolverine began to crawl off, Aliya somersaulted over a rampaging Mandroid—deftly attaching an electromagnetic pulse bomb that would render its circuitry useless—and leapt at Speedball, whom she had just seen deck Bishop. With his frictionless aura, he was next to impossible to hold on to, but the force of her charge still drove him to the floor, and sent both of them bouncing into the air. "You're our security leak?" she cried.

His face contorted with genuine pain. "It doesn't have to be like this, Aliya. You're the last person I wanted to hurt."

She wanted to kill him, but his force field deflected all her blows from his face. He felt nothing, even as he and Aliya rebounded off the head of a confused Mandroid and skittered along the bunker ceiling. "You little pipsqueak, we *trusted* you!"

"And you were fools," he replied, his words as diz-

THE PRESENT

zying as their shared helter-skelter richochets from one wall to the next. "I realized a year ago we had no chance to win. That if we went ahead with this we'd all end up captured and in stasis—just like the Avengers and the Fantastic Four and everybody else who ever tried to fight back. So I joined the X-Men and started feeding them everything I knew about Magneto, and his plans, and the other members of the PLF—even about Spider-Man and Bishop, when they showed up! I wanted to be on the winning side for once—and I wanted you with me, but you spent so much time with Magneto that you never gave me a chance to tell you."

Much as she wanted to wipe that lovelorn expression off his face, Aliya had had enough—and she knew she was needed elsewhere. So she kicked free, barely evaded the hands of a charging Mandroid, and rolled to a position of temporary safety, her battle-hardened instincts already calculating how to win this battle with one less person on the side of the good guys.

She got up just in time to see a length of chain snake across the chamber and circle Speedball's chest four times. The chain looked like any other metal, but it must have been designed to overcome the young turncoat's force field. Instead of being deflected, it bound Speedball tightly enough to squeeze the breath out of him, and stopped him dead in the middle of free fall. Then the chain retracted at high speed, pulling the helpless Speedball along behind it—yanking him all the way across the bunker to the place where Razorback stood, spinning the winch he kept mounted on his chest.

The Arkansan hero's baritone drawl was easy to hear over all the other sounds of battle. "I've long suspected as much, son—but I hoped I was wrong. You sure have a lot to learn about bein' a man."

At about the same moment, deep within a mountain of ice on another world, the Beast had just barely avoided being smashed to a furry blue puddle when half the cave collapsed at once.

He had traveled hand over hand beneath the catwalk, figuring that it would protect him from the bulk of the falling ice. And so it had—as dozens of chunks weighing fifty or a hundred pounds or more hammered the grillwork above his head, he was able to swing from one support to the other in as much of a hurry as the uneasy handholds permitted.

Then came the quake. The catwalk ripped loose of the wall, and the Beast had to leap away into space raining with chunks of ceiling the size of Volkswagens. It had not been fun, but for somebody who'd attended a school where gym class was held in a place called the Danger Room, it had not been anything out of the ordinary either. Only when the entire ceiling began to collapse at once did Mama McCoy's bouncing baby boy begin to feel he was in over his head—and even then he was able to risk everything on an all-or-nothing leap that carried him the rest of the way to the protected alcove where the wounded teenage girl lay bleeding to death.

He did not expect her to be happy to see him. His appearance had a way of startling the people he tried to rescue.

But he didn't expect her to be smiling either.

CHAPTER THIRTEEN

P*roject: Pegasus, Silo South. The battle as seen at ground level:*

Even as Razorback fired a high-voltage current through his tow chain, shocking Speedball unconscious, Aliya found herself once again surrounded by Mandroids. There were only three of them still left at ground level, their comrades either fallen or gone in pursuit of Spider-Man, but these were no longer handicapped by the confusion of battle. These only had a pair of remaining targets to worry about, as the rest had either moved on or already been taken out. And since Aliya had already established herself as the leader, and had been separated from her ion cannon during her battle with Wolverine . . .

They came at her from three sides, the human faces barely visible behind the smoked-glass visors grinning with the premature sense of victory.

Aliya considered the obvious move: jump high and let them take each other out in the crossfire. That usually worked on idiots in suits of armor; for all their technological advantage, they somehow never seemed to figure out that there was a reason firing squads don't line up in circles.

But given her mood, it was a little too hands-off for her.

So she did something a little more proactive. She picked the guy with the most obnoxious leer and went for his visor. Though transparent, the shield was probably as hard as raw diamond. It was meant to take heavy artillery without cracking, and probably had. In theory, there shouldn't have been any way for a mutant martial artist from the future to punch her hand right through that glass and poke the soldier within in the eyes.

But in theory, cinder blocks shouldn't be smashed by human hands, diamonds shouldn't be vulnerable to strikes from steel chisels, and straws driven by even hurricane winds should not be able to impale trees.

The problem with theory, Aliya knew, is that it ignored the question of focus.

She focused . . . made everything she was a straight line

THE PRESENT

that began with her will and ended with a point somewhere behind that Mandroid's helmet . . . and drove her gloved fingers right through his visor. The agony of her blow and the shattered glass slicing into the skin of his face hit the man inside the armor at once. He screamed, "My eyes! My eyes!" and staggered back, like a drunk no longer capable of remaining on his feet. He was already falling backward when she gave his momentum a little added push with a well-placed kick to his midsection.

"That's one," she said, whirling to face the others.

The faces behind the masks were no longer leering with victory, but determined in the manner of soldiers who know the battle will be tougher than they had estimated. The one on the right was particularly grim. "For that, lady, I'll rip your arms right out of their sockets."

She glanced behind him just long enough to check on Razorback's whereabouts. He was off at the farthest corner of the bunker, stashing Speedball's unconscious form somewhere it wouldn't get trampled. A fine display of principles on the part of a big lug who didn't want to hurt anybody, not even the turncoat who'd betrayed them all. Aliya appreciated the sentiment even if she didn't personally agree with it, but with two Mandroids still left to contend with she sincerely wished he'd hurry up.

The one with the creative ideas about her arm sockets went for her, his gauntlets spitting fire. She leapt over the flames, over the Mandroid's back, landing behind him, directly in front of his less vocal friend. That one didn't expect to see her at all, and when she faked a jab at his visor, he understandably panicked and fired off his entire battery of rockets.

That was something to remember, in battle situations: show them you can do it once, and they live in fear of you doing it again.

The rockets shot out with enough force to totally disintegrate Aliya on impact, even without their explosives triggered. Fortunately, she wasn't in their path. She'd dropped to her knees and allowed them to pass harmlessly over her head, so they could impact the guy with all the

TIME'S ARROW

ideas about arm sockets. By the time the explosion rippled from the back of his armor, she was already leaping between the third Mandroid's legs, using him to shield herself from the explosive concussion.

The last remaining Mandroid stared at what he'd done with something like horror, no doubt appalled, guilt ridden, and wondering how he'd explain this to his captain.

Then Aliya said, "That's two," and he whirled.

She'd gotten to her ion cannon, set it to maximum, and leveled it at his head.

"Here's three," she said, and fired. What was left of the remaining Mandroid hit the floor with a significantly wet thud.

Razorback chose that moment to return to her side. "Ooeee. Nice goin', ma'am. Remind me never to get *you* mad. Where to now?"

Aliya gestured toward the silo, which was echoing with the sounds of shouted voices and small-arms fire. "Spider-Man's alone down there, fighting the Beast, the Mandroids, and who knows what else. I have to hurry down there and help him. You get Bishop to a safe corner and come as soon as you can. We'll need you."

"Sure thing, ma'am." He hesitated. "Got a call from Night Thrasher, a few minutes ago. Sounds like he and his team . . . died, doing what they had to do."

Aliya had been too busy to pay attention to any signals, but the report was about as bad as anything she ever could have expected. "Magneto?"

"He's still fightin'. So's Sandman. But the women, Titania and Volcana . . ." His voice broke. "They're . . . gone. Cyclops killed 'em both. And . . . I was gonna tell 'em tonight . . . later . . . which one I really loved. . . . I just didn't want to do it before the battle . . . in case I went . . . but I never thought . . ."

She put a hand on his shoulder. "I feel for you, Buford. I know how you felt about them. But we don't have time for this now. We have to go and help Spider-Man, so their deaths mean something."

"I know," he said, grimly. "This one's for them."

THE PRESENT

And then came something very fast and very unexpected. The grim resolve in his face vanished, replaced in a heartbeat with something even more urgent and afraid. Before Aliya could react—which was very quickly indeed—he grabbed her by the shoulders, lifted her off the ground, and spun in place, placing himself between her and the attack that he'd seen about to strike her unprotected back.

It struck him instead. Aliya stumbled back just in time to get a good look at a gleaming, wickedly pointed spear of solid ice, projected from the hands of an Iceman now recovering from the electric shock that had temporarily put him down. Iceman had fired the ice-blast from the ground, as his first act upon rising to rejoin the fray. It was a killing blow, meant for Aliya, aimed at just the right altitude to impale her heart. She would have been killed instantly. Razorback, who was significantly taller than Aliya, and therefore took his wound several inches lower, was not that lucky. Even as the spear protruding from his chest turned scarlet with his own life blood, he had time to look down and realize that he was looking at his own death. "Oh," he managed.

Aliya cried out in rage, and returned fire from around Razorback's side. The long shaft of ice leading from Razorback's spine to the outstretched hand of a still-recovering Iceman made lining up the shot as easy as possible. She made eye contact with Iceman even as she fired, and understanding passed between them. He did not have time to cry out before her head shot struck home.

The sounds of battle from below continued. They seemed impossibly far away; she had literally a world of reasons to hurry there right now, but she could not bring herself to go just yet, not with Razorback bubbling out his last few breaths. She snapped the ice spear in twain with a single blow from her right hand, caught Razorback's huge form, and gently eased him to the floor.

She watched his face as he fought for life. It was a good man's face, the face of a brave and honest man, who'd done what he could while others ran. A face that

TIME'S ARROW

managed to gaze up at hers with total dignity even as it lay framed by the ludicrously large pig head he used as a helmet.

"Thank you," she said simply.

He coughed out a mouthful of blood, and managed, "Aliya . . . take this pig head off of me. . . . I can't use it anymore. . . ."

"Buford, I can't—"

"Take it," he rasped, with surprising strength. "I ain't bein' . . . sentimental here . . . it has my generator . . . it carries enough volts to knock out a platoon . . . an' some other surprises too . . . you might be able to use it. . . . You might . . ." He closed his eyes, shuddered, and opened them again, but this time he didn't even know she was there. "Those are . . . Big Pig's runnin' lights up ahead . . . but I can't get to her. . . . she won't . . . stop for me. . . ."

A long last breath whistled through his lips, and he was gone. Just another casualty in a war that seemed determined to leave no survivors.

She wished she had time to mourn. But Spider-Man still needed her help, down below. The sounds of battle were not getting any lighter, and the few surviving members of the PLF were fast running out of time. Just about all she could afford to do, before complying with his last request, was lower her head, blink away a wave of impotent grief, and murmur, "Rest well, Buford. You were the best of us."

Antarctica. The confrontation inside the ice cave, as seen by the Beast:

She was not human. He saw that at once. Nor was she wounded. The "blood" hemorrhaging from her open wound was too dark, too watery, too much like fuel. Her eyes, now that he saw them close, were unpainted gray spheres of metal, as soulless as the eyes of a mannequin. But the worst part was her smile: the way it arced across her face like a mechanical rictus, displaying neither warmth, mirth, nor conscience.

THE PRESENT

"Surprised?" she gibed. "Don't feel bad. You're supposed to be."

He grabbed her by the collar of her goose-down parka. "All right. So it was a nice head-game. Make the heroes think they just wounded an innocent girl. Very droll. But what's all this about? Why did Kang really put you here?"

She brushed away his furry hands with a single slap. "Do you really want to know? I'll be perfectly happy to tell you. It is, after all, one of my functions."

"Yes, I want to know!"

"Well," she said chattily, "in part, I'm here because Kang needed an agent in this timeline to make preparations for today's gala festivities. Obviously, somebody had to go around hiring the likes of Volcana and the Taskmaster and the Wrecking Crew. Somebody had to dig out this cave and set up the force field so you'd be able to keep yourself busy fighting. Somebody had to look all cute and vulnerable so you'd feel just terrible about yourself and therefore unable to exercise the primitive mound of fat you possess in place of a mind. That person was me, and for what it's worth, I think I did a perfectly bang-up job. Don't you?"

The Beast understood that the robot was not responsible for its attitude; it was only relaying the thoughts and the mind of Kang. But that didn't make the tone in its voice any easier to take. He gritted his teeth and said, "What else?"

"I'm also here because somebody had to rub in just how foolish you and your friends have been. You've obviously seen how carefully my master arranged these little encounters—letting you see where the missiles were and giving you time to get to them? You obviously knew he was manipulating you, and still you rushed in, thinking you understood the nature of this battle." She laughed. "It didn't even occur to you that the only reason he would have let you do this is *to take from you the energy he needs to finish the job.*"

The Beast could have spoken the same words simultaneously. He'd expected a hidden agenda all along, and only his various travails with the Rhino, the ice cave, and this allegedly wounded girl had prevented him from deducing its true nature. But now that it stood revealed, a sudden terrible awareness welled up inside him. After all, if Kang needed energy, there was somebody out there who was more than willing to provide it, thinking only that he was doing the right thing.

As if reading his thoughts, the robot said, "Go ahead. Stop him."

The glacier shifted again. The icefalls shuddered and collapsed, sinking with unstoppable speed into an abyss that seemed more than willing to swallow them all. The Beast was terribly certain it was only seconds before the flow of melting ice would come roaring into the alcove and slam both the robot and himself into the back wall with bone-crushing force.

Then the avalanche shuddered and slowed, and the Beast saw something impossible smiling down on him from above.

Daylight.

Only a thin sliver of daylight, of course, all that the crevasse permitted entry—and it was almost a hundred yards above him, through a crack so narrow that reaching the top would be a test of his willingness to squeeze through tight places. The top was also so far away that getting there would mean a race against the crumbling momentum of the glacier. He could very easily climb only half the distance and find himself flattened to the thickness of paper when the next shift of the ice shut the walls of the crevasse upon him. Or he could get almost all the way to the top, trigger an avalanche, and end up buried alive, with every bone in his body shattered to gravel.

Either way, it wasn't the kind of back door that gave escape routes a good name.

But it was still his only way to get to Cable before he made a terrible mistake.

"Good Beast," the robot said. "Obedient Beast."

The Beast turned his back on the cackling thing and forced his way into the shaft.

THE PRESENT

• • •

The Devil's Crescent. The fury of the monsoon, as seen by Storm:

It was like trying to gather up an explosion once it had already left the bomb. It was like trying to catch a tsunami in a paper cup. It was like being in love with something that only knew hate, something that despised her and the rest of the world so much that it wanted only to flatten everything there was into splintered, undifferentiated wreckage.

It was like holding the world in her hands, knowing it was too heavy for her, and being unable to put it down.

It was like all of that, and it was one other thing:

Glorious.

She was not just Storm, now, not just a powerful mutant woman with the temerity to name herself after forces she could influence but never fully control. She *was* the storm. She felt every inch of it, from the variable pressure fronts that were its organs to the cyclone-force winds that were its limbs. She could feel the unimaginable fury that reached from the angry clouds to the poor beleaguered ground. She could taste the terror of all the living things within, from the bent and straining trees, struggling to hold on to the earth that gave them life, to the members of the Wrecking Crew, who, as they fought Iceman, shouted threats that could not come close to matching this magnificent insane cyclone for sheer arrogant bluster.

She sensed Iceman, battling at the very limits of his endurance, using an ice scoop thirty feet high to drive the various members of the Wrecking Crew back into the waters of the swamp. She didn't pay any particular attention. Keeping track of all the storm's myriad variables took so much from her that, at this moment, names like Iceman and Professor Xavier and Kang might as well have been visions from another life.

No, right now, she had more important things to occupy her mind.

Right now, she was speaking to the monsoon.

She was taking the natural laws that governed all its

massive destructive force, and erasing them, one at a time, in favor of a brand-new set of rules. She was bringing all the power of the monsoon together, compressing it. The more she did this, the less the regions inside looked like the natural world, and the more they looked like hell unleashed on earth—and the less chance that she, who stood at its center, would survive with something resembling flesh on her bones. But that didn't matter either. Even if she died, even if Iceman and the Wrecking Crew and every living thing in this swamp died, she'd already told the storm what she wanted it to do. She'd already told it what to destroy.

Somewhere within the sphere of controlled chaos, the various members of the Wrecking Crew finally seemed to realize that the apocalypse was at hand. They started screaming, in words that the winds would never permit voice. Iceman, who had been fighting them with everything he had only a few seconds earlier, now stumbled into their midst and began using his powers to construct shelter for them all. Somehow, they didn't seize the opportunity to kill him. They were too busy wailing and moaning like terrified infants. Truth to tell, as the rains and the winds melted away his walls of ice faster than he could project them, Iceman seemed within a heartbeat of panic himself.

It didn't matter.

Not to Storm. Not now.

She was working on a scale that made them little more than insects.

She was seducing the uncontrollable.

She was showing it Kang's missile and saying, *This, here. This is what you hate. This is what you have to destroy.*

And the heart of the monsoon contracted to a single, tightly focused point of nearly infinite rage.

The South Seas. The lip of the volcano, as seen by Gambit:
Sometimes, the Cajun impressed even himself.

THE PRESENT

It wasn't every down-home New Orleans boy who ran straight up the slope of an erupting volcano while the earth convulsed like a dying thing. It wasn't every down-home New Orleans boy who battled his way onward, through a blizzard of ash that reduced visibility to almost nothing.

It wasn't every down-home New Orleans boy who was so thoroughly crazy that he actually made it all the way to the summit.

Yes, Gambit thought, with more than a little self-satisfaction, *Wolverine might have the attitude, but Remy LeBeau, he has the class.*

Another section of rim gave way, collapsing into the crater itself—more debris to fling when it came time for the inevitable explosion. Gambit paid it no mind. He leapt free of a section of rock that crumbled beneath his feet and pressed himself against the protruding surface of the missile. It was so big that, in terrain this unstable, being anywhere within a hundred yards of it was about as intelligent as daring a two-trailer semi to perform a barrel roll over his bones. When the ground shook again, the missile rocked visibly, as if trying to decide whether to fall into the volcano or slide down the mountain. Gambit, who was on the slope side, knew which choice he'd support if consulted.

He supposed that when the volcano went, it stood a substantial chance of destroying the missile all on its own.

He also supposed that it would be kind of stupid to rely on that.

So he pressed both his palms against the side of the missile and concentrated, sending forth wave after wave of explosive kinetic energy into the metal construct by his side. It wasn't easy. The missile was big, and the larger an object was, the more energy it needed to become unstable explosive matter. That was why he tended to rely on light, portable things like playing cards. If running up the side of an active volcano during a major earthquake hadn't exhausted him, then performing this little miracle was certain to cost him pretty much everything he still had left. Not a fun prospect at all, considering that he'd prob-

TIME'S ARROW

ably have to run back down and rescue Wolverine when this was over.

Somehow, he remembered somebody telling him once that life as an X-Man was going to be easy. He knew nobody would ever say such a ridiculous thing. But for just this moment, in this one insane circumstance, knowing that it wasn't true, he actually seemed to remember somebody saying that.

Silly person, whoever it was.

His normally tan complexion grew noticeably paler as, beneath his expert touch, Kang's missile began to glow.

Antarctica. The last moments in the life of the canyon of ice, as seen by Cable:

He stood on the lip of a bottomless crevasse that stretched from one end of the canyon to the other. He stood despite being soaking wet, in an environment that qualified as one of the most inhospitably cold on earth—despite simultaneous singed skin on his face and hands, courtesy of his long battle with Volcana. He stood despite being physically exhausted, despite expecting to pass out from hypothermia at any second.

He stood, and he thought of Aliya.

It was funny, how many of his memories of her revolved around having to endlessly fight for their lives in the hell his future had become. It was funny how, when he tried to conjure up the intimate moments, they came reluctantly, and only after he first found himself awash with battle memories, where her perfect face was just a crescent glowing red by the light of distant fires. He realized now—and not for the first time—that the main reason he would always think of battlefields as home is that battlefields were still places he couldn't help associating with her.

He swore now that if he found her, that would change. They would live a life far from battlefields—a life filled only with their love for each other.

But right now that was worlds away.

He aimed his ion cannon at Kang's missile and fired.

THE PRESENT

Streams of glowing energy shot from his weapon and corruscated above and around the curving walls of the missile. It didn't blow up. He kept firing, cursing at it, daring it to explode for him, hating it as he'd hated no other inanimate object in his life. He dared it to die, and he fired at it some more, hating his cannon for not being powerful enough, hating Kang for having brought such a terrible thing into existence.

He fired with such single-minded abandon that he didn't sense Volcana approaching until she was standing right next to him. And even then he didn't stop. He didn't dare. If she still wanted to fry him to a cinder, she could. She just had to wait until he completed the job he'd come here to do.

After a moment, she said, "So, that's what you were talking about before, right? That's some kind of sicko super-weapon designed to blow up the world?"

He kept firing. "The multiverse, actually. But yes."

She sniffed. "Well, I guess we can't have *that*." And she extended her arms and fired waves of searing heat at the missile. "You know, Cabe—if I can call you that—I really wish you took the trouble to mention this in the first place."

The South Seas. The last moments at the volcanic spring, as seen by Wolverine:

He was in better shape than he had been—his healing factor had repaired most of his burns and blisters, and even begun the process of regenerating the damage Electro's final attack had done to his internal organs—but he was not yet ready to go chasing after Gambit, and right now he had worse problems to think of.

One was Electro, who was just now beginning to stir. He'd be up and around and ready to start fighting in another couple of seconds. Once upon a time, Wolverine would have popped his claws and carved Electro to pieces without even a moment's reservation. He half wanted to do it now; after all, Spider-Man kept dropping the ball, and doing the job for him would at least save the webhead the trouble of having to fight this punk another fifteen or twenty times. But Wolverine's standards had changed quite a bit since joining the X-Men. Though he was still willing to kill when necessary, he would not take preventive measures against those who had temporarily fallen.

So he limped over to Electro's side, and leaned over, and growled in the stirring super-villain's ear.

"Listen up, bub. I know what you're thinkin'. You're thinkin' that you hate my guts, and you can't wait to get up so you can fry me again. You're thinkin' that this time you'll hit me with fifty times the juice, an' turn' me all black an' crispy, an' that you'll use the money you'll get paid to live high on the hog while plottin' your next attack on the bug-man.

"Well, lemme tell you somethin'. I got very good senses, and when somebody like you decides to take me on, he lets off maybe fifty different subtle cues warnin' me that he's about to strike. An' just because you took me by surprise once, don't mean you can manage it a second time when I'm ready for you."

Electro managed a moaned word: "S-so?"

"So," Wolverine grinned, "if you get off that ground with anythin' on your mind other than runnin' for dear life, I'll know it. And I promise you right now that I'll be very careful *not* to kill you."

When the meaning of Wolverine's words sunk in, Electro's already haggard features turned several shades paler.

Wolverine didn't need his sense of smell to know what the man's scent would be. The fight had gone out of him. He would make no attempt to reengage hostilities. He would simply get up and run away as fast as he could— which would be a happy ending only if Kang in all his wisdom had neglected to provide him with a boat.

That was one problem taken care of.

The other, Hydro-Man, was far more dangerous. A man made out of water had nothing to fear from Wolverine's claws. And Hydro-Man was recovering too—already, barely visible among the general volcanic haze, Wolverine

THE PRESENT

could make out a vaguely humanoid form, coming together out of mist.

Antarctica. The last moments in the canyon of ice, as experienced by the Beast:

He had returned to daylight, after a harrowing climb that had almost killed him more than once, and had wasted no time descending into the canyon so he could stop Cable from making a tragic mistake. By the time he reached the ankle-deep slush that the floor of the canyon had become, he had already spotted Cable in the distance, standing alongside Volcana as the two of them fired ion bursts and streams of superheated flame into the crevasse at their feet.

The Beast did not know what had happened to make Volcana change sides, and right now he didn't care. He just had to hurry up and stop them.

He ran, shouting. *"Cable, Volcana, stop! You don't know what you're doing!"*

He screamed the words at the top of his lungs, with as much volume as he could muster. But they were too far away, and they couldn't hear him over the sound of their own attack. He ran faster, his boots carving deep footprints in the slush, his eyes focusing on nothing but the two tiny figures who, for all his speed, remained too far away.

He hadn't covered even a quarter of the distance before he glimpsed something out of the corner of his eye—something huge and gray and glistening with crystals of ice. He whirled, but it was too late. A hand as powerful as anything he'd ever known had seized him by his left wrist and lifted him off his feet. In an instant, another hand whipped around and grabbed him by his right ankle, and he was held aloft, struggling, all his considerable strength turned to weakness in the hands of somebody whose power put his to shame.

It was the Rhino, of course. And though he looked like he'd been through a war—icicles dangled from his arms and his mask and even from the skin of his remarkably unlovely face—the single ugliest thing about him was the triumph in his smile.

TIME'S ARROW

The Beast cried out, "Listen, you Brobdingnagian behemoth, you don't know what's at stake here! You don't know what your employer's planning to do!"

"That's right," the Rhino grumbled. "And who cares? All I wanna do is teach you the price of calling me a hippo."

The last thing the Beast thought before the Rhino proceeded with his lessons was: *Oh great, somebody was the fat kid back in grade school and now wants to overcompensate.*

Limbo. The throne room of Kang the Conqueror:

The instrumentation used for measuring the currents and eddies of the timeflow had taken many forms over the years. It had been a glowing sphere of light, an impossibly complex wall of machinery crackling with eldritch energy, and—memorably, at one point—an irregular stone archway that constantly flashed newsreel footage of the great historical events of the past. Some of these methods were impressive, others not, but none among them lasted very long before the cosmic whims of Limbo replaced them with something else.

At this particular moment, the instrumentality was a dipstick.

Lireeb pulled a two-yard strip of flexible and chronally sensitive metal from its slot, used a common rag to wipe it clean of random possibility, then reinserted it and pulled it free again. After examining the level, he frowned. "My liege?" he said. "According to this, the Time Arrows are done."

Kang, who'd been watching the various battles through the flames in his fireplace, said, "Then the energy provided by the X-Men—"

"—has in turn provided us with critical mass. Which will no doubt prompt you to exclaim, 'Excellent!'"

Kang glowered at Lireeb.

The South Seas. The last moments at the lip of the volcano, as seen by Gambit:

248

THE PRESENT

The missile was glowing like a miniature sun, with so much kinetic energy that it could have been set off by a sneeze. Gambit could feel it *wanting* to explode, even as he felt the volcano beneath him *wanting* to erupt. He hated being next to either one, but he couldn't bring himself to stop. He was too afraid of giving up a few seconds too early and discovering that he hadn't done everything he could.

Left to his own devices, he might have stayed at that one spot, feeding energy into Kang's missile, until either missile or mountain exploded and scattered his atoms from here to Mount Saint Helens.

In the end, the decision was taken out of his hands.

The mountain shuddered again, and a vast shelf of rock, maybe a quarter of a mile across, collapsed into the crater, most of it one big piece, like a car skidding down a steep hill. The piece holding Gambit and Kang's missile disintegrated a little more slowly—so slowly that Gambit actually had a chance to feel the earth itself turn to gravel beneath his feet, and realize that if he didn't retreat now he'd be joining the missile and everything else within a hundred yards in the great seismic equivalent of a wok.

He didn't bother running. Running, he would not have made it.

Instead, he turned his back to the crater and leapt into open space, not caring as the slope curved downward beneath him, not caring even as the ground, already too far beneath him, disintegrated and fell a quarter of a mile in less than a second.

He only cared as gravity took over, and he started falling toward a ground that was no longer there. His only hope was for his angular momentum to carry him over the new crater rim.

It did, at what seemed the last second. But though he hit at a glancing angle, which saved him from breaking every bone in his body, he still hit hard enough to hurt. The breath was knocked out of him as he tumbled head over heels, bounced, dislodged an already weakened ledge,

TIME'S ARROW

and began a long, uncontrolled slide down the slope of the mountain.

He was aware of only one thing: that he only had a few seconds left to get back to Wolverine.

Antarctica. The canyon of ice, as seen by the Beast:

The Rhino was having a grand old time, teaching Dr. Hank McCoy the price of suggesting humiliating alterations in established self-images. In fact, he was having so good a time, holding the Beast by the ankles and slamming him against the slushy ground again and again, that the Beast honestly wasn't sure there was still malice in it. After all, the slush softened the impact, the padding on his parka cushioned much of what was left, and though the Beast wasn't particularly enjoying this, he wasn't suffering any permanent damage either. Indeed, the Rhino's main interest appeared to be complaining loudly and at length about being compared to a hippo.

And the Beast's main problem with that was that he just did not have the time to wallow in the man's angst.

So he popped his boots. He waited until the Rhino swung him in some direction approximating where he wanted to go, relaxed his ankles, and let the shouting Rhino yank the footwear right off him. Momentum carried him a full thirty yards. He hit the ground in a tuck-and-roll, which he instantly converted to a run, aware from the pounding drumbeat behind him that the Rhino was already in close pursuit.

The Beast ran faster—mostly because he was able to incorporate leaping—but even as he drew closer to the two figures up ahead, he knew that his lead was not a comfortable one. He would not be able to stop and explain. If he did, the Rhino would be upon him almost as soon as he opened his mouth.

So he just shouted again. *"Cable, don't do it!"*

This time Cable heard him. He stopped firing, and turned, his eyes wide and questioning. Volcana turned, too, her own confusion clearly visible through her mask of dancing flame. There was no malice in her eyes at all.

THE PRESENT

She might have come frighteningly close to committing murder today, but she still—somehow—radiated the well-meaning innocence of a woman who honestly didn't mean any harm.

Cable said, "Beast? What are you—?"

"No time to explain, effendi. We have to get back to the winery, *right now*!" The Beast turned to Volcana, and blurted out all he had time to say, "And you have to take your big stupid friend and get as far away from here as you can, now!"

Volcana boggled. "But—the bomb—aren't you going to explain—"

"Some other time!" the Beast said. "Just take my word for it and *run*!"

He reached into his parka and activated the TDC recall, praying that she'd listen to his advice in time.

The Devil's Crescent. The last few seconds in the swamp, as seen by Iceman:

The monsoon had reached an intensity that he wouldn't have dreamed possible, melting his makeshift igloo faster than he could generate the ice to hold it together. When the winds came in, the members of the Wrecking Crew had scattered into the surrounding swamp, seeking shelter that did not exist. Iceman would have gone after them, tried to include them in his shelter, but visibility was now absolute zero.

So he began the long and arduous search for Storm.

The winds would have blown him away if he'd just tried walking normally, so he secured each step by spearing the earth with a piton of ice, twenty feet into the ground. The pitons anchored him, as long as he moved quickly to the next one. The hot rain melted each one in seconds.

He knew he was headed in the right direction because he could feel what was happening to the air. It was becoming supercharged, pregnant with potential, filled with the sense of something terrible about to happen. He did not know whether that sensation came from Kang's bomb or from Storm herself, but that didn't matter. Ororo was this way. Ororo needed him.

Just how badly she needed him, he didn't know until the winds carried Storm's voice to him. "Bobby, get away! I can't stop it!"

Hoping those same winds would carry his own voice back, he replied, lurching toward her, "Can't stop what?"

"The monsoon! I've directed it to hit this one spot where I'm standing, but I've concentrated it too much. Any second now, it's going to hit us with all its electrical energy at once—with enough power to destroy everything within two miles of here!"

Iceman wasn't surprised. He felt it. He was sure that every living thing in range felt it.

But the nexus of all this gathering energy seemed to be right up ahead. As he staggered toward that impossibly dangerous place, with every instinct in his body warning him to turn and run, he could even make out Storm, who lay curled in a ball by Kang's missile, eyes tightly shut in the manner of a woman who'd conquered whirlwinds but had finally found one so powerful it wouldn't let even her go. He reached her, and pressed his TDC recall, just in time to see everything around them turn flashbulb-white, in anticipation of an apocalypse now less than one second from arrival.

The South Seas. The last few seconds at the volcanic spring, as seen by Wolverine:

Hydro-Man had congealed. He was a seven-foot-tall parody of humanity, constructed of water gone filthy with volcanic ash. He was filled with rage at what had been done to him, and as he ambled toward the still-not-quite recovered Wolverine, he was literally boiling with sick anticipation of the vengeance he was about to inflict. Wolverine could only stand before him, brandishing claws he knew to be useless, determined only to die with the courage of the *ronin* he had trained himself to be.

Then underground gases ignited, and the volcanic spring exploded. All its remaining water shot straight up,

THE PRESENT

with a violence that turned most of it to steam. What was left fell back down as boiling rain, liberally spiced with mud. Wolverine grunted with pain as a dozen fresh burns raised welts on his exposed back. Hydro-Man cried out as a wall of mud the size of a bus impacted him head-on, knocking him down with a force that would have crushed a man made of flesh and blood.

But what emerged from the mound of steaming mud was not a man made of flesh and blood.

Nor was it, strictly speaking, any longer a man made of water.

It was brown, and shapeless, and glistening, and only vaguely humanoid, and possessed of a face that resembled a sculpture melting in the heat. As Wolverine watched, it looked down at itself and cried out, "Aw, no, not *mud* again!"

Wolverine grinned. He brandished his claws, and took two steps forward, gratified by the arrival of something solid enough to carve.

But he didn't get his chance, because that's when Gambit stumbled into view, looking knocked around and miserable but nevertheless in time to activate the TDC recall.

It happened all over the world, almost simultaneously.

In Antarctica, a device buried in glacial ice succumbed to a combination of hypercharged ionic energy and tremendous external heat, blowing up without releasing the even more deadly forces within. The explosion further weakened a glacier already crumbling from the forces released earlier that day. The ice not actually vaporized by the heat became a torrent of boiling water, which melted a furrow miles long before finally cooling down enough to freeze once again. The resulting shifts to the surrounding glacier were significant enough to show up on seismographs all over the world.

In the South Seas, a long-dormant volcano exploded with a force that rang church bells fifteen hundred miles away. The island where it stood was literally blown off the Earth. The ocean spent days just swirling into the underwater crater it left behind. Tsunami of record size radiated outward in every direction, causing massive flooding in cities all around the Pacific Rim. The eruption would soon raise another island on the same spot, complete with another volcanic cone taking the place of the one that had so violently wiped itself off the map. But right now, the ocean was still boiling—and some of the boiling water took the shape of an anguished human face.

In Southeast Asia, a powerful monsoon ravaging a beleaguered swamp defied all known meteorological laws by just disappearing from satellite surveillance between one second and the next. The final readings indicated a power surge of almost thermonuclear intensity—followed by silence, and the revelation that much of the swamp was suddenly gone, replaced by an expanse of fused glass. Most government observers began wondering just what kind of bomb had gone off here—not suspecting that the damage was limited to only this much because the bomb that had been there hadn't gone off at all.

They were three cataclysms of genuinely worldwide import.

The good news was, they were less than they could have been. There was still a planet left when they were done.

The bad news, for everybody still alive on the planet, was that they still provided Kang with the means to create a cataclysm unimaginably worse.

Kang considered the irony and laughed.

It was a laugh that had overseen the wholesale murder of untold trillions of sentient beings, the laugh of a mind twisted enough to consider all that unimaginable carnage and imagine itself doing the right thing.

Lireeb, who stood at the entrance to the throne room holding a teakettle on a tray, cleared his throat and said, "When you're done cackling, m'lord?"

"Yes?" Kang responded with the irritation that was, increasingly, his reaction to everything Lireeb said. "What do you want?"

THE PRESENT

Lireeb placed the tray on the table by Kang's side. "Do you want to resume wreaking havoc on the multiverse now, or wait until after you've had your Earl Grey?"

There was a peculiar thrill to mass destruction that made Kang almost want to set off the timequake now, but he had other priorities. Reluctantly, he said, "We wait. We may have the means to create the ultimate timequake, but we're still searching for a timeline where my beloved Ravonna lives. And all of this will be meaningless unless I can be with her again."

"I agree, m'lord. We wouldn't want to lose our sense of reasonable perspective, would we?"

"Not at all," Kang said, his irritation rising. "As for you, don't you have anything else that needs doing?"

Lireeb smiled—a sight that disturbed Kang in ways that even he hesitated to contemplate. "Oh, certainly, m'lord. I imagine I could go ask the ten million monkeys in the antechamber whether they've finished with *Hamlet* yet. But I would like to ask one question before I take my leave."

Kang dismissively gestured. "Just make it quick."

"I just wanted to know, sir—if all you needed to do, in order to secure enough energy for your nefarious purposes, was arrange for people with super-powers to direct their forces at your devices—then why have we gone to all the trouble of hiring super-villains to take on the X-Men? Why didn't we just hire said villains to attack the missiles directly? Why not say, dear fellows, if you want to earn a fast million dollars, just stand there and blast this device here with everything you have?"

For a moment that stretched into eons, Kang sat without sound. Then, rising with the ponderous majesty of a monarch who has brooked one impudent question too many, he stood and locked eyes with his towering manservant. "Because I am a gamesmaster, playing at the ultimate tournament of conquest. Because my grand victory will mean nothing if I accomplish it without defeating foes who are worthy of me. And because it pleases me to toy with my enemies. *That* is why."

"I see." Lireeb nodded. "I'm so glad I asked. After all, I would hate to go on supposing that you just hadn't thought of it." He nodded slightly. "Until 'later,' m'lord."

CHAPTER FOURTEEN

For the last several minutes, Spider-Man had fought alone. He had been leaping from one level of the silo to another, dodging the missiles and energy weapons of the various Mandroids on his tail. He had skirted explosions, sought refuge in one administrative office after another, temporarily confused his foes by hiding in air vents and closets, and even taken out two of the Mandroids. Once, he had even reached the ground level, within sight of the room housing the stasis grid—but when the Mandroids began peppering the ground with concussion grenades, he'd had to swallow his pride and retreat up two levels, where he and the Beast reduced some poor paper-pusher's office into a riot of splintered furniture and overturned files. Since then, he'd been staying just one step ahead of his pursuers, managing to take out one or two but never quite achieving the decisive action that would once again gain him access to the stasis grid.

Now, as he battled the Beast and the two remaining Mandroids in a small lounge beyond a door midway up the silo, it occurred to him that he really ought to be winning. He was Spider-Man. And for all his pretense of being nothing more than a friendly neighborhood super hero, he had, at times, successfully defeated forces far more formidable than these. He'd even fought the entire membership of the X-Men to a standstill. There was no way that the Beast and a handful of guys in robot suits should have been able to keep him from the stasis grid.

But his heart wasn't in this fight.

This world had taken its toll. It had revealed that his career as Spider-Man had been pure poison to everybody he'd ever cared about. It had shown him a version of himself who cynically held on to his riches by looking out for number one. And it had probably left him responsible for the ambush that had met the members of the Power Liberation Front. He felt useless and deluded—and though he had managed to hold his own so far, his fighting showed it.

He clung to the wall over a sink as the Beast and the two Mandroids fanned out along the dining tables.

THE PRESENT

The Beast said, "I've got to give you credit, Spider-Man. You're almost as hard to catch as me. But you're still wasting your time. I just got word that more than half the membership of the PLF is already reported dead, and that your precious leader Magneto has already fled, in search of some more losers willing to follow him. Face it, you've already lost. Why continue to fight in a burning house when you don't have to?"

"I don't know, chuckles," Spider-Man said, with a bravado he didn't feel. "Maybe I'm just goofy that way." He flipped out of the way of a stream of flame fired from the gauntlets of one of the nearest Mandroids, scurried across the ceiling one step ahead of a series of concussion grenades fired from the wrist of another, then abruptly changed course and scrambled over to a bank of vending machines.

Probably suspecting what he was up to, the Beast leapt to intercept him. But he was too late. Spider-Man had already ripped a candy machine from its recess in the wall and flung it with all his strength at the nearest Mandroid. It was a fairly easy throw, for somebody with Spider-Man's strength—especially since it was a candy machine, whose merchandise was lighter than a fully stocked soda machine would have been.

The targeted Mandroid picked absolutely the wrong weapon to use against it, blasting the glass case with twin jets of high-temperature chemical flame. This may have made the glass shatter, and the candy inside blacken and melt (save for the microwave popcorn, which popped first), but it did nothing to lessen the machine's momentum. Now a box filled with raging flame, it smashed the first Mandroid head-on even as Spider-Man flung a second vending machine (this one a heavier one hawking a variety of fruit juices) at another Mandroid circling around for a good shot.

The Beast grabbed Spider-Man by the arm before he could make a missile of a third vending machine stocked with wrapped deli sandwiches. "I should have known that somebody like you would never be fit to join the X-Men."

TIME'S ARROW

"You're telling me," Spider-Man said, as he sent the Beast flying with a punch to the jaw. "A man who'd waste *this* much food would be hell on your annual picnics."

The Mandroid he'd decked with the candy machine hurled the flaming mass of red-hot metal away with a force that sent it crashing through the ceiling. Flaming debris peppered the lunch tables like hail. Spider-Man did not need to be invited twice. He backflipped, kicked off the wall, hopped onto one of the tables, and leapt through the hole into the blood analysis lab up above, not at all inconvenienced by the fusillade of machine-gun fire that followed him as he went. More to the point was the awareness that only four Mandroids had pursued him into the lower depths of the silo, and that the two still functioning were both in the lounge down below. They might be after him in seconds, but if he moved now there was nothing between him and the stasis grid.

He darted across the lab and smashed into the locked steel door with both feet, an impact that knocked it off its hinges and sent it crashing through the catwalk railing and into open space. For a moment, Spider-Man stood astride the now-horizontal door, riding it as it plummeted toward the bottom of the silo. Any sufficiently imaginative observer would have thought he was surfing. Then his weight made it flip over as it fell, leaving him riding its underbelly, reduced to a potential door-and-concrete sandwich. He leapt free a heartbeat before impact, scrambling across the circular walls with a speed that would have shamed an Olympic sprinter, his destination the door to the stasis grid chamber.

His destination was within reach when the Beast suddenly dropped into position to block his way. In the instant he had to gauge the depth of the murderous rage in the Beast's features, Spider-Man saw that his last punch must have been a particularly solid one, because the Beast's lips were now swollen and scarlet with blood. It did not make the Beast look less formidable. If anything, it accented his fangs, and what he could do with them if he chose. Unfortunate as the image was, the Beast underlined it by

THE PRESENT

snarling, "You've run out of chances, arachnid. Now I rip out your throat!"

"Not on your best day, Hank." Spider-Man extended his hands and with an audible *thwip* fired blasts of webbing into both of the Beast's eyes. It was an effective tactic, though one he rarely used unless his opponent was wearing glasses or goggles; there was just too much potential damage involved in exposing somebody else's eyes to one of the most powerful, albeit temporary, glues ever invented. But right now the urgency of the situation demanded it. This prompted a roar of almost unbelievable rage from the Beast.

Spider-Man then leapt over him in an all-out attempt to reach the door. It was a rare miscalculation. One he might have avoided, had he been feeling any more himself. His spider-sense even tried to warn him, but he was too distracted with his own feelings of responsibility to pay enough attention to it.

As it was, he severely underestimated how good the Beast could be without decent vision. As Spider-Man vaulted over him, the Beast leapt up, grabbed him by the ankles, swung him around, and slammed him against the ground.

The impact would have broken every bone in a normal person's body. Spider-Man's, which was considerably more forgiving of such things, merely felt the impact as agonizing pain. He twisted out of the Beast's grip, and somersaulted back to his feet, facing his opponent with new respect, aware now that, temporarily blinded or not, the Beast was still capable of giving him a fight.

Then a jab of pain from his spider-sense made him look up, and he realized that he might not have time to deal with it.

The catwalk above him was covered with Mandroids. Not just the two he'd left in the break room, but another six, who were no doubt reinforcements from the teams that had wiped out Night Thrasher and the rest of his squad. The other six looked ready to rock. What's worse, they were all aiming their weapons at him in a lethal crossfire that he would probably be able to avoid for a while, but which would keep him on the defensive until long after yet another wave of reinforcements arrived.

Spider-Man had been in worse situations. He had triumphed in circumstances that made this feel like a kindergarten picnic. But right now, facing all those rockets and gun barrels and flamethrowers and gleaming metallic battle suits, knowing that if he defeated those he would just have to face more, he did not feel his usual determination to triumph against all odds.

All he could feel was a deep weariness, and the sense that when all was said and done there just wasn't any point in continuing to knock himself out. He was alone. He was trapped on a world he didn't know. He'd screwed up and doomed everybody who had a chance of setting things right. He'd learned that all his fighting ever accomplished was pain and suffering for the people he'd tried to protect. Why go on? Why not just settle for the inevitable?

He almost raised his hands in surrender. Almost.

But then a deep, primal, integral part of him—the part that had been raised by two tough old birds named Ben and May Parker, that was husband to Mary Jane Watson-Parker, that persisted in patrolling the city as Spider-Man despite all the temptations to let others fight the good fight for once—cried out silently: *No way, Parker! Not today! You've taken us down this road before, and you're* not *doing it again!*

When the Beast lunged for him, Spider-Man ducked under the blow, grabbed his opponent by the upper arms, and flung him against the opposite wall.

And the universe rewarded him for his defiance in the form of a familiar lithe form, who landed beside him with the grace of a cat. The newcomer was Aliya, who now carried an ion cannon on each arm. There was something big and unwieldy strapped to her back, but it didn't seem to inconvenience her any as she fired strafing bursts with both weapons.

The Mandroids were startled, but Spider-Man saw at once that she hadn't been aiming at them, but at the sup-

THE PRESENT

ports that anchored the spiral catwalk to the walls of the silo. One entire loop of the catwalk broke free with a metallic scream. The three Mandroids who'd been standing there toppled over the side, too surprised to use their bootjets until they'd fallen more than half the distance to the floor. By then, their flight was somewhat less than modulated. One couldn't pull himself out of the dive and merely accelerated his headfirst plunge into the concrete floor. The other two managed to pull up, but couldn't regain full control, and smashed through the silo wall.

As debris rained down on all sides, Spider-Man shook his head. "Thugs in armor. Ya gotta love 'em."

"Glad to see you've got your spirit back, Spider-Man. For a second there it looked like we were going to lose you!"

"Yeah, well, sometimes remaining a champion of truth and justice doesn't come easy for me." The Mandroids up above were milling about, debating their next move. Spider-Man figured he and Aliya had maybe twenty seconds before they decided to press their attack. He tried to get to the stasis grid door again, but a wall of flame and machine-gun bullets and other nasty things fired from above cut him off. Instead, he leapt back, pulled Aliya over to relative shelter behind a section of collapsed catwalk, and hunkered down beside her, for the first time recognizing the large unwieldy object that she carried strapped to her back. It was a big tusked pig head. "Razorback?" he asked, afraid he already knew the answer.

"I'm afraid so. He gave his life for me."

Spider-Man's voice caught before he finally asked, "What about Bishop and Speedball?"

"Speedball was a spy for the other side; he's been taken care of. Bishop got knocked out, but I dragged him someplace where he won't be found. If we're lucky he'll join us later. As for Magneto—well, he and Sandman are still up and fighting, but I spoke to them by vocoder just a few seconds ago, and he's in no position to come and help us." She cocked her weapon grimly. "No. Right now, it's up to you, me, and one other."

TIME'S ARROW

"Leia?" Spider-Man guessed.

Fortunately, the one other revealed himself before Aliya had a chance to ask Spider-Man just what on Earth he was talking about. He appeared as a dancing speck of black, at the top of the silo, bouncing from one wall to another in a manner that resembled a contortionist acrobat performing at twenty times normal human speed. By the time he was halfway down the silo—dodging the assault of the Mandroids, who immediately dispatched half their force to intercept him—he was clearly recognizable as a man in a black bodysuit and black pullover ski mask. Spider-Man did not need to see the face behind the mask to know who it was. Delighted, horrified, relieved, awed, and for the first time in hours feeling a great dark weight lifted from his soul, Spider-Man exclaimed, "My God! That's me! I mean, him! I mean—"

Aliya's dark eyes pierced his like daggers. "I know what you mean, Spider-Man. And yes, that's him, all right. The secret heart of the PLF—a man who could have played by the rules that made him rich and famous and happy, but who instead chose to care about what's right. He's been our best information supplier for years—risking capture, death, public censure, and the loss of the idyllic life he built for himself, he even obtained the Project blueprints that got us this far. We would have been in his debt even if he hadn't insisted on coming along to help us tonight, but he said that he wouldn't let us go it alone. He's a hero, Peter—whatever world he lives on."

Spider-Man didn't know what to say. So he thumphered. "Uh—I—dammit, Aliya, why didn't he tell me?"

"Because he couldn't be sure the government hadn't sent you. He had to assume his loyalty was being tested."

"Then why didn't *you* tell me?"

"Because," Aliya said, calmly enough, "you never asked."

Somewhere up above, Wolverine's gravelly voice echoed throughout the silo: "All right, people, we're down to the wire now! No more taking of prisoners—I want the saboteurs *killed on sight!*"

THE PRESENT

The ominous words were immediately followed by an explosion that rippled through the silo with a force that tore much of the remaining spiral catwalk from the wall. Somewhere, Wolverine cried in rage. Mandroids tumbled in every direction, two trailing smoke as they spiraled toward crash landings on the ground floor. Another one, holding on to the bottom of a forty-foot section of detached catwalk, managed to get his bootjets working—but was immediately forced into a crash landing of his own by a beam of glowing energy that blasted him through the nearest wall.

The vocoder signal crackled in Spider-Man's ear and Bishop's voice said, "Spider-Man, it's me. I'm all right and on my way down. Now, stop slacking and help the lady get the job done."

Though Spider-Man's mask kept it from view, he had absolutely no doubt that Aliya saw his smile.

"Let's do it," he said.

In the end, it came down, for Cyclops, to a question of experience. Speed Demon was faster than any human being had a right to be, but so were a number of people. Indeed one of the others, Quicksilver, had been a foe and then ally of the X-Men for more years than Cyclops cared to count. And while super-speedsters were tricky opponents, they were no harder than any other as long as you learned how to anticipate their moves.

Of course, it also helped to have optic blasts that traveled at the speed of light.

Standing at the bottom of a pit of mud, pummeled by the dirt Speed Demon was shoveling in to bury him alive, Cyclops just filtered out the cold, the rain, the mud, and any fears he might have had about premature burial, and just concentrated on the circle of darkness high above, waiting for the fleeting red-and-green blur that would indicate Speed Demon's head momentarily passing within range.

When it did, Cyclops reacted with the speed of thought itself, shaming even Speed Demon's reaction time. His visor whipped open, his deadly ruby energy shot out, and Speed Demon was knocked thirty feet into the air by a blast that came uncomfortably close to ripping his head off.

Speed Demon did not even have time to cry out. He just jerked, described his unwilling ungraceful arc, and landed face-first among the rows of grapes. He did not get up.

Not far away, Taskmaster slashed at the redhead's throat with the imitation Wolverine claws around his wrist, but there was never any possibility of his actually being able to use them to cut her skin.

His hand descended only part of the way toward her neck ... then froze, held in place by the powerful mental block she'd just placed in his mind. As hard as he tried, he couldn't move his hand any closer to her neck.

And it didn't matter anyway, since without quite meaning to, he retracted the claws and was left with just a hand again.

He was unruffled. "That's okay, toots. The monofilament runs on an automated circuit. Do whatever you want to me, it'll still contract an' cut your pretty head clean off."

The strain showed on her mud-spattered face. Taskmaster trembled with anticipation.

The psychic scream that followed was a lot like being woken up by a bugle played at top volume next to his ear at sunrise. It was her mental voice, loud, defiant, and more powerful than he ever could have guessed: *No! I will not be defeated by a yo-yo!*

Taskmaster reeled. He tried to recover, but his thoughts were thick and sludgy, like mud about to freeze. He fell to his knees and remained paralyzed there just long enough to see the pretty lady manage a surge of telekinetic power that repelled the monofilament enough for her to remove her head from the noose. He tried to grab his boomerang, to knock her unconscious so he could kill her at his leisure, but somehow his hands refused to remember where the

THE PRESENT

boomerang was. By the time he fumbled for the billy club she was already towering over him, a supremely disgusted look in her eyes. He knew she would use her telepathic powers to finish the job she'd already started—and though he knew it was useless, he put all his remaining will into being ready for it when it came.

He did not expect her to haul off and deck him.

Cyclops had a hard time climbing from the pit. The walls were too soft—every handhold he grabbed came apart in his hands. His own desperation didn't make the task any easier. His mental link with Jean made him see every moment of her fight with Taskmaster as if he were right there beside her, and he couldn't avoid the terrible knowledge that he would never be able to get to her in time. When he sensed her triumph, he smiled, stopped struggling, and calmly waited for her to levitate him out.

"Ecch," she said. "You're all covered with mud."

"You too," he said.

"Good point. So I guess we can't get each other dirtier, then?"

"I guess not."

They hugged and kissed, knowing that there were still battles to be won but for the moment taking comfort in the sheer joy of finding each other at the end of the fight.

As they walked back to the house, he said, "One quick question?"

"Anything, Scott."

"I heard your psi-blast. Remember? *I will not be defeated by a yo-yo*?"

"Uh-huh."

"I'm sure he told you, but yo-yos are perfectly legitimate weapons."

"I knew that already," she said. "But I wasn't referring to his weapon. I was referring to him."

Inside, Professor Charles Xavier sat at the controls of the Time Displacement Core, wires trailing from his forehead to the control panel before him. It was a last-minute improvisation that enabled him to interface with the machine through a rickety combination of rewired backup systems and cannibalized technology. The latter came from Cerebro, the computer that Xavier had built years ago to seek out mutants for his school. Cerebro worked best when hooked up to Xavier's own powerful mind.

The strain of supplementing the TDC's damaged intelligence systems with the power of his own mind would have killed a lesser man. It was an effort even for Xavier, who needed to drive himself to his limits and beyond. Cold sweat trickled down his cheeks, and his features twitched from the regular jolts of agony. But the accident that shattered his legs had made pain his closest companion for decades. He refused to let it master him.

Through the interface, he saw time and space become distant irrelevancies. He saw everything that existed, in this universe and others, as patterns of interlocking probability—patterns that could be manipulated by anybody who knew how to make them dance. His X-Men were a very small element of those patterns. They were all depending on him for their salvation.

Obligingly, he reached out and brought them back home.

The teams returned from their various missions almost simultaneously, all of them looking like they'd been through a war. Gambit and Wolverine both arrived covered with volcanic ash, with Wolverine's costume reduced to smoking strips of tattered cloth. Iceman and Storm arrived spattered with mud, with Storm in particular looking pressed to the limits of her endurance. Cable and the Beast both arrived shivering—the Beast minus his boots—their insulated arctic clothing soaked through with freezing water.

Despite his own exhausted condition, Iceman was ebullient. "We destroyed the missiles, didn't we? All of them?"

Blaquesmith, who sat at another control panel, narrowed his already slitlike eyes. "According to my readings, yes. There seem to be major cataclysms at all the

THE PRESENT

locations you left—one meteorological, two geological—but they're all within normal tolerances. More importantly, the chronoton flow has completely stopped!''

"Oowee!" Iceman said, giving Gambit a high-five. "That's right! We bad!"

"Kang, he don't know who he playin' wit'!" Gambit responded.

The Beast snarled in disgust as he ripped the wet clothes from his body. "I'm afraid I have to dispel your illusions, my fellow marionettes, but we didn't do anything Kang didn't invite us to do. We knew that going in—and we obliged him anyway. All we accomplished was providing him with the power he wanted. The power to take this madness all the way to its logical conclusion."

Wolverine glowered. "Ain't exactly surprised to hear that, fuzzball, but do you mind telling us exactly what you're talkin' about?"

And as the Beast summarized what he'd found out in Antarctica—telling most of the story twice, because Cyclops and Phoenix arrived halfway through, and needed him to start all over again from the beginning—the expressions on the faces of his fellow X-Men transformed from relief that their battles were won, to dismay that their problems were just beginning. Like Wolverine, nobody looked particularly surprised. They'd all been waiting for the other shoe to drop. After all, they were X-Men, and when they won their battles, the stakes were usually raised for another round.

Blaquesmith moaned. "It's the twenty-five percent margin of error I told you about. The missiles weren't causing the destruction of timelines, they were just building up a well of destructive potential to be released when the missiles were destroyed. By fighting Kang, we caused the very cascade effect we were trying to stop."

Cable was grim. "Which stains our own hands with all this innocent blood."

"That's the kind of thinking Kang expects of us," Cyclops said. "He wants us to feel so personally responsible for all those deaths that we forget he was the one who

TIME'S ARROW

sent those things in the first place. Well, I won't tolerate that way of thinking, people. This was unknown technology, far ahead of anything we've ever seen. We can't crucify ourselves because we didn't know how it was supposed to work. All this does is give us more reason to bring the fight to him." He turned to Blaquesmith. "How are the repairs going?"

"We've taken a few shortcuts," Blaquesmith said, "but, thanks to the Cerebro hookup designed by the Professor and me, we'll be functional enough to carry us through until I have time to devote a few weeks to a more thorough job. We can recall Bishop and Spider-Man anytime you're ready."

"Then why haven't you done it?" Cyclops asked.

"Because—" Professor Xavier closed his eyes and, through a hideous effort of will, gathered enough concentration to continue. "I'm afraid it's not that simple. Bishop and Spider-Man have been stranded wherever they are for several subjective days longer than they expected. There's no telling what they've had to deal with. And unless they're together when the recall is activated, one of them will be left behind—perhaps forever."

Cyclops said, "Can't you just get a fix on where they are and try again if we miss one of them?"

"Under other circumstances?" Blaquesmith asked. "Maybe. But the TDC is running on spit and baling wire—not to mention Charles's brain—and the timestream is so volatile right now that our locators might be randomized two seconds after we complete the transfer. We can't even wait, because we're in danger of losing the signal at any moment. No, I'm afraid that his time there won't be any second chances."

"We'll have to send them an alert," Xavier said. "A two-minute warning, if you will. And then pray that it gives them both enough time to get into position."

Of the five remaining Mandroids attacking Aliya, Bishop, Spider-Man, and the Park, two were seriously damaged. One had lost all power in its legs and was reduced to being

THE PRESENT

a stationary gunner, firing endless rounds of razor-sharp flechettes at anything that wandered within range. Another with the same problem had already been knocked over and needed to use its arms in order to drag itself into firing position. Another two had lost all of their projectile weapons capabilities and were relying on their sheer enhanced strength to pummel the remaining members of the Power Liberation Front into submission. The remaining unbeaten Mandroid was fighting Spider-Man. As for the X-Men, the Beast was showing signs of being ready to wake up at any moment, and Wolverine was busily trying to carve Aliya into hamburger. Aliya, who needed all of her considerable skill just to keep the snarling killer at bay, had already divested herself of Razorback's helmet, which lay battered and giving off sparks at the floor by her feet.

But there were no more strategic retreats. The door to the stasis grid was just too close—and with the four of them all mixing it up within sight of that goal, the PLF would never have a better chance.

Wolverine snarled as he slashed at Aliya with both sets of claws. "You shoulda just laid down and died, lady—you woulda been better off."

Aliya flipped him over her shoulder. "I doubt it, animal. I'm *still* enjoying myself."

A vocoder signal came in from Magneto. The last surviving member of his team, Sandman, had just been vaporized by a phosphorus bomb. Magneto now fought alone.

The Mandroid fighting Spider-Man leveled his gauntlet at the wall-crawler. The tips of his fingers flipped back, revealing five minirockets about to fire at point-blank range. Spider-Man snagged the open fingertips with his webbing and yanked hard, closing the apertures just as all five rockets fired. The Mandroid screamed as the explosion blew the gauntlet right off his suit. He fell to the ground in shock, with smoke rising from that hand. Spider-Man leapt over him and *thwip*ped a thick layer of webbing to the faceplate of the Mandroid standing in place, blinding him and leaving him unable to use his weapons.

TIME'S ARROW

The crawling Mandroid grabbed Bishop's ankles from behind and pulled him down to the floor. For a moment, the two combatants faced each other from across a gulf of inches. Then the Mandroid reached out with his right arm and blasted Bishop with some kind of plasma energy weapon from his gauntlet. For a moment, Bishop stood engulfed in rippling energy. Then Bishop smiled, stood up, and stepped over the astonished Mandroid, bursting with energy now safely absorbed for his own use. He directed it at the the door to the stasis grid, which immediately flew apart from the explosion.

The Beast groped his way to a standing position, his teeth bared in an animalistic snarl. The snarl disappeared as stray machine-gun fire from one of the Mandroids strafed across the wall directly above his head, missing him by inches. With the battle raging all around him, he couldn't afford to be blind any longer. He groped for the webbing that had glued his eyes shut, and tore it from his face with one convulsive yank.

This was a very bad idea, since his eyes went with it.

As his agonized scream echoed through the silo, one of the weaponless Mandroids lunged at the Park, who flipped the massive armored figure over his shoulder and flung it hard against the wall. It made a crater when it hit, but immediately got up and began to shuffle toward him for another attack.

Spider-Man called out to his counterpart, "Hey, you're good at this! Maybe you oughta go public."

The Park leapt over an armored fist aimed at his head. "I was planning to do just that. I think I'll use an all-black costume, though. It's too good to waste on secret wars."

Aliya blocked a two-armed slash from the fighting-mad Wolverine, then struck him with a whirling roundhouse kick that sent the murderous Canadian mutant flying twenty feet over the battered cement floor. "May I remind you two fashion plates that this battle is supposed to have an objective? Somebody has to disable the stasis-grid mechanism."

THE PRESENT

Spider-Man saw his own path clear. "I'll take care of it! Cover me!"

Fighting a Mandroid several yards away, Bishop stiffened, and shouted, "No, Spider-Man, *don't*!"

Normally, Spider-Man would have gone anyway, but the urgency in Bishop's voice gave him pause. "Why not? What's wrong?"

"I just got a signal on my recall—Blaquesmith must have fixed the TDC, and they'll be summoning us back in less than two minutes! If you're not right next to me when they send the signal, you'll be left behind!"

Spider-Man didn't know whether to feel overwhelming joy or uncontrollable dismay. He was thrilled by the awareness that he'd be able to see Mary Jane again, but every instinct in his body rebelled against the idea of leaving a fight before it was done. "B-but—the PLF—we can't abandon—"

The Park alighted next to Spider-Man. "Go, Peter. This isn't your fight. You have a life to get back to—and despite what I said to you before, I'm sure you'll handle it just fine. Stay with Bishop and I'll take care of the stasis grid!"

Spider-Man shook his hand. "Good luck, Peter—and give my love to the wife."

The Park cocked his head in a certain familiar manner, that only another Peter Parker would recognize as an indication that the man inside was smiling. And then he leapt straight up and kicked off against the back of a charging Mandroid's head.

In a just universe, his leap would have carried him past the outskirts of the battle, through the shattered doorway, and into the room housing the stasis grid.

But it had already been established that this was not a just universe.

His death came in the form of the mutant named Wolverine, who charged in out of nowhere to slash at the airborne Park with both sets of claws at once. Spider-Man, who had spent years fighting for his life in arenas even more chaotic than this, might have taken sufficient warn-

TIME'S ARROW

ing from his spider-sense and been able to compensate. But the Park, whose battle experience was almost completely limited to the basketball court, reacted a fraction of a second too late. The ripping noise that followed was only partially caused by a black bodysuit being torn into long, jagged streamers. Principally it came from the skin, flesh, and organs beneath that bodysuit, most of which were also sliced into strips and some of which preceded the rest of this world's Peter Parker to the ground. He had no heroic last words, no final valiant surge of will to keep him up and fighting long enough for his companions to turn the tide. As he fell, there simply wasn't enough of him left to do anything but quickly, and very messily, die.

He didn't even have time to scream.

But somebody else did.

"Spider-Man!" Bishop yelled. "*No!*"

The web-slinger didn't listen.

With a little more than one minute before the recall signal, he grabbed an item off the floor and leapt toward the shattered door to the chamber containing the Stasis Grid. As it happened, he described the same trajectory that had only a few seconds before proven fatal to his counterpart. And for a moment it looked like his would end the same way. Wolverine was below him, his razor-sharp claws slashing like deadly streaks of silver light.

But this time Wolverine's claws did not find purchase in the chest of a man named Peter Parker.

This time, as Spider-Man passed overhead, the wall-crawler waited for the right moment, and slam-dunked Razorback's crackling helmet onto the two sets of outstretched claws. Wolverine's claws sank deep into Razorback's electrified mane. The result was immediate. Wolverine's claws became lightning rods, carrying enough current to knock out an elephant. The big pig-head smoked and crackled and gave off sparks as the generator inside fed thousands of volts into the X-Man's adamantium skeleton—a charge not capable of hurting the skeleton, but most effective in frying the man.

Spider-Man landed beside the door, found himself at-

THE PRESENT

tacked by a pain-maddened Beast, put everything he had into a punch that drove the Beast back to the ground, then ducked inside the doorway, hoping that whatever he found inside was simple enough to figure out in the less than one minute he had left.

Of course, given his trademark luck, it wasn't. The stasis grid generator was nothing but a tall cylindrical machine, humming away with the insouciance of a mountaintop still busily cooking pure moonshine. Spider-Man took one look at it and knew that he'd need somebody with the intellect of Reed Richards to figure out how to deactivate it safely.

But in less than one minute, Aliya was going to find herself alone against the defenders of Project: Pegasus.

Spider-Man didn't have time for safety.

He wrapped his arms around the great machine and, with a strength that would have startled even those who'd fought him, ripped it in half.

The Central Silo at Project: Pegasus was the largest and most closely guarded of the federal government's Unregistered Superpower Stasis Containment Facilities.

The stasis chambers were three-sided open boxes, lined up in circles around the perimeter of the silo. For years, the prisoners who stood motionless in these boxes had needed no bars to cage them. Neither had they needed food, nor water, nor custodial care. The chambers had turned them into human statues, forever trapped inside moments of frozen time. So they'd remained, their legendary forms lined up in circles around the periphery of a silo one hundred meters deep.

When the power went off, most emerged from their long imprisonment imagining that they'd been incarcerated for only hours or days. That by itself was enough to make them angry. Since they'd all been brought here at different times, it would only take them a few seconds of comparing notes to realize just how much time had actually passed—and when that happened, heaven itself

TIME'S ARROW

wouldn't be capable of protecting those who'd locked them away from their lives for so long.

Captain America recovered the fastest. After all, he'd been subjected to suspended animation before—and his experience with such things probably already led him to believe that this hadn't been just another overnight sleepover. As usual, he quickly took his place as inspiration to the others. "Come on, people! I don't know who we have to thank for this little power failure, but we have to press our advantage. Move!"

The Black Bee was older than the others, and he moved with the innate cautiousness of a man who was not quite as spry as he used to be. Still, he waved to his old poker buddy Dominic Fortune. "Come on, you old reprobate, you heard the man. Let's get crackin' and show these youngsters how it's done."

Daredevil, who'd been locked in stasis immediately after seeing his life torn to pieces by the Kingpin, reacted to all this with the dazed look of a man already teetering on the edge of madness. That didn't stop him from moving like the greatest of all Olympic gymnasts as he joined Hawkeye, Mockingbird, Moon Knight, Tigra, Hellcat, the Black Panther, the Black Widow, and the Black Cat in the race to the top of the silo.

Iron Man checked his systems, found them all operational, and rocketed upward. The Texas Twister spiraled upward, carrying his onetime teammate Firebird. The man known as Cloak wrapped his shadowy form around the woman known as Dagger, and teleported them both to the surface. She-Hulk and Doc Samson leapt up in stages. The various members of Power Pack, none of whom were older than twelve, flew up as a group, with all the pent-up energy of any children who've been kept inside for too long. On the other hand, Fabian Stankowicz, the Mechano-Marauder, tried to activate his armor's afterburners and merely caused a systems meltdown that froze all the joints solid, and was left standing in place hoping that somebody in this mad stampede upward would see fit to give him a lift. Against his better judgment, Black Goliath obliged.

THE PRESENT

Iron Fist ran into his old friend Shang-Chi on the way out. "I don't know about you," he said, "but somehow I don't think there'll be much left for us when all *these* guys are done."

Shang-Chi kept climbing at the same rate as he said, "No one misses the single raindrop in the heart of a thunderstorm. But the storm is made out of raindrops."

Luke Cage, listening, merely shook his head, and muttered, "Christmas."

Prince Namor, the Sub-Mariner, flew past all of them in his quest for the waiting sky. Yellowjacket and the Wasp were right behind him. So were Nova, the Falcon, Nighthawk, the Gargoyle, the Torpedo, a dazed-looking pudgy man wearing mechanical moth wings, and a grinning young man known as the Air-Skater, who now took his place among the champions of the world.

The Fantastic Four didn't waste any time either. Reed Richards elongated his pliable form to almost the full length of the silo, giving a lift to a number of others who did not possess the power of flight—people like Hercules, the Smithville Thunderbolt, Silver Sable, and the Valkyrie. The Thing and the Invisible Woman ascended on a column of invisible force, keeping pace with the Human Torch, who glowed white hot with eagerness for the fight. The Thing regarded the legion of other escaping superhumans with something like awe, and exclaimed, "Hey, Stretcho! Only one not here is my Aunt Petunia!"

The second Union Jack, leading a squadron of lesser-known escapees up the spiral catwalk to the top, shook his head at Black Goliath and said, "D'ye believe this? It's bloody marvelous!"

Brother Voodoo could only agree. "It's like watching something long dead come back to life."

And so it was: the hopes of a world. There were literally hundreds of them. Women dressed like white rabbits and men dressed like frogs and people in armor and people flying and people simply walking unhurriedly because they knew there'd be plenty of battle left for them when they got there. There was a man in a bulked-up fantasy

TIME'S ARROW

version of a professional football uniform. There was a caped man carrying an anvil, and another man with spookily piercing eyes who hid his features behind a slouch hat and long red scarf. There was, disconcertingly, one little guy in what seemed to be red longjohns, wearing an overturned cookpot on his head. There were great athletes and great fighters and cyborgs and robots and aliens who had made the earth their own and a thousand different varieties of mutant, and the only thing they had in common was they'd all been freed at once and they were all now raring to fight.

Their battle cries pierced the air. "Avengers Assemble!" "Imperius Rex!" And, perhaps most apropos, given what was awaiting this world's version of the X-Men: "It's clobberin' time!"

But, of all of them, one stood out by dint of his deceptive normalcy: a tall, confident bald man who strode throughout all this exploding chaos with the determination of a born leader who knew he had an appointment to keep. His name was Professor Charles Xavier, who, after years of imprisonment by the super hero team he'd been instrumental in founding, knew only that his oldest friend and greatest enemy, Magneto, was somewhere up above—and badly in need of help.

Spider-Man emerged from the chamber containing the stasis grid and returned to a scene of absolute chaos. Aliya and Bishop were still busily fighting off Mandroids, Wolverine was on the ground, crawling away from the smoking remains of Razorback's short-circuited helmet, the Beast was still writhing in agony, and the lights were strobing in what he could only assume was some kind of alarm.

Bishop, who was beginning to fade out, frantically waved for him to hurry up.

Spider-Man knew he had to go. But it also occurred to him that if he left with Bishop, then Aliya would be left to fight alone. And while she was good at what she did— literally, as good as anybody Spider-Man had ever seen—

THE PRESENT

it seemed dirty pool to leave her without allies in a chamber still filled with Mandroids. And even if she won her battles today, she'd still need a lot of help, directing all the allegedly freed super heroes to take down the power structures set in place by this world's X-Men. Somebody had to keep an eye on Magneto, to make sure he didn't try to seize power for himself. Too, there was the matter of the alternate Wolverine. He had just murdered the Park, after all, and despite the electric shock he had not yet paid sufficiently for that.

There were any number of reasons for Spider-Man to stay. Finishing the fight. Avenging his counterpart. Tying up all the loose ends. Breaking the news to Liz Parker. Even—he had to admit—meeting the children he might have had, or seeing Aunt May and Uncle Ben one last time, to tell them the things he'd never had a chance to say.

Yes, there were any number of reasons to stay.

And that was the one of the main problems with being driven by responsibility: it never stopped. There was always one more thing to be taken care of, one more crisis to face.

But he had those at home too.

Where he also had Mary Jane.

Bishop was fading out.

Spider-Man's leap carried him thirty feet across the battleground, over the slashing claws of a Wolverine lunging again for his blood, over the metallic gauntlets of Mandroids grasping for his neck, over Aliya as she shouted, "Thank you!"

With a sinking feeling, he leapt toward an empty space that had been Bishop only a fraction of a second before.

He was too late.

He wasn't going to make it.

Except that the wall faded out just before he touched it and became instead a room filled with X-Men, all of whom looked battered and bruised and filthy, and altogether as exhausted as he felt. His momentum carried him out of the TDC and into their midst, where for a moment he sat dazed, looking up at them.

It was Bishop, whose own exit from the booth had been considerably more sedate, who found his voice first.

"So, what took you so long?"

EPILOGUE

L imbo is always a shadowy place, but sometimes the shadows turn especially black, and the mists roll in like armies intent on conquering every last speck of light.

Somewhere, deep inside the castle, two figures stood partially obscured by those mists. One was a tall, cadaverous figure, with a complexion as pale as death. The other was an armored conqueror, whose life had spelled slavery and destruction for uncounted worlds. With the battles of the day now temporarily over, they gazed out a window that had once displayed a garden of unparalleled beauty, but which now—as was only typical for Limbo—showed a portrait of absolute nothingness, encasing nothing but never ending gray.

Lireeb said, "You do realize, sir, that with their Time Displacement Core now back online, the X-Men are bound to come after you?"

Kang said nothing.

"Oh. I see. Of course you realize it. I'm sorry I mentioned it. Far be it from me to waste your time with such a mundane irrelevancy. I don't know what I was thinking."

Kang still said nothing.

Lireeb sniffed, and tried another tack. "Of course, there is also a problem with the temporal field. It's showing signs of collapse. All the energy you've just gone to so much trouble to gather is in danger of dissipating."

Still, silence. The mists swirled.

"Of course," Lireeb said, "far be it from me to nag you about taking care of your toys."

Kang was a statue. Unmoving, unspeaking, unreacting. Lost in his own visions.

"You need to find the right timeline quickly, sire."

"I will," Kang assured him. "I'll find Ravonna presently. I'll even take care of the X-Men, when they arrive. I'm looking forward to it. But right now, I just want to enjoy the moment."

"Sir, this is Limbo. Time doesn't exist here. There is no such thing as a moment."

THE PRESENT

Kang sighed, glanced at his servant, but said nothing.

Eventually Lireeb had the good grace to walk away, leaving Kang to stare at the nothingness.

"Soon, my love," he said. "Very soon."

TO BE CONCLUDED

TOM DeFALCO entered the comic book industry in the summer of 1972 as an editorial assistant for Archie Comics. Learning his trade from the ground up, he pasted down character logos, proofread stories, and even served time as an occasional colorist. Within a few months, Tom sold the first of what would eventually become an avalanche of stories. Over the years, Tom has written for such diverse comic book titles as *Jughead's Jokes*, *The Flintstones*, *Scooby Doo*, and *Superman Family*. He joined the editorial staff of Marvel Comics during the early 1980s and eventually became the company's Editor in Chief. Tom has recently returned to full-time writing. He currently writes the monthly comic *The Amazing Spider-Man*, coauthored a novella with Stan Lee for *The Ultimate Silver Surfer*, and wrote short stories for *The Ultimate Super-Villains* and *Untold Tales of Spider-Man*.

ADAM-TROY CASTRO is a regular contributor to *Science Fiction Age* and the author of two cover stories in *The Magazine of Fantasy and Science Fiction*. He's sold over sixty short stories in all, including prominent contributions to the anthologies *Whitley Streiber's Aliens*, *The Ultimate Witch*, *Blood Muse*, *The Mammoth Book of Erotica*, *OtherWere*, *The Ultimate Super-Villains*, *Untold Tales of Spider-Man*, *Urban Nightmares*, and *Adventures in the Twilight Zone*. His novelette "Baby Girl Diamond" was a Bram Stoker Award nominee in 1996. At present, he is hard at work on a trilogy of Spider-Man novels. To his considerable consternation, he now lives in Florida.

TIME'S ARROW

TOM GRUMMETT started doing commercial illustration while working for the Saskatoon Board of Education's printing department. His first comics work appeared in the 1980 *Captain Canuck Summer Special*, and he went on to work on *The Privateers* and *The Shadowalker Chronicles*. In 1989, he started doing fill-in work for DC Comics, including issues of *Animal Man*, *Secret Origins*, *Action Comics*, and *Wonder Woman*. He has served as the regular penciller on *The New Titans*, *The Adventures of Superman*, *Robin*, *Superboy*, and, for Marvel, *Generation X*. Tom presently lives in Saskatoon, Saskatchewan, Canada, where he resides with his wife, Nancy, and their two children.

DOUG HAZLEWOOD has been inking professionally since 1985. After winning the inking category of the "Official Marvel Try-Out Contest" in 1986, he plunged into comic books full time. He has enjoyed stints on the critically acclaimed *Animal Man* and was a part of the death and resurrection of Superman on *Adventures of Superman*. Doug currently is the inker on *Superboy* for DC Comics. A native Texan, he lives in Victoria, Texas, with his wife and two children.

In order to stop Kang's plans, the X-Men and Spider-Man must journey to the future in the exciting conclusion...

X-MEN AND SPIDER-MAN

TIME'S ARROW
BOOK 3: THE FUTURE

by Tom DeFalco & eluki bes shahar

Here's a preview . . .

H is name is lost in history. Whole universes know him as Kang the Conqueror. Descendant of a mysterious time traveller, Kang came of age in a century of peace and brought it war.

In a galaxy two millennia removed from our own, he conquered all of known space, save for one tiny kingdom on the planet of his birth, home to the woman he loved.

The king had been old; the Princess Ravonna was his only daughter. Ravonna had defied Kang from the moment of their first meeting, on behalf of her people and her realm.

He remembered the first time he had seen her. It was early in his career. His legions had swept across all the countries of his homeworld. He held the satellites that orbited above; his battlefleet wove a steel cloak about the planet.

Only one kingdom still resisted him. It was a tiny place, a toy kingdom, holding sway over lands that were only a fragment of the planet's surface. It was so irrelevant that for years he had ignored it, intent upon bigger game.

Until now.

His legions encircled the tiny kingdom, his resources so vast against its tiny defiance. He had come to parley beneath a flag of truce. The kingdom's inhabitants had asked for this; Kang had been sure they meant to surrender.

She had come riding out to meet his battle tank upon a white horse, her dark hair flowing free about her shoulders. There were flowers in her hair, as though she had just come from the garden, and she wore a riding habit in all the colors of spring flowers. In her hand she carried the silver wand of truce, its shaft entwined with white roses.

"So you are the man who has enslaved all our people," Ravonna said.

"You mock me, child," Kang said. "I have set them free."

"Free to slave all the hours of their life for a grand design they will not live to see," Ravonna said scornfully. "Very well, conqueror, give us your terms."

"I do not make war with children, nor do I accept the surrender of kingdoms from them," Kang said crossly.

"Surrender?" Ravonna said in haughty disbelief.

She stared at him for a moment, and Kang realized she was trying hard to keep from laughing. He was amazed as he had not been in many long years, and wondered if the intelligence his spies and advisors had prepared for him could be wrong. What secret did Ravonna's people possess that she mocked him with such an easy heart?

"Oh, do forgive me, Kang the Conqueror," she said, amused. "I did not come here to bring you our surrender. We will defy you to the last babe in arms rather than submit to your tyrannical yoke. We did owe you the courtesy of telling you in person—my father would have come himself, but he had pressing business with the architect of the royal gardens."

"With the architect," Kang said, as if assuring himself that his ears did not deceive him.

"Indeed, Lord Conqueror. And so I have come in his place to assure you that you need not await our surrender before behaving like the brute that you are. Neither today nor any day will my people call Kang *master*, lord of murderers."

Kang very nearly did not hear her final insult; certainly he did not react to it. Gazing out from the turret of his massive tank at the laughing young woman on

THE FUTURE

the spirited white horse, Kang felt an emotion growing within him unlike any he had ever known.

"You are aware that my army possesses enough power to not merely subdue your kingdom, but to obliterate it entirely?" Kang asked harshly.

"So you have said, and often, Lord Kang. And so here is my father's word to you—and mine. Leave us in peace, or be prepared to slay every one of us."

It was a strange feeling. Something delicate yet powerful; of gossamer lightness that yet stayed his hand with bonds of unshatterable alloy.

"Mock me at your peril, Princess Ravonna. If Kang stays his hand, it is from mercy, not weakness. I shall give you more time to consider—perhaps to consult with your nurse?"

That insult had hit home. Ravonna had reigned in her steed until it danced and reared. Without another word, she had turned her mount and ridden away. Kang had watched until she disappeared from sight, through the wall of the city's force field.

With one thing and another, it had been two years before he returned. He came as the conqueror of an empire that stretched a hundred light years in every direction from his home star, and when he came, it was with new terms for the tiny kingdom.

If Ravonna would marry him, he would leave her kingdom in peace.

And once more she had defied him. Their clash of wills had been the clash of flint upon steel, and in the conqueror's heart there was ignited a passion to rival his love of conquest. From that moment Kang had loved the fiery princess. Years passed as he spared her father's kingdom out of love for her, hoping that one day Ravonna's heart would turn to him freely and he could crown her queen of all his far-flung empire.

But at last, frustrated beyond measure by her constant

TIME'S ARROW

refusals, Kang broke his tacit vow and turned the might of all his armies against her father's tiny kingdom.

And so, at last, Kang was master everywhere upon the planet of his birth.

But when Kang would have taken by force what had so long been denied him—the hand of the princess—Baltag, commander of Kang's elite guard, had led the legions in revolt. He demanded Ravonna's death, as all had died who had dared to defy Kang by force of arms.

It was love (of a sort) that Baltag demonstrated in that hour. He had followed his master across a thousand battlefields. He had prized the spoils that his master's victories had brought him, and when he had seen it waver because of the horrified expression in a woman's dark eyes, he had not been able to bear it.

But Kang was Kang, and he knew only one way to deal with any sort of obstacle whatever. He fought his rebellious field commanders and won; Baltag himself sat in chains awaiting Kang's pleasure. And Ravonna looked upon him with eyes of love, seeing beneath the armor to the man beneath, the expression on her face that of one who discovers, with dawning joy in the discovery, that she had at last found the man she must love through all eternity.

But such moments are not made to endure. In the moment of Kang's supreme triumph, the treacherous Baltag had somehow gained one of the guards' weapons, and used it in a final bid for mastery. He had sought Kang's death.

But Ravonna had thrown herself into the path of the bolt to save the man she had only now discovered that she loved.

She had died almost instantly.

He had executed Baltag, of course, and every member of Baltag's family he had been able to find. For a time

THE FUTURE

Kang had soothed his soul by crossing the timestream and executing every avatar of Baltag he had been able to find. A thousand bewildered men died in agony, never knowing the reason for their deaths.

It did not make the pain any less. Ravonna's death was something that the master of time lived with daily. Every hour he realized anew that Ravonna was dead, lost to him forever. And with her death, Kang had failed to achieve his objective, to make Ravonna his bride.

Kang had failed. The knowledge was nearly enough to drive him mad.

He tried to forget. Uncounted years passed, as Kang wandered the timestream, seeking to deaden the pain of this one defeat in battle, conquest, and war. Empires toppled. Queens cried out for mercy that was denied them. Heroes who had been the hope of their people fell before the man in the glittering armor who mocked them as they died.

Kang, who was his own myth, his own legend, the general who eternally returned from the mists of time to conquer again.

But always, through the branching tributaries of what might have been, he had returned to that black moment of his failure, seeking escape. Seeking to be reunited with his lost love once more. Only that would heal the wound within Kang's soul.

And now, as master of his time-twin Immortus's stronghold in Limbo—and of its one malleable defender, Immortus's servant Lireeb—he had come closer to achieving his goal than ever he had done in all his long and bloody career.

He would gain Ravonna once more.

And a thousand universes would die.

SPIDER-MAN

MARVEL COMICS · BYRON PREISS MULTIMEDIA · BOULEVARD

__SPIDER-MAN: CARNAGE IN NEW YORK by David Michelinie & Dean Wesley Smith 0-425-16703-8/$6.50

Spider-Man must go head-to-head with his most dangerous enemy, Carnage, a homicidal lunatic who revels in chaos. Carnage has been returned to New York in chains. But a bizarre accident sets Carnage loose upon the city once again! Now it's up to Spider-Man to stop his deadliest foe.

__THE ULTIMATE SPIDER-MAN 0-425-14610-3/$12.00

Beginning with a novella by Spider-Man cocreator Stan Lee and Peter David, this anthology includes all-new tales from established comics writers and popular authors of the fantastic, such as: Lawrence Watt-Evans, David Michelinie, Tom DeHaven, and Craig Shaw Gardner. An illustration by a well-known Marvel artist accompanies each story. *Trade*

__SPIDER-MAN: THE VENOM FACTOR by Diane Duane 1-57297-038-3/$6.50

In a Manhattan warehouse, the death of an innocent man points to the involvement of Venom—the alien symbiote who is obsessed with Spider-Man's destruction. Yet Venom has always safeguarded innocent lives. Either Venom has gone completely around the bend, or there is another, even more sinister suspect.

®,™ and © 1998 Marvel Entertainment Group, Inc. All rights reserved.

Payable in U.S. funds. No cash accepted. Postage & handling: $1.75 for one book, 75¢ for each additional. Maximum postage $5.50. Prices, postage and handling charges may change without notice. Visa, Amex, MasterCard call 1-800-788-6262, ext. 1, or fax 1-201-933-2316; refer to ad #563

Or, check above books Bill my: ☐ Visa ☐ MasterCard ☐ Amex _____ (expires)
and send this order form to:
The Berkley Publishing Group Card#_____
P.O. Box 12289, Dept. B Daytime Phone #_____ ($10 minimum)
Newark, NJ 07101-5289 Signature_____
Please allow 4-6 weeks for delivery. **Or enclosed is my:** ☐ check ☐ money order
Foreign and Canadian delivery 8-12 weeks.

Ship to:
Name_____ Book Total $_____
Address_____ Applicable Sales Tax $_____
City_____ Postage & Handling $_____
State/ZIP_____ Total Amount Due $_____

Bill to: Name_____
Address_____City_____
State/ZIP_____

Marvel Comics X-MEN®

star in their own original series!

X-MEN: MUTANT EMPIRE: BOOK 1: SIEGE
by Christopher Golden 1-57297-114-2/$6.50

When Magneto takes over a top-secret government installation containing mutant-hunting robots, the X-Men must battle against their oldest foe. But the X-Men are held responsible for the takeover by a more ruthless enemy...the U.S. government.

X-MEN: MUTANT EMPIRE: BOOK 2: SANCTUARY
by Christopher Golden 1-57297-180-0/$6.99

Magneto has occupied The Big Apple, and the X-Men must penetrate the enslaved city and stop him before he advances his mad plan to conquer the entire world!

X-MEN: MUTANT EMPIRE: BOOK 3: SALVATION
by Christopher Golden 0-425-16640-6/$6.99

Magneto's Mutant Empire has already taken Manhattan, and now he's setting his sights on the rest of the world. The only thing that stands between Magneto and conquest is the X-Men.

®, ™ and © 1998 Marvel Characters, Inc. All Rights Reserved.

Payable in U.S. funds. No cash accepted. Postage & handling: $1.75 for one book, 75¢ for each additional. Maximum postage $5.50. Prices, postage and handling charges may change without notice. Visa, Amex, MasterCard call 1-800-788-6262, ext. 1, or fax 1-201-933-2316; refer to ad #722

Or, check above books	Bill my: ☐ Visa ☐ MasterCard ☐ Amex _____ (expires)
and send this order form to:	
The Berkley Publishing Group	Card#
P.O. Box 12289, Dept. B	Daytime Phone # ($10 minimum)
Newark, NJ 07101-5289	Signature
Please allow 4-6 weeks for delivery.	Or enclosed is my: ☐ check ☐ money order
Foreign and Canadian delivery 8-12 weeks.	

Ship to:

Name	Book Total	$
Address	Applicable Sales Tax	$
City	Postage & Handling	$
State/ZIP	Total Amount Due	$

Bill to: Name

Address _____ City _____
State/ZIP

PENGUIN PUTNAM
online

Your Internet gateway to a virtual environment with hundreds of entertaining and enlightening books from Penguin Putnam Inc.

While you're there visit the PB Café and order up the latest buzz on the best authors and books around—Tom Clancy, Patricia Cornwell, W.E.B. Griffin, Nora Roberts, William Gibson, Robin Cook, Brian Jacques, Jan Brett, Catherine Coulter, and many more!

Penguin Putnam Online is located at
http://www.penguinputnam.com

PENGUIN PUTNAM NEWS

Every month you'll get an inside look at our upcoming books, and new features on our site. This is an ongoing effort on our part to provide you with the most interesting and up-to-date information about our books and authors.

Subscribe to Penguin Putnam News at
http://www.penguinputnam.com/subscribe